Ruthless Lessons

ARIA ZINN

Also by Aria Zinn

Ruthless Lessons

Gilded Chains

Author's Note

This book's content might be intense for some people. Triggering situations such as d-con, primal play, knife play, graphic violence, infant loss (off page), drug use (off page), stalking, mafia-related conversations, and touch her and die situations are a part of this story.

Please, take care of yourself and err on the side of caution when choosing whether to read this story or not.

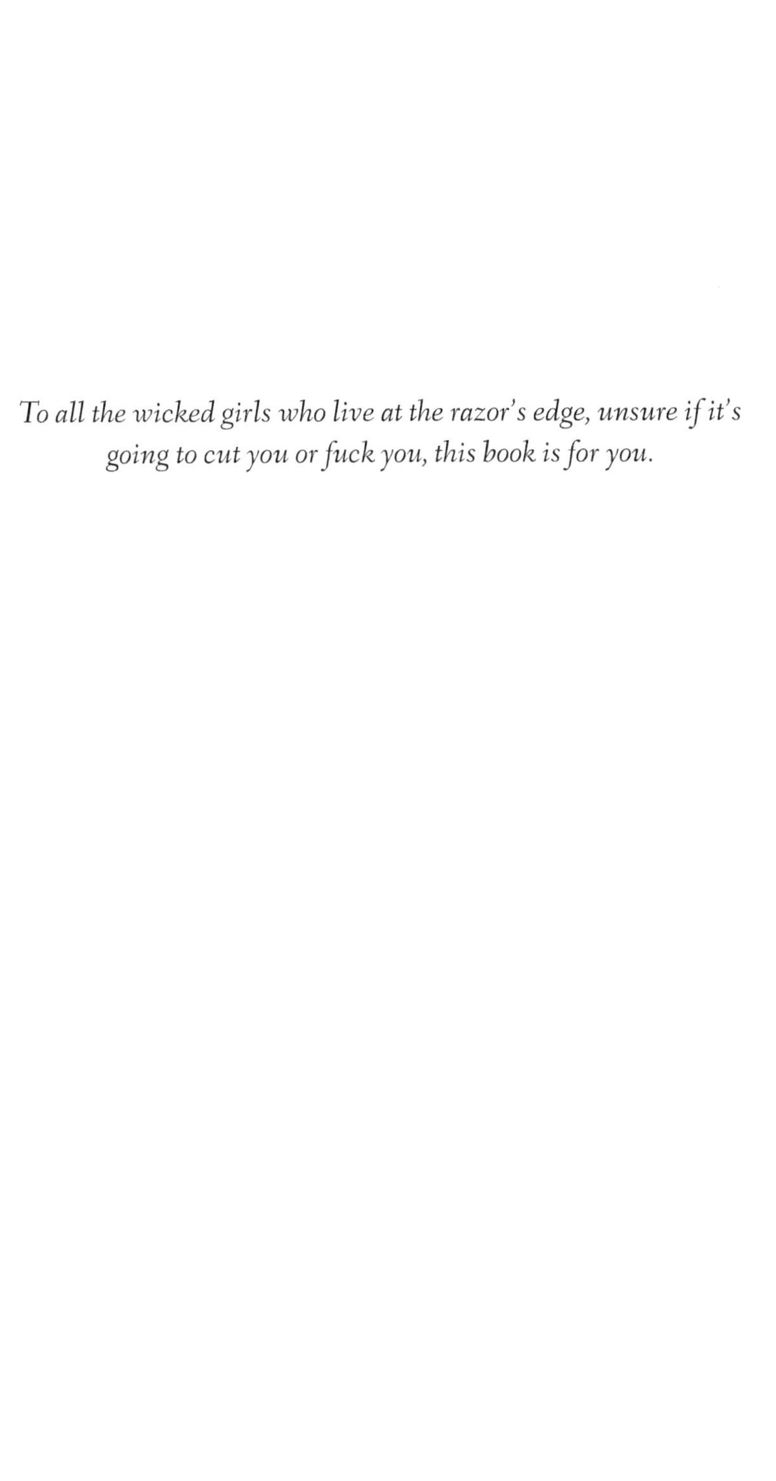

To all the wicked girls who live at the razor's edge, unsure if it's going to cut you or fuck you, this book is for you.

Chapter One

Edmond

"Did I not pay you enough, Ricky?"

I mull over the question as I brood down at the man trussed up at my feet. He looks around wildly, trying to find an ally in the stone-faced men who stand behind me. There are none here. Nor does he find mercy when he finally meets my eyes. What he sees is his mortality, his fate as certain as winter's icy arrival. Before the day ends, Ricky's going to be an example to all the others who might think to follow in his sticky-fingered footsteps.

My prisoner shudders, giving in to the terror that I've been ratcheting up for the past hour. Ever since I had him "escorted" from his office to the warehouse.

"He pissed himself," Marcus says, as if I can't smell it from where I sit or see the wetness darkening the cement.

"Yeah."

Ricky screams something behind the gag. Snot bubbles leak from his quivering nostrils. I heard it all before. His denials. His profession of innocence. As if I would ever be anything less than certain before hauling him into this one-man tribunal. It's why he's gagged. I don't need to hear any more lies.

Had he tried truth, Ricky might have survived my wrath. Instead, he's accelerated the outcome.

He's too far gone to be embarrassed. His brown eyes are blown wide, showcasing the blood-shot veins bulge across the whites. His breathing is labored, not only because of the silver duct tape muzzling his lower face. But the sheer horror show that he's imagining in his head. How many times has he seen this situation play out? Only then, he was the one having my back, not the victim on his knees. His sobbing is unending, leaving his whole face shining dully in the warehouse's dismal light.

Christ this torture shit is exhausting.

"You know how this goes. Take the consequences like a man."

I flick Iustina, my butterfly knife, open and then close. In the somber silence broken only by Ricky's muffled screams, I savor the crisp, metallic noise filling the air as the safety latch unhooks from the handles and counter-rotates, revealing the full lethal length of the blade.

Click.

Another twist of my wrist, and it closes.

Clink.

Back and forth I rotate my wrist, twirling the double handles around the knife's pivot pin as if Iustina is the scales of justice, weighing the moneymakers' fate.

Click. Life.

Clink. Death.

"Why is it always you accountants who bring out the worst in me?"

Honestly, crooked accountants are a pain in my balls. To handle the shadowy aspects of my business and keep the IRS off my back, I need accountants with a knack for creative ledger-keeping.

"Do you think I enjoy this? I don't want to have to kill you, Ricky."

But the ones I hire? They're not exactly saints; they're future criminals who can't resist the allure of fast, dirty money. When weighing the risk of obscene wealth against their desires to remain breathing, the money always wins. Personally, I'd choose life. But I'm biased. I've never had to scrape by. I'd been born into power, and I'll die by it too.

On average, it takes accountants about five years to crack under the pressure of the mafia lifestyle. The temptation of millions just a pen stroke away seems to erase any shred of self-preservation they have left. History has two unwavering rules when it comes to organized crime: don't mess with the mob, and never piss off the boss.

The first is self-explanatory.

Just don't.

Irish, Italian, Russian. We're all the same, black-hearted and murderous bastards who flout the laws for monetary gain. The only differences are our origin stories and rank structure, making us the villains in a world without heroes.

Organized crime is a vicious cycle. Once you are in or 'made', the mob owns the lives of you and your family. It sucks everyone into a multi-generational cycle of crime and corruption, greed and power.

The only way in is with blood.

The only way out is by a bullet.

I'm the boss, and Richard "Ricky" Thornton broke both rules. He lasted seven years as my accountant, but forging my signature on a check tied to my online gambling business sealed his fate. He underestimated the scrutiny that I placed on those digital transactions.

Ricky's third mistake was messing with his soon-to-be ex-wife's feelings. She tipped me off about his hasty departure from my employment without even a phone call and alongside his buxom young assistant. They didn't manage to make it out of the country, let alone the state before my people grabbed him.

I rule my domain like a third-world country. Justice is swift, brutal, and meted out with a bullet.

Ricky trembles on his knees, waiting for my decision.

"You were someone I trusted. Nadia would have taken out you and your girlfriend. Be thankful that Beth is only being relocated, and not joining you here."

My sister had hired him, and her decision-making skills were above par. For the past two years of my reign, he'd been a solid employee.

But then he stole from me.

Click. Life.

Clink. Death.

I sink deeply into the tufted, cognac-hued leather of my chair. Here, in the middle of the empty warehouse, it stands as a throne from which I proclaim the fates of those brought before me. From its gray corrugated walls to the broken windows covered in grime, there is an illusion of abandonment. I like it that way. It's not until you step inside that the modern security system discreetly tucked in a corner shatters the ruse.

This is my killing box.

Latex paint covers the floor, filling in the porous nature of the cement, and sealing it watertight. There's a big drain in the center, directly below where a meat hook hangs. An industrial hose lays uncoiled nearby; a green-scaled snake ready to wash away evidence of my sins with a pressurized blast of water. There are no shelves or equipment, no dust, and no witnesses.

There are only me, Ricky, and two of my men.

Click. Life.

Money isn't the root of evil, but it's an underpinning. A way for greed and envy to corrupt the normally unsullied hearts of good men. Ricky had been a decent man. Nobody good ever joined the *Bratva*. Now he's a thief, and the only good thief is a dead one.

Clink. Death.

With Thornton's fate settled, there's only one thing I want to know: who else is involved? I could ask Ricky why he needed the money, but the reasons don't matter to me. My interest died the moment he let lies coat his tongue.

Leaning forward, I swipe the point of my blade across the duct tape sealing his mouth. He yelps as the edge draws blood.

"Edmond," he pants, trying to foster some type of connection by using my first name. All it does is spike my anger because I had given him permission to use it, years ago.

"Don't," I grit out, grinding my molars so hard that I'm in danger of cracking a tooth. "I'll cut your fucking tongue out before I listen to any more of your lies."

Ricky flinches as if my voice is a gunshot. He knows he's out of time, and he falls forward, bracing himself on his forehead as if in prayer. I'm not religious, but at this moment I am his god. A wrathful, Old Testament deity that does not shy away from abusing his power over those he views as lesser than.

I steeple my fingers beneath my chin, brooding at the shuddering, middle-aged accountant. His woolen Versace suit is rumpled, and the pits are sweat-stained. Blood marks the collar of his white Dior dress shirt, the mother-of-pearl button torn cleanly away to expose the crew neckline of his undershirt, and a dash of the tattoos that cover his chest. The accountant is sweating like a pig, his brown hair matted, turning the modern short curtain hairstyle into an unflattering bowl around his ears.

This time I will hear his answer to my earlier rhetorical question.

"Did I not pay you enough, Ricky?"

"You paid me very well, Mr. Vasiliev," Ricky blubbers.

I grunt, already weary of dealing with my ex-financial guru. The proof of his crimes is quite literally at my fingertips thanks to technology. All my accounts send me a text notification if they exceed a certain transfer amount. You would've thought Ricky would have comprehended that. I *paid* him to understand the inner workings of my financials.

Or maybe he has a death wish.

Suicide by the Bratva.

He wouldn't be the first.

"You were excellent at laundering my money," I sigh with a modicum of regret. It's going to take me months to find another accountant who can sleep at night while dealing with the Vasiliev enterprises' criminal underbelly.

There were other ways I could make Ricky pay. I could go after his family. That had been my grandfather's favorite way to ensure absolute loyalty. But since Ricky had been planning on leaving his wife and child behind, I don't think their anguish would sway him. I also didn't like making women and children pay for the sins of their husbands and fathers. Their only sin was marrying a lying crook.

"Who else has their fingers in my treasury?"

Ricky crawls forward as much as he can with his hands tied behind his back, never quite daring to reach the tips of my black Gucci loafers. He leverages himself into a respectable kneel shuddering like a sacrifice and lifting his watery eyes to my face.

"No one, no one. I swear. I just—"

I drop my foot, the tooled leather sole slapping the cement with an annoying clack.

"Look at me."

Ricky sobs. His head hangs between his shaking shoulders. He isn't intending to deny me. Fear causes a quartet of visceral reactions, commonly known as flight, fight, freeze, or fawn. I'd have assumed that Ricky would be the fawning type.

Ricky's reaction is to freeze. His terror is convincing him to bury his head in the metaphorical sand like an ostrich, or a child hiding behind a blanket. If he can't see me, I can't see him, or some psychobabble bullshit. As if I'm not sitting above him; his judge, jury, and executioner.

"Look. At. Me."

Panting desperately, Ricky lifts his head. His eyes are red-rimmed, but the iris is dilated so tiny and the eyeball itself bulging out so violently that they show an enormous amount of white sclera.

A shiner darkens his cheekbone, the swelling half-eclipsing the corner of his eye. The damage is from where my men had sucker-punched him in the underground garage of his side piece's apartment building and then collected him here. We are miles outside the city line of Echo Bay, but still solidly within my territory. There is nobody around for miles to hear the gunshots or his screams.

I narrow my gaze at him. "I don't care why. If you'd been in trouble, if you had a sick child. Even if you owed money to the bookies or had a drug habit. You could have come to me. You know how I feel about loyalty."

Rage seethes inside of me. It twists in my gut like a viper, its scales rasping, fangs poised with the want to bite and tear Ricky's throat out. Since birth, I'd learned to honor the covenant to the *Bratva*. I assimilated the rules of this life until every breath in my lungs, and every throb of my heart resonated to the same vow: secrecy, loyalty, obedience. Men who'd lived and died by their guns had drilled them into me.

Ricky had learned them too, right before I tattooed the Jack of Clubs he wears on his chest myself. Yet here he is. A disgrace to the Vasiliev organization, and not worth the ink on his skin.

I bend closer. "Instead, you stabbed me in the back."

"I'm sorry, I'm so sor-"

My limit of listening to Ricky blubber hits its threshold. Snot and tears clot the accountant's face, his eyes wildly darting around the interior of the warehouse. I wonder if he will break and try and flee. I'd rather kill a man who stares death head-on, going down swinging instead of a coward.

The windows are grated and dust-caked, deliberately blotting out any light save for a dismal gleam. Occasionally, his gaze pings off Leon and Marcus, my diligent shadows who stand quietly behind me. I tense my leg muscles, waiting, eager for him to bolt. To prove to me that is still *Bratva* even in the face of his demise.

Then he sags as his gutlessness wins out. Disgracing his oaths all over again. I wish I had the time to cut the tattoos off his chest. He all but lays his head in the metaphorical guillotine, refusing to open his eyes and see the grim reaper standing at his shoulder.

So be it.

I shake my head and hold my hand out. I don't care whose gun is placed in it. Only that the familiar weight of the Glock 17 settles into my palm with a quickness. I rarely pack a piece, because they are traceable, and I am militant about melting the barrel assembly down after they've been used. It's hard to get attached to a weapon when you're constantly swapping it out. But my blade? That is true love. I took it off the first person I killed.

Iustina. *Justice.*

Ricky barely registers the view of the weapon before I thumb off the safety and put a 9mm bullet right between the traitor's eyes. The entry wound is the size of a pencil eraser, with the exit not much bigger. A relatively clean kill. If I wanted to make a statement, I'd have used a .45.

The meaty thud of Thornton's body hitting the cement punctuates my slow rise to my feet. I re-button my suit jacket and sear this last view of Ricky Thornton into my memories.

What a waste.

I pass the Glock back to Leon for disposal. Knowing him, he has a second holstered on him and can make a quick stop by one of my armories for a replacement weapon.

"Make sure the cleaners handle this. No evidence. Give his widow seventy-thousand and encourage her to leave Echo Bay. I prefer it if she also leaves Washington. I hear Oregon is a nice place to live."

"Yes, Boss."

I turn to leave when a sudden clamor of the alarm on my phone draws me to a halt. I flick the screen, stopping the vibration while reading the notification that's blinking at the top.

Damn it.

Swiftly, my irritation at the dead man grows. If I hadn't had to deal with him, my schedule would have been okay.

Now it's in shambles.

I swear again.

I'm going to be late for Mila's parent-teacher conference.

Chapter Two

Edmond

The drive to Mila's school gives me time to think.

As it usually does when I am forced to face the hard reality that being the *pakhan* of the Vasiliev *Bratva* requires, my mind turns to thoughts of my family.

Once, there were four of us Vasiliev siblings: Alexander, Mikhail, me, and our eldest sister, Nadia.

Pops had hailed from Russia, escaping to the States after a five-year stint in the Gulag. There, surrounded by other prisoners, he'd been taught the ways of the Bratva and been adopted by the old men who lived entire lives behind the prison's iron bars and cement casement.

In the 80's, he'd settled in Echo Bay, a post-card-perfect town in upstate Washington, not far from the Juan Islands, home of the infamous, wealthy enclaves on Orcas Island. It'd been easy to take over the city, then Seattle, before conquering the state and finally the entire west coast from the Canadian border down to Mexico's until he ran into the cartels. After a brief but bloody war with the Juarez cartel, he left California to the Italians and retained his grip on Washington.

While Pops had been traditionalist in his nature, when it came to his children, he defied the cliche mobster stereotype. He didn't wait for a son to take over his criminal empire, as many of his peers did. He chose his firstborn, gender being immaterial, with a simple decree that everyone listened to and obeyed; the eldest Vasiliev would inherit his violent kingdom.

Nadia. Our perfect *Bratva printsessa.* The very apple of Pops' eye. She had emerged from the womb ready to conquer, performing a careful balancing act between tradition and modern aspirations. She hadn't just shattered the glass ceiling that choked the future of the *Bratva* but shattered it into a million pieces that reflected her might in their splintered shards. While she'd done the duties expected of a woman by marrying into the Kiselyov family, securing fealty and strength for the two families for generations; promptly getting knocked up on her honeymoon, and giving birth to an heir that would solidify both clans' futures, she never let anyone forget that the Vasiliev dynasty was *hers.*

However, longevity is not a trait of organized crime. Being able to retire is a blessing, one very few gangsters ever achieve. Pops had been taken out by an Irish assassin when Nadia was still in her twenties. Her reign lasted five years until a fateful plane crash claimed my sister, and her husband Anton, two years ago. The only reason Mila, her now ten-year-old daughter, survived was solely because she'd had an ear infection, and the doctor had erred on the side of caution about letting her board that ill-fated flight.

As for my mother, she abandoned us shortly after Pop's assassination. Alexander had been barely ten years old, but she'd high-tailed it down to the Cayman Islands, relishing the tax haven status and balmy tropical climate.

The last time I laid eyes on her was when Nadia's lawyers broke the news that I was now Mila's guardian.

Overnight, I became a single parent to a child and a surly teenager.

With the resiliency of childhood, Mila has adapted to my new role in her life, but Alexander has not. He constantly rebels and chafes against the rules and makes my life a living hell when he's around.

Despite his behavior, Mila adores him. He is undoubtedly her favorite uncle.

I never aspired to become the *pakhan* of the family. Pops groomed me to be my sister's second-in-command, her brigadier, the intermediary, who assisted her in managing the various units under her dominion.

In simpler terms, I was the one she sent out to make an efficient, but brutal, impact. She'd represented the public face of the Vasiliev organized criminal group (Vasiliev OCG) and the *new Bratva*, exuding a modern allure and cunning that I struggled to emulate.

She'd loved being our *pakhan* and putting all the old misogynist mobsters' balls in her Chanel purse if they gave her lip.

Now Mikhail is my brigadier, and I rule all of Washington's northwestern coast with Echo Bay the jewel in my bullet-riddled crown. All for a broken family who doesn't understand the blood that saturates the roots of our family tree.

I close my eyes and let the rhythm of the car carry away my thoughts.

The drive to Harbor View Montessori, Mila's grade school, takes fifteen minutes. Being already behind schedule, I don't have the luxury to ditch my security detail, change cars, or double-check my shoes for any remnants of Ricky Thorton.

Everyone in Echo Bay is aware of who I am and my reputation. However, I prefer not to flaunt it unnecessarily, as it tends to make the "normals" uneasy. Unless I must make a statement as the *pakhan* of the Vasiliev OCG, I strive to stay low-key. My bodyguards either remain behind or discreetly follow me from a distance.

At this moment, I'm approaching the grade school, fully embodying the *Bratva* image – surrounded by bodyguards armed to the teeth, with gun residue and possibly some lingering traces of blood clinging to my clothing.

Eventually, the driver reaches our destination. He could have driven much faster. The best stunt drivers and ex-FBI personnel have trained him to evade the fastest police interceptors. However, when we need to maintain a low profile, he seldom exceeds the speed limit by more than a few miles. It's a delicate balance between avoiding the attention of state patrolmen looking for that precious ticket revenue and not annoying other drivers on the road.

Leon steps out first to scout the mostly empty parking lot. He's been with me since I took my oath of loyalty to the Brotherhood at eighteen. Despite his imposing size, leftover from being a former linebacker in the XFL in his younger years, he's a fast motherfucker. I wouldn't want him chasing me down; he moves like a jaguar hyped up on methamphetamine.

Once he confirms the area is clear, he opens the door for me, and I step out, entering the fading afternoon sun.

"Wait here with Marcus."

"Boss..."

I shoot him a glance, cutting off his complaint. The last thing I'd wanted was to arrive at Harbor View Montessori with my deadly entourage. Now that I have, I didn't want to potentially cause panic among the teachers by having the Incredible Hulk trailing behind me. No amount of luxury or modern grooming of his short, tapered locs can conceal that he's 6'3" and two-hundred and forty pounds and has maintained the gym-buffed physique that allows him to bench-press one and a half times his body weight. Nor do I want to deal with that kiss-ass Sawyer who would have panicky questions.

"I highly doubt there is an assassin waiting for me in a grade school."

Leon grunts in response, his expression still sour, but he nods in agreement.

I stride through the bullet-proof glass front doors, pass the metal detector, and navigate my way past the armed guards who snap to high alert when they see me coming. They're dressed in black Kevlar body armor over black fatigues, with holstered guns at their thighs and automatic rifles in hand.

Harbor View Montessori, along with its sister Harborcrest Academy, does not fuck around when it comes to security. Mila is not the only high-value target enrolled, but the only one who has an over possessive uncle who would bring the might of a well-funded, private army down onto the person stupid enough to snatch her.

A guard nods, meeting my eyes for a second too long, before looking away. I recognize him as someone who moon-lights on my payroll. Wherever Mila is, I make sure to have a loyal man or woman on the inside.

Like anywhere Mila goes, I've long since learned the layout and know exactly where her classroom is located. Two left turns from the main hallway, and I'm in the right vicinity.

A few doors away, Tori Malone stomps past me. She's a vulgar blonde whose entire personality revolves around the notion that big hair and big tits are the epitome of attraction. I've known her since high school, where she'd reigned as home-coming and prom queen all four years. She doesn't realize she's peaked, because Tori still believes she's god's gift to all mankind because of her Coke bottle figure. She's been after my cock since my voice dropped. Even now, despite being married to one of my men. It leaves me with a dim view of her scruples. I might have a weakness for bimbos, but why would I dabble with a cheater when I'm trying to set a good example for my niece?

Tori pauses, giving me a hot once-over that, if I were her husband, would have earned her a blistered hide. I have no idea what Drew sees in her. She possesses the loyalty of a cat in heat looking for her next hard-dicked tom to service her. If I crooked my finger at her, I could have her bent over the desk of the empty classroom in under a minute. She might drain my balls, but I'd want to cut my dick off after.

"Edmond," she practically purrs. "How are you?"

I shake my head, maintaining a cautious distance from her. Giving her even a hint of attention would be like inviting herpes into my life; easy to acquire but impossible to get rid of. Drew, despite his private life issues, is fiercely loyal. Though he's said otherwise, I know that Tori comes first for him, *then* his fealty to me. The quickest way to lose that loyalty is to mess around with his wife or give her ammo to make him *think* that I am.

"Late, Mrs. Malone."

I'm not going to indulge her advances and brush past her as if she's a gnat buzzing around me.

My memory of Mrs. Hoffman from our meeting during the first week of school is of a competent teacher with a vintage style. She'd exuded an earthmother, crunchy granola vibe, wore a flower-patterned dress, and sported a waist-length braid of long brown hair. She wouldn't have seemed out of place at a church social or an artsy outdoor wedding. Mrs. Hoffman perfectly fits the mold of what one would expect to find in Bohemian-hippie neighborhoods like Portland or San Francisco.

When I step into the classroom, I have no clue who this woman is. I don't like not knowing things, and it makes my jaw lock with annoyance. Did Mrs. Hoffman delegate her meetings to a student teacher? I did not come all this *way* to deal with a fucking college student.

The *girl* is crawling on her hands and knees beside the desk. Her strawberry blond hair cascades around her face and shoulders like an unrestrained waterfall. It's too long and unmanaged for a professional setting, I can't see much, but I discern the delicate contours of her form; the nimble curves and petite limbs that look so breakable it makes my mouth water and fingers suddenly twitch to see if she's as soft as she looks.

I'm intrigued, and don't halt until I'm standing directly over her, so close that if Ricky's blood had stained my shoes, she would have noticed the marks. Not that she could have known she was gazing at the residue of a dead man sullying the ultra-luxurious Guccissima leather.

I furrow my brow and sweep my gaze around the chic, high-tech classroom. Mila's name boldly stands out in lavender on a rose-gold chart pinned to a corkboard with a line of metallic stickers beside it, beaming out "good job" and "A+" to anyone who reads it. I'm undoubtedly in the right classroom.

So, who is this *suka?*

Then she lifts her head and I realize I've walked blindly into a trap that resembles Botticelli's Venus. She is ripe and so sweet that she looks as if she'd bruise if I were to touch her; a succulent peach just eager for sharp teeth to dig into its juicy center and gulp that sweet nectar down.

My thoughts scatter, but there is a single truth, a gravitas to this moment that I understand. Even if she does not feel the momentous pull of the world being thrown out of alignment. Then slowly adjusting to a new path, a new *future* for her and me, that unfolds with a kismet-shaped come-hither.

I feel it, and that's all that matters.

Doom awaits her. Because there is no way I will ever forget the sight of her enormous hazel eyes widening with surprise and innocent appreciation while she's on her knees before me. Her amaranth pink lips part with a shocked breath that makes me want to hear her gasp around my cock. Heat flushes into her cheeks. She blushes like an innocent, and it sends a surge of lust straight to my cock.

It only takes one look for me to know I'm going to ruin this woman and savor every tear she'll shed and moan I'll wrench from her lips.

Chapter Three

Rina

There needs to be a law that states teachers shouldn't have to deal with parents. Not unless the school boards choose to pay us more.

Isn't that why there are principals, vice principals, and administrators who earn the big bucks? They have a financial incentive to deal with the adults who think they know better than the people who've gone to school to educate their young.

I hate teacher in-service day, and for the moment, that hatred has a name and a flawless, airbrushed face.

Victoria Malone.

I look down at my papers, feeling that thief of joy start to crawl through my thoughts – comparison.

Next to her, I'm dowdy, a frumpy teacher in the orbit of the pin-thin perfection she presents in her bubble-gum pink palazzo pants, white cropped top that shows a perfect slice of her toned, tanned stomach, and fitted hourglass cut blazer with its bright golden buttons that I'm sure costs more than my rent.

She's had a baby, and yet she looks like *that*. Polished and glitzy like CEO Barbie Doll newly taken from its box. It's almost offensive to average-looking women everywhere. I didn't give birth to the teenage drama queen I live with, but I hate Victoria on principle for all the mothers whose bodies have been permanently altered by pregnancy.

"Are you paying attention to me, Miss Christenson?"

Victoria adds a mean-girl taunt and smug tone to my non-married honorific, making me feel as if I'm back in high school and not the *literal* teacher. I'm not ashamed that I'm single, but Victoria acts like I should be. I don't have the *time* to worry about dating or trying to find Mr. Right. Not that Mrs. Malone looks as if she's ever had a difficult time finding a date.

I sigh and refocus on her. I try not to let her see how she affects me. I'm here to take whatever the parents dish out, even if it's borderline abusive.

"I am, yes."

Victoria launches into another tirade, and it takes every scrap of willpower for me to sit there and take it quietly.

I wonder if I stab my eardrums with a pencil, would I still hear her? At this point, I would do anything just so I wouldn't have to hear her high-pitched screeching, which sounds as if a banshee has gotten loose in my classroom. You would think, with her beauty, she would have a sweet voice. She looks like she's some artist's ideal of an angel with bouncy blond hair and periwinkle blue eyes.

Instead, she's a harpy with zero volume control.

I choke back my request for her to use her inside voice like I would if she were one of my students. I'm sure that would go over splendidly with how angry she already is. She isn't one of my students, and I need to treat her with respect. She's a parent of one of my more difficult kids. So, I have to keep meeting with her, soaked in dread and clammy with sweat each time I see her name on my appointment log. Preparing for a one-sided battle with a woman who simply doesn't care how she comes across.

I sit behind my desk, gritting my teeth as Victoria huffs before me. She stalks back and forth across the beige and cream-dappled area rug that pads the floor beneath my desk, an enraged gazelle using the narrow space like a catwalk. Her shapely hips swish. The wide legs of her trousers swish fluidly around her trim ankles, showcasing the fuchsia satin fabric and bejeweled buckle decorations of her expensive heels. She strikes a fashionable pose even as she reads me the riot act.

I've only been teaching her son for the past six months. Shocking to no one, this meeting will commemorate the sixth time I've met her. I can practically write a script based on the monthly sound bites she slashes at me; her behavior carving invisible, bloodless wounds into me with the unerring, poison-laced daggers of her derisive words. My self-confidence is already pretty low, but it's non-existent when faced with her.

Adam isn't a bully.

He's just misunderstood.

Are you calling me a negligent mother?

Do you know who my husband is?

I can get you fired.

Victoria tosses her head, causing a sheet of flaxen-blond hair to bounce against her shoulders. It's so bright and silky, as much of a statement piece as the enormous, diamond-encrusted wedding set that glitters on her ring finger like a glacier bound in platinum. The hair toss is one of her cues, a sure sign that she is about to change tactics. Because sniping at me isn't getting her the outcome she wants. God forbid she tries talking to me. So now comes the manipulation.

I already know what she is going to say before she even opens her mouth.

"I think you're mistaken. Adam would never bully another student. He's a good kid."

Doesn't she watch the news? Every time a kid gets in trouble, it's the same spiel.

He was a good kid; except he made his sister cry.

He was a good kid; except he liked to torture animals.

He was a good kid until he got a gun.

I'm not saying that I believe Adam Malone is going to grow up to be the next Jeffery Dahmer. But he does have some alarming tendencies, especially towards kids he views as smaller and weaker than him.

I drum up my biggest, brightest smile, hoping it hides the wet shine of tears I feel burning behind my lids. It's the smile that says I believe her excuses, and that, *of course,* I'm mistaken. That *I* am the problem and deserve every nasty thing she has to say about me. Who am I in the grand scheme of her world? I'm just a teacher. A high-priced babysitter.

I swallow down the small flutter of anger flapping its fledgling wings in my chest. It only takes one student to ruin a classroom, and I'm desperate not to let that happen to my mine.

Victoria believes I am making a ruckus about nothing and has rewarded his horrible behavior. The last time we spoke, the very next day Adam came back to school with brand-new, rare-edition Nikes and then stomped all over another kid's lunch. If I hadn't separated the two, I fear worse would have happened. It's exhausting policing the kids' interactions when no one else seems to be on my side.

Honestly, what is her thought process about all of this? Does she think I'm making it up? Okay, sure. I'm not the teacher who started the school year with Adam. That had been Mrs. Hoffman, who is closing in on ten years as one of two fourth-grade teachers for Harbor View Montessori, Echo Bay's elite private academy.

Unfortunately, Mrs. Hoffman had to take her maternity leave early. Being pregnant with twins will do that to a woman.

Which left me sliding in as a full-time substitute for the rest of the year. Since I had just moved into Echo Bay, I desperately needed the job. But this grade isn't my specialty. I have no seniority and can't do much without being ignored or outvoted by my peers. That I am also an entire generation younger than the youngest teacher, at a whopping twenty-five, makes my fellow teachers question my judgment. Additionally, I struggle to connect with this age group.

Ten-year-olds are absolutely *feral.*

I'd always known I wanted to teach the lower grades. My true love is first grade. I want to help build the foundation of education that will carry my students forward for the rest of their lives.

The downside is that once a first-grade teacher gets the job, they stay on. Neither of the grade schools that service Echo Bay has a job opening in anything lower than fourth, and a ton is available in the public sector at Echo Bay Highschool, and a few more at Harborcrest Academy, the sister school to Harbor View. I know I'm not equipped to handle teenagers. They would eat me alive. I barely made it out of high school the first time.

I chose fourth grade. For now, I am stuck here, dealing with parents like Victoria.

A pang of missing my first graders back in my home state of Arizona whips through me. But I stuff down the emotion and brace myself for another barrage of denials.

"The other child probably started it."

I know this play. DARVO is a ploy straight out of the narcissist's playbook. Deny, attack, reverse, victimize, and offender.

No wonder her son is having trouble.

A discreet glance at the clock on my laptop, and I see Victoria's gone over her allotted time. That means I need to slice straight through the gaslighting. I don't have enough metal bandwidth left to gray rock her and make sure she doesn't get any emotional kibbles from me.

"Mrs. Malone, Adam is an exceptionally bright child."

I swallow around my parched throat, knowing that my next concern is going to send the woman flying off the handle.

Quickly, I take inventory of my desk, making sure there is nothing she can use as a weapon. Not seeing anything that can harm me, I forge on.

"However, I have noticed that he has trouble focusing when in a classroom environment."

Victoria narrows her eyes at me. They are a frosty, vicious blue slash through the ridiculous curtains of her eyelash extensions.

"What are you saying?" Her voice is low. Lethal. The atmosphere in the classroom shifts, making me feel unsafe in the school. I know there's guards stationed in the vestibule, but if Victoria decided to fight me, would they get here in time?

Sweat gathers at my nape and threatens to pool beneath my breasts. I'm a coward. I know I am. I hate confrontation.

Summoning my nerve, I force the words out in one breathless rush. "Have you had Adam tested for ADHD?"

I brace for the explosion, and Victoria does not let me down.

"How dare you!" Mrs. Malone smacks her palms flat on my desk.

I cringe as she curls her elegantly French-manicured nails into talons. Paper crumples and shrieks as she bunches them, tearing a few corners in her anger.

Then, she forcefully shoots her hands sideways, causing everything that had been neatly organized on my desktop calendar to scatter in every direction. Tests that I need to grade, the book reports I'm printing out from those who submitted them via E-Mail, and artwork that some of my students have drawn. It all goes flying, coating the honey-colored oak floor and plush area carpet in a blizzard of loose sheaves, a spiral notebook, dry-erase markers, and everything else that isn't nailed down.

I grab my laptop at the last second, making sure it doesn't wind up on the floor, too. I can't afford a new one if she breaks it.

Victoria gets in my face, and I flinch because I expect her to smack me. Her nostrils flare. I smell a minor hint of coffee on her breath, and the overpowering blast of haute couture perfume. The scent is heavy on the roses and deep with musk, making my sinuses burn at the affront.

I look into her eyes and feel those motes of anger ignite. Despite how angry she seems; her eyes are calm.

Bee with an itch!

She loves making me afraid of her. For Victoria, this whole thing is theater. She is an emotional vampire, and she feeds deeply when I put up a ruckus. The high from this argument will last her days. It will become a talking point that she can vent and dramatize with her friends and other parents for the next month. Until she needs another hit and plots our next confrontation.

Sometimes I wonder if she will escalate and resort to physical violence instead of mental warfare.

"There is nothing wrong with my son. Principal Sawyer is going to hear about this. And the superintendent."

Victoria's teeth are bared, and I hate myself as I turn away, giving her my cheek. For a minute I have a flash of a movie still, of the queen xenomorph in *Alien* snarling at Ripley. I feel my pulse thud in my throat, and the stress has nausea swirling in my gut. Her anger is toxic, coating me in an invisible, viscous sludge.

Then she moves, shoving her body weight against my desk. Being that I don't think she weighs more than a svelte one-hundred-and-fifteen pounds, it does nothing more than cause the wooden joists to squeak slightly. Kids like to climb on furniture, and if it's heavy like a bookshelf or desk, it's bolted down.

She pivots with all the grace of someone who has a former dancer's background. Her fluidity and confidence touch off the tiniest spark of envy in my chest. An unformed wish that I could borrow a drop of that confidence slips through my thoughts.

Then she stalks out of my classroom, culminating her tantrum with the *click* of her heels. By her direction, it's as if she's going to make a beeline straight down to the administrative office to complain. "I'm telling on you" is often her parting shot. But thus far, she hasn't actually filed the paperwork to get me into trouble.

I sag as all the tension and angst flees after her. I flop in my chair, letting loose a few of the tears I've kept at bay. Like a child dealing with a bully, I want to go home and have a good cry. Maybe dive into the bottom of a pint of ice cream. I feel as if I've been in a fight. My whole body aches from the tension, and I groan as a headache knifes the tender nerves around my temple.

I don't have that luxury.

As a homeroom teacher, I oversee sixteen students. I've blocked off a half hour for each parent who wants to meet, which eats up my entire day. Ever since the pandemic, most parents want to meet face-to-face with me today, beginning with my arrival at 8 am and ending at 3 pm. A few still like to do everything at a distance, so they will get the later video meetings that I can do at home.

Victoria is my second-to-last in-person meeting. That leaves only one remaining parent for me to talk with. Who, as I glance at my watch, is running late. A boon for me since Victoria has gone over her scheduled time.

Maybe I will have enough time to clean up the mess Victoria has maliciously left behind.

Sighing with a marrow-deep weariness, I slip out of my chair. I kneel and collect the markers which have rolled under my desk, and then gather papers which make up the bulk of the mess. Despite using digital for a lot of the kids' work, schools want to have hard copies. As if parents still stick their kids' graded tests and crayon drawings on the refrigerator as a point of pride. Now adays it's all scanned in and sent as photo attachments for digital frames or text messages.

I am almost done when the soft purr of my classroom door opening lets me know my last parent has arrived.

"I'll be right with you."

Narrowly avoiding bumping my head on the edge of my desk, I look up with a smile. Then I freeze as my hindbrain sounds the warning alarm; the visceral reaction of prey sensing a hunter and growing incredibly still so as not to catch their attention.

Except, I realize as my eyes sweep over the darkly suited, handsome man, it is already too late.

His nostrils flare as if catching my scent.

Then he smiles, accentuating his hard jaw and full, sensuous lips.

I don't have a robot flailing its arms around, but my brain screams its warning loud and clear: *Danger, Rina. Danger!*

Chapter Four

Rina

"Mrs. Hoffman?"

The unbelievably gorgeous stranger is talking, and I'm about five minutes behind on what he's saying.

I dismissively shake my head, scolding myself for thinking the boogeyman has just walked into my life. No, this man isn't dangerous. He's just an extremely good-looking parent doing right by his kid. The turmoil in my thoughts and the misfire of my instincts are just my personal demons rearing their ugly little heads.

Yet, I can't deny his captivating allure. He is awfully pretty to look at.

Sneaking another glance beneath my lowered lashes, I'm reminded of an expression I've heard but never truly understood—until now. It feels voyeuristic, almost superficial, and utterly shallow.

I think it anyway, even as I cringe inwardly at my thoughts. *God, he is sex on a stick.*

While I'm not a prude, I literally do not know how to deal

with hyper-attractive people. Take Victoria, for instance, and now this man. Unlike Victoria, who made me feel inferior, looking up at him ignites a sensation, a hot and tingling surge within. It leaves me feeling fidgety, awash with the awareness that I find him mind-searingly gorgeous, but knowing he is so far out of my league, I will never be a blip on his radar.

This is all just unreciprocated chemistry, a one-sided affair that will fuel my fantasies for months.

Reality punctures the contact high being in his orbit causes. I try to orientate my thoughts even as my pulse pummels me with the cadence of *not good enough.*

He's closer than I anticipated judging by the click of his footsteps on the hardwood. He moves like a well-dressed ninja, stealthy and sleek despite his expensive leather shoes. He towers directly above me and looks down to where I kneel at his feet. The tableau between us is both submissive and provocative, unsettling my equilibrium and sparking a subtle quiver, both in response to its implications if someone were to walk by, and the awakening stir of desire which thrums from my suddenly hardening nipples down to the gulley between my thighs.

This is not the situation I want to be in with any parent. Especially one who looks like him.

Oh. *Oh God.*

A wave of heat wafts over my skin, the first salvo of what will be a horrible, full-body, blotchy blush.

There's a certain, and mostly undeniable, truth when you're a teacher. Sometimes you meet parents who defy your expectations, for good or bad.

Occasionally, you'll meet one who is a celebrity, a politician, has more money than God, or is so delectably good-looking that they should be famous. When you do meet those rare unicorn-types of parents, it's imperative to act normal.

Nothing stops a parent from listening faster than acting starstruck. You move from the 'knows what she's talking about' category, to 'rabid fan'.

You do not, under any circumstances, gape up at them, stutter something that might have been language, or blush so hard that it's any wonder the sprinkler system hasn't picked up the rising heat. All those things make for a poor impression.

So of course, that's what I do. While I'm on my knees as if I'm about to *service* him.

If Principal Sawyer walked by, I would have to explain myself. Which would be difficult because the sheer *je ne sais quoi* this man exudes renders me mute.

A flash of amusement crosses the man's face, followed by a lopsided smirk that makes heat rush into all the tender crevices of my body, from my armpits to under my boobs, and between my thighs. The prickle of dampness *there* is as embarrassing as it is heady.

How am I wet over a smile?

Shoving my very broken instincts down, I mentally berate myself.

Get a grip!

I need to get myself in hand. It's embarrassing that it's taking me this long to find my bearings. I swallow my pride and coerce my reluctant limbs into motion. This damn man knows his effect on woman. Even from one who is already on her knees. That smirk says it all; that he commonly dodges the panties which are flung at him. He probably has a digital black book with which to pick and choose his dates like a menu; coochie on speed dial.

My thoughts are unkind, but they get me upright quicker. Unfortunately, I stand up so fast that the blood drains out of my head, leaving me lightheaded.

I wobble, catching myself on the end of my desk.

He steps closer, his fingertips ghosting along my elbow. His chest brushes across mine. The innocent pressure zaps me with an overwhelming quiver of lust. The breath I managed to draw is stolen by the scents of spicy black pepper and deep vanilla wood. His scent is utterly masculine and laced with an expensive cologne, beckoning me to lean in and deeply inhale.

There's just a hint of late-day gruff darkening what had been a clean shave this morning. I imagine the sensation against my skin. It would feel divine, and perhaps even leave marks if he were to...

Oh my God, I can't be fantasizing about a parent.

"No," I manage, so belatedly it's as if we are having a whole other conversation with our eyes.

His dark brow arches, their thick shape as dense as his hair..

Tearing my eyes away from him, I look over his shoulder at the color-coded chart of names on the back wall. I mentally recite all sixteen of my students twice until I feel calmer.

"Oh? Who are you then?"

I refocus. Taken as a whole, this man is overpowering. But in snippets? I can tolerate it.

He's incredibly tall, but for Washington State, that's par for the course. Men here tend to grow as tall as the Ponderosa pine trees that surround Echo Bay. He is draped in an expensive, flawlessly tailored suit, his attire fitting the elite setting of Harbor View Montessori. The city itself is a cozy enclave of affluence, perched on a floating peninsula separated from the mainland by the strait of Georgia, and nestled ninety miles northwest of Seattle. It offers all the nearby delights of the big city and wooded privacy for the right seven, to eight figure prices.

It's the first hop toward the San Juan Islands and Orcas Island. Commonly thought of as the Pacific Northwest haven of the rich and powerful, the only way in or out is by boat or private jet. Here, the obscenely wealthy seek refuge, hiding away from the prying eyes of the public and press. The confidentiality agreement I signed left no room for ambiguity—privacy reigns supreme in Echo Bay.

The only thing which interrupts his businessman chic are the tattoos. There's a wealth of ink that cuffs his throat and stains his chest, creeping up to cage his neck in what looks like black vines. He's not wearing a tie, and the top few buttons of his dress shirt are open, enticing me to gaze across his exposed collarbones. He has a winter pale complexion, that would probably look more like sun-kissed bronze during summertime.

More of the skin-deep artwork is prominently displayed on his knuckles, featuring boxy Slavic lettering, tattooed rings that band the joints, and a geometric rose on the top of his right hand. They continue up his wrists and disappear beneath his shirt sleeves.

He wears his brown hair in a modern style; short on the sides and long on top, with a hint of a wave brushed back at the hairline that suggests he would have curly hair if he grew it out. It's short, and elegantly styled with some kind of promenade, a posh topper to a ruggedly handsome, sculpted countenance. Overall, a look I've seen a hundred times on the average man and movie star.

He's not beautiful, but intense, drawing my attention like a uranium-plated magnet emitting low-level radiation; dangerous if taken in large doses and destructive to oneself if you get involved with him.

I know better. Or at least I thought I did.

So, what is it about him that glues my tongue to the roof of my mouth?

It strikes me when I decide to look him in the face again.

His eyes.

They are a misty gray, the type of foggy hue which reflects

the color he wears. With his black ensemble, they take on a sepulchral tint; a fog-soaked graveyard at night; a moonlit moor...

God, he has me waxing poetic.

I force on a smile and hold out my hand. "I'm Miss Christenson. Mrs. Hoffman is on leave for the rest of the year."

"Ah," he drawls, ignoring my hand. "I remember an E-mail saying such."

I drop my hand, feeling the sting of rejection, and plop the papers back onto my desk with a rustle. Then I scurry around to my chair. I need fortification, and the large wooden workspace will act as a barrier.

I glance at my Google calendar to read the name.

Mila Vasiliev's guardian, Edmond Vasiliev.

The late afternoon sun is hitting the building at an angle, bleeding interesting shadows across the classroom.

Harbor View Montessori is a posh, private school, funded by tithes, scholarships, and alumni donations from Echo Bay's private but extremely affluent citizens. With its new technology, pristine cleanliness, and beautiful feng shui layout, the academy is state of the art. It is less an institution than the school I attended, with the dismal paint and uglier linoleum of public education, and more a sanctuary of learning. One I wish that every child could experience to reach their full potential, and not just those with wealthy parents.

That is my mission statement. It calms me enough to focus on what's important in this meeting.

Mila.

When I learned I was staying on for the rest of the year, I hung white string lights and went wild with the decorations. Harbor View actually had a budget per *semester* for teachers.

Spring Break is closing in, and there are bunnies, painted eggs, and other icons of Easter and spring which are hung on the walls or draped around the borders of the desks. It looks cozy and peaceful; a retreat for all my students to learn in quiet serenity.

I stack the papers before me, creating a fortress of loose-leaf sheets and manila folders. Offside is my open laptop, allowing me to read the notes that Mrs. Hoffman had left for me about her students and their parents, with my addendums as I got to know the kids.

I am in control now, and I fix Mr. Vasiliev with a closed-mouth smile. All signs of my earlier fluster are gone.

"Please have a seat!"

Harbor View doesn't have the usual desks. Instead, there are tables and chairs, five tables with four chairs at each. The wood is protected with some type of laminate that makes cleaning up paint, markers, and crayon marks a dream.

They are also full-size, which I am thankful for. I can't imagine Mr. Vasiliev squeezing into a kiddo-sized seat like he would have had to if this had been my first-grade classroom.

Just thinking of his height draws my attention back to him. There is a chart in the doorway, allowing the kids to track their growth spurts as the months go by.

Edmond is at least six-foot-two. Almost a full foot above my five-foot-four.

He loosens the button on his suit jacket, grabs one of the brightly colored chairs, and spins it around so that he can sit in it. Everything he does is edged with elegance, as he somehow turns a school chair into a throne.

Amusement curls on the edges of his mouth. Even in such a ridiculous position, his presence commands attention. His light-colored eyes are intense, watching me with an unwavering focus that sends my pulse speeding again. Leaving a fluttery sensation in the pit of my stomach, that if I'm not careful, can reignite into a blush again.

I look away, briefly scolding myself.

I will not lust for my student's father.

I might just have to write that a thousand times on the whiteboard behind me or go Dolores Umbridge on myself. Because my libido is *not* getting the message.

I clear my throat.

"Mila's doing well," I begin. "Her creativity is... quite remarkable."

My fingers tremble as I slide out Mila's folder and open it. Art is one of my favorite subjects to teach. It isn't until the kids reach sixth or seventh grade that they will begin exchanging classrooms and following a specific schedule in preparation for high school. For now, they spend the entire day with me. Each hour is slated for a particular subject.

"She really has an exceptional eye for color."

I pick out a few of my favorite pieces Mila drew and fan them across the front of my desk for him to look at if he wants.

Tension bleeds into Edmond's face. If I hadn't been practically staring at him like a creeper, I might never have noticed. It is subtle. A slight shift of his chiseled jawline. A tick of muscle in his cheek. He nods, encouraging me to continue, but his gaze lingers, unwavering and unnerving.

"She's an artist, like her mother was."

I lick my lips, trying to moisten them. Mrs. Hoffman had left no clues behind about what might have happened to Mila's parents. Only that both are deceased, and her uncle is her legal guardian and has been for the past two years. Nor do I know why she has his surname and not her father's.

I don't dare pry into the tragedy. The wound is still fresh.

Instead, I nod, my fingers absently tracing the edge of a drawing.

"For being so young, she works with swirling colors and

bold strokes. Suggesting the shape of people, and animals, but with a surrealist bend."

"Have you thought of art lessons for her?"

Edmond sits back in the chair, his hands folded in his lap.

"Now that I know she has latent talent, I'll speak with her and see if she wants to learn."

I love parents who see merit in the arts. Even though Edmond wasn't Mila's father by birth, it seems he has taken his position as her guardian to heart.

I feel myself relaxing, and nearly forget how intensely attractive he is.

Almost.

"Mrs. Hoffman left a note earlier in the year about her math skills. I'm very pleased to report that they have improved significantly. She's working hard."

Lines branch out around the sides of Edmond's mouth as he smirks again. I know that look isn't about me, but whatever thought crossed his mind when I mentioned math.

"I'm glad to hear that. I've been trying to help her at home, but I'm afraid numbers were never my strong suit."

I blink, wondering if he's teasing me. I've never met a businessman who was poor at mathematics. I can feel myself blushing as warmth spreads up from my neck, sinks into my cheeks, and touches the tips of my ears. As I duck my head, my hair fortunately conceals that bright flush of red.

Quickly, I look down at the papers, the next layer being the math quizzes that show Mila's improvements.

"We're focusing on fractions next week; she should find it interesting."

"Fractions," he repeats. "I'll try to keep up."

He *is* laughing at me. I'm just not sure why. I glance up, finding his almost-blue eyes drilling into mine. At this moment, the classroom feels too small, the air charged with an energy that has nothing to do with parent-teacher meetings.

I break the contact and drop my gaze back to the papers.

"Mila is well adjusted."

I'm so rattled by his presence.

God, his charisma. It's enough to want to bottle it for those unlucky enough to ooze such sex-appeal.

I feel more than hear Mr. Vasiliev stand. Darting a look at the clock, I see that thirty-minutes haven't passed yet.

Is he leaving already?

By the time I look at him again, Mr. Vasiliev has crossed the scant distance and stands in front of my desk.

No. He *looms* before it. His presence eats up all the oxygen and space until it feels as if the vast room has shrunk to the size of a closet. Leaving a tiny, crackling ledge where only the two of us exist. Teetering together on the cusp above a black hole that's ready to consume us both.

I draw a ragged breath, wondering if he can hear just how fast my heart is racing. I know I'm tomato-red, blushing from toe-tips to nose with my unseemly attraction. I need to get a grip. But goodness, Mr. Vasiliev is staring at me with such a single-focused look that I swear my simple cardigan, button-up shirt, and dress slacks are going to combust. Or maybe I'm imagining it. There's no way a man who looks like Edmond Vasiliev would ever pay any attention to me. That I now have his focus is simply because of his dutiful diligence in investing in Mila's future. Maybe that's how the teachers before me did it. He flirts with them, makes them feel like the center of his world, and ensures his niece a bright and shiny grade.

It almost works. For a moment, I would do anything to keep his attention.

Then my uncharacteristic, selfish thoughts fade. I force my hand steady and tuck a non-existent flyaway behind my ear.

I'm not a teacher to be bought, not for money, new cars, or a pretty face.

"Call me Edmond."

I blink up at him.

"Wha—"

His grin is a flash of porcelain white teeth. "My name, Miss Christenson."

Oh. "Okay."

Mr. Vasiliev – Edmond – holds his hand out for mine across the top of my desk. I stare at it as if it were a rattlesnake. He'd resisted shaking my hand earlier. Now he's offering his smooth hands to me.

I guess the meeting is wrapping up. There's more I wanted to talk about, but it is just small talk. The small details to fill up the time when he's heard everything he needs to know.

Mila is thriving.

My hands are clammy, and I rub them discreetly down my thighs. I swear I see him check my ring finger. As if the Miss hasn't given it away.

No ring.

No fiancée.

No real want of either.

Our fingers brush, palms meet, and I feel the flesh-on-flesh connection jolt from where my smaller hand is engulfed in his much larger one. It sings all the way up my arms, and into my chest where it settles like a seed of potential.

Edmond's fingers tighten, and I think for a moment he's going to bring mine up and kiss them. I'm breathless, wondering how I never realized that *hands* could be an erogenous zone. His fingers are beautiful, making me think of a musician, perhaps a pianist. Someone who can create with them.

He lets me go and slips his hands into his pockets, derailing the jumbled mess of my thoughts.

"It sounds as if Mila is in excellent hands. Thank you for your attention, Miss Christenson."

I want to repeat what he said. Maybe throw in a flirtatious *'Call me Rina'*. But the words don't come. I can only stare after him as he gives me a searing look, and calmly walks out of the classroom, leaving me in chaos.

Chapter Five

Edmond

I *nearly kissed Mila's teacher.*

I don't go around molesting strange women. In fact, I don't kiss at all. Those that I do date know the drill: a nice dinner, a quick fuck, and out the door they go. Sex is a bodily function that I indulge in as I would small pastries and the occasional double-shot espresso – a treat when the stress gets too high. When I indulge, it's as effortless and easy as a business transaction, without any messy strings or annoying emotions. That I nearly pulled Rina out of her chair and ravaged her right there atop her desk nearly sends me fleeing from the school.

I don't run, even though my legs itch to put as much distance between myself and Mila's teacher. That is what I need to remind myself of. Rina is Mila's teacher. She's not someone quick fuck that I can ignore when I'm done with her.

My long strides devour the ground between the classroom and the security in the front foyer. I'm trying to outpace the confusing sensations and the urge to go back and leave my mark upon her. *Mine* my brain is saying, and my cock is throbbing and on board for that deranged notion. Except claiming her is a whole clusterfuck that I can't have in my life. I don't entangle innocents in the Brotherhood's business.

The crisp air snaps at me when I finally escape the school, and I wait for the brisk slap that cold weather brings. Hoping it knocks some sense into me.

Instead, a craving to go back in and see if Rina tastes like strawberries makes me fist my hands in my pocket.

Fuck.

I've never felt a connection like that with a woman, especially not one who looks like her. I prefer a more worldly experience. There's something about Rina that makes me think she's never done more than hold hands with a man. Let alone get shoved up against a wall and impaled on a thick cock or had an orgasm so hard her juices dribble down their balls. That I *want* to do that to her, tells me it's a bad idea.

Don't think about sticking your dick in her.

She is off limits.

I focus on Leon, anchoring myself in the here and now, and not the fantasyland that's tugging at my thoughts. He stands sentry by the sleek black Rolls Royce Cullinan, his silhouette framed by the crisp late winter sun. It smells like spring to me, the salty wetness of an urban winter mixed with a slight hint of petrichor from the encroaching rain.

As I step out from the shaded overhang, the warmth of the sun embraces me, and I reach into the inner pocket of my suit, feeling the cool, smooth texture of my shades. I slide them on and then glance over my shoulder, before forcing my thoughts forward instead of back on Rina's delicate allure.

Maybe I just need to get laid. There are any number of women I can call up for a good time.

In my world, relationships are arranged. It's a bad sport to kill one's in-laws. Which leads to a lot of intermarrying among the families. Even beyond the cultural borders of the *Bratva* and into the Sicilian and Irish bloodlines.

Historically, the Brotherhood has had close ties with the *Cosa Nostra* and the Irish Mob. There was a truce hashed out after a bloody civil war in the 80s, when both the *Cosa Nostra* and the *Camorra* were fighting over the Northeast, the Irish in the Midwest, the *Bratva* here in the Pacific Northwest, and the cartels pushing up from the south. Some of the families made a Covenant with one another, promising support in times of strife; a fraternity of mobsters.

Now, most of the fighting has remained restricted amongst state borders, and the small satellite towns with no fealty which are up for grabs to whatever group wants to take them over.

Eventually, to keep the peace, I will marry like Nadia did. She tied her fate to Anton Kiselyov and the New York branch of the Brotherhood, which so happened to be intertwined with my uncle who oversees that cell. That left my dating life easy, with no strings and no risk of attachment.

I doubt Rina would want a quick fuck. She's not what I expected. Her appearance suggests innocence, and she exudes an air of youthfulness. A good demeanor for a kindergarten teacher, but I have a hard time believing she has the kids in her classroom in hand. She's a good decade younger than Mrs. Hoffman was. There's something about her presence that permeates my senses, leaving an indelible mark.

Because I'm apparently a fucking lunatic, I lift my hand that caged hers and sniff. The faint scent of her floral perfume lingers in my nostrils, delicate and inviting.

I rarely go for the petite, elfin-looking women like her. Rina could easily pass as a moonlighting imp; soft and with the plush thickness to her hips and thighs that make a man want to sink between them.

She's a jarring contrast to my usual preference for leggy,

statuesque blondes with sharp, foxlike features and waif-like bodies. The pin-thin models who are all sharp angles and sharper tongues. The memory of their meticulously sculpted faces and the subtle scent of their high-end cosmetics floods my mind, a carousel of look-alike women I'd never be able to pick out of a lineup.

My prior flings are all the same type: women who embody the West Coast elite's obsession with perfection. They've honed their natural beauty into weapons, utilizing an army of skillful surgeons to attract wealthy men into their alluring trap. Their buoyant, silicone-boosted curves defy the gaunt physiques they've cultivated through rigorous diets and exercise regimens. Eye-catching? Sure. Realistic? No.

I never thought I'd go for a cute little redhead.

Yet, as I recall the way Rina blushed every time her eyes met mine, an electric sensation tingles on my skin. It's a tactile memory of her vulnerability, a sensation that sends a surge of heat straight to my groin. *Mine.* This time both my cock and brain chant the word.

No. Not yours.

I clench my jaw, fighting to maintain composure, determined not to let anyone see the undeniable physical response she elicits.

The discreet cough from Leon interrupts my reverie, pulling me back to the present. I shake my head, berating myself for getting lost in my thoughts.

I slide into the plush backseat of the luxury SUV, one of a fleet the I own, that I've added after-market upgrades to, like the bulletproof glass, armored shielding on the door panel, and mobile armory in the trunk.

The aroma of fine calf-skin leather and wood polish fills my nostrils. The tinted windows surrounding me, casting the interior into shadow, are an illegal shade of ultra-black, shielding me from prying eyes.

The shocks bounce as Leon lumbers into the front seat. Marcus meets my eyes in the rearview mirror.

"You okay, Boss?"

"Fine."

Or I will be once I find out some flaw that will get Rina's floral-scented burrs out from beneath my skin.

Working my phone free from the pocket of my jacket, I swiftly unlock it, the smooth glass screen cool against my fingertips. I navigate to my list of contacts and select one of my top and most trustworthy allies. He goes by D4663R (Dagger). I know his real name, but out of respect and concern for my privacy, I don't call him by it.

D4663R answers on the second ring. No voice, just a *click click* that lets me know I've connected.

"Find out everything you can about Rina Christenson." I rattle off the scant few facts I know about her.

Another set of clicks and D4663R ends the call. He's good at what he does, and he'll have a dossier on Mila's teacher by the end of the day.

As I settle deeper into the leather seat, I immerse myself in the digital world, sifting through notifications, emails, and texts that flooded in during the meeting. I focus on the task at hand, deliberately keeping thoughts of Rina from intruding, though her presence lingers in the recesses of my mind. Each mental nudge stirred by the occasional scent of lavender that lingers on my fingertips.

Chapter Six

Edmond

Killing a man is no easy weight for the soul to carry. Even one as black and malevolent as mine. No matter how many men I've slaughtered at the altar of mafia business, I remember each name and face.

Meeting Mila's teacher and being faced with a creature so sweet and delicate highlights the mortal sins which stain me, a brutal reminder of the choices I've made, and the doors eternally closed against me. I am tainted, and no amount of bleach or scouring will ever make me clean. Not enough to be able to touch such a pure creature and not sully her too.

Angels are not meant to deal with devils.

My men know my routine well. They know to stay out of my way as the ghosts come for their pound of flesh. The time I spent in the *Bratva's* Gulag haunts my steps. Those who aspire to greatness in the Brotherhood all travel the same path. Four years at one of the Covenant's covert Art schools learning Ballet, Art, Affluency, Business, and Butchery beneath a cadre of retired mobsters and hitmen. If you aspire to the upper echelons of the mafia, then you spend a year proving you can survive the lifestyle.

For the *Bratva,* its Siberia. There, in the ice-strewn tundra, you must prove that you have what it takes to *lead* in the Brotherhood's name.

I withstood it, but I sacrificed pieces of my humanity to do so.

The memories carry me steadfastly into the training room that I utilize to hone the skills I learned during the many fights I survived in the *Bratva's* training system. In this, I am a machine.

Cold.

Unfeeling.

Remorseless.

At least, that is how I usually am. It isn't remorse that scrapes long talons against my brainstem. It's something new. A nameless emotion that unsettles my usual icy demeanor.

I shove it out of my thoughts as I strip free of my business outfit and into gray sweatpants, devolving from billionaire businessman to brutish thug by the time I reach skin.

When I train, I prefer to go shirtless and shoeless because that is how I'd been taught. Warmth is a luxury, and one must embrace the painful, icy weather as if inviting Mother Russia Herself into our hearts. There, hidden amid coniferous trees and snow-capped mountains, the *Bratva* teaches the new generations the ways of the old; by putting us through our paces in forced labor camps set up to mimic the ones that the Soviet Union had been known for. Brutal is a gentle word to describe conditions there. We fought barefoot, searing our skin on the glacial stonework. Letting the elements lash at us like serrated whips, dodging the fists, knives, sticks, and kicks all trying to break us down.

In the Gulag, I built upon the foundation of ballet and

learned The System, a technique taught to Russian spies before sending them out into the world. Since then, I have maintained my flexibility with Yoga and Taekwondo, and added additional martial arts until my body is as much of a weapon as any gun.

My favorite is Arnis, the Filipino style of fighting with knives.

I wrap my fists with tape methodically, staring at the hanging bag that will warm me up.

The bag has a name, even if it's faceless. *Yevgeny.* My "mentor" spent a year breaking me into pieces beneath his heavy knuckles.

I have memories of the man that I'd been before Pops sent me to Siberia. The person who came out of the Gulag, bearing my first tattoo of service, was someone else entirely.

Pops had told me, ad nauseam, that I needed to be tough for Nadia. That I would be the iron fist to carry out her decree. That meant doing unthinkable, savage things, and learning all the ways to break a man. So that she could have plausible deniability and be free of the nightmares that awaken me in the night when a particularly cold wind reminds me of Siberia.

I throw the first punch and it's weak, leaving disgust to hang over my head like Yevgeny's deriding laughter. I haven't slacked in my training. I diligently apply myself for an hour every day, pushing my body to its physical limits. Without that consistency, I'll be a machine rusting in the rain. I never know when my enemy will come for me. While I have guards whom I trust beyond measure, whose loyalty is bought and paid for in blood, flesh, and inked vows. In the end, the only person I can count on is myself.

Nadia knew I would sacrifice everything for her. Right now, I don't have Mikhail's support.

And when he returns, he might plant the knife between my shoulder blades himself.

I've sent him to a place worse than hell. When Pops shipped me off, I wasn't sure I would ever forgive him. That he died not long after, made forgiveness easier.

Will I have to die to be redeemed in my brother's eyes?

Anger threatens to break through my carefully built walls. Emotions can make you careless in a fight.

The next punch is harder, with more force behind it. But that's not control. That's rage. It boils inside of me, surging up from the volcanic pit of my gut until I want to spew lava and vitriol.

I smash into the bag in a flurry of fists as the memories I've buried deep lurch out of their box. The Gulag befouls me, leaving a sickness behind that oozes and slops out from the fractures in my mind. Each crack is a name from my ever-increasing number of murders. Soon, I'll run out of flesh on my forearms to catalogue each death. These sooty epitaphs are etched in the old ways, with sewing needle and pen ink - pain and blood their everlasting memorial.

Thump. The terror of hands in the dark, dragging me from my narrow cot. Their jeering laughter as they herd me out of the prison cell in the middle of the night. Until I'm in the center of the yard. Barbed wire spools on the top of the cinder-block walls. Floodlights on, hot splashes of light picking out the circle of men waiting for me. By their tattoos, they are heavyweights in the Bratva.

Thump. One man steps forward, his flesh a brutish tapestry of scars and ink. Scorpions and black widows blend in with hatch marks from the hordes of men he's killed. Later, I learn his name, when I'm spitting up blood from the broken nose he gave me in greeting.

Thump. Yevgeny the Eviscerator. Because that is how he kills his victims. Exsanguination. Evisceration. He is deadly with a blade. He doesn't care that I'm supposed to return in one piece. Why would he? If I can't withstand this training, what good will I be to Nadia? He reminds me, frequently, that I'm a spoiled rich boy who isn't worthy of the stars my father intends to bestow upon me.

Thump. Pavel. The first man I kill, the one who makes Iustina sing in the night before I take her from his limp hand. A boy not much older than I'd been, intended to be a low-level enforcer for the security group in backwater Vyborg, an outlying city on the outskirts of St. Petersburg. It would be him or me. The two of us grapple and fight in the showers, the grimy tiles slick with soap scum and running water. Him full of jealousy that I have Yevgeny's attention. The fight is the perfect education, teaching me with life-long scars over the perils of fighting with anger as your furnace and how easy it can sputter out. Me, simply trying to survive this savage education, this insane initiation into the Brotherhood. In the end, I survive by smashing his head into the dingy tiles over, and over, and over again until blood and viscera leaks out of his cracked skull.

I spin away, my body heaving with exertion. Sweat slicks my torso and threatens to blind my eyes with its salty sting. My muscles croon for violence. Stalking across to the other side of my gym, I lift the lid on the wooden, velvet-lined box where a half-dozen knives are laid. None as beautiful as Iustina. She is for true work, and I would never betray her steel perfection by training her on wooden stand-ins. Nothing less than blood sates her when drawn.

Instead, I pick two simple, black-handled knives, and lapse into Arnis' familiar forms.

Yevgeny taught me much about knife play. The hand-to-hand give and take that's required to trap and block an opponent's weapon. How to control it and lock their approach. My body remembers every movement, even after eight years. I move without thought, while my memory continues to torture me. Lining up every face that has fallen beneath my hands, one after the other, until I am drowning in a river of blood.

There is no washing these stains away.

What would Rina think if she could see me now?

She would run screaming. I am the monster under her bed, not the prince I saw reflected in her eyes.

"Boss."

I didn't hear Lev arrive. The guards closest to me know not to interrupt me while I'm exercising unless it's vitally important. Like someone trying to blow up the gate with a rocket launcher. Approaching me in this state is dangerous for them. A man at my back in the Gulag meant I was dead.

At his voice, I crouch immediately, pivoting at the hip, and fling the knife before I realize where I am. Luckily, part of my mind knew that the danger is all in my head.

The knife sails past Lev's ear and *thunks* into the wall.

Lev swallows, his Adam's apple bobbing tightly. He doesn't say anything as I straighten, both of us pretending I didn't try to take his head off with a tactical blade.

I loop a towel around my neck as I clean my knives and return them to their case. Then I grab a bottle of water and turn to face Lev. Dressed in gangster couture, he's an Armani man like myself, with the only spark of light on his black-on-black ensemble being a silver wire tie-tack shaped like a wolf's head.

He is second in command behind Mikhail. My interim brigadier until my brother returns, hopefully of sound mind, to fill the role. He is loyal, his vows inked into his flesh, his body honed by blood and pain.

"Tell me."

Lev swallows again. Then he pulls his hand out of his pocket and holds a small baggie out to me. There are three round, mint-green pills stamped with a shamrock.

I pinch the zip-locked top and lift it.

"Ecstasy?"

"Yeah. Fentanyl-laced molly."

Lev flinches because this is worse than cocaine or even heroin. Fentanyl kills in micro-doses. While I can't stop people from going outside the city to get their fix, that's a 'them' problem. Because if I find out, I'd murder them for their daring. I'll help anyone who wants to get clean, but there's a limit of when aide becomes enabling.

Memories of my mother skitter across my thoughts. I'm not in a safe headspace, especially to open that door. But the rage. It surges against the cage I keep locked inside, wanting to torment me about why I have such a militant need to have everything beneath my control.

I rule more than just Echo Bay. My empire stretches south to Seattle, East to Tacoma, and all the way north to the Canadian border. With that large of a territory, it's impossible to keep a lid on everything. The Pacific Northwest is a pressure cooker of contrasting politics and ideals. Which is why I made Echo Bay my sanctuary, with one rule. One fucking rule that those who for me in some capacity and wish to live in Echo Bay follow.

No drugs.

If I find anyone dealing in the city limits, they get no second chance. They're executed, and their fingers sent to the stupid kingpins who thought to invade my territory with their poison. It used to be the cartels, before they decided to diversify into avocado farms.

I figure, if I can't keep a sixty-square mile radius clean, I have no right to be one of the *Bratva* elite.

Shoving down the seething heat rising beneath my skin, I focus on Lev.

"Where's it being dealt from?"

"You know that shitty little strip club that opened up outside of town a couple of years ago?"

Sindoll's Cabaret. As if adding a French word would make it any less sleazy.

"The one that's 120 yards outside Echo Bay's town limit?"

Echo Bay doesn't stretch the whole length of I-5. Like the state itself, there are small patches of urbanization and then miles of woodland and forests. There's a twelve-mile buffer of trees between the edge of the city and where the actual line ends.

"Yeah, that one."

The anger inside of me crystallizes, hardening into a diamond-plated knife. This isn't an accident. Someone has thought to set up shop that close to where I mark the border of Echo Bay, and then send this trash out.

"There's more." Lev shifts on his feet. His anxiety ratchets up, and beads of sweat darken his brow.

"Who is it?" There's only one thing that gets my men all antsy: family.

"Anna."

"The cousin you fostered with as a child?" Lev and Anna are as close as any siblings, even if they don't share parents.

Lev pales. He seems to age ten years in front of me.

"She's helping deal it to the customers."

Her drug addiction is why she isn't on my payroll. Anna craves drugs more than she wants financial security.

Just like another woman I know.

Tossing the baggie onto the table beside my knives, I rub the towel over my sweat-slick face, schooling my features into something less murderous before looking Lev dead in the eye. I'm proud that Lev brought this to me, even at the personal cost.

"There are two ways this can go."

"I know, Boss."

"What do you choose? I can handle it, or you can."

Lev presses his hand to his mouth, flashing the Cyrillic letters on his knuckles. He pinches and then rubs the sides of his lips. A distant look fills his brown eyes as he weighs the options before him.

If I get involved, I'll make an example of her. Should Lev choose to take on the burden of his cousin, that choice is going to be carried on his shoulders: he could kill her or get her out of the state. But this is a blood-hungry scythe that could swing back, and end pressed against his throat. It wouldn't be just Anna's head in the basket, but his own on the chopping block. If she ever comes back, ever gets herself in my business, I'll take them both out. Loyalty only goes so far.

Finally, Lev drops his hand. It shakes as he pushes it into his pocket.

"I'll handle it, Boss."

A grim resolve paints Lev's face. He looks stoic as he unflinchingly meets my eyes. He's been an excellent Lieutenant, and I hope his gamble pays off.

"So be it. Set up a meeting with the owner. Preferably somewhere other than Sindoll's. During the meeting, I want you to torch the strip club. Make sure none of the girls are harmed."

"Yes, Boss."

Lev turns on his heel and rapidly strides out of my gym, getting a start on the Anna issue. Hopefully, if I cut the head off the octopus, the tendrils will recede from just how dangerously close they are to penetrating Echo Bay's borders.

I look again at the pills. Though I don't know for certain, I have a feeling I know who is behind this new influx.

Fucking Irishmen.

Chapter Seven

Rina

Fatigue nips at my heels as I arrive home. It's an arduous task just getting out of the car. I wait a minute, catching my breath after a long, weary day that's settled into my bones. Making me feel a whole decade older than I am.

Although the townhome I rent has a garage, I don't pull my car inside. I idle on the curb, pressing my forehead against the steering wheel and closing my eyes. Stealing a fleeting, fragile moment for myself. I have so few of them, that I hoard these precious seconds like treasure.

I'm not staying, even though my whole body begs for rest. All I want to do is topple face-first into my bed and wrap myself up in fleece.

I can't, and that's just a bitter pill to swallow.

Tonight is a night I work until late. I have two other part-time jobs outside of the full-time one at the school. One is as a server at *La Baia Italiana*, a swanky Italian restaurant down at the waterfront. It doesn't serve breakfast or lunch, and its reservation list is non-existent. Dining at *La Baia* is first come first serve, which generates an odd need for people to line up and wait for the doors to open. The restaurant's specialty is extravagant, old-world dinners and wine pairings.

The last thing I want to do after dealing with parents all day is to contend with memorizing the night's specialties. Hopefully, it's something easy, like lasagna and the catch of the day. Which, with how the fishing is in the harbor, it is always trout.

I don't have much of a choice about working multiple jobs, not if I want to continue living in Echo Bay.

The sole pain in my ass reason I sacrifice so much of myself for welcomes me home with the smell of burning. Walking in the front door, I'm immediately smacked by the acrid stench of something noxious, like charred plastic. At least the fire alarm isn't blaring, which tells me the emergency has passed and this is just the remnants of it.

I brace myself in the foyer, trying not to breathe through my nose, but getting myself in the headspace to deal with whatever situation Lucia is having.

Did I say that fourth graders were feral?

High schoolers are worse. They are all mini sociopaths that you hope grow out of their craziness before they do any lasting harm. This includes my sixteen-year-old sister.

I can hear her cussing in the kitchen. While I don't know the language choice she's using to vent her annoyance, there's a cadence to swearing that's unmistakable. The vowels are guttural and sharp, rising and falling like an EKG meter tracking Lucia's anger-elevated pulse.

That I can hear her is an impressive feat because she has some music blasting from her wireless speaker perched on the narrow countertop beside the fridge, filling the entire house with the cadence of Mongolian throat singing. She's been working on the technique lately, since it's supposed to help one become a more versatile singer.

The house we're renting isn't exactly a house. It has the bones of an old Victorian, but it has been split into halves - kind of resembling a townhome but more like a duplex.

From the front door, there's a narrow beige-painted hallway that branches out toward what was likely the original sitting room or a den but is now our front room. The kitchen sits directly right of the stairs that leads up to our second floor and the attic hatch.

Straight past the stairs, an old mudroom that has been repurposed into a laundry room. That was the selling point of the rental, and why we didn't move into more modern apartments. Having a washer-and-dryer hookup right there is worth all the trouble of living in an old house; from the squeaky pipes to the constant draft around the windows that sucks out all the heat. Layers are how we survive the winter, since turning the furnace on is basically just tossing buckets of money I don't have out the window.

Past the machines, the door leads out into the shared backyard that's grown wild with scrub grass, overgrown shrubs, and maple trees. I don't have the time to weed whack the overgrowth. My neighbor is an older woman who keeps an eye on Lucia, and sometimes brings us over extra casseroles and desserts. I can't see Marianne out there handling the lawn. As for the landlord, the less I see of him the better. He's always trying to convince me that he can shave off some of the cost of rent if I do *favors* for him.

The air in the kitchen is smoky, carrying that unmistakable grit of burned food. Waving my hand in front of my face to try to clear the way through, I walk in and catch sight of Lucia standing in front of the stove.

When we'd moved to Echo Bay, I'd bought shiny new, and

very cheap cookie sheets to celebrate. One of them now has some black crusty stuff on it. Honestly, it's a charcoal briquette. I have no idea what Lucia was trying to cook.

"Luce?"

Lucia screams and spins around, dropping the sheet pan back onto the stove with a loud *bang*.

"Can you be any quieter?"

I don't point out that I can't hear myself think over the loud music filling the kitchen. A herd of wild buffalo could tromp through the house and do a Conga line and she wouldn't hear them.

Not wanting to pick a fight, I shake my head and hold my palms up. A placative gesture that I hope wards away her anger before it has a chance to brew. Then I ease around the honey-badger that's my sister and turn the speaker off.

Blessed silence.

While we moved to Echo Bay for Lucia, she hadn't wanted to leave Arizona during her Junior Year of high school.

I get it. I hadn't wanted to leave my friends and established classroom either. This is all for her benefit. Somehow, it became all twisted in her hormone-driven thoughts and now – as she tells it - she's being forced to live here, a prisoner in an ivory tower away from civilization. And I'm the swamp witch keeping her captive.

Never mind that the sole reason we are even in Echo Bay is so she can attend Harborcrest Academy. It is of the most coveted and prestigious institutions for the artistically gifted on this side of New York. Lucia's academic grades could be better, but with her talent they don't need to be. If she wants to increase her chances of getting into Julliard, NYU's School of Art, or any performance art college, she needs two years at the Academy. Back in Arizona, she'd been stagnating, having reached the limits of her private tutors and the local studios back home.

Lucia's teachers say she's a *multipotentialite*. She not only excels at singing, but visual arts, dance, and surprisingly languages. She's only sixteen and already considered a polymath.

Some days she remembers *why* we're here. On other days, she's obstinate and hates me for moving us to Washington and away from our mother.

Lucia still believes that Mom will choose us instead of another baggie of drugs or the bottom of a bottle or whichever man she's using to supply both. After twenty-five long years of hoping for the same, I know better, and I'm not going to allow Lucia to put her life on hold until she realizes Mom's a black-hole waiting to swallow up all the good in her life.

"What were you making?" I take a step closer to the stove.

It's a known fact that Lucia can't cook. Period. She doesn't have the attention span for it. She'll be in the middle of boiling water for pasta, and an hour later I'm left wondering why the smoke alarm is buzzing. Choreography, music, and art fill her head, which leaves little room for anything else. Kind of like how Einstein barely remembered to tie his shoes. The small, menial things are just that: unimportant to people on the cusp of genius. For Lucia, that menial thing is setting a timer so that she can remember to take her food out of the microwave or, you know, eat.

Lucia's mouth pinches. Her lower lip plumps out, making her look as if she's pouting. God, forbid I tell her that though, because *she's not five years old anymore*. Pouting is for kids.

I'm not sure she's going to tell me, but she finally shakes her head and spins away from the mess on the stove.

"I was trying to make some angel food cake bars with the cherry pie filling you had."

The skeptic in me looks at the charred remnants. It looks nothing like dessert bars.

She gnaws the interior of her bottom lip with her teeth. "I remembered that cherry desserts were your favorite. I figured I could do it."

She shrugs as if it's no biggie. But this is huge. It's bigger than big.

My heart melts. How can it not? There's almost a decade between Lucia and me. I can remember when she was born, and I was already an adult when her teenage drama arrived. Back then, she was my little shadow. She knew I'd protect her and would scurry into my bed when mom and her men went on wild binges, or we went a week without seeing her. Those moments trauma bonded us, at least for a time. As she's grown older, she's put up a wall between us.

It hurts.

But sometimes, like now, I see hints of my sweet little sister peeking through.

I want to make a big deal of it. Having someone remember what you like, especially with the home life we grew up in, is huge.

But, I know Lucia, and the moment I try and thank her, or say anything *nice* about the gesture, she'll shut down and turn into a prickly cactus.

Her therapist called it oppositional defiant disorder. It manifested when she hit puberty. You can say the sky is blue and she'll tell you off and declare it fuchsia. Her favorite drink is Sonic limeade, but if I try and remind her that, she'll swear its Diet Coke. Even though aspartame gives her a headache.

In her mind, I am her biggest enemy while all I want to be is her most devoted supporter.

Swallowing the longing to hug her, I poke the flaky black thing that has ruined the cookie sheet.

"Well, they look like shit."

Lucia looks up at me. A hint of surprise brightens her hazel eyes. The similarity in our eye color is the only sign we're sisters. Beyond that, we look nothing alike. While I have red in my hair, Lucia takes after our mother. She's incredibly tall and twiggy, with the lissome lines of a ballerina even though she prefers hip hop. Her hair is the pure cornsilk-blond locks our mom is known for. The Arizona sun has transformed the light color even more, bleaching a few strands until they resemble platinum. Women pay good money at salons for her hair color, and it's all natural. Today must have been a visual arts day, because she's used chalk in to turn the ends a vivid sky blue.

"Bitch." Her voice lacks venom as she laughs.

Crisis averted.

"I'm just thankful you didn't burn the kitchen down."

Grabbing the pan, I carry it out through the backyard. I don't know if I'll be able to scrape off the sugar that looks like it's melted into the pan. Either way, the non-stick sheen is beyond repair. Mourning the cookie sheet's brief life, I dump the whole thing into the black bag.

When I return, Lucia is leaning against the countertop, fiddling with the zipper on her hoodie. She isn't known to fidget, which leaves me immediately wary of what she wants to tell me.

"Sooo," she drawls.

I wash my hands and then dry them slowly on a striped kitchen towel, looking down at the soft fringe on its edges. If I don't make eye contact, she won't clam up and might actually tell me what's going on.

"I have detention on Friday."

I shut my eyes, wanting to sigh, but hold it back. For someone who *loves* being in a performing arts school, she's trying to get herself kicked out. I've lost count of how many phone calls, written warnings, and detentions she's gotten herself into in the last six months. If she gets expelled, I don't know what we'll do. The hopelessness of that future makes my pulse race and knots my stomach.

"Look."

Lucia jumps straight to bristling, taking exception to the look on my face. The expression is one that she thinks means I'm disappointed in her but means I'm just *tired*. Tired of trying to mother my little sister. Tired of working three jobs.

Just tired.

"This guy, he's been kind of bugging me. His girlfriend doesn't like it. As if I've asked for any of his attention. I don't need a fuckboy in my life."

Lucia grunts slightly.

I know she thinks teenage relationships are a waste of effort and has abstained from dating. Much to the theatrics of all the boys that are desperate for her attention.

"Anyway, the girl is a bully and has this psycho jealous thing going on. She bullies everyone cause his dad is like some hotshot in the area, or the state, or something, and her family has one of the big houses on Orcas Island. She got in my face after a test audition we had, and then continued to be a raging twat ever since."

Lucia shrugs her shoulder nonchalantly. "So, I stood up to her."

Coming from borderline poverty, Lucia *hates* the upper class. Of course, those who are affluent and don't know the struggle. Even I find them hard to tolerate.

I won't think of Edmond.

But I'm not really sure I believe Lucia's mild version. Lucia isn't a liar - perse- but she is sixteen.

"How did you 'stand up' to her?" There are air quotes all over my words that I know she can't miss.

Lucia has the wherewithal to flush as she looks away. She mumbles something, and I'm not quite sure I hear her correctly. Because detention seems too easy for the repercussions of what could happen.

"What?"

"I keyed his motorcycle and put her phone in epoxy and made an art piece about the correlation between fuckboys, cell phone use, and being a vapid cunt."

I blink at Lucia, and then blink again. Somehow torn between laughing over her bit of petty revenge and being horrified. Not only for her vulgar word choice. Because, *oh my god,* sixteen-year-olds should not be using the hard 'C' to talk about other girls. But also, because if either of their parents decide they want to push for reimbursement, be it detailing what's likely an expensive crotch-rocket, or a high-end phone, the bill could hit thousands of dollars.

We don't have that type of money. There is never more than two figures in the bank after the bills are paid and groceries are budgeted for. We have no buffer, and I've already trimmed all the fat from our budget.

I close my eyes.

I will not borrow tomorrow's trouble for today.

I focus on what I can be disappointed in.

"Did you actually use the c-word?"

"No, I used bitch. But I might as well. That's what I got into trouble for. Mrs. Sullivan is all about freedom of speech and expression unless I bring in street words. Then she gets completely bent out of shape."

I huff a breath, trying hard not to laugh. I know teachers like that.

"It's fiiine."

Lucia blows out a vocal sigh and gathers her hair in a bunch. She swiftly wraps the black elastic band she always wears on her wrist in her hair. Instantly creating a bouncy ponytail that she flicks behind her like a horsetail.

"Anyway, just in case she decides to freak out about it, I'm going to apply down at Caffeine Craze. They hire a lot of high school kids."

This is why I didn't want to work at the high school. I can barely survive one teenager. Having to deal with thousands would have me checking myself into a psychiatric ward.

"Okay." *Okay.* I need to be mellow about this. Freaking out isn't going to solve anything.

"Let me know if anything more happens." I fervently pray that things don't escalate anymore between Lucia, the guy, and his girl. Love triangles only work out in movies. In real life, they end with someone getting shot, stabbed, or set on fire.

"I work at *La Baia* tonight. Which." I glance at my watch and grimace. "I needed to leave five minutes ago. There are leftovers in the freezer and some of those frozen meals you like."

I scurry toward the hallway and then pause, whipping around to give my sister a hard look. "Don't use the oven."

Lucia scrunches up her face. "Yeah. I learned my lesson."

At least for this week, she has.

"I love you. Text me if you need anything."

Then I bolt upstairs, grab my uniform, and dash back into the car to drive to the waterfront.

<hr>

The dinner rush slams into *La Baia Italiana* like a hurricane. One with gale winds of Chanel perfume, waves of blonde hair that can only come from a bottle, and the gaunt hungriness of starving, couture-wearing sharks.

After trotting the bill over to one of my tables, I lean against the stainless-steel island where Zoe is preparing tiramisu. It, along with a small *affogato,* is our signature *dolce.* While there are a few other treats to tantalize a sweet tooth, like our house-made gelato and limoncello cake, none are as spectacular as the tiramisu.

I grab a teaspoon and swipe a bite of custard. I'm starving but won't be able to eat dinner until the doors are locked. That is one of the boons of working at a restaurant, free food.

There are two hours until close, and while dinner service is mostly over, the rest of the evening will be filled with stragglers. Those coming in from elsewhere to have coffee and dessert, perhaps a cocktail. At the most, I'll be slinging pitchers of sangria and appetizers.

Unexpectedly, in the lull, my thoughts slip toward Edmond. As if my only respite away from thinking about his intensity and mist-hewn eyes is working myself to the bone.

Curiosity gets the best of me.

I turn toward Zoe, handing her the scalloped-edge stencils that she uses to create the restaurant's logo out of cocoa powder. She's a native of Echo Bay. Her parents own the lighthouse café a few blocks over from *La Baia.* If anyone has gossip and dirt on Edmond, it will be here.

"Do you know Edmond Vasiliev?"

Zoe drops her sifter, and the metallic sieve sinks into the delicate custard.

I blink and turn to meet her wide blue eyes.

"Are you serious?"

Okay. So obviously I'm the only person never to have met Edmond before.

I reach for the sieve, rinse it in the sink built into the prep station, and offer it back to her.

Zoe is still staring at me.

I feel as if I've made a mistake, or that I'm blundering into something that I don't know the first thing about. Her reaction is not what I thought it would be. I thought she'd giggle, not look at me as if I cursed her grandmother.

Luckily, no one else is within hearing distance, so I feel that whatever mistake I'm making can be kept on the down low.

"We had parent-teacher conferences today," I say quickly. As if my being forced to meet with Edmond would absolve me.

Zoe's brows raise another inch, their points angling toward dark hairline. If she had bangs, the height of her eyebrows giving me *you have got to be kidding me* look would have been lost. Even still, her expression says it all at a loud volume without uttering a word. She doesn't buy what I'm selling. Even if it's the truth.

"Uh-huh." She picks up another tablespoon of cocoa, her wrist controlling the light flick as she decorates the dessert with the gentle chocolate drifts.

"Edmond's niece is one of my students."

"Edmond, is it?" She drops the spoon into the bowl, the clang of metal on glass loud enough that one of the line cooks turns to see what the commotion is. Zoe is completely without drama. It's why I adore her. That she's staring at me as if I've grown two heads is giving me a complex.

"You're freaking me out a bit right now," I hiss.

"You should be!" Zoe looks over her shoulder, her heavily lash-lined eyes swiveling around the whole kitchen. I don't know who - or what - she's looking for. But she must decide it's safe because she leans into me. Creating a privacy bubble where all the secrets shared within it remain and are never uttered beyond their imaginary walls.

I'd only been working at Harbor View Montessori for three months when I realized that my paycheck wasn't going to stretch to cover everything me and Lucia needed. Thus came the job here at *La Baia*. Zoe trained me, and since then she's become a friend. Maybe not as close as those I left behind in Arizona, but someone who I can count on and trust. So far, we haven't hung out after work. But that is mostly my fault. Because I have zero free time.

"First off, he's your boss's boss."

My fingers freeze above the plate, helplessly hovering as I absorb the impact of that detail. A little zap goes through me as if I'd gotten a shock of static electricity.

"He owns *La Baia?*"

"Oh, you sweet summer child." Zoe looks over her shoulder again, making sure that no nosey nellies are trying to eavesdrop.

Her husky voice drops even lower, urging me into a tight huddle as she gives me the details. "The Vasiliev family owns *everything* in Echo Bay. If they don't outright own it, they have a partnership in it. The mayor might be elected, but he's just a figurehead. The real power in Echo Bay, Seattle, you can even say all of Washington is Edmond and his family."

I stare at Zoe, unable to comprehend the magnitude of power that she claims Edmond has. If she is right, that would put Edmond on the same level as the damn billionaires who shape our country. That I've never heard of him means he's probably reclusive, preferring the quiet life instead of the limelight that it seems most wealthy enjoy.

"And here I was thinking he was just an extraordinarily handsome parent."

"Oh, he's a smoke-show." She gives me a hint of a smile, even though her focus is on plating the desserts into works of chocolate and whipped cream art.

She waves her hand about, the light glinting off the professional whipped cream dispenser to punctuate her statements. "Do you want a free word of advice?"

In for a penny...

"Sure."

"Stay far, far away. He's the kind of guy that will ruin you and never think twice when he steps over the wreckage."

I swallow around the dryness suddenly filling my throat. As far as warnings came, that one was a doozy.

"Don't worry." I force a smile on. "Edmond is just fantasy fodder."

Zoe doesn't look like believes me. There's uncharacteristic tension in her face and shoulders, and the tiny frown tugging on her mouth fans minor crow's feet around her eyes.

But she nods, and together we go back to carefully creating her culinary masterpieces. Both of us pretending that I didn't just provoke the universe by airing my questions.

Chapter Eight

Rina

That car is in front of my house again.

I'm sitting in the front seat of my Toyota, letting the engine warm up before I face a rather frosty Saturday morning, when I catch the sleek lines of a sports car.

This car looks straight out of a James Bond movie, with its inky satin finish, matte black hubcaps, and black-out tinted windows. Most of the affluent types with car fetishes choose high-end, sporty vehicles in bright, eye-catching tints with a lot of chrome. Red being the dominant color of a mid-life crisis, not this void-black beast that looks like it sucks in the light instead of reflecting it.

If Hades had a sports car, this would be it.

There is a saying that, while you might not believe in the devil, the devil surely believes in you. Over the past two weeks I've gone from thinking I'm invisible, to looking over my shoulder to try and catch the eyes I feel on me. Every day, from the moment I step out of the house, the hairs on my nape rise. A leftover evolutionary shiver from when us primitive humans were always on the lookout for hungry predators watching from the brush. Each time I have that strange, electric sensation, *that car* is right there. I've thought about calling the police, or even telling someone about my luxury phantom.

Unlike my ancestors, my suspicion isn't a bear, coyote, or tiger, but a name: *Edmond.*

If I hadn't Googled the car and seen the seven-figure price tag, I would have thought I was being ridiculous.

But that car. That freaking car is as much a declaration of *who* is watching me. Even if I don't know *why.*

Surely, a young, handsome billionaire has more things to do than follow me around. But neither can I think of who else it might be, and who can easily afford a limited-edition Bugatti that makes me feel like I'm being stalked by Batman. What that might mean for me, I'm not sure.

Does he not trust me with his niece?

Did I somehow trigger his warning alarms during our parent-teacher conference?

Whatever the reason *why,* the timing is too coincidental coming on the heels of meeting the town bigshot.

I don't believe in coincidences.

Which comes with the sticky problem of what would happen to me – and my employment – if I call the police on the most influential man in Echo Bay. I *need* my jobs, and so after the first few times, I try and ignore it.

Swallowing the mouthful of dread which makes my bagel taste rotten, I shove a pair of sunglasses on and pull out onto the road. Pretending that I'm not being stalked by that damn car that resembles a low-slung jaguar prowling the asphalt jungle.

Echo Bay is not a large town. Every road in the city leads to Willowbrook Avenue. Having a shopping nexus gives the coastal town a quaint one stop-light ambiance without losing any of its practicality or wealthy aesthetic.

East to west are residential areas, sprawling further toward open water, and deeper into the natural woodland of the Pacific Northwest, sandwiching the downtown area between the eye-catching natural wonders.

North leads towards a bridge that crosses the small rivers that fork inland from the ocean and overlooks the strait of Georgia. A band of navy-blue water which separates us from the islands dotting the coastline. Eventually, if one keeps going, they'll hit Canada. The southern road lures visitors deeper into the rather quaint-looking town, letting them gaze at the twinkle of light on the water as they travel to Seattle.

If I had a five-dollar word to coin Echo Bay with, it would be sybaritic. Whoever designed the layout took the cozy cottage core style, and then dressed it in opulence. Most of the buildings bore light-colored clapboard in beach-side colors of light blues, grays, and whites. Though no *true* seaside town maintained such a pristine complexion and vivid brightness for overlong. Here, that white remains dazzling. The colors were as perfectly saturated as when they'd been first painted.

Wear and tear need not apply.

Cute hand-painted signs hang above glass-paned doorways, and elaborate displays showcase a rugged elegance that makes me think of campfires and s'mores if one's idea of camping is sprawling log-cabin estates and luxurious RVs.

The city commerce apparently has enough money being pumped into the economy that all the kitschy, cutesy things our local government comes up with can be put into practice. Though none of the shops that won their licensing bids are practical, if I want to go to Wal-Mart, I have to drive twenty-minutes up I-5 to the next town over, I still love them. They remind me that Echo Bay caters to a rich clientele of varied tastes.

Which allows me to taste affluency without you know, being affluent.

My favorites are a tea parlor that serves a wide range of brews from simple black teas to exotic jade oblong, and a paper company that has a storefront overflowing with unique, hand-stenciled paper and gorgeous calligraphy supplies.

Once a month, on really the only day I have off, I stop in at both. Depending on my budget, I don't always buy. Which makes me the worst sort of customer, a browser. But I find serenity amid the familiar, malty green aroma of tea shops.

There is also Oliver Wright, a Londoner who has a posh upper-crust British accent. Like any American girl ever, I am a sucker for accents. He also educates me on the history of tea and serves a delicious afternoon tea on Sunday making the English Rose Garden immensely popular. Something I can't afford but always wanted to try.

Maybe in another life.

I into a parking spot a few spaces down from the English Rose Garden's immaculately gilded front window. Today I am going to actually be a money-spending customer, as I need to replenish my tin of simple black tea to get me through the upcoming week. If I'm being stalked, I need to fortify myself with caffeine.

The overhead bell tingles as I step in, sending a few flyers in the front wind fluttering in the early spring weather.

"Rina!" Oliver waves at me from behind the counter and flat-monitor cash register.

There is a snap in the air, the promise of sunshine bullying the rest of the winter season away. Still cold enough to bundle up in jackets, hoodies, and sweaters. But there should not be further snow. Of course, Mother Nature can be fickle, and she has buried the Pacific Northwest in mountains of snow before as late as May.

"Oliver."

I cannot help but smile. Objectively, he is not a super

attractive man. He has a nerdy vibe with black-framed glasses, tousled dirty blonde hair, and a penchant for corduroy slacks and button-down shirts in all manner of stripes and plaids. His idea of dressing up is tweed jackets and sweater vests. But his accent elevates him from middling attractive to incredibly fetching.

He breezes around from the countertop, then stops beside a table primly stacked with decorative canisters of tea and "biscuit" tins. It took me months to realize that biscuits mean cookies and are rather delicious dunked-in hot tea. He snatches one up, and meets me a few feet inside the door.

"I have the best surprise for you."

I don't think that Oliver likes me in a romantic way. The feeling he gives me is that he enjoys playing on both sides of the field and doesn't want any type of attachment. There are more than enough women who would not mind sharing him, and our acquaintance is comfortable—not quite close enough to be friends—with a shared enthusiasm for tea.

That almost-closeness helped thaw out some of his stand-offish British behaviors. While he hasn't quite graduated to hugging, he's touchier than he'd been before. He drops his arm around my shoulders. With his average height, that leaves him a few inches taller than me. But nowhere near the behemoth height that someone likes—say—Edmond Vasiliev has.

I stifle a scowl when I think of the devil, and studiously look to see if *that car* has followed me here.

I push thoughts of Edmond out of my mind. Since our parent-teacher conference, I have thought of him far, far too much.

"I just received my inventory of first-flush teas."

I give him a soft 'squee' of delight. "Really? What did you get?"

I have never been a coffee person. Whenever I mention

that I don't like the bitterness of the bean, those who swear by coffee tell me to doctor it. Sugar. Cream. Syrups. To me, that defeats the purpose of a drink. Why drink something if all you're going to do is mask its natural flavors?

Tea is simple, and it comes in a variety of colors and flavors; caffeinated, herbal, and decaffeinated. There is something for everyone. While there is a split among the American population who like their tea sweet or unsweetened, being that this is Washington and not somewhere down south like Georgia, 'sweet tea' is rarely found.

At least until I met Oliver. Before then, I'd never heard of 'first flush' tea.

Then he brewed me a cup, and I fell in love with the sweet, delicate flavors of the leaf.

First Flush tea is defined as the very first plucking of the tea plant during the harvest season. The new growth leaves are gathered. They are the youngest, most delicate, and tender. To me, first-flush teas are incredibly sweet, as if the brew had been flavored with honey. I am addicted to the light, fresh flavors. Oliver likens first flush teas to being the 'champagne' of teas, special and exclusive.

And very expensive.

I only allow myself one sachet when the first flush arrives. The rest of the time, I exist on second flush teas, or if I am desperate, monsoon flush teas, which is what everyone who is not a tea connoisseur knows to be more 'commercial' teas and what is packaged in boxes like Lipton.

"I got my hands on a white first flush."

My excitement ratchets up, and I spin around in front of him. I nearly bounce with excitement.

"Oh my god, really? Oliver! That is amazing!" I have never tasted white first-flush tea. Most of the time, those that make it to America are black teas, the most common type of tea on the market.

"You are—."

The bell above the door clangs like a cowbell as someone slams it open.

Oliver and I both turn, startled at the customer darkening the threshold.

Of course.

I'm not surprised. Nor am I really shocked.

My eyes narrow as I see Edmond Vasiliev looming in the doorway, his face a thunderclap that promises a storm. His gaze locks on me, and then he looks at where Oliver's fingertips are lightly resting on my forearm.

Oliver swallows loud enough that I hear his gulp. Then he drops his arm, backpedaling enough to put distance between him and me. I turn away from Edmond's chilling face, blinking in bewilderment at Oliver's reaction. He looks pale, his eyes darting between me and the man in the doorway.

"I'll go make that tea."

Oliver bolts, scurrying toward the stockroom and the adjacent employee's lounge where I know he keeps his electric kettle.

Leaving me all alone with my personal boogieman.

Chapter Nine

Edmond

I *am a stalker.*

It's taken me a week to get comfortable with the notion. But since then, I've fallen into the habit of watching Rina from a distance.

If anyone had told me a week ago I'd be giving up my precious free time to follow around after Mila's teacher, I'd have laughed.

Now, I know better.

Rina is a lighthouse beacon that draws me, her brilliance piercing the gloom and offering me sanctuary if I were to come in from the cold. Even from miles away, I feel the pull of her, the lingering zip of attraction I feel each time I catch the shape of her smile or a hint of her profile. The flicker of her warmth urges me to bask in her presence, and I find myself at a loss of how to resist.

I didn't *mean* to become her shadow.

The first time it happened, I'd only meant to drive past her house. Just to see what she was doing on a nice, albeit chilly Wednesday evening a few days after our first meeting.

Arriving just as her car pulled out of the driveway tempted me. It seemed serendipitous that our paths almost crossed. I wasn't usually a weak man, but I gave in and followed her. I wouldn't call that pivotal moment stalking. That would imply that I went to visit her with the express purpose of shadowing her like some pervy creeper leering from the shadows. It was just happenstance that my car was on her road.

Now, though?

I can't deny that I'm stalking her. Anyone with half-a-brain would hear my excuses and call it for what it is.

Like my drivers, I've been taught by the best Tactile Emergency Vehicle teachers in the world. I know how to tail a car without being seen and evade the police should they ping my vehicle for many of my criminal sins.

Tailing Rina is easy. She has no situational awareness of what dangers exist in this world. Those who want to prey on her innocent vulnerability.

I maintain a car's length of distance between her bumper and mine. Matching her speed with an effortlessness that makes me want to cut-her off and shake her for being unaware.

That first day, I followed her all over the place as she ran errands.

Then I did it again.

And again.

And again.

Today, Saturday is when she has the freest time, and she seems to spend it wandering through Echo Bay. This is the second weekend that I'm trailing after the girl like a fucking puppy. Not wanting her attention but stealing scraps of her scent whenever I get close enough.

Willowbrook Avenue is the shopping hub of the city. It isn't very long, partitioned with Lakeside Terrace and the high-end department stores and boutiques at one end, specialty shops in the center, and more regular business at the far end. All are anchored at the coast by the boardwalk that runs the entire length of the waterline. There, the kitschy tourist shops, art galleries, and waterfront bars and restaurants beckon everyone to gaze at our lighthouse and stop and grab some seashell souvenirs.

Signaling into a parallel parking spot, I choose a space that gives me an eagle's eye view of the whole area. It's a tight fit. Willowbrook is only two lanes since the founders of Echo Bay wanted to make it a walking town. Forcing people who might turn off I-5 to drive slowly through downtown Echo Bay and enjoy the affluent seashore aesthetic.

From the safety of my Bugatti, I watch as Rina jogs across the street, and stops in front of the tea shop. For a moment she hovers, her reflection subtly warped in the window. I can see indecision shape her stance. Then she shakes her head, her hair bouncing against her shoulders and making my fingers itch to weave through it. My fist curls around the doorknob, as if I'm about to jump out of the car and join her on the sidewalk.

Fuck.

What am I doing?

I can't.

After two weeks of this lunacy, there is one truth I understand about what exists in this one-sided obsession: Rina is my sun, drawing me in with her gravitational force. I'm addicted to watching her, and seeing just how close I can get before getting burned.

I exhale and pull back at the last minute. Realizing that my willpower at remaining apart from her is fraying. I need to be content with watching her from afar. My world – the Brotherhood – would break her.

I manage to remain in my seat, watching her without being seen behind my tinted windows as she steps inside. I'm fucking proud of myself for restraining my baser and possessive instincts to be at her side, shopping with her. Buying her everything her eyes linger on, her heart's desires, and spoiling her rotten like girls such as her deserve.

Then, all of my good intentions fly out the window as I watch the shop keeper *touch* her. It's as if I've been shot in the gut, leaving me wheezing and seeing red as that tweed-wearing motherfucker puts his arm around her shoulders. His thin arms squeeze her with a friendliness that I instantly despise.

I know Oliver. His store is one of many which I use to import a whole slew of goods. It's mostly a front, as are ninety percent of the specialty shops which operate in Echo Bay.

Who would spend good money at a limited-edition gallery that only uses driftwood and seashells in the artwork? Or one which sells only souvenir teaspoons?

The only time we get tourists is during the summer heyday, and right before Christmas, when those who are city-trapped crave the whole white-winter wonderland aesthetic to take photographs of.

I make sure that Echo Bay puts on the ritz, glitz, and glamour for the important holiday seasons. Enough to make it seem as if the surplus of cash comes from spend-happy tourists. When in reality it comes from me, and the kickbacks I give to the shops.

Through their imports, I'm able to stash all manner of contraband without triggering a deeper inspection from customs. Once the goods arrive at my harbors, they get waved through with a blind eye and a quick stamp of approval.

I can't begin to estimate how many of my diamonds have been smuggled in through Oliver's tea shop. Guns and ammunition stuffed into the canisters and teapots that Rina is currently looking at.

Does she have a history with Oliver?

Is that why she's letting him snuggle her against his side?

Does she know that he would sell his own mother's house out from underneath her to fund his lifestyle?

He has no code. No honor.

I might be a fucking criminal, but I took an *oath*.

I doubt she knows anything about him. If she did, she wouldn't be looking at him as if he is a knight in shining armor. If she knew what he was *really* like, I'm sure she'd avoid him, treating him like the plague rat I know him to be.

I don't even think as I shove the door open, the futuristic slab sliding up like the wing of a four-wheeled spaceship.

Checking the streets to make sure nobody is watching; I slip out of the car and stalk across the street. My intention is pure. I will put a stop to whatever budding romance is happening inside of the tea shop, without talking to Rina. Oliver will *know* not to touch what is mine. Not under my watchful eye and not with my fucking girl.

The bell resonates with my mood, announcing my arrival with an angry clatter.

Rina has her back to the door, but Oliver seems me coming from over her shoulder. His smile is a reflex, greeting me as if I'm a normal customer and not the sole reason this shop even exists.

He takes one look at me, and the hard glare I flash at him, and realizes his mistake.

I've never seen a complexion go cadaver white that fast as I give him my best serial-killer smile. The one that says he's done fucked up by touching Rina. And if he doesn't make himself scarce, he will rue the day he crossed me.

Not only will I stop paying him, but I will tear down his entire illusionary life. There are a thousand shops that would die for this real estate. It's only by my grace that he has a business in Echo Bay.

He bleats something about 'tea', and then darts away like a rat-faced fink, leaving Rina by herself.

That alone makes me want to stalk him into the twisty warren of the shop's inventory space and punch him for being inconsiderate.

The other side of me is thankful, even if this isn't part of the plan.

How long could I have forced myself to stay away?

Rina blinks at me as if she's unsure how I managed to get in front of her. The shop's lights set a torch of brilliance in her gleaming auburn-lashed hair. I don't know how she does it, no matter if she wears a ponytail, or has her hair down like it is now, it always looks silken.

I fist my hand and jam it into my jacket pocket so I won't touch her.

Suspicion teeters on her lips and narrows her eyes. I don't like that look on her. She should only look happy and sweet, not eye-fucking me as if I'm a harbinger of doom.

Giving her a benign, closed-mouth smile, I slip into another aisle. Pretending that I'm not excruciatingly aware of my proximity to her.

Fuck.

Viewing her from a distance and through the emerald-washed glare of a night-vision camera is nothing compared to her in the flesh. She is exquisite. Soft, delicate, and feminine.

I grit my teeth, stomping down another aisle so I don't do something stupid. Like corner her against a rack and kiss the shit out of her.

My good intentions last for all of a minute. I don't know dick about tea.

What the hell is artemisia?

Then there are the special imports, many from Asian countries, whose names are kanji instead of letters.

Not knowing what I'm reading, it's not long before I've swiftly browsed around the shop, doubling Rina's pace until I wind up right behind her.

She is focused on a miniature aluminum canister. The whole of it is painted in a watercolor splash of cerulean blue and then decorated with white flowers detailed in violet and pink. Her mouth is parted as she holds up her trophy. Captivating me with the intrigue that I read on her face.

I creep closer until I am right behind her. The scent of her tickles my nose. Rina smells soft, not unlike freshly washed linen, a hint of lavender, and something soft like chamomile. I don't think it's a perfume she wears, but a holy trinity of shampoo, laundry detergent, and her.

Rina strokes the canister.

I read the sales tag on the shelf that has been translated from its original language into English.

Jade Oolong Imperial Green Tea.

Rina shakes her head, sighs, and then sets the container back on the shelf.

While I'd been raised with a silver, bullet-riddled spoon in my mouth, I understand the need to be frugal. Not only does Rina work as a teacher at Bay View, but she also apparently tutors every night from the sanctity of her home and works swing shifts at *La Baia Italiana.*

Three jobs. And she can't afford a tea that costs seventy-five dollars for 30 grams. Considering I can walk into a grocery store and buy fifty bags for under five dollars, that seems exorbitant.

But I also don't understand the market for imported teas. I know cars and artwork, drugs, guns, and the cost of taking a life. Still, I want to reach over her shoulder, take the canister off the shelf, and buy it for her.

This uncharacteristic obsession with Rina makes me feel

twitchy. It makes me want to do things that I never thought about before.

Like learning what the fuck oolong is.

I glare at the offending container.

Rina turns around and then squeaks as she runs right into me.

Poor girl needs better awareness. There had been a beast breathing down her neck and she'd been clueless.

"Edmond." The way she says my name makes my pulse throb. It is innocent and lush, a wispy, breathy gasp of shock that she tries to rectify with my name.

I don't have any good intentions when it comes to Rina. Those ended the moment I read D4663R's dossier on her, and I realized she is exactly as she presents herself; family oriented, smart, sweet, caring, and selfless. Despite her being Mila's teacher, I can't stay away. And now she's gone and hammered the last nail in her coffin by letting another man *touch* her.

She doesn't know who she belongs to. Not yet. But she will soon, because I need to consume her. I need to taste her. Touch her.

Fuck her.

Gold starbursts encircle the pupil of her hazel eyes, drawing me in as they lift to mine. I know it is naivety that makes her so bold. Nobody who knows me, really knows me, can meet my gaze.

Those who do see death in it.

I wonder what Rina sees as she holds my stormy stare.

"What are you doing here?"

"I'm here for the tea, of course."

"Mmm."

"Do I detect sarcasm, Miss Christensen?"

Her attention skips down my body, before catching on the hint of ink that flares at the neckline of my pull-over sweater, and cuffs. I wear them like armor. But to the uninitiate, my tattoos are just stark, dark ink. For those in the lifestyle, they declare my fealty, rank, and other unsavory tidbits meant to inspire terror.

"I would have assumed your favorite drink was something harder than this."

"Oh, it is." I dip my head, voice lowering into a husk. "But I suddenly have a hankering for sweet...tea."

Rina's pretty pink lips part into an oval. Her cheeks flush into that fetching blush that makes me wonder how far it travels. I bet it stains her tits and leaves pink blotches on her thighs. She is so fair with a hint of freckling dusting her nose.

"That sounds like a horrible pick-up line."

I can't help the laugh that rumbles in my chest. "You wound me. Are you saying I'm bad at flirting, Miss Christenson?"

"Are you flirting with me, Mr. Vasiliev?"

Feisty little kitten.

Her sass surprises me, but I enjoy it too. Even as I press my luck and move closer, slathering her in the darkness of my shadow. As if that is her one and only warning to the stain I'll leave on her world.

"Edmond. I told you to call me Edmond."

"Or what?" Her eyes spark with gilt fire as she challenges.

Oh, she's definitely flirting back. While I didn't think this narcotic attraction between us was one-sided, now I have irrefutable proof that I'm in her thoughts as much as she's in mine.

"Do you really want to know? It involves my hand, and your pert ass." I don't touch her, but I come close to brushing my sleeve along her shoulder when I curl my fingers against the shelf just behind her.

She blushes so prettily for me. Her nerve breaks as she

looks away from me, snagging her bottom lip between her teeth as if that prim, buttoned expression would contain her embarrassed and shocked breaths.

"You're terrible."

"I am." I am not going to lie about who I am. I am terrible, and every other adjective you could attach to a man like myself.

Her expressive gaze flickers around the British-inspired shop. Oliver still hasn't returned. I doubt he will while I remain in the shop. Any man worth his nuts wouldn't sacrifice a tender, innocent young thing like Rina to the wolves.

Yet Oliver has done exactly that.

I might just have to teach him a lesson.

Shoving the weasley British tea shop owner out of my head, I focus exclusively on Rina.

Her teeth nibble her bottom lip, assailing me with the urge to replace her mouth with mine.

Fuck what is wrong with me?

I get hot over a nice piece of trim. But I don't kiss. Kissing is intimacy. Connection. Neither of which I do. Any woman who tangles with the *pakhan* of the Vasiliev OCG needs to have a spine of iron and a trigger finger of stone.

Neither attribute that I notice in Rina. She is sunshine and flowers, laughter and fucking butterflies.

She would make a wonderful mother for Mila.

Rina finally locks eyes with me again, and I read some decision in the faint hardening of her eyes. When she wants to look tough, she lets her lashes list downward, casting her liquid pupils in shadows. I'm sure she thinks it makes her look hard, tough. But to me, it makes her look sultry.

"Have you been following me, Edmond?"

Maybe her situational awareness isn't as bad as I first thought.

I dip my head, close enough that anyone walking by might

think we were kissing. Except my mouth is still a few inches away. Hovering. Threatening to sting her with the venom of my affection.

"Do you want me to be stalking you?"

Her eyes widen. Her throat tenses around a hasty swallow. And those luscious breasts heave as she inhales deeply, making the ripe curves almost brush my chest.

"No." She shakes her head so vigorously that whips of rose gold lick at her pink cheeks. "I... no, Edmond. I don't want someone to be following me. It makes me feel unnerved. Soon Lucia is going to notice, and I don't want anything to interrupt her routine."

Her love and devotion to her sister is impressive.

It also gives me depraved, dark ideas. Thoughts of using that connection as a weapon, a tool to graft her into my life whether she wants to be or not.

"You care a lot about your sister."

Rina doesn't flinch from my dark gaze. She holds it, nervously licking her lips as if that would moisturize her parched mouth. "She means the world to me."

I barely stifle my grin. She makes this too easy.

Ghosting my fingers in the air near her cheek, I bend my head and whisper.

"Perhaps you should leave your window unlatched tonight, to ask your stalker what he wants without waking up Lucia."

Rina whimpers softly, a thrilling commingling of pleasure and betrayal that shoots carnal lust into my groin.

I am an absolute bastard for my suggestion.

But I hope she'll do it anyway.

Chapter Ten

Rina

He can't be implying what I think he is.

Right?

I can't look away as motes of heat collide with quivery bubbles of nervousness inside of me. Despite the evidence to the contrary, I really didn't *believe* Edmond had been the one following me. But here he is, all but gloating over the fact that he's had his eyes on me for *weeks*.

I should be disgusted. Any sane woman would be dialing the police right now. Not having a conversation with her stalker.

But I don't feel like myself when around Edmond. I didn't the first time we met and he strutted into my classroom, and I still don't now that he's had a fortnight to fester in my thoughts and fantasies. The emotions he wakes in me make me feel as if I am straddling a huge crevice between fear and lust. I don't know *what* emotion is going to win out.

Maybe the fear is fueling the shameful arousal that thrums through me at his suggestion.

Or is it the ghost of his touch and the nearness of his

athletic body, almost pushing mine into the shelves behind me, that has my nipples hardening into tiny spikes beneath my sweater and the damp heat sweltering between my thighs.

I suck in a deep breath, trying to read Edmond's face. His smoky eyes burn, as if their hearts are fire-licked coals, hiding the devastation beneath swirls of mystifying smoke.

My knees threaten to buckle as I sway toward him.

I'm entangled.

Trapped.

Aching for more.

Luckily, Oliver returns right before I make a huge mistake. Such as throwing myself into Edmond's arms and begging for a kiss.

My previous promises to myself emerge from where they'd been choked by lust.

I will not get involved with a parent.

Maybe I need to carve it into my skin. Because I am *not* remembering my promise when faced with Edmond's seductive pull.

"Boundaries, Mr. Vasiliev," I breathe, hauling myself away from the cliff face of horrible decisions.

Edmond's lips curl, a hint of a smile shining through that damnable smirk.

"Of course, Miss Christenson."

The pressure of his presence eases as he steps back. He shoves his hands into the pockets of his slacks.

Which is right about the time Oliver navigates down the aisle and finds us. His eyes grow into saucers behind his glasses when he notices Edmond is still in the shop. He holds a flower-patterned, porcelain serving tray with two cups of hot tea, and a couple of 'biscuits'.

Edmond's face turns stony. His eyes ice over until I feel a chill just from being in their proximity.

What the devil is Edmond's issue with Oliver?

Oliver clears his throat, squares his shoulders beneath his long-sleeved shirt, and moves toward the round table he uses to treat his best customers with samples of exotic teas.

"Here we are."

The silverware clatters as he sat the tray down before he palms the dancing teaspoons.

"Would you like a sample, Mr. Vasiliev?"

Am I the only person in Echo Bay who hadn't met Edmond?

Edmond strolls down the narrow aisle. Somehow, the closer he moves to Oliver, the larger he seems. Until the entire shop feels as if it rides a knife's edge. The menace is coming from Edmond. It ignites that squeamish feeling in my belly. One that feels like knots and writhing snakes.

For some reason, I feel like Edmond wants to hurt Oliver. But since I am a witness, he won't risk it.

Why would Edmond want to fight Oliver?

Am I losing my mind?

Have my instincts gone that wonky?

I need more sleep, or a therapist, or both.

I shake my head, slowly following behind Edmond. The aroma of tea beckons me. I can't quite decipher the notes that are in the white that Oliver has steeped, but it makes me smile.

Oliver and Edmond speak in low tones. Well, more like Edmund is talking to Oliver. Whose face grows tighter, his eyes a little wide and white around the edges. I can't hear what he is saying. Then Oliver's rather terrified gaze flicks over Edmund's shoulder, and their conversation ends abruptly.

Edmond turns. His smile is all sharp edges and a flash of white teeth that make me think of a damn shark.

"I will leave you to it."

Edmond closes the distance, his head lowering to brush my ears with his pantherine voice.

"Remember what I said, little lamb. Will you be the prey for your stalker?"

He is *deranged*.

I shudder as he brushes by me. The only part of Edmond that touches me is the edge of his cuff, but I feel burned by the contact.

Being the glutton for punishment, and the poster child for bad choices, I watch Edmond leave. He is too good-looking. Beyond anyone I've ever imagined would have an interest in me.

He frightens me.

He intrigues me.

He desires me.

How can a girl say no to a man who looks like *that?*

I know enough about myself to know that I am quite properly screwed. Right now, I hold the line between us. I've erected my boundaries and I'm holding him at bay. But I can feel my resolve to keep him at arm's length faltering.

I am weak when it comes to tall, suited, tattoo-clad men.

Even those I know are bad for me.

I sigh and turn toward Oliver. He looks grim. His eyes are fretful as he watches Edmond leave his shop with relief. Then he smiles at me. Though it is strained. As if my presence has become bothersome during the time between my arrival and Edmond's departure.

"You need to be wary of him, Rina."

I falter as Oliver refuses to hold my gaze. He drops his view to the tea setting.

Two warnings from two residents of Echo Bay.

I would be a fool to ignore them.

Running my finger along the edge of the bone-China, I trace the navy-blue strip that is glazed on the white porcelain. The whole tea setting is gorgeous and luxurious, and it makes me feel as if I could take tea with the Queen of England, or maybe the Princess of Wales and know what I'm doing.

"I know." I smile sadly, my voice a whisper.

Oliver isn't telling me what I don't already know. Zoe gave me the first warning; this is just another red flag being waved in front of me. It's up to me if I adhere to it or ignore it and crash with my eyes wide-open at the wreckage hidden out of view just around the bend.

I might not understand the animosity between Oliver and Edmond. I do know that there are things about Edmond that are hidden. He is much more complex than the intimidating, intensely handsome man I first thought him to be.

He has secrets, and deep down where the truth lives, somewhat concealed by my libido and sexual attraction to Edmond, I know they are the big kind. The ones that will ruin my life if I get any closer to Edmond.

I exhale a shaky breath as I doctor my tea. White teas are delicate. You can easily make them taste bitter if you steep too long. Milk would be terrible. So, I give it a tiny squeeze of lemon, adding some acidity to the pale tea. I won't need any honey because it's a first flush, and it will be sweet enough.

Lifting the teacup, I look over at Oliver. He still looks ruffled.

"I'm sorry for whatever he said to you."

Oliver gives me a pained smile. "He's fixated on you, and I am so sorry for you that he is."

Fear grips my chest, making my lungs feel tight. Oliver knows enough about Edmond to offer a warning, to give me his empathy. As if I've somehow caught the eyes of the beast, and the outcome is now preordained.

No matter if I might want something different.

Chapter Eleven

Rina

The sunset should delight me. Echo Bay loves to show off its natural splendor. The light fades, and though I can't see the bay from where I live in the poorer section of the city, the sky doesn't discriminate. A palette of coral stains the inky approach of evening, its brighter rays staining the azure which darkens slowly into indigo.

I hold onto those sunbeams for as long as I can.

Because once night falls, Edmond is coming to get me as if he's the Lord of the Underworld and I'm his destined Persephone.

I scurry around the house. Making sure all the doors are locked, and the windows are secure. It isn't like the townhouse Fort Knox. It's old, one of the original Victorian manors built back when the mills dominated the area. Though the hardware is newer, it would only take a swift kick to get through the paltry security.

Though I don't think Edmond would do that. He seems to want me to submit. But one can never be sure when dealing with men who think stalking is okay.

I ignore the quivery feeling that steals into my limbs. The surge of excitement sends my pulse racing in ways that have nothing to do with the exertion of locking down my fort. Or the eager, unhinged throbbing between my thighs.

I am not getting off to being hunted.

I tell myself that while running up and down the stairs. Before finally, I pause in front of Lucia's door. She goes through moods. Some days she's a social butterfly. Others, she locks herself in her room. During those days, she has her tablet and will let me know if she needs me.

I don't know what version of Lucia I'm going to get. But that's the way of living with a teenager - it's a tempest in a teakettle always.

I tap lightly on her door.

"What."

Angry Lucia.

Got it.

"Can I come in?"

There's a heartbeat of silence, and then she answers in a way that I can hear the begrudging, capital letters in the word she chooses.

"Fine."

I open her door and peek in.

Lucia is cuddled on her bed, and I'm only vaguely surprised that it's filled with a toy store's worth of stuffed animals. Usually, she only has a weighted blanket, smooth sheets, and enough downy pillows to make it cozy. The rest of the time the animals live in the closet. When she has them out like this, she's feeling some kind of way. Not quite the D-word, but poor enough that she seeks the comfort of childish things. Even if neither of us had a childhood we'd want to remember or hold onto.

Colorful fabrics hang around the four-poster bed, making a

diaphanous canopy that catches the fairy lights she has strung all around the room.

In the far corner, a hanging egg chair hangs from the ceiling. More pillows and cushions are packed in the oversized seat. The wicker frame bumps up against a wall decorated with light-colored string lights. When they are turned on, the lights pulse, looking like bubbles gurgling down the wall.

I hesitantly approach, barely able to see her where she's buried in the stuffed animals. The largest one, a bear I got her for her fifth birthday, is tucked in her arms.

"What's wrong, Lu?"

"Nothing." Her voice is husky, a hoarse rasp from crying that I know well. It breaks my heart. I know she's homesick. Not from where we left, because that wasn't a home. But because neither of us had that sense of belonging.

I hover beside the bed, wanting to figure out a way to fix whatever's upset her. But if she doesn't let me in, how can I? It can be anything. Lucia runs emotionally hot, her moods swinging from happy to dark as frequently as a clocks second hand.

Finally, I let my hands drop, worrying my fingers down the seam of my blue jeans. "Okay. Do you need anything?"

Lucia burrows herself deeper, giving me her back. I can only see the tangle of her light hair, and the stiffness of her shoulders. I don't understand the pressures she's under. Harborcrest is both a dream and a nightmare, offering incredible results in her confidence as a performer and artist. If you put in the back-breaking labor, not only in her chosen art form but in all academic subjects.

The teachers had been adamant that a talent like hers is generational. She has a love-hate relationship with composing music. Her passion is art, her fallback dancing.

Lucia doesn't move from her position, but she mutters a snarly 'No' at me.

I back away. She's alive. She's breathing. That's all I can hope for.

"I love you. I'll see you in the morning."

Shutting the door behind me, I head down the hallway and shake my head clear of the fog Edmond has bespelled me with.

Lucia is my main - only - priority. I don't have the mental bandwidth to deal with a man like Edmond.

As if there's anyone out there like him.

I stuff that nagging thought down, seal it in an iron box, and bury it.

Even if this is a once-in-a-lifetime sort of attraction, I can't afford the entanglement. Not when every time I see him, I see danger peek through his mask of civility.

With that decision firmly, soundly, and reasonably, made, I slip into my bedroom.

It is still too early to go to sleep. Though my bedtime is early, because I get up at Six AM to get ready, get to school, and get my room prepared by seven-thirty, right now is even early for me.

I change into a pair of sweatpants, a ratty old t-shirt, and thick woolen socks, practically mummifying myself in plush cotton and nothing sexy or lacy. Who has time for that type of lingerie when you're single? This is my usual sleeping attire.

Then I stand in front of the only window that looks out of my second-story bedroom. The streetlights ward away the shadows, rendering the outside road well-lit. Nobody who lives in a residential area likes to have pitch-black streets. Lucia has black-out curtains because it is a lot brighter when the lights shine in through her windows.

I nibble on my bottom lip. Nothing stirs out there, but I

have to make sure that if - and it is a BIG if - Edmond tries to pay a visit tonight, he will know that it is unwanted.

Turning toward the narrow writer's desk that serves a dual purpose as a makeshift vanity, I tear a piece of paper from a notebook. Then I grab a sharpie and write a single word in large letters.

BOUNDARIES.

I tape my makeshift sign facing outward, and step back, hating how hard my heart is racing when I see the sheet obscuring half of the window. It might cause a spark of gossip if someone walking their dog sees it. But it is dark, and only a person with ill intent and a zoomed-in camera or binoculars can make out the words. I'll take it down in the morning.

Slipping into bed, I prop a few pillows behind my back, turn on the television to let a movie play as background noise, and haul my laptop across my thighs. There are a few assignments I need to grade, and I have to check my E-Mail and the message boards tied to the online tutoring site I work for.

As I work, I try not to think about Edmond or his audacious suggestion. Not thinking about him is harder than it should be, but I eventually push him to the back of my mind and focus on the pages before me.

Book reports are some of my favorite assignments to read. Not every student is a reader. Most of the fourth-graders do the bare minimum, parroting back a short synopsis and quick thoughts about the subject. Occasionally, one of my students uncovers a passion for books. You can always tell during the early grades that, as they grow older and their vocabulary grows with their education, they will be voracious.

I have a reader in my class this year, and she'd chosen to write about the ultra-classic *Alice's Adventures in Wonderland*. Her editorial takes on it are hilarious. *Why is she drinking random things, didn't her mother ever teach her not to follow strange rabbits*, makes me giggle whenever I come across them.

The hours pass in work, on-line browsing, and *The Princess Bride* quotes. Eventually, sleepiness slinks through me. It is close enough to my usual turn-in time that I don't feel guilty for maybe falling asleep thirty minutes early.

Grabbing my phone, I type out a quick text to Lucia, letting her know I am going to sleep. There's a fifty-fifty chance she's asleep too, watching a television show, or perhaps working on a composition for her classes. I am more of a creature of routine than she is, which surprises absolutely nobody when they get to know me.

Yawning slowly, I begrudgingly turn off the television right when Princess Buttercup learns her *twu luv* isn't dead. Tucking my phone on the charger, I drink a quick gulp of water from the bottle I keep on the nightstand, and then click off the light.

Sleep claims me easily, where dreams of Edmond wait to torment and titillate me. There, I am safe to indulge in the *what ifs* and *might have been* between us.

Chapter Twelve

Edmond

I am not visiting Rina tonight.

I am not a creature of impulse. Being impulsive leads to mistakes, which leads to men dying.

My men.

Visiting Rina in the middle of the night on a weekend is impulsive. It's also dangerous for her. Though my little teacher doesn't know it, the skeletons in my closet have skeletons. Her instincts are honed well, warning her away even as I draw her closer.

But there's no denying the magnetism between us. Or the intrigue I read in her eyes. My mind keeps offering up the memory of how she looked when she blushes. How her cheeks grow all pink, and her breasts quiver with shock. On the surface, she'd been scandalized by my suggestion.

Underneath those flashing hazel eyes, something turbulent and hungry had risen to the bait.

I know that look. I see it on my own face every time I think about Rina and what I could do to her. She's interested in just how far I'll go. I wonder how far she'll let me. Those two thoughts have me in a fucking chokehold.

Work keeps me occupied for the rest of the evening. There's no murder on the docket, but that might change. I visit two warehouses, and one of my local suppliers who buys my imported diamonds.

The West Coast elite are always hungry for glamour and sparkle, and very few things gleam as beautifully as a diamond.

One of my recent Brazilian mines turned out to be a node for rare reds, and I only part with a half-dozen of them yearly so as not to drive-down their rarity factor. Manufactured scarcity puts more money in my pocket, and the Vasiliev name rubbing elbows alongside De Beers, ALROSA, and Dominion formerly the Harry Winston Diamond Corporation.

While I have no interest in being the world's largest diamond company, being a top-tier operation encrusts my illegal activities with protection only obscene wealth can supply.

The millions don't hurt either.

That my drive home happens to take me through Rina's neighborhood is a coincidence. And since I'm in the area, I figure a stop by just to make sure she hasn't left her windows unlocked for any pervert to climb through is imperative.

From the street, it's impossible to miss the note taped to her bedroom window. Though I can't read the words, not until I pull out the night-vision binoculars and focus it on that square scrap of paper.

Boundaries? Who does she think I am?

Drumming my fingers on the steering wheel of my Bugatti, I lower the binoculars and frown. Some hot emotion drags through me, and it takes me a breathless minute to understand.

Anger. I'm fucking pissed that little bitch told me *no*. The audacity of it gnaws at the edges of my thoughts.

Even heroes have vulnerabilities. That I adhere closer to the villain, means I have more than a few chinks in my psychological armor. Being told *no* is at the top of the list. It makes me want to break not her house and show Rina just how big of a mistake she's made by leaving me that sassy note. By making her cum on my cock and scream herself hoarse and breathless from just how hard I fuck her.

Lust cooks into the anger, forming an unholy duality that burns inside of me. It makes my throat feel tight from how my pulse spasms beneath my tattoos. My jeans are tight from how engorged and thick my cock is pressing against my zipper.

I want to break Rina.

I want to own her.

I want to see just how *pink* the little teacher is when I spread her thighs wide.

What had been just harmless flirting, is now becoming a declaration of war. I haven't touched her. Haven't kissed her. Haven't made her share her part of this erotic burn that claws inside my veins.

Rina needs to be taught a lesson.

How can she *understand* if she isn't experiencing the same mind-scorching craving as I am?

There's no room for guilt in my world. I left that worthless emotion back in Siberia.

Patting my pocket to make sure Iustina is secure, I pop open the glovebox and grab handful of small, pocket-sized items, among them zip ties, a torque wrench, and a small light. The three kings of any burglar's kit.

Now, I know *normal* people don't just keep random handcuffs and zip ties on them. That I'm ever ready to kidnap someone and haul them of, or break into a secured building, puts me strongly in the realm of psychopathy. At least I don't have body bags on hand. But in my world, being unprepared usually means death and having to deal with the police. Even if most will turn a blind eye to a six-figure payout, despite what the general populace might think, there are some good cops out there. Those who can't be bartered and bought will only be pushed so far with threats. The only way to deal with those badge-wearing cowboys is with a bullet. I don't like shooting policeman, so the less I have to involve them in my work, the lower the risk.

It's those wild cards that keep me working in the dark. Restricting my illegal enterprises to the criminal underbelly where gangsters such as me belong.

That I'm now bringing my brand of felony into the working-class residential areas not known for it would raise a few eyebrows. *If* I got caught.

The smile curling my lips would scare the devil. I avoid looking in the rearview mirror as I slide out of the Bugatti, and jog across the street.

I stay away from the streetlights, slicing into the darker shadows that border those sodium-orange puddles discoloring the asphalt, and using the night to camouflage my path. What I love about the layout of the neighborhood is that there is a lot of space between the houses. Allowing me to slip into a gulley between them and use the easement of the privacy hedges to work my way around back.

From there, I have an unfettered and private view of the house. Though it takes me a minute to figure out the layout. Then, I slip between the narrow gulley between the houses.

A lot of the old houses in Echo Bay are partitioned into two or three units. Back in the day, these enormous, rambling monstrosities were both a way to showcase one's wealth and to house their giant, multi-generational families.

Now if someone is rich, they build a modern mansion near the water, or higher in the hills. Never down here with the commoners. Since living space is at a premium world-wide, these old houses became multi-family apartments. Sometimes the houses are separated by floor, instead of down the middle like this one is.

The basement is a no-go. I can get in through the rather thin glass since a piece of it is patched with particle board. This isn't Rina's space.

Ah. Now here's a way in.

Using a flip LED light, I scout the backdoor and the flimsy lock that isn't worth the metal it's been manufactured with. It's the kind that comes built the doorknob, a set you buy at any home good's store like Home Depot. I scope the area again, and shake my head. With the way the houses are clustered, soaking the yard with shadows, no porch light, no automatic floodlights, no dog to bark an alarm. It's as if Rina is *begging* for an intruder.

I'm really going to have to teach her a lesson about poor security measures.

Pulling out the wrench, I jab the flat head in between the door jamb and the lock plate. A quick smack of my palm, and the lock pops with a faint metallic gasp, as if *shocked* at how easily I've broken it.

Pocking my tools, I crouch beside the door, waiting to see if anyone inside heard me. This is what separates professionals from amateurs – we don't rush.

After ten long minutes, when nobody appears, I let myself inside.

This is far too easy, and my feral instinct has me stopping just at the threshold.

Pulling out my phone, I type a text to Lev, telling him to send one of our security specialists to Rina's address for a full lock repair and surveillance package in the morning. That I'll be getting unfettered access via a key is secondary to my desire for her to be safe. Echo Bay isn't known for its crime, since I run it both the legal and illegal side, there is still the occasional property theft from adrenaline-seeking teenagers and the occasional skulking tourist who doesn't know whose territory they're messing with.

With that taken care of, I navigate through the kitchen and out into the hallway.

Breaking into old houses can be tricky. Wood creaks with the slightest step, and these old mansions are all hardwood, from the frames to the floors. It's why I couldn't live in one. I like my silence, and hearing every person as they walk around based on how the floorboards groan would drive me insane.

Luckily, when this one was renovated to switch over to a rental, they'd modernized it. While they would have been stupid to pull up the natural hardwood, they had buffered the noises by adding wall-to-wall carpeting. The thick kind with a tight nap that doesn't show footprints. Nor does it let the worst of the squeaking tongue-and-groove construction groan through.

I walk swiftly, as nimbly as I can. Ballet, of all things, taught me how to be fleet-footed, putting my weight on the balls of my feet so that my strides are barely heard. It is the heel, and the levered motion of walking, that makes the most noise. And why dancers seem to glide like ghosts, weightlessly and eerie when they are poised on their tiptoes.

Rina's bedroom is on the second floor, or at least the sign is. I creep up the stairs, feeling the excited thud of my pulse in my chest.

I know I'm a bastard. I know I'm all sorts of fucked up for getting off over breaking into my niece's teacher's house.

Yes, Rina is more than that *now*. But that doesn't change the truth of our association.

In her eyes, I am Mila's guardian.

A stand-in father figure.

Is that the allure for me? Rina doesn't look at me with fright in her eyes because I am *Bratva*. Nor does show me any respect because I am the *pakhan.* Her insult is refreshing, a snap of summer air in the tundra of my soul.

Her fear is pure, sexually based. She took one look at me and knew I'd ruin her.

That much is true. I will destroy her.

Not because of *who* I am.

Not because of *what* I am.

But because the attraction between us is too large to not shatter lives and break worlds. When we come together, it will be a fucking collision that will set off the seismic monitors that are embedded all over the fault lines from Washington to California.

At least, that's how it feels to me. It's a *knowing* that has increased over the past two weeks that I've tried to keep her at a distance.

If Rina doesn't feel this *yet,* it will only be a matter of time.

I'll make sure of it.

Finally, with only a few creaky steps in the second-floor hallway, I stand outside Rina's doorway. She keeps the door half-cracked. Probably for her sister to come to her if she needs to.

Rina is a mother without a child. Her maternal instincts are on razor-sharp, especially for one who hasn't honed them on the whetstone of pregnancy hormones. While there are parallels in our lives – her with Lucia me with Alexander and Mila – I'm not the person they would come to in the middle of the night. Nor have I had to sacrifice what she has. From what I'd read of Rina's past - financials, job status, college transcripts, and the like - she sacrifices her present to give Lucia a brighter future, without any help from either parent.

On paper, Lucia and Rina are half-sisters, blood shared by their mother with different deadbeat fathers who hit the road whenever the elder Amy Christenson got herself knocked up. In actuality, Rina doesn't acknowledge any difference in genetics.

They are a family.

In this is our strongest similarities. I would do anything for Mila, Mikhail, and even Alexander despite him being a thorn in my ass. I would protect all of them with the very breath in my lungs, the blood in my veins, and the marrow in my bones.

So too would Rina do that for Lucia.

I am, unsurprisingly, fucking proud of her for it.

Reminded of that, my irritation over her smug little note calms. But not enough to leave her to her much-needed sleep.

After all, my girl needs to learn and the best way to learn is through hardship.

Boundaries? Who the fuck does she think she's dealing with?

I elbow her door open and push my way inside. Before shutting it behind me with a quiet click. A twist of my wrist, and the flimsy lock in the handle is secured.

Nobody will be interrupting my plans with Rina. Tonight, I will force Rina to admit the chemistry between us. And the best way for that to happen is to get her to cum for me.

My cock leads me forward, hardening into iron at the idea.

Rina sleeps in a taut bundle, curled up on her side with half of the queen-size mattress free. As if she were waiting for a man to come fill that empty niche. She is bundled up in cotton, with one leg flung out from the nest of sheets and duvet, to reveal the wool socks encasing her feet.

I can't help myself as I reach for my phone again. It's stupid of me to bring it when I'm in the middle of a criminal misdeed. Cops can track people from records of cell tower pings. If Rina calls the cops after this bit of breaking-and-entering, I am dead to rights the moment they see my cell pinging in this location.

But I know she won't.

Tapping the phone icon, I snap a few photos, holding the phone still so that 'night mode' can activate. Which pushes out photos that look almost as if a flash has brightened the scene.

Then I set my phone beside hers on the nightstand and nose my way through every aspect of her life. The ones that couldn't be uncovered without old-fashioned breaking-and-entering.

It takes only fifteen minutes to prowl through her dresser drawers, finding them packed full of simple cotton and only a few pairs of lace panties. The urge to steal one has my fingers quivering in the gusset of one particularly racy red pair. But I can't take them, not unless I plan to replace them. I don't want to leave Rina without, and taking them would be cruel to a woman who is living on the edge of poverty – one health bill, or job loss from ruin. Not unless I plan on replacing them.

We're not yet at a place where she'll accept help from me, especially not underwear. But soon, I will see her dressed as she deserves. In a fortune of cashmere, silk, and expensive merino wool.

Muttering at myself, I slide the dresser drawer shut and turn to the sleeping beauty on the bed. Her dreams most likely filled with unicorns and flowers. Not knowing that the monster has crept out from beneath the bed.

It's time to wake up my angel and show her how wrong it is to deny the devil.

Chapter Thirteen

Rina

Something tickles my face and throat, creating an irritation around my nose that draws me slowly from the comfy slumber I'd fallen into. I don't often dream, and I'm pretty sure I'm not dreaming now. But I was on the cusp of a deep, deep sleep, about ready to dive head-long into the embrace of the Sandman and let him have his wicked way with me.

Alas, that isn't in my future.

My eyes open to darkness, the only light seeping in from around the edges of the blinds pulled down across the window. For a moment I don't know where I am, let alone *who* I am. My subconscious is suspended somewhere in between the waking and dreamworld, slow to reboot as if it's a personal computer running on drivers years out of date. Eventually, the fog clears as I work through the fuzziness of sleep, remembering the ticklish sensation that caused my brain to jar me awake.

God, I hope it isn't a spider.

I go to scratch my nose, maybe swat away whatever creepy thing that is crawling over me. This is the Pacific Northwest, and with the congregation of trees, all kinds of insects manage to find their way inside.

Instead, my hands jerk against the headboard. The hard bite of plastic gnashes at my wrists.

The shock brings me fully awake. The back of my head digs into my pillows as I follow the line of my arms to where my wrists are tied together and then lashed to the headboard.

What..the...

I know I didn't fall asleep while in the middle of performing some self-bondage. How would I even zip-tie my wrists by myself? Nor do I have any interest in being an escape artist.

That must mean...

Panic bursts in my chest, a firecracker of fright that sends a heavy dose of adrenaline pumping headily through my veins.

Oh my God.

Before I can fully freak out, a darker shadow separates from the gloom surrounding my bed. Though I should be stunned, I'm not, as I look up at Edmond looming over me.

Edmond Vasiliev is in my bedroom. He has me *tied* to my headboard, trussed up like a piñata waiting for his attention.

The words he'd whispered to me earlier in the day scream through my head. *"Perhaps you should leave your window unlatched tonight, to ask your stalker what he wants..."*

"I left a note," I blurt because a little piece of paper is surely going to stop an unhinged man. Ask all the women who take restraining orders out. Paper does nothing, and here I am trying to hold it up as a shield.

I'd badly misjudged the whole situation. Because the note had done nothing. Not a damn thing.

Suddenly, Edmond's hands are on each side of my body as he leans over me, filling my vision with his handsome face as the weak light and shadows cavort across it. He is ruggedly beautiful, all hard angles and sharp-cut planes that leave me trembling beneath him. Craving things which I don't have a name for, but can read their definition in his gimlet eyes.

"Boundaries are for those too weak to take what they want."

My heart gives up trying to resist the roar of adrenaline rushing into it. It jumps into my throat, pounding so hard that I can feel the quiver of my pulse between my temples. I'm going to have a heart attack as my body slingshots between fear and arousal. He has me completely *helpless* beneath him.

And oh *god* do I like it.

His lips are a promise above mine, their corners twitching up in a resemblance of a smile. It's a scary expression, because all I see is a shift of shadows, and then a brighter gleam of teeth. Before his breath brushes across my mouth.

"And I want you. Thus, I'm *taking* what I want."

"Edmond." My voice shakes, and I want to applaud myself for being able to speak. My brain has taken a hiatus, unable to deal with this situation. Which leaves my body, my hormones, in the driver's seat. My ovaries are egging me on, encouraging me to give him everything he wants. While self-preservation is building a scream in the back of my throat.

Right before I let it loose, I remember I'm not alone. I draw back the leaking, shrill decibels with a shocked inhaled. Belatedly realizing *his* game, and the ammunition he has with which to get me to do what he wants.

Lucia. I don't want to wake Lucia. She's a spike of ice in the sauna of my lust. Her being a few doors down means that I can't scream, I can't do anything. Because I don't know what Edmond would do if someone caught him here.

I can't risk it. Which means I need to be quiet, even if half of me wants to scream for help, and the other half wants to squeal with pleasure.

The bastard knows it too. He reads my expression, and

then slowly he grins, a malicious hike of his well-shaped, generous lips when he realizes that *I get it* now. I understand the game.

Edmond backs away, all but vanishing into the deeper shadows that shroud the area near my closet.

"Not going to scream, *solnyshko?*" His voice mocks me, filled with sarcastic humor that rubs my predicament in like salt in a wound."

"I hate you."

I can almost make out where Edmond is in my bedroom. Since there is no light ruining my night vision, when he moves, I can strain my eyes just enough to make out his shadow; darker even than the dusk at the peak of midnight.

"No, you don't," he whispers, and then he is right there by my bed again.

His bare hands cup my chin, jerking my head up and tilting my neck at an angle. My hair is caught beneath me, and the position makes the roots tug, sending a thrill down my nape from my annoyed scalp. He looks at me as if he's inspecting a priceless bauble or sculpture, covetous and ready to acquire it by any means necessary.

I whimper, feeling that strange surge of heat that decides to joyride on the paralyzing fear that grips me. My body throbs at the way Edmond manhandles me. How he makes sure I am completely vulnerable to him. My pussy very much likes where this is going. But I can't even call her a traitorous bitch. As every bit of me is excited that I've managed to snare the attention of a man of Edmond's caliber.

My brain makes one more last-ditch effort, screaming 911, before it falls silent. The war between my brain and body is brief, lost during the first salvo as Edmond's hand leads the first charge. He thumbs my bottom lip, tugging on the tender flesh until my jaw unlocks and mouth opens. Giving him enough room to wedge the blunt digit between them. I gasp as his roughened finger-pad pushes down on my teeth, demanding a way in. My core clenches, and I squeeze my thighs tightly as if that can help me ignore the wet neediness pulsing between them. He hasn't given an order, and my cheeks are already shivering with the want to suck on his finger.

"You look like you want to be kissed."

I try shaking my head, but his fingers tighten, biting into my cheeks. I mewl. Both because it hurts, and he has me absolutely at his mercy.

Mercy?

No, Edmond is a man distinctly lacking in mercy.

Merciless.

"Now isn't the time for lies, Miss Christenson," he taunts.

I groan, unable to get my tongue to work and propel the words my mind is shrieking at me.

No.

Stop.

Please.

Of course, it's the last one that I give voice to.

"Please," I whimper. Surely, I mean 'please no'?

Instead, it sounds as if I'm begging him for more.

Edmond grins down at me, his lips parted slightly to allow me a hint of his teeth. He looks like the Cheshire cat when he smiles like that, all teeth that stretches ear-to-ear.

"I love it when you beg." His head lowers, once again filling my narrow viewpoint with his handsome face and those sinful eyes. His breath whispers over my mouth, making the spot where his thumb tugs burn with heat.

He's going to kiss me. And oh, *oh* how I want him to. I've wanted to kiss him since I first laid eyes on him, kneeling at his feet as if that meeting was a premonition of what would come next.

Then, right before he touches that lush, cruel mouth to mine, he pulls back.

"Only good girls get kisses. And you have been a bad girl."

"Ba-bad?" I'm dying as he teases me. Jerking me around until my head spins as if I'm caught in a tilt-a-whirl.

"Mmhm. That note, Rina. Is that what you want? Do you want boundaries?"

He might sound as if he's playing, but I can hear the heat - the anger - that burns furnace-hot behind his half-joked words.

Before I can answer, or scream, he claps his palm over my mouth. He reads the panic in my eyes that desperately wants to get free. His fingers forced my head to move, and I realize with a jolt of surprise that he's making me shake my head 'no' at him. As if my brain isn't crying out the rules of engagement.

That boundaries are healthy. Having the autonomy to say no is important in a relationship. Not that we're dating let alone involved in a relationship. But I want a partnership. Someone who will take my 'no' and not change it, or outright ignore it.

Edmond is not that type of man. He's in touch with his Neanderthal side. He has to be because that's the only reason he acts the way he does.

"I thought not. You want to be *my* good girl."

The way he growls 'my' causes a wave of pleasure to roll from head-to-toe, leaving my toes curling in a way that I thought was reserved just for the movies.

Slowly, Edmond uncoils his hand from my mouth and drags his fingertips down across my chin. He paints my flesh with the slickness gathered from keeping my mouth captive.

His hand travels lower, brushing a light touch between my straining breasts. They're lofted high, threatening to choke me with the way their weight pushes into my throat. But he doesn't stop and indulges in their silent plea. Even though my nipples are tingling and as hard as rock candy against the soft cotton of my much-worn sleep shirt.

His knuckles caress my belly, making me tense when I realize where his hand is headed.

"Ed-Edmond," I squeak, stuttering in full-body shock.

Edmond continues his descent as if he doesn't hear the half-begged 'stop' in my voice. Though I'm not sure I really *want* him to stop. It's just that nobody has touched me like that before, and that he wants to – with or without my consent – leaves me burning red-hot and trembling.

His touch is light, a playful flicker of his fingers across the waist of my sweatpants. Fanning his hands to the side, that softness suddenly turns hard and brutal as he grabs my hips.

I cry out as he yanks me down the bed, forcing my arms taut and the plastic to dig painfully into my wrists. I'm going to have marks, if not outright bruises, in the morning.

My pussy grows slick, outright soaking my panties.

I lift my head, catching snippets of Edmond's motions as his fingers curl, capturing a wad of cotton and fleece. His doesn't seem at all bothered that I'm swaddled in layers of warm fabric, and nothing sexy.

Then he pulls, and I whimper as he peels my sweats *and* panties down. He doesn't stop until they are completely off, leaving me naked from the waist down with only my fleecy pink socks on. I feel so, so naked. Despite being half-dressed. I twist my face, pressing my feverish cheeks and closed eyes into my raised bicep. My thighs snap together, trying to chastely guard my sex from his hungry eyes. I know he can't see much in the dark, but I'm still blushing at the idea of what he might see – might feel – when he touches me.

Edmond jostles the bed as he climbs onto it. His knee crashes down onto the tender flesh of my inseam, making me whimper as he wedges my thighs apart. Heat ravages me, making every brush of air feel icy when it touches my over-heated body.

"Mm, there we go, *solnyshko*."

"Edmond..I-I haven't, I..."

I can't spit out a secret that when most guys I've dated, finds out falls into two categories: disgusted or fetishizing.

"Shh. While I have plans for you, I'm not going to fuck this sweet cunt tonight. I want you begging for my cock before I let you feel me."

His words are scandalous. My pulse jerks in my throat and that throbbing is echoed deep, deep inside.

"Then wha—."

Edmond lowers his head, his meaning unmistakable.

Oh. *Oh.*

He isn't. He is no...

He is.

I cry out when he lays a kiss on my pussy lips.

"Mm, there she is. My good girl."

That first kiss might have been soft. But the next one isn't.

Edmond presses his whole mouth over my sex. His tongue slinks inward, a ticklish invasion that laps from my dripping slit, all the way up to the hard button of my clit.

I'd never trusted, or really wanted, to get naked with a man. Let alone find one who wanted to give me such an intimate kiss. Now a man I barely know, whose broken into my bedroom, has his tongue flicking and swirling around my clit. Every soft, wet pass makes my hips lift, seeking that slick connection.

Edmond's head lifts, his growl a deep, vibrating basso that I can feel between my thighs. "Never?"

A hot blush burns through me as I realize I must have been sputtering that all aloud. Letting him know my biggest, darkest secrets.

I want to close my eyes and remove the view of Edmond's baleful eyes stabbing me into the bed.

But I can't. Not when his mouth is shiny with my juices.

"Never," I pant.

Something feral grows in Edmond's eyes, darkening all of that silver until it looks like gunmetal.

He lowers his head again, a starving man let loose at a buffet. When I clap my thighs around his ears, he shoves them wide, forcing my knees toward my chest and exposing *all* of my charms. He grows comfortable between my trembling legs, laying flat on his stomach. I get a glimpse of his wicked smile, before his face disappears between my thighs.

I look down, meeting this lethal gaze. His eyes are the only thing visible because the rest of his face - his mouth - is driving down onto my pussy.

I lose it then and there. I have to turn my face into my bicep, smothering my cries into the flesh as his tongue flicks and traces. The slick muscle undulates against the underside of my clit, making sparks flicker behind my closed eyes.

I moan his name.

The bastard chuckles into my pussy. I know he wis toying with me. Each time I feel that coiling, tightening sensation that warns me my orgasm was close by, he stops. Pulling back to lazily lick all of my juices trickling out of me as if I am an ice cream melting beneath the heat of his breath.

"Edmond," I plead.

"Keep begging, *solnyshko*."

I writhe as he feasts. And right when I'm sure I can stand the tension, he ratchets up the agonizing pleasure by wrapping his lips around my clit and sucking gently.

A scream locks behind my teeth. My thighs strain against the width of his heavily muscled shoulders.

I'm so close. The edge rears before me, beckoning me to

crash over it. Then he teases my slit with one large finger, surprising me with the callous-roughened touch on such vulnerable flesh. I tense when I feel the intrusion, the size and just how blunt the digit it is threatening to stretch me open.

Until he wriggles it inside, creating a delicious friction that has my hips arching off the bed.

"Oh God," I breathe.

His teeth rake gently over that little nubbin that is the epicenter of my pleasure. When I touch myself, I focus on my clit. Working and rolling that bundle of nerves around without really sliding a finger in. I don't have any hangup about fingering myself. But I've learned that I can get off just by clitoral stimulation, and Ihaven't felt the need to explore further.

Edmond teaches me how wrong I've been with my thoughts.

He hooks his finger, finding some spot inside that I haven't explored, but dimly knew existed. I assume it is my G-Spot he is toying with. But I never, ever expected it to feel like *that*.

My toes curl as all the tension in my body arrows between my thighs. I feel fragile, brittle even, as if I'm going to shatter.

Edmond's finger stroke a little circle 'round and 'round that hot patch of pleasure. Until he's spooled the tension into that narrow arrow, piling it all up on a cliff's edge that I've begun to crest.

Then, he sucks again, manipulating my clit with his tongue and that spot that feels like it is right *behind* my clit with his finger.

Somehow, I put my teeth into the pillow beneath my cheek. The scream he wrings from me as makes me cum on his fingers and face is loud enough it would have woken Lucia. God, it would have woken the dead it is that loud. Now, with cotton bunched between my teeth, I smother it enough to let loose.

Giving up control and worry and all the things that always used to hinder my climaxes. Beneath Edmond's touch, I have no such problems.

My pussy grows wetter, louder as I gush, filling the bedroom with the obscenely wet sounds of Edmond's finger working inside my flooded cunt. Time is immaterial as I soar into the stratosphere, lingering in the euphoria and body-melting pleasure of my orgasm. Dimly, I'm aware of my earthly body and the man who is ardently keeping the pleasure-train chugging. He is a relentless conductor, keeping the pace perfect and steady despite how I shudder and rock beneath him. Until the last tingle fades away.

I remember to breathe, inhaling loudly as I sag between the painful hoist of my trapped arms. God. The French named the orgasm right. I have died, and now I'm resurrected by a gray-eyed devil. My mind is quiet, and my pussy coos with pleasure.

Slowly, Edmond tugs his finger out, smearing wetness between my thighs.

He kneels there, hooking my gaze so that I can stare at the glaze of my arousal smudging his chin. I did that to him. I know I should apologize for creaming his face, but I can't unglue my tongue from the roof of my mouth. Let alone muster enough fake guilt that would make the apology sound sincere.

"You taste like sunlight and honey." Edmond smudges his thumb against his lips, gathering up the wetness I left behind before licking it free.

He moans in appreciation.

"I could eat you for breakfast, lunch, and dinner, *solnyshko.*"

I have quite literally died and gone to hell, because there's no way the angels in heaven are this debauched and sensual.

Edmond stretches out over the top of me, his fists knuckling the pillows beside my head. His mouth lowers until I can smell *me* on his breath. It is so raunchy that my core throbs to life, a weaker pulse but one of obvious approval.

He rubs his cheek against mine, his nose tucked into the crease as if he were nuzzling my face.

I breathe him in. Desperate now for a kiss. A real kiss.

Edmond rises a fraction, reading my craving in my face.

"Remember this feeling for when you try to deny me again."

Then, the bastard pulls away. I hear a knife, maybe a switchblade before the tension around my wrists suddenly lets loose.

I whimper as the blood rushes back into my arms. Bringing with it that painful pins-and-needles feeling. I curl on my side, rubbing my wrists as Edmond slips into the shadows. He grabs his coat from the chair in front of my desk. I catch only a flash of his silhouette, so large and intimidating in the dim light.

Then he's gone, vanishing into the dark like a thief in the night, while I replay the hardest orgasm of my life until dawn crests on the horizon.

Chapter Fourteen

Rina

Not only does Edmond snatch my precious sleep away, but he also infects my brain. To make matters worse, the plastic cuffs have left bruises. Purple-black marks ring each wrist as a testament that the night prior wasn't a dream. I have to wear long sleeves, and I am petrified that someone will notice the marks.

Luckily, no one seems any wiser.

The entire school day drags by, and I feel flighty and preoccupied. It's made worse by the fact that Mila is in my class. I blush when I look at her and try to stop thinking about the deeds we'd done in the middle of the night.

All day long, I expect Edmond to pop up like a bad penny. Just to torment me with that knowing smile and watchful eyes.

I tell myself I am relieved as the final bell rings without any sight of him. Mila rides home with her bodyguards and driver. The former stands in the wraparound drive where the high-target kids are protected by a cement wall as they climb into their bulletproof cars and then are ushered home.

Mila sees me watching, alongside a few of the other teachers, and Principal Sawyer who likes to oversee that nothing happens during these vulnerable moments. Where the kids are leaving the protection of the school and climbing into mobile fortresses.

She waves and I wave back.

She is such a sweet kid. It's a shame that her uncle is a daemon in a three-piece suit.

I tell myself I'm not feeling disappointed that I haven't seen hide nor smile of Edmond.

Tonight is another tutoring day. Which means I go from one job to the next. Albeit my second job is done in the privacy of my own home. It's a surprisingly busy tutoring day, which leaves me scrambling to make dinner in between sessions.

Edmond's memory is a passenger in my car. He occupies my thoughts way too much. I'm still not sure how I feel about him or the situation that I find myself in.

Honestly, Edmond is too much. Like, way too much. He kind of scares me with how intense he is.

My dating life is nothing to write home about. While many of my college friends date around, and live that hook-up life, I have never been interested.

Sure, there'd been a boyfriend or two. I even managed to get to second base, which is some mild petting overtop of the clothing and kissing. But I always stopped before we reach anything deeper. I simply didn't want to sleep with any of the boys I date.

Perhaps because what I needed was a man.

Edmond knows exactly what he wants, and how he wants it. I know I should feel something or even acknowledge that he's broken into my house and accosted me in the middle of the night. But I can't summon the outrage. I'd never had an orgasm that hard. Just thinking about it leaves me hot and bothered.

I squirm in the front seat of my car, ignoring the sudden rush of wetness soaking my panties.

Before I'd met Edmond, I hadn't known how to classify my libido.

Healthy.

Average.

I masturbate at least once a week, usually to help me sleep. A good orgasm is nature's Ambien. Chamomile can't touch how relaxed I feel afterward. Had I been able to get eight hours after that mind-blowing climax, I'd have felt like a new person. Instead of an exhausted and overworked hag.

Frustration eats at me as I drive home, trying - and failing - to force the larger-than-life prowess of Edmond Vasiliev out of my head.

Would it be so bad if I just...gave in to him?

Okay, yes. I always tell myself I won't involve myself with a parent. But I could bend on this hardline. As long as it's just a one-time thing. A way to scratch the itch, as it were.

"Hello, Luce," I call as I breeze through the doors as if my thoughts are lighter than they are.

Marianne surprises me by calling, "In here," from the kitchen. Peeking around the edge, I find her putting a casserole dish in the refrigerator.

"You shouldn't have."

I love this woman. She has a sixth sense when I need a home-cooked meal, and I'm too exhausted to do it myself. Then she shows up like this, toting sweets and treats as if she doesn't work harder than I do. She has custody of her granddaughter, because her daughter is caught up in a drug and abuse cycle with her current live-in boyfriend, and the daddy is in prison down-state.

"I had time."

I hug Marianne and then grab a bottle of water before she can close the door.

"You've had a lot of company today."

I school my face into a mask that I hope doesn't look too guilty, while trying to figure out what she means.

Did she see Edmond leave last night?

"I grabbed your mail, it's on the table beside a delivery your received from the English Rose Garden Tea Shop. And the locksmith was already here and gone. He fixed the back door and put in a bunch of sensors and an alarm system by the front door. There's a dictionary-sized instruction booklet for you to read."

I freeze with the bottle halfway to my mouth. I didn't order anything off of Oliver. I hadn't had the chance because Edmond had stolen all of the air out of the shop and scared the shopkeeper. Then the whole lock thing.

I shake my head and take a swig.

So, that's how he got it.

At least he had it fixed before Lucia noticed it. Perhaps the alarm system is his way of apologizing.

"Thank you for handling that."

"One can't be too safe. Echo Bay might be cozy on the surface, but it's anything but."

I raise a brow, wondering what Marianne means by that. Is it the same pseudo-warning that I've gotten from Zoe and Oliver?

What the hell is under the surface of Echo Bay?

Marianne clamps her mouth shut. She shakes her head at my look and then hauls her tote bag onto her shoulder.

"Nothing. If you don't know, you don't need to."

Mari gives me a hug and a kiss on the forehead, then goes to say goodnight to Lucia.

Curiosity pokes at me with spiny fingers. I wonder if her

assessment has to do with the eclectic assortment of kids who attend Harbor View Montessori. There is barbed wire atop the brick wall that surrounds the school's entire footprint, which sits on a plot of land that is at least three acres, bulletproof glass in all the windows, and armed security guards who roam the hallways, making it feel like a well-fortified castle.

I simply assumed that all of the wealthy who live on Orcas Island, ship their children over to attend school.

But maybe all that money isn't exactly legitimate.

I frown, biting on my bottom lip.

Then I shake myself, deciding not to borrow trouble from tomorrow.

Curiosity leads me to the letter and package that Marianne said arrived. A set of boxes decorated in the powdery blue of the English Rose Garden tempts me, sitting stacked like Christmas morning in the middle of the table festooned with navy-blue ribbon.

While Lucia tries to find me things I'd enjoy for my birthday and the holidays. The truth is neither of us have much money. Her due to her age and class schedule. Me because I'm trying to keep our heads above water. Even when we are flush with cash, the gift before me is so far outside of my range that I can't believe it's real and sitting in *my* kitchen.

For me. I don't need to speculate on who sent the gift. I've known Oliver since the first weekend we moved to Echo Bay. He's never sent me a care package, let alone anything this extravagant.

I stroke my finger through the extravagant loop of the ribbon's bow, savoring the satiny texture. Oddly, tears gather in my throat, putting a surreal type of pressure on my chest that I can feel gripping my heart. I know it's silly and stupid to cry over a gift, something that Edmond probably sent his assistant to purchase. But it means something to me. Something I can't put a word on. Only that for the first time in my adult life, I almost feel…cared for by someone other than my sister.

I tug the ribbon, unraveling it so that it swirls away from the stack of boxes.

Then I reach for the lid of the first one and open it.

The tears that threatened break past the gates of my teeth, and drip silently but steadily down my cheeks. I need to sit down, as my knees have turned to mush.

Along with the stony walls I tried to build up around my heart.

For all of my tea obsession, I don't have a legitimate tea set. I have an electric kettle and a mismatched set of mugs that I picked up over the years. Honestly, nothing in the kitchen matches. Everything from the silverware to the plates are cobbled together, picked up individually from stores or purchased from thrift shops. I've always felt a tiny bit embarrassed that I'm an adult and don't have grown-up dinnerware. Let alone a tea set.

The first box holds a fine porcelain, hand-painted teapot. Its delicate floral motif makes me think of a sun-soaked field of wildflowers. With watercolor blooms of warm pink and gold on a silky white background. A brush of mint green, a flush of pinkish coneflowers, a delicate spray of blue-tinged violets, it's a romantic portrait overlaid with a flight of butterflies winging around the body. Delicate gold bands outline the edges, from the rim, handle, base, to the knob that tips the cap-style lid. A matching creamer pot and sugar bowl are nestled on each side of it. I don't even need to check the mark. It's a Wedgewood, the Mercedes Benz of teapots.

Gently shifting the large box aside, the next one is even bigger, and holds a matching full teacup set. Four cups and saucers, and a sandwich tray to serve with if I want to make my own Sunday Tea at home. The tears drip steadily, followed by a ridiculous sound that escapes my clasped lips that makes me think a cat is loose in the kitchen.

The final box dispels my belief that Emond sent an assistant to buy this gift. He'd gone in and picked it out himself.

Nestled in crinkly packing filler is a canister of jade oolong. The same imported tea I'd been drooling over when Edmond had barged into the shop, breathing down my neck like a pissed-off dragon.

I cover my mouth, trying to hold back the tiny animal sounds I'm making.

This gift…

This fucking gift…

It's exquisite.

Expensive,

And so thoughtful that I can't stop sobbing over it.

It also makes me realize just how dangerous Edmond is to my well-being. He slinks into my bedroom in the middle of the night. Conjures danger and fear, and gives me the hardest orgasm of my life, then vanishes with the sun as if he's a midnight phantom. Only to tug at my heartstrings by giving me the best present I've ever received. On a weekday morning no less. For no other reason than he can.

It takes me the better part of a half-hour to calm down. The tears refuse to quit, no matter how often I wipe at them. Finally, though, I can breathe and look at the tea ware without breaking down again. The frugal side of myself tells me I should send it back or put it on a shelf and never use it. But gifts are meant to be enjoyed, and I promise myself I'll brew a big batch of tea with it later.

The mail sits stacked beside the boxes, along with the inch-thick manual on my new alarm system. I shake my head as I skim over the directions for setting the code. This is ridiculous. The security guy installed a cutting-edge system that is meant to protect the vault of some mega McMansion. Not a dingy little duplex on the edge of respectability.

Flipping through the letters, I wrinkle my nose as much of it is just junk mail. But the logo on the top of a cream-colored envelope makes my fingers tense. There's nothing good about receiving a letter from Lucia's headmaster.

I hope she's not in trouble again.

Slitting the seal, I pull out the letter inside and unfold it.

No, Lucia's not in trouble. This is worse.

Much, much worse.

My heart stops beating. I forget to breathe, or maybe I Just can't through the constriction that's starting to throttle my lungs. The quivery feeling of a panic attack begins behind my eyes, brought on by my earlier off-kilter emotions from the sweet gift, now plunging to the opposite end of the spectrum.

Certain words jump out at me.

Tuition hike.

4.8% next semester.

Enrollment costs.

Not covered by...scholarship.

I smooth the paper flat on the table, staring blankly at the financial grenade that just dropped in my lap.

How am I going to afford another five thousand dollars on top of all the other costs? We live on a shoestring budget, paycheck to paycheck. And that's if it's a good month, without medical costs or car issues or dental problems. Most of the time, I barely keep our heads above water.

If the landlord decides to raise our rent next year too, which knowing the housing market throughout the entire country, is likely. We are going to sink.

I can't do this alone.

But I have to. Because there's nobody else. It's just Luce and me against the world. The only thing she has is her future, the promise that her talent will make all her dreams come true. She could be the next Merce Cunningham, the renowned, local-born artist who pushed the creative boundaries of dance, music, and visual media. The same type of complexity that drives my sister, and the progenitor of the school she now attends.

The ache of oncoming tears blooms behind my eyes. My lower lip quivers, and I suck it in past my teeth. Pressing my fingers against my eyelids, I will myself not to have a meltdown.

Such is life.

And oh, how it is bitter.

On one hand, I receive an expensive, impractical gift.

With the other, the balance I'd maintained for the past six months is shattered.

I will not cry.

My nose burns from my earlier sob-fest and the want for more. I want to break down into tears. A knot of frustration laces around my throat, turning every breath into a struggle.

I already have two jobs.

If I had been hired for the year by Harbor View Montessori, I would be a salaried employee, with all the bells, whistles, health care, and union protection that teachers enjoy.

Right now, I am a little more than a substitute, paid a fraction of my worth. But and this is the important part, I have a foot in the door. I am hoping I can springboard this term into a legitimate position for the next year.

The alarm on my phone beeps, prompting me up and out of the kitchen. I need to log in for my tutoring job.

"Luce, I'm logging in to work now. Do you need anything?" I yell toward her shut door as I jog up the stairs. From inside, I can hear the faint melody of music. Not loud enough to be noticeable, and the repetitive thump of sticks on the rubber-headed, electric drum kit I got her for Christmas.

Knowing she can't hear me if she's practicing with her headphones on, I send her a text before sliding into my seat and logging into the application I use for my tutoring job. Online tutoring sustains us, because there are always students who need assistance, that they might not be able to receive in person.

It takes me an hour to settle my student into a mock test. Tonight isn't a video session day. It's a screen share so I can watch how my student shows his work before his upcoming exam.

Pulling up another window, I type in a few choice searches and begin my job hunt. The only free time I have is on the weekends. Luckily, certain industries are calm during the weekday and kick off into a frenzy on the weekends. Mostly restaurants, bars, hotels, and other service industries. I don't want to put added stress on my car, so delivery driver and ride share are out.

Finally, I narrow it down to a handful. Before realizing that they are all for the same parent company.

Apply in person at Timberhaus I-5, five miles before exit 183.

Just watch it be a strip club.

I email myself a link so I can investigate them more thoroughly later before I return to watching as my student finishes his exam. Closing out the browser window, I focus on my tutee and try not to think of the invisible clock now ticking down over my head.

Chapter Fifteen

Edmond

Money doesn't buy happiness. What it does give is time. Everyone has the same twenty-four hours a day, but if you can hire out all the small, dreary aspects, you suddenly have a whole lot more free time on your hands.

The time my wealth affords me is spent obsessing over Rina. After my nocturnal visit like Dracula sneaking in her window at night, I manage to keep myself away.

Mostly.

Before, I'd used the Bugatti to observe her. Now, I use one of the G-wagons reserved for the fringe members of my business. It's more rugged than the Rolls Royce, making it easier to blend in with all the other off-road, luxury SUVs which populate the roads throughout Washington state. This distance is for my own sanity, and her safety. I need to rebuild the wall between the tempting Miss Christenson and myself and try to put us back on professional footing.

A week passes, and I think perhaps I have managed to work her out from beneath my skin.

Until Mila takes a wrecking ball to that wall, and it crumbles so swiftly, that I realize it had been a mirage.

Mila bounces around the kitchen like a hyperactive hummingbird. Neither Eve, her live-in nanny, nor I are quite caffeinated enough to withstand the endless chatter. Luckily, our chef knows that our breakfast is often liquid and has pulled me a shot of Blue Bottle espresso. The crema is a perfect brown sugar shade that matches the naturally sweet notes of caramel, almond, and dried cherry.

"Oh, Oh! Guess what today is!" Mila's voice is a pip of excitement. She nearly vibrates around the cabinets to stand at my side.

Though it is March in the Pacific Northwest, you wouldn't believe it with how cheery and sunny she is clothed. I am confident that the daisy-yellow dress she wears with the frilly skirt is more appropriate for summertime. But Eve has made sure Mila is dressed for warmth by adding layers, with a pair of tights underneath and a white cardigan overtop, creating enough of a buffer between my niece and the precocious weather.

"Hmm, *pchelka.*"

"Miss Christenson is going to show us a movie about the stars."

My good work at blocking out her tempting teacher shatters, leaving the image of the innocent redhead slicing through my mind.

I swallow a methodical sip of coffee, feeling the itch of obsession dig its tether hooks beneath my skin. I've grown familiar with it over the past few weeks, ever since I got gut-punched by it the first time my eyes met those bewitching hazel hues.

I don't obsess over women.

Sex is a biological function. Nothing more.

No matter how often I repeat my mantra, it's not sticking.

What I want to do is drag Rina into my arms and ask her how she liked her present. The security cameras hadn't been recording when she received her gift. But I did enjoy watching her use the tea set that night. Seeing her curl up with a delicate cup of hot brew made a spot in my chest ache.

That night, I dreamed what life might be like having Rina in my home, cuddled against my side, with her feet in my lap and the pair of us watching a movie alongside Mila. A homey vignette plucked straight from a Hallmark special that has no place in my real life.

"You'll have to tell me all about it tonight at dinner."

"Okay!" Mila flings herself against my side, hugging me tightly before she bounces over to Eve.

Eve swallows a mouthful of her coffee as she's tugged out of the kitchen by the small-statured dervish. It's rare that I see her eyes brighten and lips tweak with a curling grin, she's a Russian nanny and ice runs in her veins. But I know, based just by watching her, that she's happiest around Mila. It's what makes her an excellent companion for my niece.

Hosting her travel mug in farewell, Eve allows her charge to yank her away, leaving me alone to brood.

Lunch begins its rapid approach a few hours. The morning has dragged by, and the afternoon looks as lackluster as the AM had been. The imminent emergencies I expected in the wake of the encroaching drug problem haven't materialized.

You wouldn't think that running what amounts to a criminal enterprise would be so menial when it comes to administrative work. I blame it on the fact that some of the businesses under the Vasiliev umbrella are legitimate. It is, on paper, where the bulk of the family money comes from. As far as the IRS and other financial agencies are concerned, the Vasiliev family is made up of millionaires. Nothing extravagant, and never enough to draw unwanted eyes. Our legal bank accounts hold a realistic sum in the scope of our official work.

It's all the offshore accounts that reveal the truth. Most of them hidden behind false fronts and shell companies.

The truth is that if we ever were to declare our true income from all sources on our tax forms, the billions in profit would send up red flags everywhere. Dirty cash is both the bane of my existence and the grease that makes the wheels of Echo Bay turn. Nearly every business that has a storefront down Willow brook is in my pocket. I don't bother with the small-time protection rackets but store my servers for my online operations in their back rooms, conceal my imports in their inventory.

The legitimate hides the illegal, allowing me to all but print money which then goes right back into the community. While I might dabble in a bit of everything from arms dealing, to gambling, loan sharking and every white-collar crime under the felony code, I won't touch the drug trade.

My reasons are personal, and my methods of ensuring that the city streets stay clean are just shy of being militant. Weed is allowed because it's legal in the state, and while the Vasiliev name isn't attached to the dispensaries and farms, I have allowed my men to have personal stakes in this new money tree.

Bored of refreshing my E-Mail, I shut the lid on my laptop, and glance down at my watch.

Mila's lunch hour at Harbor View Montessori begins in thirty minutes. I know my niece's schedule by heart, down to the minute. Occasionally, I show up during recess and eat with her. It's been a while since I've done so, and the weather is nice enough to indulge in a makeshift picnic.

That I've decided I will do it today has nothing to do with Rina.

Leon, as usual, protests when I choose to leave the compound alone.

I arrive just in time to watch the flood of children exiting the school, ambushing the playground. Despite the seasonal chill in the air, the kids are warded against the cold with knit caps, colorful mittens, and down-filled jackets. Resembling shadows, a half-dozen bodyguards patrol the perimeter of the school, and a sniper has made a nest on the roof across the way.

The kids are boisterous with energy, filled to the brim with it after being stuck in a classroom for hours. It needs to be purged, and the yard is the perfect place for it. Plastic slides, monkey bars, and other assorted playground equipment is scattered about the rubber-topped surface of the outdoor, fenced-in area.

I pull into the parking lot, and casually stroll to one of the wrought iron gates where the teachers and various bodyguards, and the occasional Secret Service agent, are collected.

I don't see Rina, but that's likely due to her class being on the opposite side of the playground. As I grow closer, being swept in through the gate with a once-over from a hand-held x-ray wand, I catch view of Mila's bright yellow dress as she chases a boy around the playground.

I grin at the sight, then shutter my expression as Principal Sawyer turns at my approach.

"Ah, Mr. Vasiliev." The man has a voice like a foghorn. It booms through the brisk air, drawing the ears of everyone around him.

Rina startles like a doe sensing a hunter at the sound of my name. Her amber-flecked eyes flicker, landing on me and then jerking away as if the sight of me burns her.

I rake my teeth with my tongue, tasting the memory of her hot honey beneath my lips. Her blush is neon pink, scalding her cheeks so deeply that the twin patches are visible even at the distance.

It seems I'm not the only one affected. I might have left her alone for the past few days, but her memory hasn't left me.

Gritting my teeth, I force my gaze away and give Sawyer a tight smile. "How are you?"

"Quite well. I take it you're here to see Mila?"

"Of course." I lift the container that's packed with treats for us. Likely Mila has already eaten, but our cook has packed a few delicacies that no reasonable person would be able to resist.

"Miss Christenson." Sawyer walks toward where Rina stands stiffly on the edge of the playground, holding herself separate from the others with her boot heels planted in the red cedar mulch.

His voice lowers, too quiet for me to hear. Knowing the man, he's probably telling her to *be nice* to me. Since next year, it will be my family name on the new gymnasium being constructed.

Then he turns toward me, beckoning me closer while Rina eases around the jumble of flying limbs and squealing third and fourth graders to get Mila's attention.

I see Mila's face when she realizes I'm here to visit. Her smile dwarfs her round cheeks, and she swoops down the slide with her loose cocoa curls tumbling behind her. I swear the last time I'd seen her there had been braids in her hair, but the ribbons are long gone, and *snarled* is a polite adjective to describe her hairstyle. There are already dirty patches on her tights, and I hide my grin thinking about the tirade Eve will have later when she notices them. She loves dressing my niece up in frilly, girlie things. But Mila is solidly in her tom-boy phase, and would rather climb, jump, and rough house than worry about keeping herself clean and neat. I don't interfere, because there's little things worse than having a Russian nanny being angry at you for overstepping. Even though Mila is *my* blood and I pay Eve's wages.

Mila hurtles past her teacher and friends, skidding to a stop before me. "Are you having lunch with me?"

"I am, lead the way, *pchelka*."

Mila grabs my hand and drags me toward the lime-green, thermoplastic picnic benches which are tucked a few yards away from the playground. They are protected from inclement weather by the overhanging roof which encapsulates the outdoor corridor that runs lengthwise between the school and playground.

I sit on the bench while Mila decides that the tabletop is appropriate. Her sneaker-clad feet scuff across the seat beside me.

"Look what Maria packed for you." I unzip the leather bag that holds a portioned container. My lunch is inside, so too is a nest of fresh fruit, and the foil-wrapped cookies earmarked for Mila.

"Ooo choco-chip." She eagerly unfolds the tinfoil pocket and inhales it with an exaggerated sniff. "It's still warm too!"

Mila bites into the gooey cookie, and a glob of chocolate sticks to the edge of her lip.

I look over toward Rina, meeting her eyes and giving her a grin that is - perhaps - a touch sadistic. Giving a ten-year-old sugar is always a recipe for disaster.

Lifting out a second box, I waggle the container, beckoning Rina over. I am a horse breaker offering a sugar cube to a dainty little filly.

Will she accept?

And if she does, just how much sweetness will it take to tame her?

For having had a screaming orgasm beneath me, she's maintaining her distance. Something I don't like.

I don't like it at all.

So, I wait patiently, listening to Mila chatter, until curiosity and the magnetic pull of our shared attraction propels Rina toward me.

Being the gentleman I am, I hide my smug smile when she joins us. It's the least I can do when she's being a good girl today.

Chapter Sixteen

Rina

There is nothing quite as intimidating as watching *that car* glide to a stop outside the school. A Bugatti. I hadn't known the name until curiosity got the better of me and I looked it up.

I shouldn't have. Because now I know the price tag on Edmond's limited-edition midlife-crisis. A few of the other teachers take notice of the matte-black vehicle, and though I know that Susie, a second grade teacher is married, it doesn't stop her from fluffing her hair – and her breasts, trying to appeal to his male gaze.

I'm not immune to the spectacle that he presents. But I don't want to stare. Because there's something torrid about seeing him in daylight, after knowing what the two of us have done in the dark. He slips out of the low-slung car, smooths a hand through his well-kept hair as if patting a strand in place, and then he prowls across the parking lot.

I look away then because he's not here for me. He's here to see Mila. While my ego might say otherwise, I just can't picture Edmond acknowledging what's gone on between us in a public setting. He's a man who has secrets, a load of them if the warnings I keep receiving are any indication of the skeletons in his closet.

And I'm not going to be any man's secret.

Crossing my arms tightly over my chest, I sink my fingers into the warm cable knit of my sweater. It helps to hide my quivering fingers. While I tell myself it's from the frosty nip in the air, I know it's because of the man who stands on the opposite side of the yard. I'm hyperaware of him as the gate opens.

When Principal Sawyer jovially greets Edmond like a politician would his constituents, I jerk, swinging my attention back around. He's wearing a full-length wool over coat, and black leather gloves, both which look striking against his suit. I've never seen so much black in a man's closet before. At least not someone who isn't a mortician. But he makes it look good, not ghoulish or like a car salesman trying to appear posher than he is.

The edge of Edmond's mouth quirks when he catches me staring.

I berate myself and look away. It's so damn difficult. I can't help myself. He's like a solar eclipse, tempting everyone to look at nature's painful beauty, knowing it would scorch my retinas to do it.

My eyes water as I stare unseeing at the playground. All of my focus is on avoiding looking at Edmond. Let the other women gawk at him. They can feed his ego.

Eventually, it works. I pay little mind to Edmond and Principal Sawyer's conversation, and instead focus on my class.

They are burning off excess energy that learning boring fractions has generated. Adam has been incredibly resistant to sitting still this morning. Which has told me all I needed to know about Victoria's parenting style. She is going to ignore my gentle encouragement. There is nothing more I can do. Not unless his acting out turns violent or increasingly disruptive. Right now, Adam is borderline. His inability to focus could go either way - toward further bullying and bothering his class-mates, or internally into depression and self-harming thoughts as he realizes he is just slightly different than his peers.

In comparison, which I hate to do, Mila is a bright ray of sunshine for a dismal afternoon. I can't help but smile as she chases John around. He dared to cut in line at the water foun-tain, and his penance is being chased around with the threat of Mila's surprisingly dirty hands wiggling at his back. That girl has no fear when it comes to messes.

Suddenly Principal Sawyer is at my elbow. "Mr. Vasiliev is going to have lunch with his niece."

There is no question about allowing it. Or even mentioning that Mila has already eaten a hot lunch at the cafeteria. The lunch ladies pride themselves on making a delicious, well-rounded meal for all the students. They dish out gourmet foods that no brown bag could compete with. Though I doubt that Edmond came with cold cuts and a juice box.

"You are new to Harbor View Montessori this year." Prin-cipal Sawyer's voice pitches even lower, a mild-mannered tenor that hides a wheedling, nasal tone that I dislike immensely. Behind his back, the other teachers call it his Willie Nelson voice. As if he were about to break into a country croon.

I shift my face slightly, just enough for eye contact.

"It's in everyone's best interest." *He means his.* "That you give Mr. Vasiliev whatever he wants."

I blink and try to absorb the meaning of that warning.

Did he... no that's too far even for Principal Sawyer.

"Of course," I say with my brightest smile. The one that hides the trembly feeling that wavers between my chest and belly.

Principal Sawyer turns and treads back to the other

teachers and is enfolded in the hive of gossip that I am now going to be the main focus of.

I sigh inwardly but go ahead and grab Mila. She stands at the top of the s-shaped slide, waiting her turn nearly at the cusp of the stairs.

"Mila," I call. "Your uncle is here to see you!"

Her face is so expressive. After two years of teaching, it's easy for me to tell when a child feels safe, loved, and cared for. Mila's cheeks puff up, and her smile is as brilliant as a summer sun. Whatever sins follow Edmond, that makes people like Zoe, Marianne, and now Sawyer assign a warning to him, his niece loves him.

Mila swoops down the slide, slips slightly on the pebbled rubber mat that covers the playground, and then skip-bounces over to her uncle.

There's a catch in my chest as she leads the two of them to a picnic bench.

I look away, feeling a tidal wave of emotions threaten to suck me down. Edmond so easily demonstrates what I want for Lucia and myself.

Family.

These types of thoughts aren't meant for men like Edmond. That he broke into my bedroom, ate me like a starving man, is immaterial. I'm mature enough to call it what it is: a one-night fling. Even though he got nothing out of it but my moans and pleasure, I don't expect a repeat of it.

Shunting my thoughts to the back of my mind, I head toward my spot at the edge of the playground. It's far enough away from the other teachers and gives me a bird's eye view of all the kids romping around during recess. My attention betrays me, though. I keep looking over at Edmond.

On my third peek, he holds up what looks like a bento box. He wags it as if tempting me.

I resist, up until he curls his finger and beckons.

Did he use that particular finger on purpose? Because I know what he did with it, and so does my pussy. My inner muscles flex, tightening at the memory of his finger sliding deep.

The heat flushing through me is hot enough that I want to tug at the collar of my sweater. I don't dare. Not when Edmond is watching me like I'm his favorite meal and entertainment all in one.

That he's brought extra food completely shatters my self-delusion that he only came to visit Mila.

He's here for me too.

And...

Oh God.

And...

He wants to eat with me in public. In front of my other teachers, and the assessing eyes of Principal Sawyer.

I don't know what this is.

This feels like dating, though we've never discussed it or the ramifications.

I can barely breathe around the rushing tempo of my heartbeat. It races and kicks against my ribcage. For a moment, a crazy, self-preserving second, I consider denying him.

Maybe I can turn away and pretend I don't see his summons. But then I realize that, deep down, I don't want to resist. It's so flattering that a man as good-looking as Edmond wants me. It feels as if every adult's eye on the playground is focused on us. The gossip of this will be far-reaching.

Victoria Malone will likely hear about it.

My cheeks prick with heat as I cross over to where Edmond and Mila sit. I am hyperaware of feeding the school's rumor mill, especially as a young, single teacher.

But Principal Sawyer has all but given me an order, and who am I to say 'no' to the Principal?

"Do you like desserts, Miss Christenson?" Edmond's voice is sin-laced as if he is substituting baklava for another word.

Two can play this game.

"I've never tried it." I sit beside Edmond, with only Mila's feet separating us.

He turns and straddles the bench. The exquisite fabric of his charcoal pants pulls tightly over his well-muscled thighs.

"Now that is a shame. You should try everything. At least once. Just ask Mila."

Mila rolls her eyes. She sprays a few cookie crumbs as she huffs, "He made me try brussel sprouts."

I mock gasp at Edmond. "That is inhumane, Mr. Vasiliev. Brussel sprouts? The horror."

Mila giggles as she finishes her cookie, and before she can lick the sticky chocolate off her fingers, Edmond pulls out a wet nap from where it is tucked in a zip pocket of his fancy lunch box. Dutifully, she scrubs her face and hands and then hops off the table.

"Uncle Edmond, watch me on the monkey bars! I can go all the way across without stopping!" Mila bounds from the top of the picnic table, and darts full speed ahead to the monkey bars.

Edmond's voice is low as he admonishes. "I told you to call me Edmond. I'll have to punish you for that."

I freeze at the sudden steamy words, the image of his elegant fingers on my skin and the bite of the zip-ties a sharp reminder of his methods. "Punish?"

"Oh yes." Edmond leans closer, his fingers cool against my flustered cheek. He tucks a lock of hair behind my ear and scorches me with his sizzling whisper.

"I've been thinking just how delectable you would be on your knees for *me*. The past few days, that's all I have been able to think about. Don't you think it's fair that I get that mouth, after you so prettily came on mine?"

I look around in a panic, thinking someone might overhear what he's saying. But everyone is giving us distance, suspiciously letting us have a private moment in an area filled with screaming children.

"I don't hear you protesting, *solnyshko*. Have you been thinking the same of me?"

I finally jerk, acting on his sinful words. Clamping my fingers together on the plastic tabletop, I give him a side-eye.

"Edmond, you can't talk like that. We're at a school."

"We are, and nobody can hear us."

"You're shameless!"

He fastens his wide, enigmatic grin on me. But gives me a reprieve from his ruthless flirtation. I'm sweating beneath the thick knit of my sweater, my inner temperature suddenly boiling and steamy.

He opens the dessert container, showing me what lies within. "Do you like baklava?"

"I've never tried it before."

He plucks one of the flaky, honey-drenched triangles from a nest of waxed paper.

"Open."

When coupled with what he had *just* been talking about, that he's telling me to open my mouth sends all the heat rushing south. I pant softly, focusing on his face and the intense burn of his intoxicating mercury eyes. I lick my lips, and his pupils dilate, as he tracks the faint flutter of my tongue. Both of us are thinking about what the dessert is substituting; his dick sliding into my mouth, thrusting to the back of my throat instead of the pastry.

Our eyes hold and lock as I bite into the gooey snack. It immediately dissolves on my tongue, sending a trickle of honey and syrupy sugar over the rim of my bottom lip. Before I can catch it, Edmond's thumb is at my mouth. He strokes the luscious droplet away, and then carries the combined flavor of my lips and honey sweetness to his mouth.

The way his eyes burn reminds me of just how intent he'd been devouring my juices. It's as if he's tasting nirvana.

"Delicious."

Desire lashes at me. It flares through me like a hydrogen bomb going off in my womb. My ovaries are on-board for whatever raunchy things that Edmond wants to do with me. Punish? Hell, yes if he keeps looking at me like that.

"Uncle Edmond, Miss Christenson. Look!"

Saved by the child.

Mila's voice squeaks through the erotic thrall Edmond is spinning around me. Dutifully, we turn to Mila.

She hangs from the monkey bars, a triumphant grin on her face. Her knees are curled, making sure that she doesn't accidentally touch the cedar-mulched ground. Once Mila knows she has both of our attention, she swiftly crosses the monkey bars. Swinging from one bar to the next before ending at the opposite side.

She jumps down and does a fist-raised flourish like a mini Olympic gymnast, flushed from exertion, but laughing.

Edmond claps riotously, lauding her with boisterous accolades that her athleticism demands.

Mila hops forward a step or two, then spins around and races right back to wait her turn in the three-person line for the monkey bars again.

I have a better lid on my emotions, and libido, by the time Edmond's attention is back on me.

"Edmond, we can't do this." I hate that I have to say it. Every part of me wants to fling caution to the wind, but my boundaries are there for a reason. We come from two different worlds. That he drives a seven-figure car and I bought mine second-hand for five is the least of our differences.

I sigh and let the words rush free.

"I am sincerely flattered by your attention. But I must inform you that I don't date the parents - or guardians - of my students."

Somehow, I get my rejection out without tripping over my words. My voice is unflinching steel. I even have time to admire my bright and shiny backbone.

Before Edmond ignores them entirely.

He stands from the bench, and smooths the cashmere lapels of his outer jacket.

Then he leans over me, suffocating me in the dark shadow of his presence. Nobody can see the sudden snap of his tattooed hand curling against the side of my neck. The position of our bodies, so close together, and the wave of my hair, hide the bite of his fingers. They dig into my skin, biting, bruising, as he brings me closer, a lurid promise of stolen intimacy whispered right against my ear. From afar, I'm sure it looks like he's nuzzling me, not promising violence with the palpitation of his hand and the barely restrained growl of his voice drizzling into my eardrum.

"That is a pretty speech. Nobody said date, Miss Christenson." He taunts me with my title, stroking it with the flick of his tongue over the vowels. "But I will be fucking you and making you mine. It's already too late, *solnyshko*."

I gasp, trembling in his hold. If I hadn't been sitting, I'm pretty sure I'd be on the floor in a dead faint. He's single minded. Absolutely ruthless.

And it arouses me painfully.

How can a man like Edmond want *me*?

"You are *mine* Rina." His words are a vow. "And soon, I'm going to shove my very hard cock straight into that virgin cunt."

I should be disgusted by his vulgarity, not burning white-hot for want of it.

"Be a good girl until then. I'll see you soon."

I can't speak as he lets me loose.

He turns, the length of his jacket fanning behind him like a cloak, making me think of a Gothic lord as the fabric billows around his thighs. His strides slice him across back across the playground.

He stops by the slide, where Mila had gotten distracted with a few of her little friends, and his goodbye carries over the playground.

"See you after school, *printsessa*. Be good." Somehow though, that instruction isn't just for Mila. His words echo for me to.

Be good.

"I'm always good! Bye Uncle Edmond!"

Edmond casts one more lidded look over his shoulder. A ghost of a smile creases his supple lips. Then he disappears through the gate, leaving me shocked and aching wet.

Chapter Seventeen

Edmond

"If it gets into Echo Bay, it *will* be your head I put the bullet in," I snarl into the phone.

Ever since Lev told me about the drugs creeping around the border of my territory, an uptick in overdoses has been hitting Echo Bay hospital. Though every police officer, paramedic, and emergency worker carries a kit of Narcan with them. There is always the chance that whatever junk the patient took is more powerful than the nasal spray. The real addicts seek out the 'strong' stuff. The blend that puts people in the ER, or the ground

Anger and frustration duke it out inside me, leaving me on edge and snappy. Barrett has been cagey, not agreeing to a meeting. Probably until he has more personnel to back up this little power play.

I barely listen to what is being muttered about on the other side of the conversation.

"Fucking fix it."

I stab 'end' on the call, and then fling the cell onto my desk.

Loyalty is an ever-shifting commodity. At times I feel as if I built my entire enterprise on Florida swampland, ready to crumble and sink beneath the tides with one magnificent storm. Other times, I feel untouchable. The truth is somewhere in the middle. There are always people eyeing the throne. The smart ones don't come straight for the prize, but try to chip away at the power structure from the edges. Like right now, where I want to slit the throats of every one of my men who let the Irish's drugs seep into my territory like poison.

The Vasiliev OCG isn't just Echo Bay. This is just where I built my fortress. Each of the *Bratva's* elite groups has four cells they control, led by a brigadier. Usually far enough away from each other to give those who rule in my name a feeling of being in control and a taste of power. Yet close enough for me to bring the hammer down if they decide to buck my control.

Alongside the Vasiliev family, the combined morass of Ovechkin, Sharapova, and Kiselyov own Seattle, Tacoma, Bellevue, and Olympia. My territory is a hook-shaped slice of Washington's northwestern coast with the San Juan Islands - and Echo Bay - cupped in my palm.

Most don't expect that the head of Washington's *Bratva* OCG to lead from here. That I import and export anything from the harbors and waterways inside my territory makes it a linchpin in my organization, with Canadian waters a stone's throw away. I haven't yet made a move on Vancouver, partly because the Sicilian Mafia had a prior claim on America's northern neighbors, and war is costly. Not just in ammunitions, but in men. I have enough power to not throw away my people needlessly and don't want to expand just for expansionist's sake.

Tension rides me, making me feel walled in, though the bars of my cage are nouveau rich, all extravagance and excess.

I've built my office on the second floor of my mansion, a more modern beast of architecture than my father had, more masculine than my sister's former estate. While there are not any outward signs of ostentatiousness. No gilded ornamentation. No sculptures to be found. The vastness of the space is declaration enough of the money I spent on having such a palatial office space at home.

From here, and beyond the many windows that overlook the property, the panorama of the gardens, fountain, and the whole of the diligent landscape are laid out before me.

I stand in front of the window, watching as the army of gardeners kept the land tame.

Then I sink into the enormous leather chair, staring at the mahogany desk that looks surprisingly naked for a man of my prestige. My laptop is stored in the drawer below. Only my forlorn, neglected phone remains on the leather blotter.

My thoughts stray to the other things stored in my cell.

Like photos of Rina.

I'm a bastard. That is a mild word for my regular way of being.

Not only had I broken into Rina's bedroom while she slept, tied her up, and devoured the absolute sweetness of her pussy.

But I'd also taken pictures, mementos, trophies, whatever you want to call them. A reminder of the time I'd had with her. Though nothing vulgar. I don't want to put her in a position should my cloud get hacked. There are always hackers, governmental and freelance, both Russian and American, trying to find dirt on me. While there is a fair share of pornographic images and videos I enjoy looking at, none are as intimate as the clothed photos I took of Rina. The only suggestive nature is that she had been tied to her bed. Asleep and looking so fuckably innocent.

I close my eyes, trying to push away the memory. The thoughts of Mila's teacher invade my thoughts more and more often. Ambushing me in the quiet moments of the day, when I seek solace and quiet.

The blood thunders in my veins, eddying lower, and lower, does not want peace. It wants violence.

It wants Rina.

I bite back a groan as I snatch my phone off of my desk. I don't use any type of biometric password. In a world as violent and blood-bathed as mine, that type of security is asking for someone to cut your finger off - or gouge out an eyeball. I use a simple pin, one that I can tap in with my thumb.

My phone clicks as it unlocks, and I immediately open my gallery. Traveling pathways I have already voyaged too many times to count. There are only five photos, taken in the darkness of Rina's bedroom, with only the enhancement of technology to separate the soft shape of her from the darkness.

I flick slowly through them, reliving the memory of her writhing beneath my hands. The sweet wetness that melted on my tongue. How she'd cried out and gushed on my face when she came.

Fuck.

Rina is not someone that belongs in my life. My father, and sister's deaths taught me well. At any moment, I run a risk of falling to the machinations of the enemy. Pops died to an Irishman's bullet, the sniper's shot drumming through his temple while he'd been on a fishing trip. Eventually, the *Mob* took credit for it. But they got nothing for their trouble, except war that wiped that particular branch from the face of the planet.

The culprit behind Nadia's plane crash remains a mystery. The Kiselyovs blame themselves. Eventually, I would figure out who took the hit out on my sister. If not for my sake, then for Mila's.

All of that death proves that Rina is too innocent.

Is that why I'm drawn to her?

I stroke the delicate image of her stretched-out body like a blind man seeking braille in the picture of her petite curves. I can't remember the last time a woman captivated me this way. Maybe never. This is why I should delete these photographs, and delegate Rina Christensen back to the category of 'Mila's Teacher".

My cock thinks otherwise. The second I'd opened the photos, my shaft hardened, bloating to its full length until the pressure of my zipper was uncomfortable.

I try to ignore it. I'm always in control of my emotions. But Rina is proving to be fucking hypnotic to me. I feel that control slipping, leaving me exposed.

"Fuck." I groan as I drop my hand to my lap, digging my palm down on the tent I've pitched in my slacks.

My cock refuses to cooperate. I could call up Lev, and have him bring one of the working girls to me. Use their soft, wet mouths to suck the release from my balls.

But it's not *their* lips I want around my shaft. I want to watch Rina's wide eyes brim and run with tears as I choke her on my cock.

Knowing I'm not going to get any work done, not with the pictures open on my screen, and the empyreal scent of Rina's soft lavender perfume drawn out of my memories, I take matters into my own hands.

Literally.

The bite of my zipper lowering rasps in the air before I reach in through the seam and fish my dick out. The cool air chills the moisture beading on the head of my length. Then I roll my palm across the tip, gathering up the slick wetness of my pre.

It isn't just Rina's mouth I want. But her sweet virgin pussy, and innocent ass. I'm a greedy bastard, and though she's forbidden - the worst sort of trap - I want to take everything.

I still can't believe she's a virgin. I've always avoided them. In my world, they're unicorns. The women around me are already broken in, if not by the family business, then by their own choice, trying to drown out reality with a cartel of men.

What the fuck would I do with a virgin?

Make her bleed all of your cock.

Fuck.

I drag my fingers down to the root of my shaft and grip. Forcing the blood into the veins which stand out lividly along every inch. I choke my cock until the flesh darkens before I stroke myself., thinking of breaking open Rina's cherry-ripe pussy. She'd been so wet for me.

Wet enough to take me?

Doubtful. So fucking doubtful. That tinge of pain she'd feel makes it all the sweeter to me.

Would she cry?

Fuck I hope so.

I drop my head back, losing myself in how I pump my hand. I stroke slowly, then pick up the pace until I'm fucking my fist. Shifting the mental image of Rina through my head, I begin with those pouty pink lips, and end with her pussy spread incredibly wide around my dick. I imagine the ways I could take her. Bent over, with the apple of her ass sinking into the fulcrum of my hips. Or on her back, with those doe-like eyes of hers staring up at me in shock. Leading to eventually teaching her to ride me. Bouncing atop my dick, working her soft, silky twat until she creams my shaft. Her dainty curves undulating as she writhes through her own orgasm.

I would let her scream when she comes. Instead of choking her breath away.

Thinking of shattering her - ruining her - thrusts me over the edge. My ass flexes as I drive into my fist while pushing my thumb into the sensitive tissue beneath the crown. I groan as my balls tighten, sending frissons of pleasure from toes, to taint, to fucking tip of my dick. I have to swallow the loud growl that thrums in my chest as I orgasm, barely catching the surge of my release in the divot of my palm.

Panting through the exertion, I tear my handkerchief out of my pocket and clean myself up. Telling myself this is a one-time thing. That I'm not going to wedge myself into Rina's life. That her virginity isn't mine to claim.

And knowing I'm lying about it the whole time.

Chapter Eighteen

Rina

This isn't my scene.

My nerves are stretched wire tight, jangling like the neon sign that flickers above the bar's entrance. There's a drunk quality to the animated logo, that of a lumberjack chasing after a cartoon pin-up who wears Daisy Duke shorts and a flannel bra. It looks like a joke, but by the staggering number of cars, pick-up trucks, and shiny chrome motorcycles that fill the parking lot, it's a happening spot. Especially being so early on a Friday.

I don't know *Timberhuas'* reputation, but the clientele looks rowdy, full of lumberjacks and other roughnecks. I can imagine that the uniforms are risqué; one step above a strip club in that my boobs would be covered. But I'd probably be treated just as badly like a tasty slab of meat to be pawed at. I need a job like this, though. The good thing about parading around in barely there clothes, in a place that slings alcohol, is the tips are monumental.

I left for the 'interview' straight after the kids had gone home. Looking down at the cream-colored sweater dress and ankle-high boots I'd worn for the day, I realize this outfit isn't going to cut it. I look like a teacher, because I am one. I hadn't thought of changing, as if I have anything sexy in my wardrobe, and now there isn't anything I can do about it.

Squaring my shoulders, I forge ahead. The door's hinges growls as I jerk it open, followed by a swish as I step into a tiled foyer, and then through a decorative pair of double doors. A wall of noise splashes over me, a haze of chatter and jukebox music. Later, there will be live music, maybe a blue grass band or one of the million Rolling Stones Tribute bands that work along the state. The air is rank, thick with the reek of stale beer, sweat, and a faint undercurrent of lemon-scented bleach that does nothing to cut through the odors. Energy buzzes through the air, loud and drunken, followed occasionally by a squeal of a girl who gets too close to the long, clutching fingers of a patron.

My stomach sinks when I see the uniform. Because yeah, it's bad. It's a replica of the sign out front, though the shirt is more of a crop top than a bra, with the *Timberhaus* logo stretched vulgarly right across the center of the chest - a titty slogan. I lock my knees, refusing to back out now.

Mustering my courage, I approach the bar, my rather short legs scissoring and eating up ground with fake confidence. However the closer I get to the bart, the stickier the floor grows. Until the soles of my boots make tacky sounds as I walk. Ugh. I hope that the stains and marks on the floor are just a collage of spilled liquor and not anything like a biohazard.

The bartender casts a look at me as he whips the cap of a bottle of beer and slides it toward a waitress. He's a burly man whose hair is as long as his beard; both long and dark and shaggy.

He doesn't smile when he sees me. If anything, he looks skeptical.

"Here for the job?" he asks, his voice rough like the sawdust that litters the floor around the bar, and does a piss-poor job of sopping up the stains.

I try to sound more confident than I feel. "Yes, I worked at *Bombshells* in college."

I even printed out my resume. I offer the sheet to him, which he takes and slips under the bar without looking at it.

He rotates his finger. "Turn around."

I stiffen, wanting to tell him to go 'eff' himself. By the smirk on his lips, he's expecting it too.

Piece of meat time.

You can do this.

I pivot in place, making a slow circle so that he can suss out the shape of my body. I'm a bit softer in places than I'd like and need a padded bra to fill out my bust. Tiny. Petite. True words, but the real one is 'elfin'. If I dyed my hair pink or thought about getting a tattoo, I'd easily be labeled a manic pixie girl. Maybe a few generations too late, but the potential is there. If I wasn't so strait-laced.

I turn back to face the barkeep. "

You understand what working here entails, right? It's not your typical bar."

The uniform and the raucous antics that I've seen and overheard since stepping foot in the bar are a crash course in what's expected. More than a few of the girls have been manhandled and forced to perch on the thick, jean-clad leg of a patron. I stifle the shudder, knowing that I'll have to deal with that and nod.

"As long as the money makes up for it."

"It does. The only way to make more in a short amount of time is by stripping." His grin turns lecherous. Those beady eyes lock onto my tits.

"If you want to show a bit of skin, Sindoll's Caberet is hiring."

"No." *God no.*

The bartender shrugs and then points toward the door that's adjacent to the bar. "Go through there, change into the uniform, and let's see how you do."

Wait. "What?"

"You look like a prissy Sunday school teacher. As if hearing someone say 'fuck' is going to make you faint. I'm not putting you on the schedule until I know for sure you can hack it. The best way to do that is to see you in action."

He makes a 'shoo' motion with two fingers. "So either put up or get the fuck out."

Shimmering heat warms the base of my neck. My skin prickles beneath the soft knit of my dress. Even my eyes sting because I want to cry. I want to break down and rage over the desperate situation the working poor creates.

Swallowing the bitter, metallic tang that fills my mouth, I pivot and march stoically through the double doors. A narrow corridor leads into what looks like a multi-functional backroom. The bulk of the cramped space is the kitchen, with the walls clad in a utilitarian, easy-to-clean material that bears marks and scuffs from hurried service. Non-slip floor, a lot of stainless steel countertops, and the essentials for a bar like this: a grill and a deep fryer with a large freezer/fridge in the back. On the left side of the corridor, opposite the kitchen, is the employee locker area. A row of personal lockers, each assigned to a staff member, marks this section. Only a couple of the dingy cubbies have locks on them. I pick one at random, shove my purse into it, and then find the stack of uniforms that are folded in clean piles on a back table.

The uniform is exactly as I fear: tight, revealing, and designed to draw attention. The fabric is cheap and rough against my skin, polyester instead of real flannel or cotton. The titty-logo draws attention to my breasts, and the few inches of cleavage the v-neck top reveals.

Cringing, I step in front of a Wal-Mart special full-sized mirror, feeling a blush of horror and embarrassment. Everything from my ribs to my pubic bone is exposed. Thank God I shaved. I check the side profile, and hate how my buttcheeks seem to swell out around the denim. Somehow, this is worse than being naked. Maybe because there's enough hidden to give people ideas.

You're doing this for Lucia, I tell my reflection.

I need to make enough money to cover the tuition hike, pad my bank account for the eventual rent increase, and try to hold us afloat until I'm hired by the school district. This is temporary. Refusing to be cowed by a slutty uniform, I leave the privacy of the locker room and march back into the bar. My bravery lasts all of ten seconds.

As I step out, I swear I feel hundreds of eyes turn my way, their gazes a tangible, lecherous weight. I look over at the bartender, watching where he stands with his arms crossed over his leather vest-covered chest. The badges and patches on it no doubt mean something. Nothing good. I hike my chin and set out to survive my first Friday shift at *Timberhaus*.

An hour or so later, I'm trotting back to the bar with an empty tray when a voice snags me. I pause, trying to place the lyrical vowels that are rolling from a conversation nearby. As a red-blooded American girl, surrounded by the same types of voices, when something new and palatable hits my ear, I want to listen to more of it.

It takes me a second, but I pick out the brogue and smile to myself.

"Irish," I mutter.

Before I can continue heading to my order pick-up at the

bar, a heavily ringed hand catches me by the pockets of my thin shorts.

I squeak at being suddenly manhandled as I'm swung around. The man doesn't so much as tower over me, as he's on the shorter side. But he's three times as wide, with a build that can only be described as a brawler, and a head that looks surprisingly small compared to his road-enhanced muscles.

I look up and freeze. He has the face of a pugilist. Attractive to some with his vaguely squashed nose and flat cheekbones. But only if you like your love with a side of bare knuckles. There's a small tattoo of a four-leaf clover under his eye. And a whole pot of gold with a skull-faced leprechaun around his throat. The ink travels further, interspersing motifs of death with common images of the Emerald Isles.

He's dangerous. In a way separate from Edmond is.

I can see my death in his flat gaze. That he has his hands on me, someone he doesn't know, tells me that he will - and has - dished out his anger on a man, woman, or child at the slightest provocation.

I glance down at the fist which has migrated, now wrapped around my wrist. I'm almost sad, or maybe relieved, to see that he doesn't have 'pain' and 'punishment' tattooed on his knuckles.

He sees my gaze, and his hand tightens until it hurts. I bite back a hiss of pain, not wanting to encourage him to leave more marks behind.

There's restrained violence in his voice as he snarls, "What did you say?"

I quiver, looking between him, and the silent men at the table. There's no help from that quarter. Two of them have matching tattoos on their faces. And equally hard eyes.

Swallowing thickly, I whisper. "You have an Irish accent."

His face grows surly. "What's it to you?"

Oh my God, he's going to punch me.

I flinch and cower away from him as he gets in my face. Intimidating the answer from me.

"Nothing," I stutter. "I just thought it was nice."

One of the men shakes his head. "Oh leave her alone, O'Malley. By the looks of her, she's new here. She doesn't need your attention."

"This is your only reprieve," O'Malley growls down at me. Then he flings his hand off me and gives me a little push.

I stagger toward the bar, my heart racing in my chest.

The lesson stings, but I learn it well. I'll be keeping my mouth -and thoughts - to myself about my customers.

Chapter Nineteen

Rina

I never felt so grateful to be back in my normal, boring clothes. Though the work at *Timberhaus* isn't physically exhausting, there's a mental toll that can't be denied. One that comes from too many forced smiles, and trying not to flinch at the grabby hands of men who think wearing booty-shorts is an invitation to touch me. I'm fairly sure I have a few bruises on the meat of my butt cheek.

Now that I'm covered from neck to calf, I feel better. I feel more confident in my "performance", but only the bartender – likely the manager – can tell me if I have the job or not.

Bracing myself for rejection, but hoping I have the job even though I hate it, I step out of the locker room and push into the wide-open area of the bar.

It's empty now that the neon lights are turned off, and the brighter overhead lights are blaring. The halogen lights reveal the dingy grime of old cigarette smoke caked on the wood-paneled walls, dried beer stains, and the moldering hints of mildew in the sawdust.

I hope that gets changed frequently because that is such a health hazard.

The man who temporarily hired me isn't behind the bar when I approach it. Instead, there's another guy, slouched in a lean-to against the wood, his lanky, long-limbed body taking up the whole hi-top seating. He flicks some ashes off the burning tip of his cigarette and takes a puff. That he's smoking inside, when cigarettes and vapes and anything that would give someone lung cancer has been banned for years, means he's not one who cares about rules or laws. He catches my reflection in the logo-decorated mirror, and spins slowly, blowing out the fumes through his nose.

"Gunner said you did well tonight. It's not every day I get a fresh-faced beauty like you in here."

"Gunner?"

The man ticks his chin toward the backside of the room where the bartender is lugging in a case of new liquor bottles to restock what he used.

Ah. Of course, his name's Gunner.

He beckons me closer, and while I don't want to get nearer to him, mostly because of the smoke, secondly because I don't like the way his eyes keep running over the fit of my dress, I do so because I need the job.

Tuition.

Rent.

Food.

I swallow my disgust and slip against the empty chair beside him.

"The name's Barrett." He doesn't hold his hand out. Instead, he slides a wad of bills my way, the tips I earned from all the credit card receipts and bar-tabs. There are quite a few twenties in the bunch. "I own *Timberhaus,* among other places around here. You get paid nightly. Your tips are your own. I don't do the taxes bullshit, so whatever you make is off the books."

"Thanks," I say as I reach for the cash.

His nicotine-yellowed fingers coil around my wrist, a dirty manacle suddenly locking me against the bar. He leans in closer, bringing with him the stench of alcohol-laden breath and cigarette smoke. "I'll have Gunner put you on the schedule. But, there are other ways to make a lot more cash than that."

I tug my hand, trying to extricate myself. He holds me for a few seconds longer, enjoying my discomfort.

"Let me know if you need that kind of money, sweetheart."

I don't even need to ask what he's implying. While I'm not going to look down on a girl for doing *that* type of work after hours, neither is that lifestyle for me. If I can't see myself stripping, I definitely wouldn't be able to work as a prostitute. Especially with you know, the whole V-card issue I have.

"N-no thank you."

Barrett twitches his nose and then thumbs the side of it. "Suit yourself."

I back away, nervously clutching the money, half-afraid he's going to grab me again. When he goes back to his glass of whiskey and half-burnt cancer stick, I turn and bolt out of the restaurant and don't stop running till I reach my car.

My nerves don't calm down until I put *Timberhaus* miles behind me. Then I sit at a stop light and count the tips I made.

Three-hundred-and-twenty-three dollars.

I drop my head back.

That is a great amount for a half-shift on a Friday night. If I can make six-hundred dollars a week, by the time the tuition is required I'll have enough. And a small nest egg for whatever else might pop up.

And unfortunately, that kind of fast money makes the whole skeezy situation worth it.

Gritting my teeth, I finish my drive home. Vowing to wash the scent of *Timberhaus* off of me the moment I walk through the door.

Whatever happens, I can't let Lucia know just how far I'll go to make sure she has what she needs.

Mom never did it for us, but I'll sacrifice just about anything to give her a good life.

Chapter Twenty

Edmond

Rina is not home when I let myself in through the back door.

The locksmith who works for Echo Bay Security Solutions did a great job. He secured every entryway, added a bolt to the back door and a privacy chain for the front, double-checked the windows whose latches were shaky, and placed a variety of cameras throughout the house – inside and out. There's even a new shiny alarm at the front door, that Rina set with her birthdate.

I need to speak to her about security precautions. She's probably the type of person who uses her name and birthday as her E-mail passwords.

There're only two rooms that aren't being monitored: the bathroom and Lucia's bedroom.

I slip up the stairs, and into Rina's bedroom before dragging the chair from her vanity into a corner by the closet.

Then I wait. Because I don't know where Rina is, and I don't like that feeling. I noticed her leaving too late to have one of my men tail her. She isn't working at *La Baia Italiana*, and I didn't see her car anywhere in downtown Echo Bay when I drove through. When ten PM rolled around, and then midnight, and I didn't get the alert that she's returned home, I decided to make a housecall.

It's now after one AM.

So where the fuck is she?

Did she agree to go on a date with Oliver? I thought I'd scared him off, but maybe I need to visit him again.

Or perhaps one of her fellow teachers asked her out for the evening.

My thoughts stew toward jealousy and anger as I brood in her bedroom. Watching from out the window to the darkened street outside.

Finally, sometime between two AM and three, which would be the last call for a bar, I see headlights flick up the street. Then the rumble of the garage door opening, before killing engine she parks. I don't see or hear anything more until I finally get the alert that *Rina's home* as she sets the alarm.

A few minutes later, I hear her bootheels click tiredly on the stairs. Each one carries her closer and closer, making my anger grow until it feels as if a volcano is rumbling in my chest. Ready to explode.

The door swings open, and Rina flicks on the light. Somehow, she sucks back a scream of fright when she sees me, part of her recognizing me before she alarms Lucia.

"Edmond!" Rina's breath is a hiss as she looks over her shoulder, checking to make sure Lucia's door is shut. It is. Then she quietly closes her bedroom door.

Rina's dressed in what I call her teacher's clothes. All buttoned up, without a hint of extra skin to be had. Unless you call the tiny sliver of pale flesh above the shaft of her boot and below her dress hem 'provocative'. I don't, but it helps calm me down. If she had a hot date, I know Rina would have dressed up more.

My calm shatters when the smell reaches me. I'm up and out of the chair, pinning her up against her bedroom door with a growl on my lips.

"You smell like a bar."

Cigarette smoke. Old beer. Overpowering cologne. There's a mélange to dive bars, and instead of Rina's sweet lavender and herbal perfume, she smells as if she spent the night cozying up to a beer keg.

"Because I've been in a bar, Edmond," Rina snaps. She pushes her hands against my chest. "Move. All I've thought about on the drive home is taking a shower."

I don't budge an inch.

"Why were you in a bar?"

"Because I was working?"

"Bullshit." I know Rina's schedule. And nowhere in her work history is 'bar wench' as a job title.

"How would..." Rina shakes her head, fatigue making the circles under her eyes look stark; bruise-black against the veneer of her moonlight skin. "Never mind. Forget it. I don't want to know how you would know or not. It's a new job. I just got hired. Tonight. So if you can please unbunch your boxers, I would really like to wash the smoke off of me."

I want to push for answers and bully her until she submits to everything I want. But I also know that if I apply too much pressure on Rina, she might break instead of bend. I might want to ruin her, but not irreparably. Just enough to put her back together with me at the center of her world.

I relent and brush a kiss on her brow. "I'll be here after to talk."

"Talk?" Rina's pale brows quirk upward with skepticism.

"Talk," I emphasize. Though my dick has other notions

because now that she's here, looking up at me with those big lagoon-like eyes, 'just talking' is the last thing on my list.

I step away from her.

She huffs a laugh at me and then collects her bed clothes. I know them by rote, sweatpants, t-shirt, socks. Her warm and cozy cotton-wrapped cocoon.

"I would love it if you weren't here when I get out of the shower, but I doubt that'll happen."

Rina sails out of her bedroom like a queen, her slim chin elevated just enough for her to look down her nose at me. I have one last look at her shapely hips, and that sumptuous heart-shaped ass wrapped in snug cable knit, before she disappears down the hallway. Leaving me sitting on the edge of her pristinely made, colorful stained glass duvet stewing in my thoughts and a residual wash of anger.

Chapter Twenty-One

Rina

The shower is everything I'd been dreaming about since half-way through my shift. I groan as the hot water drills into my tired muscles like needles. Making my flesh ache, but sending zips of energy that helps rejuvenate my fatigued body.

There's not much to say about the place that we're renting. It's kind of shabby, and while some parts of the old Victorian have been refurbished, the bathroom was not part of the makeover. Its penny tile-floor matches the black and pink tiled walls and the built-in bathtub monstrosity that's a few inches too high. I've nearly killed myself each time I don't lift my leg high enough to climb out.

But the water pressure is amazing. The pipes and water pump were primed from a time before water conservation was written into residential building codes.

I should feel guilty about how much hot water I'm wasting, but when I'm getting my very own massage from the torrential downpour gushing from my the shower head, I can't muster the emotion.

Still, I only linger for a few extra minutes. Until my skin takes on the hue of a freshly cooked lobster, and a thick haze of steam fills the whole bathroom. The exhaust fan is unable to clear away the condensation with its labored whirring, leaving the interior swaddled in a mist that blunts the edges of reality.

Wrapping my hair in a towel, I slather on a quick layer of moisturizer before getting dressed and bracing myself to face Edmond.

That he is waiting for me while I shower is just so intimate. It sends little quivers running through my body, ending in a toe-curl that bunches my socks between them.

Ready or not.

I sneak out of the bathroom, glad it's not an en-suite but still worried about waking Lucia as I creep down the hallway, dodging the floorboards I know creak. Then I slip into my bedroom. Only to come to a halt with my back against the closed door as I find Edmond sprawled out in my bed.

Shirtless. Shoes off. The snap on his jeans unbuttoned to show a tantalizing slice of his happy trail veering off into the forbidden area beneath the waist band of his boxer-briefs. And completely out cold.

How long has he been waiting for me?

That warm feeling returns, filling my veins with a heavy sweetness that almost makes me want to cry. The sob catches in my throat, and it takes me a few minutes to untangle the sudden flurry of emotions, teasing a strand free so I can figure out my reaction.

Then it hits me.

I've *never* had someone wait up for me. With her school load, I'd explicitly told Lucia not to wait for me during those late nights.

My heart trembles in my chest as I approach my bed. Drinking in the way Edmond looks so much younger when he's unguarded. His eyelashes are surprisingly lush where they lay against his cheekbones.

The tension he carries around his mouth is gone, revealing rather supple-looking lips that are slightly parted. He is utterly relaxed, and I can only stare at him as one would an exotic animal they've happened across. Despite how relaxed he looks, even asleep he exudes a dangerous air. As if I were to get too close, or make a wrong move, he'd spring awake and tear out my throat.

Am I a masochist that I can't help but get closer? Knowing the risk? He's already proven how much of a stalker he is. That boundaries mean nothing to him, and that his pursuit of me is completely single-minded. To what end, I'm not yet sure. Men like him don't fall for women like me. I'm a mouse in a lion's den, prey to be gobbled up. Not the lioness to rule over his pride. The only outcome of this dalliance is heartache. Mine. But I can't help how I'm drawn to him.

I stand at the edge of my bed, watching him sleep.

I've always known he was built. The way his tailored suit molds to his body, and the breadth of his shoulders gave that way. But this is something more. He's sculpted in a way that reminds me of a dancer or martial artist. The muscles in his chest and abdomen are clearly defined. His shoulders and arms are a woman's wet dream. At least *this* woman.

Then there's the tattoos. He's absolutely *covered* in ink.

I swallow thickly, conflicted over what I should do. I'm so tired. Fatigue tugs on my muscles, and the temptation of sinking beside Edmond and covering us both up pulls at me. It's as if there's a cord at the center of my body attached to him, tightening and drawing me closer.

Edmond's lips tremble as he exhales a deep breath, an almost-snore that leads to a murmur. It's enough that the vision of the villain in my bed shatters, humanizing him and making him seem approachable.

Knowing I'll probably regret it come morning, I crawl into my bed beside Edmond. Thankful that when I moved I splurged on a queen-sized instead of the full I'd had back in Arizona. There's enough room for me to wedge myself under Edmond's arm, becoming a little spoon against his mostly immobile body.

He doesn't stir as I arrange an extra blanket overtop us. Reaching across the nightstand, I click the light off and settle down for what I expect to be an uncomfortable sleep.

Instead, I find myself drifting into sleep the moment my head hits the pillow. While at times Lucia and I slept wrapped around each other when she was younger, especially during the times our mother had a very unwelcome male guest over, it's been years since then.

I never realized just how cold and isolated I've been until Edmond's warmth seeps into my back. Lulling me into a fragile hope that this could be the start of something beautiful.

Chapter Twenty-Two

Edmond

Rina is a cuddler.

She's using my chest as a pillow, completely oblivious to the world. I'm pretty sure she's even drooling a bit. There's a smudge of wetness on my skin. But I don't want to move. Because waking her up when she looks like an elfin princess snuggled in my arms would break my heart.

I didn't intend to fall asleep while waiting for her. Her bed looked comfortable after spending a few hours in the thin-cushioned chair waiting for her. So, I got comfortable. Perhaps too comfortable, because dawn is on the horizon. Bringing a touch of gray onto the inky dusk of the night sky.

I should leave. Being here is a mistake. I don't sleep with women. Sure I fuck them, but none of them are warm enough – enticing enough – to make me want to linger in their beds once the fun is over.

I can't say that about Rina. She's all tactile sensation and affection, wrapped tightly around me as if she's seeking my warmth. Her unconscious mind probably doesn't recognize who she's tucked up against.

Closing my eyes, I will myself to get up. Except my body is no longer at the command of my brain. It's completely enamored with Rina's softness. It's not only the clothing she wears, which is simple and cozy. But the sweet warmth of her radiates from where her arm lays spread across my waist. Or the gentle pressure of her petite breasts crushed into my side. Hell, even the way her breath fans across my shoulder is searing my senses.

It's kind of ironic. I thought I would be bringing doom to Rina. Instead, she's the one leaving the wreckage behind. I can't afford to be soft. Tender emotions are all but foreign to me. While my cock is definitely on board with fucking Rina, I never intended for it to be more than that. Especially not with someone who isn't already part of the mafia lifestyle. But all of my bad intentions are morphing, becoming something a little scary. As if my obsession for Rina is gaining permanence. No longer just a skin-deep hunger to taste her. But a bottomless craving to share my life with her. To have her sweetness and light illuminate the darkness, and burn free the bloodstains from the brutal corners of my world.

I'm a selfish bastard. Because I linger, knowing the harm that will come. My mother is the fucking poster-child of a fragile, gentle woman who couldn't hack being a mobster's wife.

Right now, I don't care. I want this.

I want her.

I brush my knuckles against the soft contour of her cheek. Following the angular hollow beneath the bone down toward her lips. Knowing that I'll probably wake her, I steal a kiss, a first one plucked and not given like a thieving prince taking what he can from sleeping beauty.

She stirs against me. Her dewy mouth shifts, lips parting. Before she languidly kisses me back. I savor that groggy affection, drinking in the pliant feel of her in my arms. Before she wakes fully and withdraws some. That tiny bit of distance she erects between us causes an ache in my chest. Making me want to pull her tighter into me and never let her go.

Instead, I loosen my arms just enough to stare down at her.

"You're still here." Her voice is almost kittenish because she's groggy. It makes me want to kiss her again.

So I do, stealing another sip of my favorite flavor off her lips. Never mind that I don't kiss. Now that I've sampled Rina's mouth, I'm ditching that rule just so I can continue to savor their pliant softness.

"I need to be going soon."

"Is that why you woke me?"

"Yes. Are you going to tell me where you were last night?"

"I told you, working." Rina sounds like a grumpy kitten as she burrows her face into the pillow. She's hiding something, and I can't figure out why.

"Where?"

"It's none of your business."

"Everything you do is my business."

Rina sighs, but I don't let her flop away from her. I clutch her tighter, pinning her to my side as if that would keep her brain from continuing to flee from my man-handling.

My bare chest distracts her. Her fingers twitch slightly as her beautiful hazel eyes trace my criminal biography indelibly inked into my skin.

I freeze when she strokes and circles the bare spot of flesh over the top of my heart. The reserved one that I suspect might wear 'Rina' sooner rather than later. Even if I never make her mine in all ways. She's wormed her way in, and she deserves that recognition on my skin.

"Why is this blank," she muses. Her nail flicks above my nipple.

"Why do you care?"

"You're covered almost head-to-toe with tattoos. Yet this little sliver here looks abandoned."

If she only knew the truth of that word.

Abandoned.

I tense against her. She feels me withdraw, and her fingers slip away from my pectoral muscles.

"You're hard to read. Do you know that?"

I'm in a rare mood, reflecting her questions with my own. Forcing her to explain to me why she wants in deeper, why she wants to know about me and not just accept what I'm offering.

"Why do you want to read me?"

"You won't take 'no' for an answer and stay out of my bedroom. It seems prudent to know about the person who keeps breaking in."

She does have a point, and I sigh in concession of it.

The problem is I don't know if I want her mired in my world. If I let her close, will she run and hide?

Will she turn to drugs to numb the memories, pain, and isolation as my mother did?

Could I stand by and watch it happen as my father did? Letting her drift away from her children on an opiate haze.

I knew the answer to that. I have since I was ten years old.

Fuck no.

I sit up, preparing to leave. This is a mistake. I forgot myself, getting addicted to her warmth and sweetness.

But Rina won't let me go. Her hands tighten, and I'm shocked as she pushes me back down. She's not strong, but I'm weak, and I don't put up much of a fight.

"You're not running from my questions." She scolds me as if I'm one of her students, much to my delight. It's not often that people are bold with me.

I curl my fingers against her throat, yanking her toward my lips where I steal a kiss.

"You get one," I acquiesce. "Make it a good one."

"Do you promise to answer it no matter how much it might make you uncomfortable?"

I grunt. She's backing me into a corner. But the thieves' vow says I must speak with honesty and integrity if I give my word.

So be it.

"Yes."

Rina's lips press into a thoughtful little moue. She snuggles down beside me, quiet and introspective for a few minutes. Mulling over that singular question that will pry the most answers out of me.

Then she smiles, and I know I'm going to regret promising her. But how can I? That smile is as if the sun is peaking out from behind a fog bank. Immediately brightening my dismal world. I realize that in here, in this little cocoon away from the world we're somehow carving out together, I can't deny her anything. It's a shocking revelation for someone who spent his entire life saying no to everybody.

"Tell me a secret," she demands with a mischievous little smile.

Little Minx is goading me.

I have a lot of secrets. The skeletons in my closet have skeletons.

But there is one that very few people who aren't family know.

I wrap my arm around her shoulder and enjoy having her pressed against my side. Creating a nook with my body. Because I will need her warmth to excavate the badly healed wound she's digging into. I know it festers beneath the scar. But there's nothing to be done about it.

Still, it takes a while to bring the words up. To pull them out of the box it's sealed in, along with the memories. I buried them deep, and it's bitter to utter the truth I've kept locked inside for twenty years.

It begins with a story.

"My Pops always wanted another girl. He loved doting on a daughter. But with Nadia, as his heir, he could only be a girl dad for so long. Before he had to be the pakhan teaching his successor."

"Mom, well, she was ambivalent about the idea. They didn't start as a love match. I don't think they ended as one either. It was an arranged marriage between two heavy-weight *Bratva* families. As time ticked on, there was less affection and romance between them."

I lick my lips, looking over at Rina. Her eyes are speckles of gold and green, with swirls of umber that look like chocolate drops in her irises. She's riveted on the story, even as it twists my guts.

"When Alexander was four or so, and I was eleven, mom got pregnant again. Honestly, it was a fucking miracle. She probably figured she was in the clear with her change of life being only a few years away. Isn't that always how it goes? An older woman thinking she can't get pregnant winds up with an oops baby in her forties."

I close my eyes, inhaling the soft floral scent which clings to Rina. Chamomile and lavender.

"Nobody knew that during the interim years after Alexander's rather difficult birth, mom had turned to drugs. The doctor had given her a long-running prescription of Vicodin. And as far as I know, she stayed on it way too long. She probably started as most do after she was cut off. You know? With booze. Maybe took the edge off her depression with marijuana. When that didn't cut it, she tried the harder stuff."

The taste in my mouth is ashes, and I lick my lips slightly as if I can get the flavor out of it.

Rina's hand steals into mine. Squeezing tightly, as if helping staunch the bleeding that I feel in my chest. Right around where a mother's love should be.

"Where was your dad during that?"

"I don't know." That lack of knowledge digs into me. I really have no fucking idea what Pops was doing while Mom devolved into a drug addict.

"Eventually, her whole life became chasing the high. Forget her kids. Forget her husband. Fuck, forget even enjoying life. Her true love was heroine. You would never see a track mark on her arm. Later, we learned that she shot up between her toes. Where she learned that junky trick is a mystery. When she got pregnant, well. That wasn't enough to stop her habit.

Bitterness sputtered inside of me.

"It wasn't until she was seven months pregnant, and she went into premature labor that Pops learned the scope of her addiction. She'd been fucking a dealer behind his back, a man who was on the fringe of the *Bratva* but only at a low level. And when that stopped working, hid the cost amidst a shopping addiction. She would do anything to serve that demon."

I stare up at the ceiling, thinking of a name I haven't spoken in so fucking long. The future that could have been flickers in the shadows. I tell myself the burn in my eyes is because I'm staring at nothing as if I can bore holes through it with my eyes.

"They named her Adina, a book-end for Pops' life. He had his Mafia Queen in Nadia, and his little Mafia Princess in Adina. She spent her very short life in the neonatal intensive care unit. Back then it was simply Echo Bay Children's hospital, now it's the Adina Vasiliev Children's Hospital-Echo Bay. Pops made a huge donation after her funeral."

"I never got to meet her. The first and only time I saw her was when she was in her tiny little casket."

Funerals are commonplace in this way of life. But that one,

that one stays with me. It took years for me to not see the extravagant floral displays and the numb, empty look on Pops face whenever I closed my eyes.

"Mom didn't show up for the funeral. The moment she gave birth she was out of the hospital looking to score. Never mind that her drug use caused Adina's premature birth and eventual death."

"Fuck, *solnyshko*. I don't even have to tell you, that a child being born with an opiate addiction is a terrible, horrible thing. Her entire life was the pain of withdrawal."

"Afterward, Pops sent Mom to rehab. She was gone for a year. Sometimes she'd come back for a few months. Then she'd relapsed and she was gone again."

I exhale as the secret crystallizes, letting Rina see the true man behind the mask. In the *Bratva*, there's no room for vulnerabilities. To show a wound this deep is asking my enemies to gouge it out and exploit it.

Mom had abandoned us all for her drugs. Long before she moved to the Cayman Islands. That's why she's not here. As soon as Pops was gone, and she felt free, she took her inheritance and vanished so that she could spend the rest of her sad, albeit wealthy life coked out of her fucking mind.

Wetness splashes across my chest. Shaking me from the memories and painful thoughts which grip me.

I look down at Rina and see that she's crying. It shakes me. Mostly because nobody has ever cried for me. When mom was gone, Pops refused to let us talk about our mother. Not until she could prove that she was worthy of being one of the family again.

"That's a horrible story, and I hate how alike it is to my mother."

Her empathy, the shared pain, slips into me. It's gentle rain on an out of control wildfire, taking the sting away.

I've keenly felt the abandonment of my mother and Pops disinterested air. Nadia was mostly grown by then and had always been Pops favorite. Mikhail's memories were fuzzier and eventually faded. Alexander never knew her.

Then Pops set my path for me by sending me to Russia. The sacrificial son. Either I'd thrive in the Gulag or I'd die. I never had parental love. That dearth shaped me as surely as being part of the *Bratva*.

"You have a heart too big for this world, *solnyshko*."

I pull her tighter against me and press my forehead to hers. Demanding she give me her eyes so I can drown in their sweetness.

"If you don't watch out, someone's going to take advantage of you."

She laughs and its melody soothes me.

"Oh, you mean more than the scary tattooed man that keeps breaking into my bedroom?"

Warmth drifts through the ice floes around my heart, cracking the glacier that encases it. Her affection is digging out chinks in my armor. Making me feel fucking exposed.

I turn abruptly, pinning her beneath me. She giggles, pushing against my chest as if she can leverage me off her.

I kiss her, just to taste the mirth on her lips.

Chapter Twenty-Three

Edmond

The last thing I want to be doing on a Saturday evening is spending it in a dive bar. Make no mistake, despite its attempts at rebranding as a gastropub, *Timberhaus* earns its low-brow reputation.

It should be condemned. Instead, it thrives as a place where secrets are exchanged, crimes are committed right out in the open, and sexually charged slurs are part of the conversation.

I want to burn the fucking place down and I've only been inside for a minute.

Once upon a time, the log-cabin-style bar might have been considered 'rustic' and charming. But now it is a spectacle that caters to lumberjacks, oilmen, truckers, bikers, and other rough-neck vagabonds that ride the axle down I-5 between Seattle and the Canadian border.

This is Barrett's kingdom, and if I want to know where the drugs are coming from, here I need to be. Though I'm not entirely sure that this isn't going to be bait and switch. The flesh between my shoulder blades itches, as if I'm in the crosshairs of a sniper. It's dangerous for me to be here, but not coming would be worse for business.

"Edmond! I'm so glad you could make it."

I barely stride past the swinging doors, with Leon and Marcus hot on my heels, when Barrett appears like a demented red-neck from a pool of neon light that vomits gaudy color all over the bar. Every brand of booze is advertised in the white-hot glow of colors, with the Coors logo brightest of all.

Timberhaus' proprietor makes a big spectacle as he meets me halfway. His jocular welcome distracts me from the eyesore of the bar's decor.

Does he think rusted chainsaws, axes, and stuffed animal heads are engaging?

My regret deepens as we shake hands. His meaty fist pumps mine, though he is smart enough not to make an ego trip out of it. I would crush him if he tried.

The two of us stand in the only well-lit area of the entire shadow-choked bar, probably to make sure that his regular patrons know who he is meeting with.

"Barrett."

"Welcome to my pride and joy. Anything you want is on the house." Barrett oozes smugness as he invades my space. "Including the girls."

Barrett signals the bartender, two fingers held high as he orders drinks. Then he weaves through the bar, glad-handing a few patrons like a politician on the campaign trail. He waves me toward a wooden booth.

Nodding at my bodyguards, who station themselves in the booth behind me, I slide in.

Barrett takes the position opposite of me. "I appreciate you meeting with me. I know this isn't your usual scene."

"You could say that again."

"That's what I wanted to talk to you about."

Before he can launch into his business spiel, one of the waitresses materializes. One look at the country Barbie schtick, and I can understand - distantly - why *Timberhaus* is popular. If you like slutty lumberjack, this is the place to be. The 'uniform' is cut-off jean shorts short enough that daisy dukes look modest, a flannel shirt cropped high and straining across the girl's overlarge tits, some fetishist's concept of a leather toolbelt, and work boots worn with open laces.

"Here you are, sugar."

Barrett feeds me a smug grin. Then his hand arcs out, connecting with the waitress' ample ass. She squeals, throws an extra hitch to the swing of her hips, and spins around, balancing the now empty serving tray expertly.

"Whiskey," Barrett says when he notices me eyeballing the glass. "I hear it's your favorite."

My reputation transcends even the borders of Echo Bay, by design. That doesn't mean I like loose lips who know that I prefer whiskey over vodka. Should that reach the wrong Russian ears, I'd have a problem on my hand. That he knows this, and is offering me my preferred drink, is a clumsy move. What I can't decipher is if Barrett is trying to piss me off or butter me up.

"You have quite large ears."

I lift my tumbler, mutter a Russian toast, and take a polite sip.

Surprisingly, the whiskey is fucking good. I'd assumed that whatever schlep Barrett serves his patrons would be watered down.

Barrett watches me closely, and grins widely when he reads the approval on my face.

"What do you think?"

"Pretty good."

"Not just for a place like this or this area. It's pretty fucking good for anywhere. I imported that from Dublin. That's Teeling, new to the scene especially for Dublin, but making big waves with their liquor."

His arrogance makes him drop nuggets of information. *Finally, I'll get some traction on the drugs.* The faster he spits out his grand scheme, the sooner I can get home, return to my my stalking of Rina. She's gone again, and I don't know where. That she's out of my reach and away from my brand of protection is making me paranoid.

I can't think of her now. Now it's time for business.

I sit back, arms braced on the tabletop in front of me. Through the constant haze of smoke that permeates places like this, I look around. Making it seem as if I am interested, or too dim to realize Barrett's already told me who he's working for.

Every *pakhan* has their kryptonite. Mine is the Irish.

Timberhaus is dimly lit, ensuring that the sins of its decor are witnessed solely through beer goggles. The sickly-sweet stench of vape smoke fights for supremacy with the reek of spilled booze. Considering its clientele, there is a heavy musk of body odor and the sour stink of old grease. The menu consists of what you can drink: as long as it is beer and whiskey. Food comes straight out of a fryer and could be rat tails or chicken wings. I can't tell based on the breaded monstrosities that I see one of the waitresses has served up.

I strive to keep disgust off my face.

"That's quite an import," I say finally. "Why do I think that's not the only thing you're buying from the Irish."

Barrett laughs. He looks like a rat with his thin face and pointed nose.

"That's because you're a savvy businessman. Like me."

The kiss-ass is already getting on my nerves. He's lucky I'm not packing heat, because I'd already have put a bullet in him and made his toothsome grin into a jack o' lantern smile.

"You wanted my attention. Well, here I am. Give me your best business proposal."

Barrett leans close, making it hard to hear his spiel over the reedy thump of the music. "I've been eyeing the city for some time now. I put out some feelers about where you might be losing money. There are a few areas ripe for diversification, and I believe I have the means to make that happen."

There it is.

I love when a plan comes together.

Studying Barrett, I realize two things simultaneously.

One: he doesn't know as much as he thinks he does. If he were as informed as he tries to make me believe, he would know that I would never let the Irish Mob into my city. I barely tolerate the *Cosa Nostra* at the harbor.

Second: he is a shit businessman for not knowing. Instead of seeing the drug-shaped void in my business deals and thinking it's a deliberate act on my part, he sees it and thinks I have a blind spot.

Anger creeps through the cracks in the back of my mind. I keep my growing rage at bay as I swirl the scotch-whiskey in my glass. Studying the interplay of smoggy light on the amber-colored liquid. I can't act on it, though. I need to keep him talking until he coughs up a name.

"Diversification is a loaded word. What exactly are you planning?"

This fuck-wit thinks I am nibbling at the cheese in his whiskey-baited trap. He sits up straight, his chest puffed out with misplaced pride.

"Why the usuals of course. I've already seen a great return on the molly we've been pushing. We're going to expand that, and maybe add *tranq*. Not the usual weak shit hat's made state-side. I want to invest in business with you. Beyond the usual scope that I could do myself. You name it, the two of us could do it. *Timberhaus* and *Sindoll's* are primed to be distribution points."

Excitement ratchets up his voice. "Fuck, Edmond. We could take over the whole west coast if we think large enough. Echo Bay is thirsty. Washington is booming. There's money to be made here."

"And why should I trust you with this endeavor? You're stepping into my territory."

Barrett's manic smile dims when he realizes I'm not leaping into his idea with both feet. He drains his drink, slams the heavy-bottomed glass down, and waves his hand high enough that the bartender would be blind not to see him calling for another.

I run my finger around the rim of my glass. A few droplets of liquor stain them, which I lift and lick off carelessly. As if I'm not aware of the hostility starting to brew in my host.

"I have connections you don't have, Edmond."

No shit. Give me the name.

The only thing Barrett has are connections I don't want. Willingly putting yourself into the mob's back pocket is stupid and risky. They don't play well with others, and once they get what they want - a foothold in Echo Bay – they will send a hit squad up and take Barrett out.

I hate stupid, low-level criminals.

Before I can work Barrett around to coughing up the name of his Irish contact, a delicate whiff of perfume reaches out and grabs me by the balls.

I know this scent. It is evocative of lavender and herbal tea - a sun-soaked, powdery innocence that doesn't belong here.

My head whips around, staring at the waitress who has come bringing Barrett a refill of his drink.

No. Fucking. Way.

Rina stands dressed up like a lumberjack slut. The frayed

denim shorts look painted on, showcasing the pale swathe of her thick thighs and petite legs. The low angle of the waistband and the tied-up hemline of her barely buttoned red-checked flannel show off an appetizing amount of flesh.

Before seeing that shadowy divot, I hadn't thought belly buttons were sexy. But the way Rina's peeks an inch above the brass button of her jean shorts makes me want to lick and nibble all around it.

What the fuck.

Is this the bar she's been working at?

Possessiveness seeps into my head like a Tsunami sucking up the waves, preparing to unleash a devastating strike. My anger collides with the ice-cold demeanor I need to handle business. I need to find the name of Barrett's supplier, but how the fuck can I do that when Rina is *here* and looking like *that.*

Nobody but me should see her dressed like that.

Heat nooses my throat above the open collar of my Henley. Blindly, I grab the whiskey glass and shoot the rest of the liquor down. Burning away the words locked-and-loaded on my tongue with the burn of pure distilled alcohol.

The whole scene slows down.

Rina hasn't quite noticed who is sitting with her boss. Her lips are painted scarlet and turn up in a smile that's so fake even as it bewitches the men around her. I've seen that half-flirta-tious looks on a dozen waitresses doing some mild teasing to earn big tips. A smudge of some woodsy-looking eyeshadow makes her hazel eyes pop. She balances the drink tray expertly, resting it near her hip which is cocked out to accentuate the contour of her delicate curves.

"Here you go, boss." Rina delicately lifts the fresh cocktail and places it in front of Barrett. She bends down slightly, reaching for the empty glass. The position allows both of us to get an eye full of her cleavage from how low-buttoned her top is.

The roar in my skull returns, threatening ruin. I can practically hear Iustina whispering from inside my pocket, promising to gouge out the eyes of any man whose gotten an eyeful. It might mean the whole fucking bar, but so be it. Nobody looks at my girl.

Nobody.

"Ah, that's my girl." Barrett's attention rakes over Rina, but I barely notice it as my awareness goes hyperdrive at hearing *my* and *girl* fall from the bastard's lips.

Then he seals his fate, and all of the anger falls away. Leaving behind the cool calmness I learned in Siberia.

Barrett's wrist sweeps out, and I know exactly what he's aiming for. Who wouldn't want to cop a feel of Rina's sweetheart ass barely covered by those shorts.

Of course, I can't allow that. Neither can Iustina.

Iustina screams her metallic cry, a crisp snarl like a steel-beaked war hawk as I pluck her from my pocket and flick her open. Exposing the nearly four-inch length of razor-sharp lethality. The haste with which the pivot pins sing is a blur to the untrained eye.

Rina finally notices me. Shock crosses her face, bleeding out the rosy color in her cheeks until she looks pasty and ill. I hate that she has to see this violence, but it was only a matter of time before the truth of my work would reveal itself.

Welcome to my world, solnyshko.

Time speeds back up as I slam the point of the knife straight through Barrett's hand, pinning it palm-flat to the table, with only the decorative handle visible above his knuckles.

Barrett's mouth flops open. Shock blunts the pain, his bulging eyes stare at his maimed hand as if can't quite believe he's just been stabbed.

The icy calm continues as I place my hands flat on the table, leveraging myself upright. Blood spurts from the wound, a growing puddle from the slow trickle that's eventually growing quicker as Barrett's body gets the message that he's been wounded.

"Ed-?" Barrett's voice shakes.

I yank Iustina out of his hand. The wet *slurp* of his flesh giving up the blade is a noise I'm intimately familiar with. But the rage that's boiling just behind the glacial wall pushing it back isn't soothed.

I need more.

More of Barrett's pain.

More of his blood.

I need to take his fucking hand for thinking to touch *my* girl.

Iustina slashes down again, slamming through the meat of Barret's palm in a different spot.

"She."

Stab.

"Is."

Stab.

"Mine."

Stab

By the third word, Barrett is bleating like a stuck pig.

Iustina withdraws, showcasing the shards of bone through Barrett's gouged flesh. The middle knuckle is in danger of being severed, and I think for a moment of cutting it off entirely. Just to shove it into Barrett's howling face so that he can choke on it.

But his cries are drawing unwanted attention. A few rougher, leather-clad bikers leave their table, looking as if they want to get involved.

They stop when Leon ambles into their path.

The bikers raise their hands and back away, leaving Barrett to his fate.

What a shame his Irish suppliers aren't in house. Then I could deal with the problem all at once. For now, business is going to have to wait.

I turn to the next person who is in desperate need of a lesson.

Rina.

My little sunbeam, you have no idea the monster you've awakened.

Chapter Twenty-Four

Rina

I'm *having a stroke.*

Edmond's angry silver eyes clash with mine as he glares, the fury in them pinning my feet to the floor. Everything has happened so fast that I can't make any sense of the situation.

Violence, even in a place like *Timberhaus,* where barfights are as common as a dart game, doesn't just erupt out of nowhere. Especially with me as the apparent epicenter.

In a bid for self-preservation, my brain refuses to acknowledge that my boss looks like he's bleeding out at the table. Instead, I look up at Edmond. He is wrath personified, radiating the most primal, primitive fits of anger that I lose feeling in my knees.

A common occurrence around him, it seems. Once, I'd thought all those damsels fainting in distress was just theatrics for the sake of art. Now I know that in situations where my nervous system is entirely overwhelmed, my knees would rather kiss the ground then do something useful like run.

I surely would have fallen if he hadn't invaded my space.

He's so tall. I keep forgetting how much larger than me he is, until he's right there, looming and huge and very, very angry.

"This is your new job?"

Edmond's voice slices into me, making my skin feel tight as I meet his piercing pewter eyes. I want to shy away from how embarrassed I am over him seeing me dressed like *this*. Barrett's version of the happy-good-time-lumber jack.

"I needed the money."

The truth inflames Edmond's temper. His fingers latch onto my arm right above the elbow. The grip is hard enough that I know I will have contusions in the shape of his finger-prints later.

"For what? If this is how you want to make money, Miss Christenson." I flinch as he smacks me with my honorific. Reminding me that he's an influential parent at the school. "You can earn it flat on your back in my bed."

His comment stings, as it's meant to. Shame washes over me, chasing away the fright that lingers in the pit of my belly over the one-sided knife fight.

"There's not enough money in the world!"

Edmond yanks me into him, reeling me like a captive until the whole of my body is flattened against him. He's dressed down, the soft cotton of his black Henley and casual-fit, dark-wash jeans showcases how sculpted his body is, highlighting the strength and power. Seeing him so *raw* makes him even more attractive. Like this he is accessible, and I can almost forget he's filthy rich.

The fabric of my uniform is thin, and there's no hiding the stiff peaks of my nipples. I'm oddly aroused by the whole damn situation, and with my heightened senses, I can *feel* every inch of Edmond pressed against me.

Including his very thick, and very hard cock where it grinds against my belly.

Before this already insane situation can get worse, Edmond wraps his arm around my waist. The sleeves of his shirt are rolled back, revealing strong forearms which are nearly covered in tattoos. Interspersed between the stark, monochromatic designs are hatch marks. I don't have time to count how many there are, but at first glance there's a lot.

Edmond snaps his fingers at his bodyguard. I just now notice the pair of them, who are still both dressed in black suits. The big one shrugs out of his coat, revealing a holster and the butt of a gun at his side. He's packing heat, and the leather straps look shiny against his short-sleeved black dress shirt.

Grabbing the guard's jacket, Edmond drapes it around me. It's so large I feel like I'm swimming in the designer fabric.

"You're going to burn this sorry excuse for an outfit." Edmond's voice is icy and clipped, and I jerk as if he's physically slapped me. Did he miss the part where the only reason I'm here, working at a place like *Timberhaus,* is because I needed the money?

Of course, Mr. Moneybucks isn't asking me why. He is completely out of touch with the realities of life and things like *cost of living.* I doubt he's ever had to struggle to pay the rent *and* grocery bill before.

As suddenly as my anger spikes, my emotions flip. Because I'm embarrassed. I'm ashamed I need to scrape by. Before agreeing to work at *Timberhaus,* my biggest fear had been a parent – or someone else I knew – seeing me like this.

And here is Edmond, paying into that fear by reacting like a deranged lunatic over the fact that I'm in a shitty dive bar, showing a lot of skin to earn tips.

Tears well in my eyes, and I'm wordless as Edmond manhandles me. There's no fight in me as he draws me against him. I'm sandwiched against his back while his bodyguards flank either side of me.

There are a few customers who look like they are spoiling for a fight. They stand between the neon-lit bar and the table where Barrett's screams have faded into gasps.

I can't believe Edmond stabbed my boss.

Why is he here?

How does he know Barrett?

Never in a million years would I have pictured Edmond having a casual drink in a country bar. I have a thousand questions, but the foremost one is simple, and something I should have asked long before.

Why is everyone afraid of Edmond?

It has to be something seedy. Why else would he be meeting with Barrett? There is no way that they run in the same social circles.

I have a thousand questions. The topmost one being that I don't know what Edmond does for work beyond what Google coughed up. Suddenly, I remember what Edmond had said when he'd begun stabbing Barrett. Three little words that most girls never knew they wanted to hear.

She is mine.

Oh. *Oh.*

Edmond implied that I was *his* before. Now I realize just how far he'll go to lay his claim. Whether I need to worry about that, I haven't decided yet.

My fears are quiet as the four of us exit *Timberhaus'* stifling, sweltering interior, and into Washington's crisp night air. Suddenly, I'm thankful for the jacket. Not because it hides my skimpy 'uniform', but for the warmth it offers. My bare legs are immediately freezing.

"Where is your car."

I blink up at Edmond as he turns to look at me.

"Back there, that's the employee lot."

"Boss." The smaller of Edmond's bodyguards' steps close to

him. They are about the same size, now that I see them side-by-side. And I realize that Edmond doesn't physically need a bodyguard.

Wow, I know he can take care of himself.

Is having them just for how?

A delicious shiver skates across my skin that has nothing to do with the cold. There is something powerfully arousing, and intoxicating about being with a man who is so physically intimidating.

"You and Leon will follow behind us, Marcus."

Marcus - and he looks like his moniker with his buzzed-down haircut - gives me a hard look. Then, he nods to the big one and the pair blend in with the night as they step away from the parking lot light and toward wherever they've parked Edmond's shiny SUV.

"Wait," I say as my brain suddenly came online. "Wait. I'm still on the clock."

I probably don't have a job, and it's doubtful that I'm going to get paid for the time I worked tonight. But I needed to know for sure, as well as collect my purse and other personal items I left in the employee locker room.

Edmond's anger manifests in a sharp motion as he yanks me out of the well-lit parking lot and shoves me into the shadows that congregate on the building's backside. I didn't realize just how dark a rural, gravel-strewn parking lot is until I'm pushed out of the light and shoved against a darkened wall.

I gasp as the brick bites into the backs of my thighs.

Edmond is backlit by the LED lights. I can see the shine of his inky dark hair. But his face is a blur as if the shadows are a mask. Concealing everything but two swathes of light that bounce off each cheekbone, making them seem sharper, more dangerous.

He leans closer, just enough so that I can see the burn in his eyes.

"You won't be coming back here. If you are that desperate for money, we can work something out."

Those pitiless eyes flicker, stroking whiplashes of heat across my cheeks, and my nose, before locking like smoldering embers on my mouth.

Outraged tears well in my eyes. "I'm not going to fuck you for money."

"If you go back in there, I'm going to kill him."

Edmond lowers his face. His intensity sends frissons of fear and desire darting up and down my spine. I can't look away from the unspoken dare which gleams in the pitiless voids of his eyes.

His voice lowers, each syllable a humid pop of breath against the underside of my jaw. As if he is nuzzling me, instead of keeping me caged by the brutish grasp of his hand. "Is that what you want me to do, Miss Christenson?"

Oh, how he mocks me.

"Do you want me to slaughter all those men who dare to look and think about touching what's mine? I'll make the wood slick with blood, and then I'll torch the whole fucking place. I've wanted to since the moment you bent over my table and shoved your tits in our face."

Edmond pulled back enough so that I could read the truth in his face.

I shudder, because I know, deep in that primal part of my hindbrain, where the genetic memory of human ancestors running away from the dark exists, that he would do it too.

And like the insanity that has colored this entire night, he'd enjoy every second of it.

"You can't do that." I'm trembling like a leaf against him,

trying to implore him with my eyes to back away from whatever psychosis edge he's teetering on.

Edmond growls, and then he clenches his hand around my throat, making a tattooed necklace that squeezes and cages me.

"Shut. Up."

Then he ravages my mouth, kissing me until the only thing I can do is melt into him.

Chapter Twenty-Five

Rina

My bottom lip throbs from where Edmond bit me. Hard enough that my tongue keeps worrying over the swollen mark, feeling the bruise that's rising there.

After the kiss, he dragged me into my car. Somehow, the kiss made him angrier. He doesn't hit. Nor does he rage. But his fists tighten on the steering wheel, making the synthetic material squeak beneath his palms.

"I don't kiss," he snaps at me.

Sure. If you don't kiss, what do you call that? Or all those sweet ones you gave me in bed?

I don't say it, but I think my snark at him. Hoping he can pick up on it through ESP or something.

Muttering beneath his breath, he starts the car, and cranks the heat. We sit there, waiting for the interior to warm up. But it's not the cold that has me trembling beside him, as fragile and wayward as a wind-tossed leaf.

It's him. Edmond. Preparing to drive my car. Who just threatened the lives of an entire bar full of men, and nearly degloved Barrett's fingers. All because they liked the look of me in my skimpy little uniform.

I dare a glance at Edmond's profile. I'd gaslit myself during all of our interactions, telling myself that he's not dangerous. Despite the very air of lethality he exudes. He wears it like a reaper would a cloak of shadows; a mantle that flows and melds to him. That, if you are naive like I had been, you would see and think he is just intense.

Apparently, intense is my codeword for *ruthless murdering psychopath*.

First impressions are always right: Edmond is dangerous, and I'm the fool who got herself caught up in his web.

I swallow a hiccup that might be a sob or a laugh. I'm not entirely sure what my emotional state is other than fragile.

Edmond glances away from the road. Though calling it a highway is being polite. It is a two-lane country road that weaves through the verdant wonderland. There might be urban hubs and cityscapes here and there, but most of the state is wilderness.

It would be far too easy to dispose of a body.

Has Edmond used Washington's natural landscape to hide his criminal deeds? There are enough pockets of unmapped terrain and mines to conceal anything.

Edmond's brow rises, a sinister slash that makes him look positively diabolical in the diffused light that bounces off the pavement.

"If you keep looking at me like that, I'm going to shove your head in my lap."

I gasp, eyes widening as I give him a once-over.

How is that a normal reaction? I'm not sure if I should be petrified, or if I'm going to live to see the morning, and he's threatening to force me to give him roadhead.

"Yes," he says as if reading my mind. Though I'm pretty

sure every thought in my head is a ticker tape scrolling an S.O.S across my face. "Your fear makes me hard."

"If you even try, I'll bite it off."

Edmond laughs, a low, sinister baritone that makes the car's interior shrink to accommodate it.

"You'll do no such thing, *solnyshko*. You'll be a good girl and suck my cock down as if its candy filled."

"You are such an arrogant prick!"

Somehow, I realize that I'm seeing the *real* Edmond for the first time. He wore a mask for me, a mirrored one that reflected all of my yearnings and expectations. But now it's cracked, letting me see the darkness that exists behind his sterling eyes. He's a volcano, a pent-up, natural disaster that is one eruption from destroying my whole world.

Minutes pass as I stare mutely out at the passing scenery. I don't dare ask him to slow down. Maybe if he crashes the car, he'll die, and I'll survive. It will get me away from his nefarious clutches.

"You are so innocent." A panther purring couldn't have sounded more velvety seductive than Edmond did just then. He made 'innocent' sound so, so dirty.

My thighs clench at the sudden, inexplicable rush of heat that pools in my core. While my mind is screaming danger and trying to figure a way out of this madness, my girlie bits are on high alert.

Hasn't this been my body's consistent reaction to Edmond? I inwardly shake my head at myself. Was this the missing ingredient that none of my former boyfriends had? Homicidal tendencies?

I finally find my verve, enough to ask the question that's been battering around my skull. Though it takes a few thick-sounding, loud swallows to wet it enough to push the words out.

"Who are you?"

Edmond's smile dissolves into a grim expression. He is a master of lopsided smirks, and he gives me one now. Allowing me to watch the interplay of thoughts as they slip across the devastatingly handsome planes of his face.

"You know who I am. I'm Mila's uncle."

I scoff loudly. "You're more than that."

"I don't know what you're talking about."

"Don't insult my intelligence. I just saw you almost cut the hand off my boss. Yeah, you're *just* Mila's uncle. Did her parents know you were like this before they made you her guardian?"

Edmond shakes his head, the amusement back on his face. I hate how the devil can look so good while we are discussing the violence he has just committed in my name.

"Nadia was worse. Her violence was all mental. At least with me, my enemies know the torment will eventually end."

His off-hand remark about his sister sucks the questions from my brain. This is way deeper, and much larger in scope than Edmond just being the run-of-the-mill murder. There's a dark road here, and we're at a crossroads. I can turn back and pretend that I didn't brush up against this seductive violence and return to my simple life.

Or go deeper.

Think of Luce.

You can't get involved in Edmond's lunacy and criminal shenanigans.

Edmond flashes another dark look at me in the headlights of a lone oncoming car. In that single expression, he dares me to follow him like Alice toddling after the white rabbit, except this isn't the wonderland that he is offering to reveal to me, but a blood-soaked nightmare. There will be no delicious tidbits, but violent delights instead.

The lights grow brighter, flaring over the high points of Edmond's model-worthy good looks; the breadth of his forehead; the sharp angle of his high cheekbones; that cruel, sensuous-looking mouth.

Then the car passes, and we're both cast in the dim glow of the interior electronics.

I hate myself for being selfish. For the first time in my life, I'm going to do something that's for me. I adore my sister. I love her to pieces and would sacrifice my very life for her own.

But right now, that protective instinct is far, far away. A reckless girl I don't recognize has emerged. It's she who speaks.

"Tell me," I whisper.

Chapter Twenty-Six

Edmond

The blood caked around my knuckles flakes away when I tighten my fists on the steering wheel. I'm not worried about Barrett filing a police report. Especially this close to Echo Bay. Criminal activity begets violence. Everyone knows that.

I'm still not entirely sure I'm going to let Barrett live. Not only because he's touched Rina. But because of his Irish ties. His life means less to me than the hassle it would take to deal with them.

Beside me, Rina continues to quiver. Occasionally, I catch a glimpse of her bare thigh from beneath Leon's jacket. Then the rage over what she is wearing reignites, and I provoke her with another smack of my arrogance.

I really should have taken off Barrett's fucking hand.

I hadn't wanted Rina to see that part of me. Not only because she is utterly naive about what Echo Bay is and my role in it. But because she is one of the few threads of legitimacy I have.

But a deeper part of me roars with approval. She sees the

way I shed my skin of civility in favor of the violent, hungering beast inside. She saw it and didn't run away. Fuck. I don't think she even screamed as I stabbed Barrett. Nor did she do anything but look up at me with her dewy, doe-like eyes when I called her mine.

Now, she is asking me in that kittenish voice, all shivery and wispy to tell her who I am.

Minutes pass in the wake of her tentative courage. I see the awareness in her eyes over how different her life will be if I bring her any deeper into mine. The indecision shines as bright as the north star in her eyes. Any reasonable woman would turn away and choose self-preservation over getting into bed with an obvious violent man.

Instead, she surprises the ever-loving hell out of me by taking that first, tentative step into the darkness. All on her own. Without my prompting.

God, it makes my cock hard.

Before meeting Rina, I would have said there wasn't any goodness left in me. At least if it doesn't come to Mila. Not even my brothers earn a light touch. If they fuck up, they are educated under the old-school law passed down straight from the Soviet Union. Though the Vasiliev family is a whole generation removed from the old country. Pops was the last in the line who spoke with a minor trace of an accent. Though we all speak the language. The edicts are maintained. Carved onto the tender flesh of the heir, and by proxy all the spares.

I should shove her back into the light. Keep her away from the shadows, and preserve her innocence.

Except I want to shatter it and cut myself in the pieces.

I am a bastard.

"Do you know what the *Bratva* is, *solnyshko?*"

The term has come up more frequently in the past year.

Mostly because of the war between Russia and Ukraine. There are members of the brotherhood on *both* sides of the fighting.

Rina shakes her head.

Of course, she wouldn't know.

I squeeze the edge of the steering wheel, fighting against the lure of needing *her* flesh beneath my fingers.

I lose the battle. Using one hand to guide the car, the other finds the supple curve of her upper thigh. Her shorts are more like hot pants, only covering her crotch and probably half of her ass. I hadn't looked when I had the chance. I'd been more interested in stabbing Barrett to see what I'd yet to uncover.

Rina tenses beneath my palm and then makes a move to squeeze her thighs together. As if that would deny me what I want.

I tighten my hold, clamping my fingertips down into the soft meat that pads her inner thigh. The backs of my knuckles graze across the stitching of her jeans, right where the material cups her delicate little pussy.

Deliberately, I dig my knuckles against the seam and feel the answering surge of heat bloom across my skin.

In the low light, I glance over, getting a dark surge of possessiveness when I see the blood-stained, ink-marked caress of my hand engulfing her thigh.

Coaxing her thighs back apart, I stroke the edges of my nails along her skin. Tenderizing it with a *scratch, scritch, scratch.*

"*Bratva* loosely translates from Russian to English as brother or brotherhood."

Rina's thigh jerks beneath my hand. "Russian?"

"Mmhm. Russian organized crime, to be exact. I am the *pakhan*, boss if you'd like, of the Vasiliev OCG. My father, and his father before him, on and on have all been part of the collective. My grandfather ruled out of St. Petersburg. It was my father who arrived to begin his cell here in Echo Bay."

A cruel smile edges the corners of my mouth. I know Rina can see it.

She tenses beneath the caress of my hands, while a soft, almost panicked breath teases apart her lips. Glancing away from the road, I fix Rina with that smile. Letting her know she is now in the lion's den. And there is no escaping me now.

"I am *Bratva*."

Chapter Twenty-Seven

Rina

A gangster, of course. *The most handsome man I've ever seen, and he kills people for a living.*

Hindsight is twenty-twenty. There's a reason that phrase is a cliché. Because it's so true. Now that I know, I can see all the signs and the sea of red flags I either missed or ignored.

Edmond is quiet, allowing me to absorb what he's told me. It's a bombshell, but it explains so much that I'm kind of thankful he's not a raving serial killer and only murders people for business.

Yeah. As if *that* is any better.

Edmond hand doesn't move off my thigh. Though his fingers retreat from stroking my pussy, letting me think since it's hard to do when he's touching me.

"And Mila's mother was in the mafia too?"

"Yes. She was the Boss, and after she died, I became the head of our organization."

Wow, talk about breaking the glass ceiling.

Occasionally, as if to remind me about the traitorous reaction my body has for him, Edmond strokes the back of his hand against my core.

In a way, it reminds me of an evil henchman petting a kitty. His touch is featherlight, almost absent-minded. While yes, that is my pussy under his hand, it is not a cat. And every new amount of pressure on my clit sends need pulsing inside of me. It isn't long until a steady drip of wetness makes my panties stick to my lips.

Somehow, I manage not to moan each time he caresses me. I can't disguise the increase in my breathing, though. Or the thick, soft gasps that puff into the air.

Through it all, Edmond seems unaffected. His free hand is loose on the steering wheel. Looking casually as if he were behind a Ferrari instead of my beater.

Finally, finally, he pulls down my street, before coming to a smooth stop in front of the old Victorian. Not even a half-minute later, Leon and Marcus park behind us.

Edmond turns the ignition off, pulls the keys free, and holds them out to me.

How chivalrous.

I hesitate. Because now that we're in a residential area, the lighting is much better. And I can see the smudges of blood he's left on the metal.

I swallow and hastily accept them. I can bleach them later.

"Your sister is safe and sound asleep."

In the wake of all that I've seen tonight, my first alarm triggers. I'm not a violent person. My nature is to live and let live, but all of that inflames in a burst of temper as I swivel on Edmond. Just *hearing* Luce's name on his mouth makes me want to take a swing at him.

"You might have some sick fascination with me," I hiss. Because that's becoming very obvious. "But you leave Lucia alone!"

Just as suddenly as my anger rose, it faded out as realization punches me.

I'm the witness to a crime.

Don't criminals put cement shoes on people who can squeal on them? I know that's the Italian mafia - thanks to The Godfather.

What do Russians do?

I suck in a breath, staring up at Edmond as if he were a python ready to gobble my whole life whole.

"Please," I beg as reality shakes through me. Shattering the stupor I've been in through the car ride. "Please don't hurt Lucia. I'll do anything. Just...leave her out of whatever you have planned for me."

Edmond's face is unreadable. It's as if I'm staring into a statue carved from imported marble; expensive and hard.

"Is that all it takes to get you to beg for me?"

He isn't smiling, but there's heat in his eyes and sin in his voice.

I'm in emotional turbulence, because I'm right back to where I started when we got into the car; blushing around aroused.

I turn away, but he catches my chin, his tattooed fingers gripping hard enough that I can't wrench it free.

His tattoos take on a new, nefarious allure.

I rack my brain, trying to remember a movie I saw in college about the Russian mob in London. How every tattoo had a meaning, ranging from rank to murder tally.

Is that what Edmond's tattoos mean?

Are those what the hatch marks on his arms mean, how many people has he killed?

Will he kill me and Lucia now that I know about him?

The questions are a swarm of angry bees, roaring in my head. Suddenly, I feel myself panicking. There's not enough air in the car. Not with Edmond so close to me. His hand is only a few inches north of my throat. He could strangle me here and now. Lull me into a false sense of security. Then have his henchman dispose of my body. The house keys are on the keyring with my car fob.

"Shh." Edmond's face fills my line of sight. His eyes anchor me, drawing me out of the spiral my fear has been sucking me down into.

His hand splayed across my cheek. While rough and calloused, his touch is light. As if he doesn't want to get more of Barrett's blood on me. I'm already stained with it.

"I won't hurt you."

"Why?"

"Don't you know, *solnyshko?*" His head dips until his words kiss my lips. "You're my everything."

I hadn't understood what Edmond had meant when he'd told Barrett I was his. I'd assumed, days ago, that when he said that he hadn't an interest in dating, that meant he was only out for a quick fling. Something that was without strings so neither of us would get entangled.

Hearing his dark promise, I realized that wasn't what he meant at all.

This is more than dating. More than a relationship. More than anything I've ever experienced thus far, meager as my relationship history was.

He wants everything, and if I even muster the strength to say 'no, I'm not sure he'd listen to it anyway.

Chapter Twenty-Eight

Rina

Sunday is meant to be a day of rest, though I'm not sure how restful my sleep is. It's fitful, stalked by the burn in Edmond's eyes when he tells me of his affiliation.

Edmond is a Russian mobster.

He's the villain. No matter how attracted I am to him, there's no fairy tale or happily ever after with him being a criminal.

Why does Echo Bay let him get away with it all?

Is this whole town corrupt?

God, and I brought Lucia here.

I wake up before I'm ready too. As if I can pretend in my dreams for a little while longer. I refuse to open my eyes, even as the first light of the morning filters through my curtains. Unlike Lucia, I don't use blackout shades. I prefer rousing the soft, diffused glow of the rising sun drifting across my bedroom. Painting it in watercolor shades of rose and coral that tiptoe across my beige walls.

That I'm already middling aware, my consciousness skimming the surface of my mind, allows me to slip easily from the layers of smothering sleep even while I stay smuggled in the nascent warmth of my blankets.

My body feels heavy. An uncustomary weariness steals into my bones. My mind is foggy, thoughts and memories drifting like leaves in a slow-moving stream.

I roll over, and in the spot, I haven't slept in, the sheets cool against my skin. They smell faintly of lavender, a scent I've chosen for its aromatherapy properties of calming and vitality. But rejuvenation is far from what I feel. There's a rawness inside me, a vulnerability that lies just beneath the surface, aching and exposed.

As I stretch, trying to shake off the remnants of sleep, a sound catches my attention—a soft, almost imperceptible creak. My heart skips a beat, and I freeze, before I peek my eyes above the duvet's rim and scan the room. And then I see him. Edmond. Sitting in a chair in the corner of my room, his presence as jarring as a cold hand in the dark.

Somehow, I'm not surprised. He's the shadow in my world now.

Slowly I sit up, pulling the sheets to my chest. As if he hasn't seen me mostly naked and made me cum in this very bed a week ago.

"What are you doing here?" Sleep makes my voice extra husky.

Edmond leans forward, planting his elbows on his knees. He doesn't immediately respond. He just sits there, staring at me with his intense, diamond-bright eyes that see straight through me.

It takes me a moment to realize he hasn't changed from the night prior.

"Have you been here the whole night?"

His smile is ruthless and utterly heart stopping. It really should be illegal for a man to look like that this early, especially when I know my hair is all tousled in a titian-red rat's nest. Being this close to the water, there's always humidity in the air. And if I don't tame my hair with anti-frizz serum, the wildness grows out of control.

I mentally smack myself.

Why am I worrying about what I look like when there are more pressing matters to deal with?

I sigh. The air in the room feels charged, heavy with his unspoken words. I can smell the faint trace of his cologne, that sharp, peppery scent with a touch of dark vanilla, and the lingering odor of cigarette smoke from *Timberhaus*. This is not a happy good morning to my lover. I didn't invite him to stay overnight, and I'm not at all armored to deal with him first thing in the morning.

"How did you get in here?"

"I had the locksmith make a copy of your new keys for me."

He has no shame whatsoever.

"Of course." Because I'm beginning to learn that whatever Edmond wants, he can get. He can do anything, and nobody is going to stop him.

Except, maybe me.

"Do you want me to stop?" His voice is a silken challenge. Daring me to deny the connection that throbs between us.

All you have to do is say yes.

But do I want to? Do I want Edmond to go back to his life and relinquish his claim on me?

His stalking.

His obsession.

His violence.

Why don't they bother me more?

Because for the first time in my life I'm being *seen*. His obsession makes me feel warm, creating tingling awareness that spreads through my attention-starved body. Even though I know I should be upset about his constant night-time prowling into my bedroom, the only sanctuary I've ever had, I look forward to it. Because in those nocturnal visits, it's as if we are the only two people in the world.

I love Lucia. I've loved her ever since she was born when I was six years old. I didn't believe our mother intended to have another baby. But a drug-induced binge later, and out came Lucia and I became Lucia's caretaker. If I didn't do it, nobody else would. I couldn't ever let her out of my sight. There was never enough time, enough energy, to pay attention to me.

Am I that broken now as an adult that I crave any type of affection? Even if it's disastrous?

I don't have the answer. All I know is that when I'm around Edmond, I'm caught in his orbit. He drags me in, making me feel alive. He shatters all my illusions about what I thought about myself. That I'm good and wholesome.

He makes me feel wicked and wild.

I should be angry at him. I should be feeling betrayed over the underhanded tactics of his violent outburst and his stabbing Barrett.

Instead, there's just sheer carnal heat. His behavior is out of control. Unorthodox. Fucking criminal.

It seduces me.

I should feel unsafe with him. But the opposite is true. He makes me feel cherished and cared for. I believe, truly believe, he would destroy the world just to protect me. Maybe I'm daft in the head, delusional, or have watched too many drama movies where the toxic love interest throws red flags like roses. But I don't feel just fright when he shows me his true self.

We're at a crossroads, Edmond, and me.

Do you want me to stop?

I lick my lips and then lower the sheet I've raised as a flimsy barrier between us.

His pale eyes grow hot. All fire and ice as he watches my hands, tracing the slow descent of my pastel floral sheets until they and the comforter bunch at my waist. I don't wear the sexiest clothing to sleep in. T-shirt and sweats because it's cold in Washington in, but the offer is symbolic, letting him in instead of shutting him out.

"No," I whisper. "I don't want you to stop."

Edmond's eyes take on a hungry expression. It's not one of lust, but something deeper that he craves but neither of us can put a name to it.

"You're going to destroy me." He sounds almost vulnerable, and it pierces my heart like a million Cupid's arrows.

"Never." The vow surprises me, but I know what he needs. I know what we both need, and the words tumble free even as I wiggle over and invite him into my bed. "You're safe with me."

Chapter Twenty-Nine

Edmond

S *afety.*

Its definition is simple: to be free from risk and danger. Rina is offering to be my safe harbor when I've never known such a simple concept. I was born into a violent lifestyle, raised by nannies, shoved into my first dance class at three, learned how to shoot a gun when I was seven years old, and ballet and martial arts by eight. Though my first weapon had been a BB gun, the lesson was a vital one on how desensitize myself from killing.

Rina has seen the worst of me. The beast that lives beneath the mask and fine trappings of my expensive suits and affluent polish.

And she's inviting me into her bed, offering me *safety* as if she's offering me everything my lovesick self craves. I'm not worthy of it – or her – but I'll take it anyway. I'm not a good guy, even if I keep the worst of myself from her.

My exhaustion lifts, and wonderment drives me out of my seat. I know it's creepy, but I sat here in the dark, watching her as she slept. Wondering what to do about this little ray of sunlight that is wrapping herself around my very dark heart.

I got up to leave at least half a dozen times. Then she'd make an adorable noise in the back of her throat, or fling herself over to snuggle into the pillows, revealing the delicate curves of her bottom, and I sat right back down. Watching over her as if I were an avenging angel.

And not a daemon thirsting to possess her.

The soft aroma of lavender reaches out to me, wreathing her scent around me. But it's those huge hazel eyes that draw me in, along with the echo of the word which steal shapes her lips.

Safety.

I take off my boots, and stand, hooking my fingers in the hem of my shirt and reel it off.

Rina licks her lips, her attention skittering down to the flesh I'm exposing.

That's right solnyshko, *look at what's yours.*

My body is a roadmap of my life in the *Bratva*. A tale told in jet-black ink and symbolism. One of my first, back when I was simply Nadia's brigadier, had been the dagger tattoo which looks like it is piercing from one side of my throat to the next, and the beginning of my kill count inked in Roman numerals down one forearm.

As I gained infamy, more tattoos came. Until I took on the mantle of *pakhan*. Then what flesh I had left on my chest became a banner for my criminal enterprise.

From the twin, eight-pointed stars that perfectly decorate the front caps of my shoulders, the spider and webs on my elbows, the matryoshka doll that inclines along my side, to the crowned skull that wraps around my throat, the enormous cross on my chest, to the scrolling *vor v zakone* along my abdomen.

It would take Rina's touch to feel the raised scar tissue and read the braille left behind by the knife wounds and bullets I've taken and survived. As is the way, once they'd healed, the tattoo gun came out and replaced the scar with a symbol of strength or a vow of revenge.

And finally, the many, many *Bratva* symbols which decorate my forearms and the stylized tattooed rings on my fingers. The Vasiliev family insignia is that of a rose blooming on the top of my right hand.

Rina stares as I drop my shirt, and I wonder if she regrets welcoming me into her sanctuary. Where she is soft and sweet, I am hard-edged and violent.

I stop beside the bed, watching the unconscious flick of her tongue as she drinks in my body. Her attention lingers on the sharp definition of my well-muscled abdomen, and the angular line of my defined Iliac furrow.

"Do you want to touch me, *solnyshko*?"

Rina squeaks and I watch as her cheeks flush a fetching shade of red. She tries to scurry her way beneath her sleep-rumpled sheets. But I stop her by grabbing her hand, holding it in the snare of my diabolical hands.

"Don't be afraid, I'll only bite you if you beg me to."

I love making Rina gasp. I've already made her cum and she's still as innocent and sweet as if I've never laid my filthy hands on her soft skin.

Her fingers tremble as I draw her hand closer, before setting her palm flat against my stomach. Only a hand's breadth above my belly button, and not *lower,* where my cock aches for her touch. My dick is hard, twitching involuntarily behind my jeans. She'd have to be blind not to see the tent pole I'm pitching.

But she wouldn't be my innocent *solnyshko* if she leers my erection. She steadfastly keeps her eyes above the waist.

"What does that mean?" Her fingers trail the Cyrillic

lettering, occasionally digging the edge of her nail in and leaving goosebumps in her wake.

"It translates to thieves within the law."

"So, you're a criminal that follows the law?"

I bite back a laugh, and instead lean down and brush a kiss to her forehead.

"No, it means I am one of the criminal elites in the *Bratva* and follow a specific code of conduct in how I do business. The thieves' code is a set of unwritten rules which I adhere to, and the guidelines referenced in the tattoo."

"A thieves' code." She sounds skeptical, but she accepts my explanation for what it is.

Her fingers continue their voyage, pausing whenever she comes across the rough, gnarled flesh of a scar. Her eyes widen when she reaches the perfectly round bullet wound that pierced my side. The mark is self-explanatory, and she doesn't pry, which I'm thankful for.

That bullet nearly ended me when I sought revenge for my father's assassination. If Mikhail hadn't been there, pulling my ass from the literal fire, I would have buried at the same time Pops had.

I let Rina's hand drift away as she wiggles back against her pillows.

"There are so many."

"It would take me a long time to explain them all. Russian organized crime is very big on symbology."

The bed shakes as I plant a knee in the mattress, digging my thigh against Rina's hip.

She gasps as she looks up at me, prowling over her until she's trapped not by my body weight, but by the force of my presence.

"All you need to know *solnyshko* is that I'm a very bad man."

Rina squirms as the memory of the night before invades into the present. There's a look in her eyes as if she's regretting letting me so close.

I don't let that seed get a chance to germinate.

Curling my fingers into her hair, I fist a hank of her sleep-tousled strands. "Give me your mouth."

"Edmond." She breathes my name as if it's a prayer, filling me with the heady power that I hold over her.

I am a sinner, but when Rina's melting beneath my grip, I feel like a saint.

She shakes her head, flushing pink across her pretty peaches-n-cream complexion.

I don't like 'no' in any form.

"And why not?"

Her blush darkens as if I've smeared blood across the apples of her cheeks. "I have morning breath."

Christ.

"I don't care. Give me those lips."

Her pulse jerks, spasming like a living thing caged beneath her skin.

Finally, she obeys. Her lips part, offering me hints at the tender pink cove of her mouth. One that I will soon sink my cock into. Along with the matching, sultry pair between her thighs.

I give another yank on her hair, not letting up until she draws her fingers up over my naked chest. She pauses when her palm hovers near my heart.

Letting her hair go, I lay my hand over top her own, pressing the heel of her hand into the naked flesh there. It's not marked. Not a single hint of ink dares seep across that pectoral muscle. Long ago I'd reserved that patch of skin for my future wife's name.

"Do you feel that?"

Her eyes search mine as she nods.

"My heart beats just for you. Until I met you, I wasn't sure I even had a heart."

"Are you always so intense?"

I give you a fiendish grin. "When it comes to you? Yes."

Her forehead scrunches, causing her nose to lift. I can tell she doesn't believe me.

But she will. Because she's mine and I don't let others play with my toys.

Losing patience, I pull her into me, crushing her beneath the weight of my body.

She grows soft as I lower my head, forcing her to look into my eyes as I close the scant distance between our mouths. I catch her bottom one with a rough snag of my teeth. Hard enough that when I relinquish this kiss, there will be a bruise left behind. Marring her sweet skin with the testament of my attention.

I don't have to tell her to let me in. Her lips part, and she grants me unfettered access. I sweep in, my tongue, teeth, and lips ransack her mouth until the air we share is filled with wet suction.

The soft, musky scent of her arousal, coupled with the light grind of her pelvis against my thigh, wakes the possessive need inside of me. I had only meant to kiss her, and then tuck us both into bed together for another few hours of sleep. Dawn has barely broken on the horizon, the sky outside more midnight blue than light, fostering the tranquil, cocoon-esque ambiance of Rina's bedroom.

But when I feel the needy squirming of her body beneath mine, my thoughts divert from sleep into making her come for me.

I lift my head, freeing her lust-bruised mouth. The glint of arousal plays in her eyes. Their color is akin to a fine aged whiskey, with hints of amber and moss, and making me feel drunk off of her attention.

"Do you want me to play with your sweet little pussy, Rina?"

Rina's mouth jars open, but she doesn't quite gasp. The noise gets stuck in her chest, thrumming there like a moan.

I love shocking her. I crave seeing the painted heat of embarrassment and pleasure smudging her face. She makes an incomprehensible noise in the back of her throat.

"That sounds like a yes. I'll make you come before I tuck you in."

Rina's head drops into the cozy pillow cluster beneath her head. Her hair spread around her in a fusion of warm blond, revealing the subtle reddish undertones.

Stripping her bare would be too much temptation. Though I hesitate for a split second, thinking about all the liberties I could take when she's so warm and supple in her bed. I could violate every inch of her and pluck that sweet cherry.

"Tell me yes. I want to hear your consent."

There's a lot that I can take. But this is important. I want the first time, whether it's *her* first time, or just the first time between us, to be special.

Rina trembles with erotic delight beneath me. Her body arcs, fitting all of those soft, splendid curves into my body.

Then she says the magic words that doom us both.

"Yes," she moans. "Yes. Please, fuck me, Edmond."

Chapter Thirty

Rina

Edmond groans against my throat, warming it with the humid busk of his breath. That sound shoots straight between my thighs and sounds as if my consent is the most important thing in the world to him. The noises he makes is almost indescribable, relief edged with a growl.

It's the sexiest thing I've ever heard.

I'm completely lost in the heat of him. Seared by the way he craves me. He's dazzled me with his intensity, and no matter what might happen in the future, I won't regret *this*.

This moment.

This man.

This experience.

"Have you touched yourself thinking of me, *solnyshko?*"

I'm on fire both by the lust he ignites in me, and the blush that makes my entire body burn. On a cerebral level I know there's so many things wrong with this. That I'm basically signing myself up to one of those *Mob Wives* programs. God forbid Edmond gets arrested and throw in jail for a million years. But I can't help it. He's taken hold of my mind and emotions, and I don't want to get them back.

"Yes." I choke out the admission as his lips continue their devastating caress down along my neck.

His rumble of approval kisses my lips before his mouth claims them. Once more stealing my breath away but giving me his as he plies my lips apart and jousts with my tongue.

"Do you know how long I've thought about holding you down? I've wanted nothing more then to fuck you, pin you beneath me and plow into your sweet little pussy. I've gotten off to you, remembering how fuckable and submissive you looked tied up to your bed. And how hard you came on my face. I've wanted to ravage you since the first moment I saw you on your hands and knees in your classroom."

His confession spikes me, making me quiver beneath him. He plants his fists in the mattress, leveraging himself above me so that I can't shy away from the impact of his words or the fire that melts the silver of his eyes.

"I knew I would ruin you. I didn't realize you'd destroy me too."

I can't breathe through his confession. My pulse is a volatile *thump* in too many places to keep track of; my head, my ears, my *fucking* pussy. I tremble as he catches me up in the torrent of his lust. The only thing to hold onto and keep my head above water and not *drown* in his fervor is *him*. I clutch at him, giving myself over to his attention.

"Good girl. My good girl."

His mouth feasts on mine until I lose track of everything. The two of us slowly combust. Each kiss leads to another one, until I'm in a lust-drugged stupor beneath him.

Then he touches, and I want to cry out at how sensitive my skin is. His palms aren't calloused, but his hands are manly, just a touch rougher than my own. Reminding me that those are not *my* fingers sliding beneath my shirt to cup my breast. I only remember that I need to keep quiet so Lucia doesn't hear us when Edmond shoves my shirt up, and his sinful mouth hovers above my turgid nipple.

"Mmm, you might need to bite the pillow when I make you cum, *kisa*."

There are too many layers between us. Edmond takes his time, unwrapping me like a treat. For a brief second, nothing more than a momentary flare, I wish I owned sexier clothing. But he doesn't seem to mind that I bundle myself in cotton to sleep in. He voices his appreciation, planting a hot, open-mouthed kiss on each patch of skin as he frees me of the fleecy layer.

"You are so beautiful." His breath turns into a staccato, and he rumbles some deliciously sexy Russian words against my breast.

I'm beginning to think Edmond is a tit-man, even though I've not been bestowed by the breast fairy in *any* way. He worships the small, pert globes, and nips and suckles on each nipple until I'm a writhing mess beneath him.

"Oh my God," I pant. I want more. I need his hands, his touch, his *mouth* all over me.

"Not God," Edmond says, so damn smug as he looks up at me. "But you can praise me like I am one."

Then he rakes my pants and panties off in one fluid move, letting me feel the cool rush of air across my sizzling-hot flesh.

"Ahh so wet for me. I love how you melt when I touch you."

I don't have time to *think* let alone formulate a response. His mouth falls, and those devastating, *hungry* kisses he'd given my mouth are introduced to my pussy. He *devours* me, and I yank the pillow over my head to smother the cries he's pulling from me with every flick of his tongue.

"So sweet, like the best fucking candy." I squeal as Edmond

nips his teeth into the tender flesh of my inner thigh. "I want to sink my teeth into every inch of you."

I'm so close to climaxing. My thighs flutter around Edmond's face, trembling while he pins them open with the width of his shoulders.

"Mm not yet, *solnyshko*. When you cum it's going to be all over my cock."

He yanks the pillow away, bunching it to the side of my head. I lay shuddering beneath him, thighs akimbo, breasts bouncing with my ragged breathing.

"You look so good coming undone for me."

"Please, Edmond, please."

"Keep begging for me." His voice is a panther's growl. I've always suspected Edmond has a dancer's background. He moves so gracefully, as if he should be on *So you think you can Dance?* or one of those other amateur dancing shows. That fluidity to his movements is more apparent as he disrobes in half the time it would have taken me to remove my shirt. His every movement is economical.

Then he's naked before me, and I'm completely wrecked by the sight of him. I drink him in. He preens above me, stroking his hand down across the breadth of his chest, surfing his palm over the rock-hard washboard of his abdomen, before he encircles the base of his cock with his tattooed hands.

"Look what you do to me."

My mouth *and* pussy waters as he strokes his cock with one rough jerk from the root all the way to the swollen, bulbous tip. He's thick, but to me his shaft is the perfect length and girth. Not porn-star big or anything overlarge, but wide enough that I know he's going to stretch me so, so good.

"I need you in me." Desperately I stretch my legs wider, hooking my knees on the outside of Edmonds. Instinct demands I lift my hips, and I don't feel a lick of embarrassment as his eyes drop.

"So wet for me. Fuck." He's a man undone as he slides between my thighs. Big and heavy and everything I want.

His fingers curl against my nape, tugging on my hair so I'm forced to look up at him.

"Am I the first?"

I swallow the huge heart-shaped knot that makes breathing difficult. Trembling, I force a single word free. "Yes."

Edmond's eyes darken to pewter, not as if a shadow has crossed his eyes. But as if a fiery forge has turned their light color igneous.

"I'll be the only."

I'm not prepared for the blunt pressure of his cock-head probing at my opening. Nor the sudden strain of flesh parting as he rubs himself against me. It's tantalizing, teasing me with the want of more.

Edmond groans above me. "So tight and so hot. You're going to be the death of me."

My head sinks into the pillow as he eases in, letting my body adjust to each inch he feeds me.

"Oh my God," I chant, breathing those three little words as he pulses in, then eases out, working my pussy open as if his cock was a magical key and my pussy the eager, soppy lock.

There is a tiny pinch in one of those deeper thrusts, followed by a sensation I can only describe as burning. I gasp around the almost painful pressure, before he pushes through, filling me to breaking with the full girth of his cock.

I cling to him, trembling as my body clenches and spasms around the thick invader between my thighs.

"Good girl, such a good girl taking my whole cock. Fuck." Edmond's brow touches mine, putting his mouth in range of mine. I cling to his kisses, soaking in the pleasure and heat between us while my body relaxes.

A minute might have passed, or ten. Time is immaterial. But he eventually settles atop me, pinning me beneath the largess of him.

"Better?"

"Yes."

His grin is devilish. "Good."

I thought I'd been prepared. But Edmond shows me how wrong my thinking had been. His body is a piston, relentless, as he strokes his cock in-and-out of me. I'd asked him to fuck me, but this isn't carnal or a quick finish.

Edmond makes love to me.

He knows it too. His eyes don't leave mine as he drives into me. Filling the bedroom with the obscene sounds of sex. All while caging me in the protective grasp of his muscled arms.

As the ache in my muscles vanishes, I wrap my legs around him. Holding onto him as he shows me just how *good* it is between us.

I can only whimper his name as he pounds into me, pushing me into an orgasm that makes fireworks detonate behind my fluttering eyelids. And sends whorls of effervescent heat shooting all through my veins.

He silences my wild, pleasure-filled cry with a kiss. Tasting my ecstasy. He powers through my climax, never stopping that perfect, *ceaseless* rhythm. Until he joins me. Driving into me so hard, so deep that it's as if the two of us are fused together. His animalistic groan vibrates my lips as his shaft pulses, and he comes inside me.

Chapter Thirty-One

Rina

"**I** made a mess of you."

The two of us drowse in bed together, tangled up together beneath my sheets. I can feel the evidence of Edmond dripping between my thighs. But I'm not in any hurry to clean up. That requires leaving the bedroom, and dashing to the bathroom and hoping that Lucia doesn't see my post-sex glow.

I blink as I realize a vital part that we missed. Though I'm not too worried about it, since I'm on the shot for hormonal reasons.

"We didn't use a condom."

While I don't teach sex-education, I'm a teacher for heaven's sake! I know the risk of single birth-control. And I didn't even have a thought about protection.

"I haven't had a partner since my last screening." Edmond hoists himself on his elbow and looks down at me. "You can't catch anything from me. Are you worried about pregnancy?"

I can't read the look in Edmond's eyes. It makes my heartbeat faster, and my girlie bits suddenly flutter with warmth. His gaze is possessive, *hungry*, as if he's imagining filling me up with his seed until I get pregnant.

Honestly, he's the type of virile calamity that would overpower even the most robust birth control. He could probably impregnate an entire city with just a smile.

But bringing a baby into Edmond's world?

What would we do if he was assassinated?

I have such an easy-to-read face. Everything I'm thinking flashes over it. And Edmond is far too good at deciphering it.

"Hey." His free arm wraps around my waist, hauling me into his side until I am caged in the mountain of his body. "No matter what happens or what you decide, I'm here for you."

"I would love to have a family." I didn't want to be emotional after sex. I never thought I would be. But having such a powerful orgasm, and realizing that I'm *falling in love* with Edmond, petrifies me. Now thinking of a family, the one thing I've always wanted?

I dissolve into tears. They swim in my eyes, blurring my vision.

Edmond holds me, letting me sniffle and cry softly into his chest.

"Family is everything. In a strange way, that's why Pops got involved with the *Bratva*."

Sniffling softly, I lay back and look up at him.

"It was only him and his younger brother after our grandfather died. They took care of them, and Pops showed his loyalty, his fealty, by becoming one of the Brotherhood on his own merit."

Edmond's thumb strokes a soft design across my cheekbone.

"I joined because I wanted to make him proud, and after everything our mother did. I wanted them to be protected if I couldn't. It's a dangerous life, but each of us chose it."

"Is it a choice if you've been raised with that expectation?"

In a way, Edmond is a victim of indoctrination. Did he really have a choice if his father pushed him from the start?

Edmond's brow furrows, as if he's never quite thought about his life and choices in that view.

"I wanted to protect Nadia, I wanted to be sure nothing happened to my siblings and any family I might have. You're probably right that I didn't have a choice, but protecting those I care about is the most important thing to me."

A knight in blackened armor.

His confession makes my heart ache for him.

"You would be a great father," I whisper against his chest.

He stiffens against me, and for a fearful moment I wonder if I've said something wrong. Then he relaxes, and I'm swept up in a surge of his roaming hands and ravenous kisses. My head spins through the onslaught, each feathery caress and nip of his teeth feeds the starving spaces inside me. Until I feel as if I'm flooded with warmth and light. Edmond kisses me as if the air in my lungs is the very breath he needs to survive.

By the time he's done with me, my lips are kiss-bruised and a steady, wanton pulse has kicked up between my thighs again.

"How can you see the good in me?"

Edmond's eyes are bright, but there are shadows on his brow and a tick of anger tugging down the corners of his mouth.

"You are so soft and sweet, the light in my very dark world. You should be disgusted with me. You should hate me."

Hate? How do you hate someone who makes your heart feel full to bursting?

"Because there's good inside of you. I see how you are with Mila. And how you treat me? I feel like a princess. That you pledged your whole life to protecting your family. People don't just do that. No matter what you *need* to do to protect them, you'll do it and that means more to me than anything."

Edmond's eyes close, as if he's dazzled by my words. "You're too good for me."

I drag my nails down his chest, until my knuckles brush along the iron-hard length of his awakened cock.

"Or maybe I'm just bad enough."

I tug him against me, leading his slick, sticky shaft between my thighs.

Edmond groans, not needing any more encouragement as he claims my lips in a hungry kiss. And then sinks into my slick core with one rough hip thrust.

I'm sore, but it feels so good being filled up with him again. There are words between us – three of them – that we can't yet speak. At least I can't. I've never been in love, and I don't know if this is just the heady high of my first lover, or if the fire can build into something everlasting.

While I keep them to myself, I let my body show Edmond what he means to me.

And he does the same, fucking me into the mattress until the two of us shatter together in a burst of passion and mind-melting heat.

Chapter Thirty-Two

Edmond

Mondays are not restaurant-friendly. That a few days passed since I taught Barrett his lesson, doesn't work in his favor.

It leads me to plot, deciding that he'd gotten off too easy. I still have questions. Our meeting got interrupted by Rina's appearance and my single-minded need to get her covered up and out of *Timberhaus*.

The lack of neon lights doesn't do the old wooden building any favors, leaving it fading into obscurity. Just another hulking building in the middle of Washington's woods set back away from I-5

Leon and Marcus drive ahead of me, arriving fifteen minutes before me. Keeping watch of the few drunken patrons, and the staff, while making sure that Barrett doesn't slip through my net.

I sit in the driver's seat, staring out the tinted windows of the G-Wagon we swapped out for the Rolls Royce since we're 'off roading', and waiting for my Bluetooth headset to connect a call that needs to be handled *before* I entered *Timberhaus*.

"It's me," I say when the person on the other end picks up.

There is a beat of silence, which I imagine Rogers is smothering a curse that he doesn't want me to hear. He's been busy this weekend, what with the fire at *Sindoll's Cabaret*. My people had given him the heads up that time.

Fire Chief Rogers blows out a sigh which crackles through the wireless connection. "Again?"

"Just think of it as the same. It's owned by the same person who would have had an unfortunate accident on Saturday if other matters hadn't gotten in my way."

I wait to hear the words that I pay him good bribe money for. Thirty seconds of silence pass, and I begin to wonder if I need to fix the next election for fire chief when he rolls over and shows me his greedy, corrupt belly.

"What do you need me to do?"

I grin in the dark, my attention focused as a laser on the bar's dull sign. "Off I-5. You shouldn't get any alarm notifications down at the station, but if you do, just ignore it. It's isolated out here."

"It's the dry season, Mr. Vasiliev. If a spark ignites a tree or shrub, we'll be looking at a forest fire. And I won't be able to keep that quiet. The state fire brigade will be all over it."

"I'll have it handled. Have I ever let any of my burns get out of control?" Over the years I've learned to master the art of a 'controlled burn'.

"No," Rogers says begrudgingly.

"You'll receive your evergreen bouquet in the morning."

I end the call and put the Chief out of my thoughts.

Marcus materializes from the shadows at the far side of the building. Where the heavy metal door that leads out to the dumpsters and employee parking lot sits. He has a pair of bolt cutters over his shoulders just in case Barrett increased his security since my last visit.

Raising his hand, he flashes two fingers at me, indicating how many people are inside.

My opinion of Barrett plummets.

Did he think almost losing his hand was the end of our business?

The car door swings open, and I step out onto the gravel. Feeling the bite of the stone through the rubber soles of my work boots. It feels freeing to put on the fatigues that I used to wear as Nadia's brigadier. Despite wearing the power suit for the past two years, it still feels like a costume.

Dark-wash jeans and a black T-shirt help me blend in with the night. The shadows wrap around me, helping to obscure my arrival at the back entrance.

"Security?"

"There was an outside line that looked like it fed the cameras. Leon cut them. We tested the push-bar and looked inside. Nothing. No alarm. He's in the office with one of his servers."

"No bodyguards?" I'm surprised. Anyone who wants to go toe-to-toe with the *Bratva* would hire cannon fodder.

"No, Boss." Marcus shrugs his shoulders as if he too is perplexed by the lack of muscle.

Carefully, the pair of us slip in through the back door. It's a straight shot through the dark kitchen, where the scent of lemon-scented bleach tries to cover up the stench of old grease from the twin set of fryers that bracket the flattop. Instead, it makes a stomach-turning odor that I associate with dive bars like this.

It doesn't get any better as we navigate the narrow corridor right outside. A cheap beer, heavy on the hops, seeps into my nostrils.

I glance through the open archway that leads out into the bar. The dim emergency lights cast eerie shadows on the sawdust-covered floor. The bar stools are empty, showing their wear in the cracks and white stuffing spilling out from the forlorn leather.

Burning this place down is a mercy.

Leon leans against the wood-log wall beside a closed door. A pebbled glass panel fills half the frame, the glass covered in grime until it looks amber in the light.

I run my fingers against the imperfections in the wood, then drop my hand to the battered brass knob, opening it with a brutal shove.

Barrett has a girl bent over his desk. He's mid-stroke, the rough slap of flesh-on-flesh from how he pumps in her continues for one more thrust before he catches sight of me.

"Fuck." He pulls out of the girl, hurriedly trying to zip up his pants. As if I care about seeing his stubby cock flop around. He should have gone for a weapon.

The girl squeals. Her shorts are down around her ankles, her flannel shirt unbuttoned, and her lacy bra raked underneath her breasts, showing off her abundant rack. She wiggles off the desk, trying to right herself. Just seeing her in that position beneath the greasy pig makes me think of Rina, and how he'd *dared* touch her. My anger is reignited, leaving me to want to punch the slimy fuck with my life, until he's a ruin of chopped meat at my feet.

Barrett's the type of guy who tries to fuck every one of his employees. I wonder about the girl that she's letting him. She's older, probably closer to my age, with a faded beauty that reminds me of Harley Davidson's rallies and barflies. Not ugly, but having spent years rode hard.

"Leave."

She stares at me, her jeans half-undone, shirt barely covering her tits. But she nods, doesn't even look at Barrett, and flies past me. Trailing the stench of sex and cigarette smoke behind her.

Leon and Marcus shut the door behind me as she leaves. Now that it's just me and Barrett, they're on guard duty. In case there is someone else lurking in the closed bar.

Barrett gapes at me. His long face was enhanced by his hound-dog expression.

His hand is wrapped, and I'm disappointed to see that he has all five fingers secured in a soft-sided cast. I might have to sharpen my knife.

"Edmond." Barrett looks past me, takes note of the two shadows just beyond his perception, and pales. "Wha-what is this about?"

"Did you think our conversation was concluded?"

"You maimed me, you son of a bitch!" He holds his hand up as if hadn't already appreciated my handiwork.

I reach into my pocket and pull out Iustina, the blade singing free with a mild twitch of my wrist.

Barrett backpedals, trying to put distance between us. He's already up against the back wall, his knees pressing into the edges of a loveseat. I don't try to guess what the stains on the upholstery are.

"Sit." I casually flick my blade hand. The low light, cast by the overhead fluorescents, makes the steel blade gleam. Iustina is hungry to taste Barrett's blood again.

"Edmond..." He holds his hands out, reminding me of Chris Pratt from Jurassic Park. When he's trying to calm down a velociraptor as if it won't just tear his throat out for trying. The sheer hilarity amuses me, making me drop the mask I've cultivated to hide my true self, and let the lunatic's smile shine through.

Barrett drops into the seat as if his limbs have turned to jelly.

I avoid his desk and grab one of the wooden chairs along the wall. The legs growl as I drag it behind me, moving only a few feet away from the cowering manager. I spin it and then straddle it, propping my arms on the wooden back. Crossing my wrists, I let Iustina gleam between us. Barrett can't look away from the knife, as if he's having flashbacks to when I'd sunk it over and over in his hand.

I cut straight to the chase. I didn't want to spend all night interrogating Barrett. If I finished this up in time, I might be able to break into Rina's house again.

"The last time we spoke, you tried to sell me on letting your 'backers' push drugs in my territory."

Barrett finally looks away from the blade and stares at me with a haunted look. As if he's realizing now how badly he mishandled the situation.

He nods.

"And were you aware of my stance on hard drugs before you started dealing Fentanyl out of Sindoll's Cabaret?"

Barrett jerks like a marionette, letting me play with his strings as he realizes just how far I've shoved my fist into his business.

"That was you?"

"Everything is me. Are you really that stupid? Christ." I can't believe this chode.

Barrett withers in front of me as if understanding the outcome of crossing me.

"A couple of the girls told me you wouldn't like it," he mutters.

"That's putting it mildly. Who backed you?"

"Can we cut a deal? I give you the name and this ...goes away?"

"Do you think you're in a position to barter? You got into bed with those fucking leprechauns. If they didn't kill you after they were done with you, you should have realized I would."

I watch Barrett as I would an insect. What is his fear response going to be?

Barrett turns out to be flight. He bolts from the battered couch, scrambling over a low-slung table marred with rings from numerous bottles and wet glasses left to stain on the wood. He leaps over it like a hurdler, fingers outstretched as if he will be 'safe' if he can touch the door.

This is amateur hour.

I slip out of my chair, grab the sides in both hands and swing it like a bat. The wood creaks, but doesn't shatter, as it nails Barrett in the solar plexus; an immovable object battering into a frantic, fragile human body.

Barrett wheezes and topples, landing painfully on his back atop the coffee table. Glasses shatter as he knocks them askew with his flailing arms. Immediately whiskey fumes fill the air.

I take a sniff, placing it as the same distillation that he'd tried buying my goodwill with. With all this imported booze, I can make my Molotov cocktails.

I move to stand over Barrett. He looks like an upended tortoise, rolling side-to-side as he clutches his good arm over his ribs.

"That was stupid," I say mildly.

Then I skewer Iustina into Barrett's shoulder. One of the first lessons Pop taught me was about human anatomy. There are so many weak points on the body, that it's no wonder humans as a species have survived to be at the top of the food chain. I wedge the knife between the humeral head and humerus, cutting through flesh and severing the coracoacromial ligament without getting caught up on bone until he's pinned to the table as surely as a fucking moth to a collector's dissection board.

Barrett's screams break through his terror-driven sobs. They wash over me, a balm on my twisted soul.

"Now, shall we begin again?"

"O'Malley, Brian O'Malley," Barrett pants.

Why is it always the O'Malley's? I should have eradicated them when they took that shot at Pops, but I'd only taken out the old man and let all the other cockroaches live.

A mistake that I'm now going to rectify.

Blood mixes with the booze as I retrieve Iustina, then I lean over him, my whisper the last thing he hears before I send him to hell.

"This is for touching Rina."

I twist my wrist and slash Barrett's throat wide open with one quick swipe. He doesn't realize the wound's mortal as his hands lift, clasping at the second smile that gapes across his neck.

I don't watch him die as I wipe the blade clean on Barrett's sweat-grimed shirt, then stow her back in my pocket with a pat.

I leave Barrett where he lays dying and open the door for Leon and Marcus.

"There's about a half-dozen crates of the Teeling in the office. Use that as fuel."

"Yes, Boss."

I leave the two of them with Barrett's body as I stroll through the bar. I hop over the counter, looking at the swill that Barrett had been pushing to his customer. He didn't have a single top-shelf brand.

Fucking animal.

Picking one at random, I grin as I dump another bottle, and then another, and another. Until the wood is flooded with the noxious fumes of low-brow hooch. When I reach the Grey Goose, I take a shot from the bottle and then tuck it under my arm.

Navigating around the bar, I grab a pack of matches bearing *Timberhaus'* logo. Striking the match, I toss it onto the rag soaked with the alcohol.

The liquor flares up, bright, and blisteringly hot.

I watch the bar top burn for only a second before I leave the way we came in; out through the kitchen and into the back lot.

Only a couple of minutes pass before Leon and Marcus join me beside Mercedes Benz. I pass vodka to Marcus, who takes a swig, and hands it over to Leon.

The three of us sit there, leaning against the SUV's hood, occasionally sipping from the cheap-as-shit vodka, watching *Timberhaus* burn.

It takes a little over an hour for the whole thing to burn down to its foundations, turning Barrett into little more than a footnote in Echo Bay's history.

And as I promised Rogers, not a single ember dares ignite the surrounding woodland.

Chapter Thirty-Three

Rina

"Did you hear?" Zoe's voice is a conspiratorial whisper as she sneaks up beside me. I nearly smack her with the metal ladle I'm using to scoop out perfect portions of the wedding soup for table twelve.

"Hear what?"

"*Timberhaus* burned down last night."

I freeze, dripping soup onto the stainless-steel countertop. Is it a coincidence that the bar has burned down only a few days after Edmond threatened to do it?

I wasn't born yesterday. So no, it isn't a coincidence.

Why had Edmond gone back?

This morning, when I woke, my bedroom had been filled with a faint smoky smell. As if a candle had just been blown out, or someone had stood close to a campfire and carried the smoke in with them.

Now I know where the smell came from, and obviously who'd tracked it into my bedroom.

Edmond visited me last night. After apparently torching a

bar. He didn't wake me up, and he's been distant the past two days since the night we shared tangled up in my bed.

Carefully I hang the ladle above the soup station, and busy myself with wiping up the spilled broth. I don't want to ask the question that is banging on my temples.

It rushes out anyway. "What about the owner?"

Zoe grimaces, and I know the answer, even as she says. "He's missing, but it doesn't look good. The firefighters and cops aren't saying, but Raul, one of the busboys, claims they found human remains in the ashes."

Acid churns in my gut, searing a queasy feeling that runs from my belly to my throat.

Did Barrett deserve to be murdered and his business annihilated?

I don't know. Edmond thought so. I just hoped he had a better reason than how Barrett had treated me.

I don't have time to dwell on the macabre gossip. Vince, the manager on duty, bursts through the double doors that separate the kitchen from the serving area.

Zoe turns around, grabbing a plate and skedaddling toward the cold bar. As if she is simply preparing a Caesar salad, instead of churning fodder through the rumor mill.

I navigate both bowls onto a tray, and nearly drop them when our manager's voice cuts over the general noise and ambiance of a working kitchen; the constant hiss of hot water through the pipes as the dishwasher rumbles; the clang of plates and the clink of silverware; the exhaust fan purring as it sucks up heat and smoke from above the stoves; and the sizzle of flame and heat as food is prepared.

"Rina," Vince barks like a drill sergeant.

All the noises seem to fade away as if someone has turned off the background soundtrack, leaving me in the spotlight. I don't have any beef with, Vince. He's a hard worker and runs the upscale Italian restaurant with a precision that can almost be considered micro-managing if it doesn't work out so well.

"Yes?"

"I need you to go down into the cellar and pull this bottle." He hands me a sticky note with the title on it because I will never remember the year let alone the grape he's requesting.

"Oh-oh, a high roller!" Another of the waitress's crows as she swings into the kitchen.

I know nothing about wine. Only what's printed on the wine list we hand out to our customers, and the little notes about pairings, like how red wine is great with beef and white for fish. There are a few bottles on the menu that are in the high four figures. I can only assume the bottle Vince needs is one of them.

"Can you see that table twelve gets these soups?"

"I got you."

I hate going down into the wine cellar. It's exactly what I imagine would be in an old Sicilian estate; a basement kept chilled and dark to preserve the numerous bottles of wine stored there. I always feel as if I am one step away from tumbling down the stairs and breaking my ankle.

I swallow my annoyance and carefully descend into the underbelly of the restaurant.

The wine cellar isn't as vast as say, a wine bar. Our list is only four pages. Not like *Vino Venue*, a place I'd visited with friends back in Arizona. The wine list was three times the length of the normal menu.

Here, at least, the shelves are color-coded by varietal, so I can figure out the general vicinity of where the bottle I need is located. But I still need to roam around the cubbyholes to get to that point.

Usually, it gets rather warm in the kitchens, but I'm glad I wore a long-sleeve shirt today. Instead of a black polo, which was the only other option we were given for our uniform. Rubbing the damp chill away from one arm with my other hand, I decide to begin my search at the far end of the basement. The bottles are dusted pretty religiously, but there's a patina on the really old bottles that no amount of buffing can eradicate.

I crouch down, pulling a bottle free to see if I'm in the right varietal, and then hopefully be able to narrow it down to year.

A soft scuff of what sounds like a foot on the stone distracts me.

I frown. There shouldn't be anyone else but me down here. So why does it sound as if another person is walking on the stairs?

I hold my breath, waiting to hear movement.

When nothing more disturbs the quiet, I shake my head. I'm jumping at shadows.

Striking out with this particular row of reds, I stand up and make my exit to check the backside of the aisle and its cubby. But I run straight into someone quietly lurking in the gloom. They spin me around, only letting me see a flash of jet-black clothing before they shove into me from behind. I'm pushed and dragged back toward the darkest crevice of the basement. Where the light barely shines because the wooden shelves are too tall.

I try to scream, but a hand slaps over my mouth from behind. Cutting off any plea for help. Hot and cold battle it out inside of me, leaving my skin feverish, but the quivery chill of fear infusing my veins.

I'm in the middle of a panic, digging my heels into the ground, and throwing my body weight against the person holding me by my arms and face, when I'm pushed forward. My hands jerk out, catching myself from slamming face-first into the brick. I don't get much leeway, because the person - a man by the sheer size of him - crowds me in.

I try and remember the self-defensive moves I'd read about online. There's never enough time in a day, so I've never actually gone and attended a class. Luckily, you can learn just about anything through YouTube. They don't connect. Instead, the man *laughs*. As if my self-defense is funny and not intimidating.

I freeze as he wraps his free arm around my waist, holding me flush so that my bottom fits into the crux of his. There's no hiding how hard he is. His cock is an iron bar nestling between my buttocks, kept from more lurid contact by my pointelle-knit slacks and what I know is a pair of really expensive suit pants.

The fight fades away, leaving me trembling for another reason entirely.

Edmond.

"Mmm. You walked into my trap so innocent, *solnyshko*." His voice is a predator's growl in my ear, while his hot breath strokes the sensitive nerves against the side of my neck. "When did you realize it was me?"

He spins me around so that my back is pinned to the wall, and his hands fall away from my mouth, before finding a purchase on my hips.

"You're a bastard. You scared me."

"That," he murmurs as he leans over me, snagging me in the heady intoxication of his chameleon eyes. They look bluer today, dark and intense, and remind me that he'd likely *killed* a man last night. "Is entirely the point."

He doesn't give me time to talk or complain about being afraid. He attacks my mouth as if he's starved for the taste of me. Honestly, I'm desperate for his kisses. Those deft fingers dart up along my side, before curling around my ponytail. He uses it as a leash to yank my head back so he can attack my mouth with a deeper, harder ferocity.

I'm swept up in him, holding on to the violence-edged cyclone that is his attention. His teeth rake my lips, while his tongue sweeps in, conquering the sweltering depths with the ardent dip of muscle. Somehow, either I bite my tongue, or he bites his but there's the unmistakable bloom of copper pennies on my tastebuds.

Edmond groans and slowly ends the kiss. His mouth is red as if he'd been eating strawberries instead of my lips. He lifts his thumb to his mouth, wiping away the crimson. Holding it up, he grins down at me. The look is the most demented, deranged thing and it makes my knees buckle.

He holds me up effortlessly. "You bit me, *solnyshko*."

I bit him?

"Maybe I should call you *Kisa* instead."

"What do those mean?" I'd meant to google a translation if I could only figure out how to spell it.

"*Solnyshko* means 'little sun'. You are the ray of light in my dark, dismal underworld."

His grin is wicked as he lowers his nose to my neck, drawing shivers up and down my spine with how his cheek roughs against my skin. He's clean-shaven, as always, but Edmond has a perpetual five o'clock shadow, which makes the gruff tenderize my skin with a rasp like sandpaper.

"*Kisa* means kitten."

What's a girl supposed to do when faced with such endearing, adorable pet names?

I melt, as the bastard knew I would.

Edmond

"You shouldn't be here." Rina scowls at me as if her angry face doesn't look like a pixie trying to look tough.

I wrap my arms tighter around her until her soft breasts crush into my chest. "I can be anywhere I want. I own the place."

Rina huffs, still squirming in my arms.

I pin her in place, a warning growl rumbling in her ear.

"Is that what you want? Do you want me to close the restaurant, send everyone home, and then have you cum on my face?"

The fight evaporates from her in a shocked gasp, capitulating her into my greedy hand.

"I'd do it for you too. You're worth everything."

Rina has her hair up in a bun, and the bastard part of me wants to unwind it. But I don't. Instead, I stroke my knuckles against her jawline, lightly pinching the skin between my forefinger and thumb.

"Go out with me this weekend."

Rina blinks up at me, mouth agog that I'm asking her for a date. "I shouldn't."

"Why not? It's not like you have to work."

The expression that flashes over her face tells me she's heard about *Timberhaus* and Barrett. I hold still, wondering what her reaction is going to be. Is she going to rage? Shy away? Shun me for murdering her former boss?

Her teeth flash as she worries her bottom lip. A tiny line beaches the soft sorrel of her brows into the furrows there.

"Do you regret what you do?"

I drag my fingertips down along her neck, leaving my mark on her. Though it's invisible, I know they're there. That I'm the one, the only one, who touches her.

"I don't think either way about it. I do what needs to be done. Barrett needed to go, and so I put him in the ground."

"That's so brutal." Rina shifts against me as if she wants to cross her arms and physically block me out.

I won't let her. Instead, I push closer until she can feel the war-wrought length of my body against hers. My war isn't fought in the sands of Afghanistan or other far-off countries. But in the shadows that stretch from Seattle to Tacoma and all the way here to Echo Bay. I protect what's mine.

"My life is brutal. I need someone sweet and soft to help buff the edges away."

I look at her from beneath my brows, knowing just how susceptible she is to my charm and the steely glint in my eyes.

"Will you be that softness, Rina?"

My girl tries so hard to be tough. But she melts against me, wanting to believe that the love of a good woman might change me. And not that letting me in will ruin her.

I'm okay with that. As long as she's mine.

"Fine," she mutters. "I'll go out with you."

That's my good girl.

To show her my approval at how easily she agrees, I slip down her body, intent on making her forget the stress of working and steal these few moments of pleasure with me.

Her dainty fingers flex on my shoulders as if she's trying to yank me upright.

"Edmond, you can't do that he—oh my God."

I grin up at her once my knees hit the cement. She's doe-eyed, shocked that I'm face-level with her pussy. Even though I've seen and had ever bit of her. Her innocence remains, untouched by my passion. As if it's made of diamond and not something easily destroyed like tissue paper.

Ignoring the possibility that someone will enter the wine cellar and see me feasting on her luscious cunt, I continue my seduction. No one will come down. Those who frequently fetch the wine saw me stalk down after Rina. They'll stay away until one of us comes back. Vince will serve excuses if someone does order one of the more expensive bottles, and not the more common mid-range wine bottles that are always kept on hand in wooden cases in the manager's office.

"Yes here. Are you going to be my good girl?"

Rina's eyes slit, and I feel her toes crunch in the cage of her work shoes. Those three words are magic to my girl. They unlock her thighs and get her so wet that I know, once I strip her down of her pants, she's going to be soaked for me.

I rub my knuckle along the seam of her pants. "I didn't hear you, *solnyshko.*"

"Yes!"

I love playing with her. Her innocent reactions fuel the fire in my veins. "Good girl."

I watch the blush stain her cheeks as I curl my fingers in the waist of her pants. The relaxed knit flails beneath the pressure of my hands when I rake them down, leaving them in a puddle around her ankles with the fabric trapping her as effectively as any shackles.

"Mmm. Were you expecting me to get between your thighs?"

The previous times I'd had my taste of Rina, she'd worn cotton hipster panties. No pattern, just plain fabric that covered her delicate bits.

I've just unwrapped a present decked out in black lace, the material scalloped high along the outside of her thighs. Slipping my palms up the back of her thighs, I squeeze her bare, naked ass. This style is not quite a thong, even though Rina has ample assets to show off in one, but the cheekier-type cut that shows off her underbuns.

"No. I..I needed to do laundry."

I grin up at her, showing her my hungry smile. Then I smack her, leaving the shape of my hand in bright red on her inner thigh.

"Good girls don't lie. I know you have enough panties to last at least another month."

Rina jerks against the wall I've crowded her into. "Did you look in my pantie drawer!"

Among other places. "Yes."

"You're a devil."

I pry her thighs open, wedging myself between their quivering length.

"I am, and don't ever forget it."

Her panties don't last. Once I place a light kiss on her mons, and I taste the silky wet heat of her cunt drenching the material, I rip them down too. Revealing her well-kept pussy. Only the slight hint of flossy curls cover her mound in dark wisps. Not shaven or a landing strip, but a neat patch of hair that makes her look as innocent as she is.

My cock throbs painfully, making me growl as I try and be gentle with her. It's a fucking battle within myself not to simply take what I want. I could have been balls deep inside her a half-dozen times by now, but I'm teaching her. Introducing my innocent little sunbeam to the ways of pleasure.

Rina's half-mad with pleasure, proving that my patience is reaping tactile rewards. Her hips tilt, rolling that buttery-hot core toward my questing mouth.

I flick my tongue, wedging the tip against the top of her split. Then I lick down, a firm, rough swipe that ends at her slit.

"Oh my GOD," Rina moans. Her earlier protests are gone as she pants for me.

I pull back, just enough to show her the sheen of her juices glistening on my face. The rush of heat wafting off her body is a precursor to a blush. I watch it start slow, staining her creamy skin until she looks like a ripe, delectable strawberry.

Then I feast, and I don't let up until she's riding against my mouth.

I suck gently on her clit, curving it out from its tender hood, and making it swell between the taut knit of her nether lips, with my tongue. She makes soft keening noises, scaling higher and higher until she realizes just how damn loud she's being. Her moans and passionate cries bounce off the cellar's stone walls.

She clamps her mouth shut, sealing her wanton noises behind the press of her palm. A few dribble free, and I endeavor to make her scream.

Riding my fingers between her thighs, I inch my middle one into the velvety heat of her core. The muscles clench, milking the finger and leaving signs of her pleasure smudging all over the tattoos marking my skin. I work her relentlessly, keeping up a steady piston, an intense pressure, before I hook my fingers *like that.* A come-hither motion that her pussy knows means I want her to cum. Being the good girl she is, her pleasure unlocks in a near flood of arousal.

But I want more, and right as she's on the precipice, with her muscles clinging skin-tight on my finger, I suck on her clit, until the potential for climax hits her as a certainty.

She forgets she's being quiet as she cries out, her hips bucking in a frenzy of motions as she tries to fuck my fingers. Seeing her need a bit more pleasure than a single finger can give, I slam another in, stretching her open.

The orgasm I mouth-fuck out of her lingers. She is left wrung out and leaning against the wall, holding it up with the way her soft, curvy body is angled.

Slowly I withdrew my fingers, holding her eyes as I lick the sweet flavor of her off my fingers.

"Mmm. The best fucking dessert, Miss Christenson."

Climbing to my feet, I lean over her, pressing her into a smaller bundle between the cage of my arms. I feed her a taste of herself, the sweet musk that's seeped into my breath and shines on my skin. Her mouth opens, letting me in as I kiss her mouth like I did her cunt.

Deep and hungry.

When I pull back she's staring up at me, those big hazel eyes lagoons in her face.

"I'll have seconds later."

She chokes on a noise as I step back, adjusting the raging length of my cock into a more comfortable position.

"I'll pick you up Friday evening."

Throwing her a wink that lets her know I've gotten what I came here for, the taste of her in my mouth and a date, I stroll back out of the cellar to attend to business.

***

Rina

Edmond is a bastard. I can only stare at his black-clad back as he struts out of the wine cellar, leaving me trying to right myself from the earth-shaking orgasm he's just given me.

I groan as the feeling finally comes back to my legs. He's left me disheveled. Pants and panties all around my ankles. The wetness of my release is sticky between my thighs.

Slowly, I pull my clothing up. Trying to make myself look presentable. As if the damn owner of *La Baia Italiana* didn't just have me coming on his face.

I flush, pressing my palms against my cheeks. I hope that their cooler temperature might calm down the constant heat I know is flagging in my cheeks. Warmth over him noticing my panties and liking the lace, blooms in my low belly. Not even knowing he's invaded my privacy, multiple times, quells the giddy butterflies winging around beneath my ribcage.

Finally, I've dwaddled as much as I can. Squaring my shoulders, I stride up the stairs, skimming my fingers along the cool metal railing that's there to prevent ungainly creatures like me from falling and breaking my neck.

The kitchen is still hustling. Not quite the breakneck pace of the dinner rush, but it's not quiet in any way. I try to find Vince to ask over my tables, but everyone is conspicuously absent. Which I'm thankful for. I'd never thought I'd be doing a walk of shame at work, but here we are.

Zoe cranes her head toward me, waggling her brows at me in a way that I can't mistake. She suspects what Edmond and I did, and she's not letting me cringe away or pretend it didn't.

I slink toward her side, clearing my throat and washing my hands as I return to preparing a salad.

"So," she draws out the word, letting the 'o' turn into a teasing hoot. "What was that about?"

My cheeks are on fire. I can only imagine what I look like. Do I look like I just had an amazing orgasm?

"Mr. Vasiliev asked me out on a date."

Zoe snorts. "Is that all he wanted?"

I can't answer her, because I'm pretty sure my throat's closed up in residual embarrassment and cringing horror that I'm so transparent.

Is the kitchen staff being otherwise occupied a gift from Edmond to spare me my shame?'

Zoe sobers slightly, letting the shared high of my exploits evaporate.

"I hope you know what you're doing." She worries, and I hear the brittle edge that prods at me.

I hope so too.

It doesn't dawn on me until much later, that nobody asked me about the wine. Which I'd forgotten all about. Making me realize the strings Edmond had pulled to get me right where he wanted me.

254

Chapter Thirty-Four

Rina

The days pass in a hurry. I don't have any more shifts at *La Baia Italiana* for the week. Only the days with the kids, and the occasional tutoring session. Despite not working myself to the bone, I'm not worried about the money.

I can't stop staring at the new zeros Edmond added to my bank account after I agreed to go on a date with him.

It's a nest egg that would have taken me *months* working at *Timberhuas* to build up. For the first time in what feels like years, I can exhale.

I spent the time I would have been working with Lucia. Harassing her about school, and bonding over a mani-pedi session. Somehow, she'd heard about my date with Edmond, and declared the state of my cuticles to be 'nightmare fodder'.

The day of, I'm in a state. I have nothing to wear. Even if I did, I don't know how to coordinate an outfit that isn't work related. The last time I went on a date was in college. Back then, I wore jeans and a blouse.

Somehow, I know that wherever we are going, if I am going to be escorted on Edmond's arms, I need more than denim.

That leaves work clothes, but nothing says 'sexy' in my wardrobe. I'm around kids all day. I've built a small selection out of knits that don't stain, and loose-fitting silhouettes. That is how I survive the occasional spill or accident that might happen with my students.

My crisis draws Lucia into my bedroom. She slings herself across my bed, above the mass of clothes I've pulled off the hangers. I think I've gone through everything I own, holding it up to myself in the mirror fastened to the back of my door, and then discarded just as quickly.

"I can't do this."

I've already showered and primped, shaved, perfumed, powdered, and even curled my hair. My hair is very fine, but the humidity of living near the water often leaves it in a frizzy mess. But it's holding up, looking surprisingly silky thanks to the anti-frizz stuff I'd splurged on.

"Is this the state of your wardrobe?"

Lucia lifts a pair of black and white checkered pants, before moving on to a black ankle-length skirt that works with everything.

I sink on the edge of the bed, in the small corner where only a sleeve is flopped into the space.

"Yes." I'm twenty-five dressing twenty years older.

I sigh, then stand up, and begin the search for my phone beneath the piles of clothing.

Lucia sits up, eyeing me with suspicion. "What are you doing?"

"I need to cancel. I can't embarrass Edmond by showing up in any of that."

I'm near tears, trying to stifle and push the disappointment down.

Why didn't I go shopping? I'm sure I would have been able to find something at TJ Max or even Marshalls. Maybe not a designer label or even an outfit like Victoria Malone would wear. But spades better than *this*.

"No!" Lucia dives into the bed and finds my phone before I can.

She spins around, and I swear she's typing a text. Her fingers rapidly move across the screen as her forefinger loops and flicks on the touch keyboard.

I don't worry about it, and instead flop into the backless, velvet-covered chair that's pushed beneath my vanity-slash-desk. I use it more for the latter when sitting in bed grading papers makes my back hurt or causes the sleep demons to come after me. Makeup is another foreign concept. I'm lucky that my complexion has been clear for most of my life. Other than a spot of concealer, I restrict my daily routine to lipgloss, mascara, and a touch of bronzer.

Finally, Lucia stops whatever she's doing on my phone, and approaches me. She stops right behind me, and I stare at her reflection in the tri-fold mirror. The LED light brightens as I push the touch button in the middle of the mirror.

"Stay here. Let's do your makeup. Makeup can distract from even the worst outfit."

"How did you get so smart?"

Lucia grins at me. "Someone has to be. You are ridiculous at being a girl."

Guilty as charged.

I consider my reflection in the mirror during the few minutes that Lucia's gone. I have zero idea what Edmond sees in me. I'm no beauty. I'm average-looking, with smooth skin and hazel eyes that look muddy in most lights. If I were quizzed, I'd say my best feature is my hair. I loved that I was one of the only redheads in my school, even if my hair is a washed-out version; a watercolor strawberry instead of fiery locks. I'm short, and a bit soft because I would rather curl up with a good movie or book instead of exercise, and I don't have any assets to write home about. But when Edmond looks at me, I feel like the sexiest woman alive.

I sigh and prop my chin in my hand.

Lucia finds me scowling at myself. She hustles up and presses her forefinger against the angry furrow which ridges my forehead.

"You're going to give yourself wrinkles."

I feel like the younger sister when Lucia sets a makeup case down on my mostly barren vanity. The black and white striped design is easily recognizable, the flash of pink on the inside as she opens it just as iconic.

"Wow." I stare at what looks like a million shades of eyeshadow, blush, gloss, lipsticks, pencils, and makeup brushes stuffed in the collection.

Lucia has loved makeup since she was thirteen, but I hadn't known she'd advanced from Maybelline to some high-end brands. I guess that's where all the gift cards she's accrued during birthdays and Christmas have gone.

Her smile is wide and proud. "Makeup is just another art form. It's all about shading and contrast."

Pinching my chin, she tilts my face toward the light, angling it side-to-side so the soft white LEDs highlight my features.

"You really should wear more makeup. You have great bone structure. Not as gorgeous as me, but passable." She winks, and I am overcome with sisterly affection.

I throw my arms around her, hugging her tightly. Her hands hover above my shoulders, and then she squeezes me before pushing me back into the chair.

Somewhere along the way, Lucia grew up. It takes sheer

force of will to hold the tears back as she daubs some cream on my face, and begins buffing it in with a hot pink sponge.

As she works on my face, my phone beeps. Though she doesn't let me get it. She grabs it before I can reach it, taps in my passcode that I have no idea how she knows, and reads a text. She hums in the back of her throat, pleased with whatever she's read.

"Who are you texting with my phone?"

"Don't worry about it." Lucia pockets my phone and turns me around so I can't see my reflection.

I have enough to fret about for this date. I don't borrow the trouble and let Lucia work her magic.

And it is magic.

Lucia turns me around, and I blink at the fetching image in the mirror.

That can't be me.

I've always hated my fae-like appearance. I've always thought the only thing missing from the illusion that I belong in some mythical, fantasy court is a frothy dress and pointed ears.

Lucia downplayed my narrow features and gave me a more adult, vampy style. Her advanced sense of color theory, and her light hand at playing with highlights and lowlights, are evident in the makeover she's given me. My eyes have become foxy, the cat-eye liner elongating them until they look more almond and sensual than their wide reality. She's enhanced my cheekbones, carving out hollows beneath them, and then added a dusting of shimmery powder on top. It's a mixture of old-world glam, and pin-up aesthetic, with a modern, sexy allure.

I gape. That's the only thing one can do when one's sister turns her from a frog into a princess.

"Don't you dare cry!"

Lucia knows me so well. I clamp my lips shut as she moves in front of me, waving her hands dramatically in front of my eyes as if that would somehow dry up the wetness gathering on my waterline. I've never thought false eyelashes look good. Maybe because I'm biased against Victoria's caterpillars. But Lucia's used some wispy type that makes my eyes pop and doesn't blind me with their minky curl.

"You have a talent."

"Yes, for painting. Your face is just another canvas."

The doorbell rings, startling me from my mirror gazing.

Lucia bolts, tossing a 'don't move' over her shoulder.

I squint at the alarm resting on my night table. The green numbers tell me I still have thirty minutes before Edmond is going to arrive. Unless it's that pest of a landlord, nobody should be here right now.

An anchor of dread settles into my gut, and drags down my mood. I don't want to deal with the landlord. Not when I'm preparing for a date. He would definitely up the ante on his suggestive rhetoric if he sees me looking like this.

I stand up from the vanity's chair, pacing as the worry lodges beneath my ribs. But when I don't hear the sleazy boom of the landlord's voice, I allow myself to relax a bit.

Then I turn toward the tough, hair-wrenching job before me. I need to put together an outfit out of the contents of my closet. I know it's a Cinderella fantasy, but no fairy godmother has bopped her wand over my clothing. They are still drab, shapeless frocks in primarily black, white, and gray. I never realized how restricted I kept my wardrobe until seeing it laid out like this. It's a capsule wardrobe, of sorts. Everything I own can be paired with everything else.

No matter how Lucia did my makeup, it's not going to be enough for people to overlook this mess.

Glumly, I pick up a dress. When I'd purchased it, I loved its white sailor collar and calf-length. While cute, it's boring.

I hear Lucia's footsteps pound on the stairs as she climbs up them. Another dress is sifted from the pile, and I hold the marble swirl of gray, white, and black that patterns the shift dress in front of me. It hits just below the knee, but it's short-sleeved. It might work.

"Oh god, not that one." Lucia's breathless as she re-enters the bedroom.

"This is hopeless." I turn to face her and then stop when I see the beribboned white box she's holding in her arms.

"Oh. You are, but this is going to fix it."

"What did you do?"

Lucia's smile is enigmatic as she drops the delivery atop the soft nest of my clothing.

I'm helpless as I come up behind her, watching over her shoulder as she tips her fingers under the snug lid, and lifts it. Tissue paper conceals what lies beneath until she twitches it aside and reveals something silky and gold.

"Ohhh." Lucia coos. "He has impeccable taste."

"What did you do!" I'm in a panic as I suspect I now know who she was texting on my phone, and what this gift foretells.

"I told Edmond you were spazzing out about not having anything to wear. He had one of his goons drop this off for you." Her hands are light, careful as she shakes out the cocktail dress, and holds it between us.

The two of us stare at it before Lucia flicks the tag so we can see the designer.

I gasp. We might be poor, but both of us have wished for a better life.

Lucia whistles. "Herve Leger. Damn. He's loaded, isn't he?"

I nod, because he is.

Slowly, I accept the dress and step into it. It's a foiled bandage minidress, fitting tightly from the shoulders, with its straps and texture that crisscross along the back, to mid-thigh, with a cutout that offers a hint of my cleavage without showing too much skin. The whole of it is embossed with a rather iconic bandage texture.

Lucia zips me up and rests her chin on my bare shoulder. With the makeup and now the dress, I don't recognize myself.

"Oh wow." Lucia is speechless too as we stare at the impossibly perfect gift. It's difficult being a redhead with fair skin. It's so easy to look washed out. Gold is *the* color for my complexion, along with greens and darker, jewel shades.

I run a hand down the perfect fit. It's slightly lose around the bust, nothing a tailor can't fix. For something that's not really meant to be off the rack, it hugs my figure like a sublime, gilded glove.

"How does he know what size I am?" I wonder aloud.

Lucia snorts, and then the two of us are giggling. Somewhere, we've shifted from me being her quasi-mother to sisters again. My heart soars as she bounces to my closet, as happy as I am that I'm going on a date. She digs through my pitiful shoe collection. Luckily, black will go perfectly with gold, and she hands me a simple pair of pumps that aren't too beat up.

I balance on one foot, and then the other as I slide into them. Then I'm ready. The high of this makeshift bonding session pops like a needle puncturing a soap bubble.

I'm going on a date with Edmond Vasiliev. A gangster.

Am I crazy?

"No." Lucia's hands clamp on my biceps, turning me toward her so that I can stare into her hazel eyes. She has blue flecks in the iris that I've never noticed before. I've always thought it was unfair that she's taller than me. It makes her seem older than her sixteen years. Now, she uses the few inches she has on me to bully me, and get me to do what she wants.

"You're not going to think this to death. He's not proposing marriage. He's not asking you to run away with him. It's dinner. Enjoy yourself."

It's not like I can confide in Lucia that Edmond's idea of 'dating' is a lot more intense than just 'dinner'. I can't offload the worm eating my brain about him being a criminal. I have no one to confide in that I know Edmond has murdered at least one person in the brief time I've known him and committed arson. It's a lot of information to keep locked in, the weight of the unfamiliar baggage leaving me uncertain. But, I don't want to ruin her happiness and good mood.

Instead, I flash her a smile that folds the edges of my scarlet-glossed lips upward. "Okay."

Then, the two of us head downstairs, where I await my knight in black, blood-stained armor.

Chapter Thirty-Five

Edmond

A flurry of soft voices seeps through the front door in the silence left in the wake of the doorbell.

My breath catches in my chest as anticipation seizes me. I don't know why I'm so keyed up. It's just a date. I've been on thousands, parading gorgeous women from socialites to mafia princesses, on my arm. This just feels differently, and I don't have a fucking clue as to why.

The knob creaks, and then the door swings open, revealing a vision in gold that steps onto the sagging porch.

When Lucia informed me through text about Rina's meltdown over clothing, I felt like an idiot. I'm not normally this far outside of my depth. The women I've had flings with always seemed put together. I'd forgotten that this is my Rina, and she's anything but composed. She is as fragile as spun sugar surrounding a frenetic core of empathy. She takes care of everyone *but* herself. And I need to be the one to support her.

The answer to the problem of Rina's wardrobe had been instantaneous: I gave Evelina my credit card and sent her post-haste down to Echo Bay's high-end boutiques with a bribe - If she can find a dress for Rina, and get it to her in under an hour, she can then buy whatever she wants as repayment.

When Eve returned, her smile had been the cat with the canary as she'd carted a glossy Louis Vuitton shopping bag up to her suite.

Mission fucking accomplished.

Behind Rina, Lucia gives me a thumbs-up, before she bundles a jacket in Rina's hands and shoves her out the door.

She squeaks as her heel clicks, and I immediately cup her elbow. Drawing her small frame into the warmth of my body.

The porch light illuminates the metallic sheen of the cocktail dress which hugs her body as it's intended. My stare travels the swerves of her petite curves, appreciating Eve's eye for fashion. I'm riveted by the way her breasts thrust against the fabric. Bandage dresses were made for the male gaze because I can't look away from that peek-a-boo of flesh the cut-out allows me.

"You look..." I'm never at a loss for words.

Her hair falls in soft waves, barely controlled by some bobby-pin magic behind her ear. It reminds me of a 50s pin-up; the style enhanced by the exaggerated eye makeup and glossy slick of deep red lipstick.

I tuck my free hand into my pocket so I don't tug at my collar. 'Cause *god-damn* am I a lucky bastard.

"Cat got your tongue, Edmond?"

The little minx dares?

I secure Rina against my side, helping her down the stairs and to the Bugatti parked against the curb. Marcus and Leon are in the SUV, waiting for me to leave before they tailgate us to *Merce's.*

"Not yet," I murmur against her exposed ear. "But later, a pussy will."

I love making Rina blush. She turns beet-red, which makes the green in her hazel eyes pop like fireworks.

"You're terrible, you know that?"

I lean in, draping her coat over her. "You keep saying that, *solnyshko*. But you're still here with me."

Shutting the door, I stalk around to the driver's side and slide into the ebony leather seats. A Bugatti is utterly impractical for Washington's winters and twisty roadways. It's a statement piece, meant to catch eyes and curry envy. Which is exactly why I'm driving it on our first date. I want Rina to know that with me, everything she could ever want - let alone need - will be provided.

These thoughts are dangerous. I can feel the warmth and heat that Rina sparks in me thaw out the cold aloofness that I've armored myself with. If I don't let anyone in. If I keep them at arm's length, shoving them away by the hoarfrost-coated walls that armor my emotions, then they can't leave me.

It's worked for years. Until now.

All it's taken is one little sunbeam and I'm completely fucked. Stranger still, I don't hate it.

As I navigate out of Rina's neighborhood and head toward I-5, I let my hand drift to lazy possessively on her bare knee beneath the jacket.

Truthfully, I want more of it.

***

"**Y**ou're very efficient, Milo," I say to the maître de as he ushers us into *Merce's*.

I didn't just call ahead for a reservation, but I booked out the whole restaurant. That leaves only the four of us seated beneath the upscale restaurant's velveteen, star-studded dining room.

Marcus and Leon are at a table near the front, in line of sight to the double doors and vestibule. Outside, two more of my men keep watch. Leaving Rina and I in an elegant bubble lit by mood lighting conjured by candles, string lights, and the crackle of a fire in the fireplace that separates the two dining rooms; the dual-sized, river-rock hearth is as much of a statement piece as it is a heat source.

"Thank you, Mr. Vasiliev." His hand slides against mine and the bundle of twenty fifty-dollar bills I've palmed immediately vanishes into his pocket.

Rina stares up at the stars with the pinpricks of light shining through the gathered material reflected in her eyes. She looks like a fairy princess, holding court, with starlight in her hair and warmth in her cheeks.

"This is phenomenal."

The tension I nurtured since getting that wild hair about taking Rina on a real date, instead of being just a creeper stalking her, fades. In its wake is a damn kernel of heat that's lodged like a bullet in my chest. The sharp, odd sensation isn't dissimilar, though this wound isn't one packed with cold metal. But a fiery ember that makes me feel as if I've been hit by a meteorite. The flame pulses, making me uncomfortably aware of my heart beating in my chest.

Rina picks up the menu that Milo left behind. I can tell when she notices there are no prices attached to the dishes. It's a multi-course dining experience, with different delicacies and protein to choose from. The receipes themself full of locally sourced ingredients. Her lips tighten, and she shoots a look at me through the weight of her lashes. Wisely, she doesn't say anything. Not until our waiter arrives, pours us twin goblets of water, and introduces himself.

"I'm Kyle and I'm pleased to be taking care of you this evening." His attention flicks to me, and I see his Adam's apple bob when he notes the tattoos across my hands and knuckles. But he doesn't stutter as he launches into his spiel.

"Would you care for wine, or perhaps a cocktail from the bar?"

Rina smooths the leather-encased folio on the table. And I can see how her hands shake. Not from the cold, but nervousness. I need to go slowly with her in how I introduce her to a life of wealth.

"I don't know what to get," she whispers at me. As if the waiter isn't hovering expectantly beside our cloth-draped table.

I slide my hand beneath the linen and press my fingers soothingly against her knee. "Do you want me to order for us?"

She looks askance at Kyle, but his face is an impassive mask. Completely polite and impenetrable without judging her. That alone is going to earn him a fat fucking tip.

"Please."

I squeeze her thigh, and then rattle off our order; choosing differently for myself so that we can share each of the courses. The plates are small, as restaurants such as this are wont to be. But the drinks are strong, and the service is white-glove and impeccable.

"And a bottle of the Pauillac red blend."

"Excellent. Thank you, sir."

Kyle slips silently away, taking the menus with him, leaving me to face Rina's flushed cheeks and wrath.

"Pauilliac?" she asks.

The edge of my mouth quirks shamelessly.

She shakes her head, laughing ruefully before taking a sip of water.

"Tell me about your family."

"You're not going to warm me up, *solnyshko*? Just lob hardball questions at me right off the bat?"

"How else am I going to get answers out of you? There's no one else around, except your people. It's the perfect time and place for it. Why, do you want me to ask casual questions?"

Tension skitters through my throat. The last time I was in the metaphorical 'hot seat' was when Pops was still alive, and I got caught flashing my guns on social media. When I messed up, not even Nadia took me to task. She simply let me do as I would as long as it furthered her goals for the *Bratva.*

This time I'm the one reaching for the water glass, stalling as I drink a few gulps of mineral water.

"How much do you know?"

"Google has a lot to say. About Nadia, and the accident. That you're one of Washington's most eligible bachelors. About your Brazilian diamond mines and other businesses and how you took over as CEO after your sister's death. A few smaller gossip sites declare you as the head of the Pacific Northwest mafia syndicate. The pages on the *Bratva* were more detailed, but I still can't see you as one of those old man mobsters from Russia."

"They're not wrong." I shrug nonchalantly. "The Brotherhood has many excellent public relations people that spin whatever story we want them to. Let people think the *Bratva* are obsolete. That way, nobody will stick their nose in our business or assume a man with a Cyrillic surname is in the mafia."

"I'm really surprised that all of that is just out there on the internet." Rina shakes her head, and I can well imagine the kind of stories she's read about me and the Brotherhood.

"I was never meant to be the leader of anything." I don't know why I'm confessing this to her. While I've grown into the role of *pakhan,* the first year was a rough fit. I chafed against the confines and boundaries of my new role; and the thieves' code which I was now forced to uphold.

"Nadia was everything Pops wanted in a successor."

Rina's head tilts head as she listens. We've brushed across this subject before, but now it seems she wants more in-depth knowledge. As if she's educating herself to make a decision.

"Don't get me wrong. He was the most misogynist, hard-as-nails Russian mobster you'd ever meet. But because Nadia was *his* daughter, she alone was the only female worthy of leading. If any of the other families thought to put a woman in charge, he'd have cut out the tongue of the person who suggested it. She was taught to be the iron fist wrapped in a silk glove."

"And you?"

The edges of my smile turned sharp, as jagged as the shards of my soul. "The weapon the fist wielded."

"That sounds like an intense way to grow up."

"I survived it. We all did. Now that Nadia's gone, Mikhail is learning how to become my brigadier." At Rina's confused look, I explain. "He'll be my second-in-command."

Guilt gnaws on my bones when I think of my younger brother. He isn't meant for this life.

"You look sad."

"Do I?" Fuck her for being so perceptive.

I force my arms along the table, holding my palms down so I don't curl my fingers into fists.

"Before Nadia died, Mikhail found a career he loved. His reason for living, he used to say. And I've had to take it from him. He hates me for it."

"What did he do before he...became your second."

"I'll show you." I flash her a look from beneath my eyebrows, and then dip my fingers into my interior pocket, fishing out the jewelry case tucked there. This is her second gift, and one which will serve a dual purpose. Though I'll make sure she only ever thinks of it as a pretty bauble.

The black package is stark and elegant against the white tablecloth. *Mikhail* is embossed in gold on the top of it. These cases had been one of Mikhail's final purchases before he'd shuttered his fledgling business and gone to Russia.

Rina's hands remain in her lap, her breath a shocked, sharp rapport in her chest.

"What is this?"

"A gift. Open it."

Rina snags her bottom lip, tugging on it with her teeth before seeming to remember her lipstick. Then, she slowly curls her fingers around the box. She slides it free from the paper sleeve, revealing the black leather case with the gold clasp and gilded tooling which screams luxury. Mikhail's eye for detail is second to none, and he knew his market well.

Another wave of guilt kicks me in the chest. This time I rub at the spot before letting my fist drop into the shadows beneath the tablecloth.

Rina acts as if a spider or snake is going to leap out of it as she opens the lid. The low lights dazzle on the ruby-red diamonds and emeralds that form the shape of a petite rose on a seamless golden bracelet. In the center, amid the velvet, is a small screwdriver.

"Oh my god."

"Importing jewels is one of my businesses, *solnyshko*. One of my mines produces a surplus of red diamonds. Rare and priceless to some."

"But not to you."

I smile. "Not to me. But, if you hate it, you can sell. You'll get enough money to buy a house."

I don't tell her that one of my more recent red diamonds I put on the market sold for fourteen-million dollars. If she knew, I'm confident that her reaction would be to throw the bracelet at me and refuse to wear it. Which defeats its purpose. I need her to never want to take it off.

"Edmond." She's scandalized, but the haunted look in her eyes is gone.

"Come, give me your wrist."

Stubbornly, Rina keeps her hand from me. "Are you really going to screw that onto my wrist?"

"Of course. Mikhail borrowed the design from Cartier's love bracelet, but made it more lavish, with larger and more colorful diamonds."

Rina's hand shakes as she lays it across the table. Carefully, I loosen the two screws which keep the piece together. Then I tuck Rina's wrist into the bottom half of the gold circle and click the top on it. Before screwing it back together. The sizing is perfect, with just enough give for it to easily move around with her movements.

Once it's secure, I pocket the small, golden tool. Because one of those diamonds, buried on the underside, conceals a tracker. One that will let me find Rina *anywhere*. When it comes to my girl, I've taken my stalking to another level.

That is Mikhail's true gift. His fusion of high-tech espionage with haute couture jewelry. That I've taken his joy from him fills my veins with iron and my gut with lead. The Brotherhood's hierarchy demands I have a second, a successor to take over should an assassin kill me. If I want to follow Pops, and Nadia's vision and keep the Vasiliev in charge, that means Mikhail, at least until Alexander comes of age. That Alex is seventeen and denies my authority as if every vowel he utters is made of wrath, doesn't bode well for him ever willingly stepping into my shadow.

Rina doesn't seem to notice that I've taken the screwdriver. The only other way out of the bracelet is to cut it off. But by the how she watches the firelight cast brilliant carmine prisms in the diamonds, I don't think she's going to be doing that any time soon.

Which is exactly what I want.

Our dinner continues with small talk, interspersed with the quiet, stealthy delivery of appetizers and food.

I've lured Rina closer, until she's at my side. Allowing me to feed her from the *tapas* plates arranged on the tablecloth.

Rina accepts a morsel from my fork, her lips smudged in the sauce that coats the lamb. I've never felt this need to feed someone before. But watching her accept each tidbit I offer her, and then hear her low murr of pleasure, has opened up a whole new kink to me. My cock agrees. I've been suffering in rock-hard agony as she nibbles off of my plate and hers.

I tuck my thumb against her glossy bottom lip, smearing away some of the juice that remains behind. Then I flash her a wicked grin and lick the taste of her *and* the meat off my thumb.

"Delicious."

There is a commotion just past the dual-sized fireplace. I catch sight of one of my men, one of the two left outside to keep an eye on our perimeter. He strides through the hallway, meeting my eye before he pauses like a good soldier at Marcus' and Leon's table.

I stifle a sigh as the threat of *business* looms.

I ignore it for now, keeping watch behind Rina as the guard bends low and whispers in Leon's ear. The three confer, speaking in hushed tones that don't carry above the soft music that's piped in from the discreet, overhead speakers.

Picking up my stemmed glass, I swirl the dark currant-colored wine and take a small sip.

"Is something wrong?" Rina notices my distraction, and I cut her a warm smile. I'm already putting back the wall that this interlude has brought down. It's surprising how the company of a good woman makes one forget the realities of life.

Such as I'm a gangster in the middle of a brewing war with the Irish.

Leon unfolds from his table, drops his napkin in his seat, and heads my way.

The guard returns to his post, disappearing beyond my view as if knowing I want his head to roll for interrupting my dinner.

Leon stops at a polite distance. He gives Rina an apologetic smile, but his eyes are burning with information that I need to know.

I beckon him closer.

"Boss." Leon's voice is a rough basso, rolling over my title with a cut of apology in his breath.

He approaches, and bends low, making sure that this round of 'telephone' is for my ears only.

"Cody and Ryan are outside. They routed one of the Irish safehouses near Olympia. Things got ...rough. They believe the guy they have has information, but it's now time sensitive."

Even in privacy, there's a code to what he's telling me. A few key phrases send the rest of my good mood plummeting in a fiery crash.

Translated: Cody and Ryan went in, guns blazing. There's only one mick left, and he's probably bleeding out right now in the trunk of their car. If I want to interrogate him, I need to do it now, or else hire a fucking medium to contact the dead.

I nod, and Leon backs up a few paces. Behind him, Marcus is already standing. They knew what my answer would be. Business always comes first. I learned that during my year of training in Russia. Nothing supersedes *the work*.

"Something needs my attention."

I shove my chair back and rise. Rina has a pout on her face and a few wrinkles furrow her brow. She looks gorgeous in the candlelight, and I stop and take a mental snapshot of this moment. Just in case I never get to see her like this again. The wine gives her a soft flush and a wanton look in her eyes that makes me want to take advantage of her.

Pausing at her chair, I cup her chin and draw her toward

me for a lingering kiss. "Be a good girl and stay here, *solnyshko*. I won't be long."

Then I put Rina out of my thoughts, and stalk toward the opposite side of the restaurant.

"Commandeer the manager's office. It should be in the back. They usually are so they can keep an eye on their staff. Have Cody and Ryan bring the package in that way. Then dismiss the rest of the staff. *Merce's* is closed until further notice."

If the mick is bleeding like I think he is, the whole area will need to be sanitized by my cleaners.

"Got it, Boss." Marcus goes to do my bidding, and I vanish down a tastefully appointed corridor, heavy on imported marble tile and elaborate, baroque decorations. The area is not far from the bathrooms and a storage room. But I was right. There's nothing but a few feet between the back exit, through the kitchen which is completely tiled in easy-to-clean stainless still. I approve of its setup after a brief look. There's nothing tiny and crevice-like for blood to slip through.

Cody and Ryan come in through the backdoor, dragging a half-conscious man between them. His t-shirt is ripped open to his navel, exposing the gauze taped on his side. Blood is already seeping through, the tint dark enough that makes me think his liver's been clipped. A slow, painful bleed-out, but he has enough time left on God's green earth for me to get what I need.

I jerk my chin into the office. In a few minutes, Leon's already grabbed a roll of industrial plastic wrap from the storage area, and pushed the soft, chintz-patterned chairs and desk aside.

Cody drops the man on his knees atop the plastic and then crosses his arms as he leans in the doorway. Ryan mirrors him, neither stepping inside since there are already three of us packing the rather small room.

I stand in front of the man, taking note of the pallor of his skin; the fish-white shade that's gone cold and wan from blood loss.

Reaching into my pocket, I pull out Iustina, and get down to the interrogation.

"The first question is hard. Because I know you don't want to be a traitor. But I'll get the information." I pivot my wrist, listening to the familiar hum of the butterfly blade pivot on its pins.

Clink.

Click.

"Who told you to push into my territory?"

Chapter Thirty-Six

Rina

I don't know how long it's been since Edmond disappeared in the back with his two goons. Long enough that I'm growing bored, even if my lips still tingle from the promise I felt behind his kiss.

I squirm in my chair, feeling the angry throb of my bladder. I never could hold my liquor, and I'm two glasses of delicious red wine in, plus at least eight ounces of water. I need to pee.

He told me to stay here.

It's not like I'm going to go run around and shove my nose where it doesn't belong. I just need to find the bathroom.

Like now.

Whatever emergency has led him away is taking a while.

Edmond might have said this business won't take long, but it feels like an eternity. Especially when I'm doing a potty dance that would put my first graders to shame.

I wiggle out of the booth, feeling the impact of the wine hit me as I wobble on my heels. Steadying myself with a hand on the table, I go in search of the ladies' room.

It's not too difficult to find once I figure out it's not in my area but on the other side of the empty restaurant. Occasionally, I see the wait staff peek in from the bar area, notice Edmond still hasn't returned, and vanish into the kitchen again.

Relief is a spacious, empty bathroom. Though I don't take overlong, even if I want to linger and look at the sample-sized lotions and soaps that are organized on the counter in a small onyx dish. After using the facilities, I wash my hands and check my reflection in the mirror. I look flushed. And it's not just the wine. I don't know where the evening will lead, but I hope it will end with more of Edmond's kisses.

His touch.

His everything.

Two rounds of good dicking and I'm turning into a nympho.

I giggle and boldly meet my reflection, feeling wanton as I fluff my hair and touch up my lipstick.

Then I step out into the abandoned hall. Across the way is the men's restroom, but there's a whole other section through an open doorway with a sign above that reads, employees only'. I have zero intention of trespassing there. In fact, I've already turned on the point of my shoe. Pivoting. Ready to return to my table.

Then I hear it. That fucking knife. The sound of the switchblade unfolding haunts my memories. In my dreams, I can still see the way the blade comes together, swishing and singing lethal, murderous intent every time Edmond opens it.

That Edmond has that knife out, means that whatever is going on in that area is more than just a bit of business.

Oh God, is he doing what he did to Barrett to someone else?

I hold my breath, and though every instinct is telling me not to be nosey because we all know that curiosity killed the cat, I follow the noise as I slip through the archway I shouldn't be passing through.

Immediately to my right is the manager's office. The door is open as if Edmond and his crew don't care who catches them. More than likely it's because the small office is stuffed with big burly men, each inked to the nth degree as if blank skin is an affront to their natural order. If the door was closed, it would be claustrophobic.

A man I don't recognize kneels before Edmond who looks like a dark avenging angel as he looms above his captive.

He twirls and twists the butterfly knife in front of the man's eyes. Terrorizing him with how the low overhead lights play off the blade's silvery sheen.

I press a hand across my lips. This is utterly different than the protection - if you can call it that - which he showed me at *Timberhaus.*

This is sadistic.

He's pulling terror from the trembling man as if it were his favorite scent. I can smell it from where I stand, flattened against the wooden walls. It's adrenaline-induced sweat with a sour note, and ammonia because I'm pretty sure Edmond's captive has pissed himself.

I shouldn't be watching this.

I need to return to my seat, but I can't look away. My feet are glued to the floor, watching this horror show play out.

Edmond leans into the man, face-to-face as he murmurs something.

The man whimpers, but the noise is subdued, and I realize it's because the his jaw is broken. There's mottled bruising ripening on his skin, and angle of his chin is all wrong. Blood leaks from a dozen cuts and slices which mark his face, torso, and arms. A swatch of gauze is stuck to his side, but it's flooded and drips gore from beneath the bandage, staining his jeans a gory shade of red.

Then Edmond moves, and it's so swift and vicious I'm not prepared for it. He's a dancer, a fucking maestro as his fist moves, and slams into the man's head. I barely understand what is happening, until I see see the knife all but disappear. Edmond stabs the blade into the man's ear, cutting through cartilage and flesh. There's familiarity in the motion, something I might have seen in a zombie show. It's a quick, smooth way to get to the brain. An immediate, bloodless killing blow.

The man doesn't utter a sound. He simply topples, his body hitting the plastic stretched across the ground. As he falls, the knife slips free, the hilt still caught in Edmond's hand, and I swear there's *brain* matter on the cutting edge.

I don't think I scream. I'm in too much shock. But I make a noise. Because all of the men in the office whip their heads around.

Edmond's jaw clenches. His eyes narrow, becoming pinpricks of wrath and ice that score me so intensely that I nearly fall to my knees.

I thought I could be his equal. I thought I could handle the bloodstains on his hands, and the savagery with which he rules his empire.

I was so fucking wrong.

I don't think. I just *react*. I turn and rabbit, becoming prey for a hunter who already has the taste of blood in his mouth.

Chapter Thirty-Seven

Edmond

A weightless sensation grips my head when I meet Rina's horrified eyes. It's as if someone has wrenched my head off the stem of my neck, and leaves it floating in the ether like a balloon.

The dark parts of myself, that I stuffed in a cage when dealing with Rina, have a vested interest in what reaction Rina would give into when her protective instinct kick in. The sadist wants Rina to get on her knees and fawn, promising to suck my cock as long as I don't hurt her.

Unfortunately, *flight* wins. The icy walls I'd erected while interrogating Cian O'Malley crack, then fell beneath the blistering waves of angry heat that blast from my core.

She. Fucking. Ran from me.

Fury pounds between my temples. It bubbles against my throat. I choke out my breath until I feel air-starved.

Cody makes a move as if he's going to be the one to go after Rina.

"Don't," I bark, and all four of my men balk. They hear

death in my voice, the rage unconfined. "I'll get her. Get rid of this mess and bring my car around."

I realize as I hear the exit door bang against the doorjamb, that I've been entirely too *gentle* with Rina. Instead of showing her the real me, I've anesthetized the darker parts of my psyche. Giving her a watered-down version instead of the fucking *pakhan* of the Vasiliev Bratva. I've been trying to get the red-haired filly to trust me, when I should have broken her like a fucking mare being presented for a stallion.

And for what? For her to run from me when she sees my true face? For her to *abandon* me after I've peeled myself apart to let her in.

Adrenaline thumps through me, as if I'd kicked back a shot of Kerosene and hyper fueled my focus.

Cody and Ryan edge away from the office door, scurrying away.

It's Marcus who tries to reign in my rage. He can see the madness bleeding out of my eyes and carving my face into unfeeling marble. But that's not true. I'm not unfeeling.

I feel fucking everything. My lungs are tight. There's a troop of soldiers marching in time with my pulse between my temples. My heart is racing so fast I feel I'm about to have a stroke and join Cian on the ground; dead from one upstart little bitch.

"Boss, don't kill her. You'll regret it."

Only he and Leon can get away with being so blunt. But not right now. Not with *her*. I slam my fist into Marcus' face, feeling flesh split around the signet I wear on my forefinger.

"Stay the fuck out of it."

I've already decided that Rina's going to bleed for me when I catch her. I should have fucked her, tore into her ripe, cherry-lush cunt the first night I broke into her bedroom. I must have lost my fucking mind that I'd simply given her an orgasm, and went on my merry way. And when we did have sex, that I'd *made love* to her, and not simply taken what I wanted.

I've been pussy whipped. I've neutered myself for her attention. Her affection. And what do I get in return?

Abandoned.

Slowly, I tug off my suit jacket and pass it to Leon who holds his arms out. They're long, keeping him out of striking distance, while Marcus cusses behind the handkerchief he's holding to his face. I unlatch my cufflinks, the same blood-red as Rina's bracelet. For a minute I think about opening the application on my phone and track her. But that's not what my brain is roaring for.

I want to hunt. This instinct is primal and as old as time, and rubs the violent edge off of my anger.

"I won't kill her," I concede to Marcus as I drop my cufflinks into the pocket of my jacket. Slowly, I unbutton the cuffs on my shirt and roll the sleeves up to my elbows. Revealing the tattooed numerals that have kept track of how many men I've murdered.

Sixteen. I haven't added Thorton or Barrett yet. Can would make nineteen. Rina isn't going to be lucky twenty. But she's going to wish she is when I'm finished with her.

I crack my neck, the satisfying pop of vertebra sending tingles down my spine. Limbering my shoulders with a quick roll, I breathe deep into my sense of purpose. I ignore the pain in my chest. Because it's as if in that one stroke of thoughtless betrayal, Rina has torn my heart from my chest.

I'm *Bratva,* I don't have a fucking heart.

With that oath, I stalk out the back door of *Merce's.* Ponderous pines, towering maples, and other conifers border the backside of the restaurant. There's a patio, closed until summer, with a short , light-festooned fence around it off to the side. The rest of the space is blacktop which angles toward the front of *Merce's* and I-5. Rina might have gone that way, but she'd run into my men and they'd hold her before she got far.

I take a few steps, getting my bearings, when I see Cinderella has left her heels behind. They're placed a few strides apart as if she kicked the pumps off as she ran toward the woods. If I were a better man, I might give her a fairytale. I could be her prince, carting her shoes for her until she returns.

But I'm not.

In this story, I'm the ogre under the bridge. Worse yet, I embrace the ideals of the pussy-hungry wolf from Little Red Riding Hood's erotic tales, the beast that senses a vulnerable, tasty morsel and intends to take her for himself.

Blood surges south, lengthening my cock until it pushes against the front of my slacks. I savor the pain in my balls, knowing that I'll be emptying them in Rina's cunt before too long.

Then I hunt, charging straight into the heart of the forest with a single thought in mind.

Ruin her.

Chapter Thirty-Eight

Rina

Merce's backdoor leads into woodland. All of those trees aren't what I wanted to see when I burst out the exit and sought freedom and safety in the outside world.

Luck is not on my side. I'm miles from home, without a car, and at the mercy of a man who just killed another.

I bite back a curse as I run across the parking lot, realizing that there's nowhere I can escape. Out front are all of Edmond's men. They can easily run me down in their monster-sized SUVs, if they didn't just shoot me in the back whenever I cross their line of sight.

I spin in a circle, feeling my heart thunder in my chest. I'm not safe out in the open. That leaves only one direction.

The forest.

I jolt forward, nearly twisting my ankle due to my unfamiliarity with my heels. Kicking off my pumps, I bolt for the cover of the pine and maple trees. I don't feel 'safe' until I dart into the cold shadows of the trees. But even this is an illusion. I'm not safe, even if I'm camouflaged by the elements. Damp soil, loam, and decaying leaves slither through my toes.

I ignore it as energy flickers through me, lightning strikes that make me feel as if I'm burning up inside. I have no direction. No way to get myself out of this mess.

Weaving around the thicker tree trunks, I almost scream when I startle a hawk from its roost. Its agitated birdsong competes with how loudly my pulse rages in my ears.

If I can cut around the backside of *Merce's* through the wood, maybe I will find the road.

I don't want to be lost in the wilds of Washington. I will die out here. If not from exposure and thirst, then because of the bobcats, coyotes, and moose who claim this territory.

But right now, a worse predator is hunting me.

"Rina." His voice fills the darkness, echoing through the eventide somewhere behind me.

I flatten myself against a tree. The rough bark digs into my chilled skin, and snags on the fragile threads of my golden dress.

He isn't going to let me go.

Am I going to be next to feel the bite of his blade?

I shudder, searching the vicinity in front of me. Everything looks the same. Without my phone or any sort of navigating equipment, I'm going to be running blind.

Footsteps crunch on a branch, the wood breaking as loud as a gunshot.

I whimper and scramble forward, feeling like a damn doe as I escape the hunter's crosshairs.

Without thinking, I dart deeper into the thicket. Risking the danger in the dark instead of the devil on my heels.

I'm not a sprinter. The muscles in my thighs burn. A stitch zips up my side. I pant through the physical exhaustion and breathless flaring of my lungs, laboring to get enough oxygen in my body to fuel my organs and continue my madcap escape.

Time loses all meaning in the dark. I could be running around the woods for an hour, or five minutes.

Glancing over my shoulder, I try to figure out if I'm running in circles, and if Edmond is still hunting me.

I can't see him, but I know the answer.

He isn't ever going to let me go.

He's vowed it over and over to me.

I don't see the shadow in front of me, or how it separates from the tree. Not until I nearly plow into it. I flinch as I collide with a muscled wall, reeling sideways, trying to get around it.

There is no escape.

There never was.

Edmond's hand sinks into my hair, long fingers pale in the darkness tangle in the roots. My scalp screams with pain as he reels me backward, trapping me against his side.

He is so strong. So fast. I tremble as I lurch, flailing sideways with my whole body sinking toward the ground.

Edmond doesn't let me fall. He uses his fist in my hair like a leash, urging me up, and up, until he can wrap one of his thickly muscled arms around my waist.

I scream again, writhing and thrashing as he picks me up as if I weigh nothing. He is a brute, manhandling me as he walks the pair of us to the tree he'd been using as cover. He is all over me, filling the space between us with the scents that are purely him; peppery and sweet, with a flourish of red wine and the unmistakable metallic tang of blood.

He still has blood on his hands.

I scream until his hand slips out of my hair and fans against my throat. He doesn't relent as his fingers tighten, threatening to crush my larynx in his murderous claw. The pressure is just enough to silence me, informing me that my continued breathing is by his will. A notion which subdues me. I feel myself weakening. Though I don't stop fighting. I want to hurt him. To kick him. To wound him for letting me think that we had a chance and that he isn't a murdering son of a bitch.

You knew all of this before you fucked him.

Why is it different now?

"Shh," he growls in my ear.

His body weight smashes me into the tree until pinpricks of pain flare from where the hard bark digs into my spine. Each time I squirm and wriggle, the ache blooms wider, promising bruises from how hard he has me pinned.

Holding me by the hand-necklace, he pulls back just enough to wedge his hand beneath the back of my thighs. He lofts me, forcing my legs to spread and wrap around his waist.

I shudder when he grinds himself into me, letting me feel the thick outline of his cock trapped behind his zipper.

This is madness.

Because not only is he iron-hard, but I'm drenched. The pressure of my lacy pants digging into my pussy pulls a whimper from my lips. It barely reaches air, but I know Edmond hears it. His head lowers to my mouth, ransacking the rest of my oxygen as he devours my lips in a kiss.

Somehow, I go from pushing him away, to gripping him. My fingers rake across his shoulders, curling in the lapels of his dress shirt. He shucked his suit jacket at some point, leaving only a thin layer of fabric against his overheated skin.

"Fuck, *solnyshko*," he moans against my cheek.

I know when his control snaps, as if still had any shreds of humanity left. His shoulders shudder, and when he lifts his head from mine, there's intent in his face that - had I not been pinned against a tree - would have sent me rabbiting again.

His gaze dares me to deny him as his hand slips down my thigh. Those blood-stained fingers pinch the hemline of my dress before he tears it up. Shoving and bunching the soft fabric until it is wadded around my waist.

"N—." Edmond doesn't let me get the word out. He doesn't even care to hear it. His mouth slams over mine, swallowing my denials, my pleas, while his hand slips between my thighs.

He pulls, forcing the fabric to bite into my hips. Lace doesn't tear easily. It abrades my pussy with how hard he yanks, the material refusing to give. Until finally, there is a shrill cry of seams pulled to their limits before they give way with the sharp sound of tearing fabric.

I tremble as he tosses my shredded panties away. Before his hand is right there, stroking roughly over my exposed sex. I can't hide how turned on I am. My pussy makes obscene noises as he slides his fingers between my lips.

I groan against his mouth, feeding him my lust, this demented pleasure that is making my needy juices dribble down my thighs.

Edmond pulls away from the kiss. His breathing is as labored as my own. There is no moonlight to cast its judgmental gaze upon us. It can't penetrate the thick overhead canopies. Instead, there is the dark of velvety night and the gleam of Edmond's eyes.

"You are so wet for me."

I close my eyes and shake my head as far as the hand on my neck allows me to.

A loud *smack* pops my eyes open, followed by the sting of my clit from how hard he smacks my pussy.

"Don't lie to me. You're panting for my cock. How did you keep this pussy so cherry when you're nothing but a dirty little whore?"

Oh my God.

My eyes widen as I stare up at him, shocked by the vulgarity of his mouth. And so painfully turned on that my core clenches and sends more wetness drooling from my slit.

Edmond smirks, his mouth twisting in violent suggestion.

There is nothing gentle about the way he pries his fingers between my thighs. His middle finger seeks the hot, aching core of my body. When he shoves his finger in, I have to force myself to keep my eyes open.

"That's it, *solnyshko.* Squeeze this tiny twat around my finger."

I'm on fire. Every nerve ending flares with pleasure. He draws his finger out almost all the way out, before ramming it back in. He shifts his whole hand until he is cupping my pussy in his palm. One finger buried deep, with his thumb swiping across my clit.

I ride his fingers, my thighs tightening around his waist. Another finger thrusts in, widening me until I scream into the night.

"That's it. Take my fingers. If you don't let that pussy relax, you're never going to fit my cock."

I arch against him, the fight to get away turning into a sultry writhe that rocks me atop his hand. I can hear the soppy wetness he is finger-fucking out of me. Stars began to ignite in my head. I'm blinded to everything but the addictive haze of pleasure that has my head dropping backward. The dark is a huge void above me, as if a heavy curtain has fallen around the world, concealing us from sight.

"I'm going to..." I pant, chasing the sensation of my oncoming orgasm.

Edmond pulls his fingers out, leaving me empty and aching.

I moan, painfully turned on and denied any release.

"Please let me come. Please, Edmond." I am so close to crying. He has me on the edge, thighs quaking. I wish I could wrap them tighter around him and pull him against my needy sex.

The unmistakable jangle of his belt loosening strikes out at me from the gloom. I should feel dread because this is not how I imagined sex would be - pinned up against a tree after witnessing the violent murder of another man.

It is wild.

Unhinged.

Animalistic.

Edmond doesn't give me a chance to protest. The moment his cock is free, the swollen head glides across my clit as he settles himself between my thighs.

His thumb swept across my lower lip, holding me steady with how his fingers cuff my throat.

"When you come, it's going to be on my cock."

I tense, knowing what is coming.

Needing it.

Craving it.

Begging for it.

I'm still not ready when he fucks me.

His hips pound forward, and pleasure-pain jolts through my body as he buries his cock inside of me in one rough thrust.

I scream as the hot friction rushes through me. I am so full. So impossibly full that I swear my pussy is going to tear apart. But just behind that ache is pleasure. It makes me wild. My thighs push at him, my hands coming up and clawing at his shoulders, as if I'm trying to get him closer to me.

He is relentless as he hitches his hips back a mere inch. Then he pounds forward until I hear - feel - his balls slap against my pussy.

A pleasure-soaked sob flies free. My head is all messed up

over how *good* it is to be caught and fucked without any say in the matter. But only because it's Edmond. I know that intimately. That this madness inside of me, making my pussy milk his cock, is because I trust him. And that while violence is between us in this moment, he would never really hurt me.

I'm just the vessel he's using to fuck free his demons.

And I am so here for it.

"That's it. Cry for me."

I cling to him as Edmond's eyes close. His head is tipped back as if he's having a holy experience by bottoming out in my pussy.

"Mmm fuck."

Thrust.

"Your pussy is so tight."

Thrust.

"So fucking tight."

Edmond's rhythm is brutal. He never lets me adjust. Instead, he is relentless. Barely giving me time to find air as he draws his shaft out to the head, and then hammers it right back in. Each impalement fills the air with the sounds of sex. The brutal way his flesh slaps against mine. The obscene wet sounds of my pussy tightening around his cock. The smack of my thighs as they jiggle around his undulating hips.

I gasp as Edmond tilts his pelvis, angling the spongy head of his cock against the backside of my clit. That spot. That damn spot he'd found before with his finger. Now he is working it with his cock.

"Oh my God," I groan.

Oh my God.

I shudder as I grip him. Holding on. Not wanting to let him go. Caught in the endless tide of his hips battering against mine. Tension coils through me, beginning low in my belly. My nipples tighten. My clit tingles. I feel as if I am going to die because of the intensity of the sensation.

If this is death, take me grim reaper!

"There you are my little slut." His head drops to my shoulder, and those cruel lips bite and suck at my throat. "God your pussy is trying to strangle my cunt."

I can only whimper. My skin feels as if it is pulled too tightly across my body. I'm one wrong way from shedding my skin, at least that's how it feels. I claw at him, needing something more.

Needing...

Edmond's hand drops between us until his fingers find my clit. He pinches, tugging on that delicate button. He feels me quiver, trembling as he brings me closer.

And closer.

"That's it. That's it my beautiful *solnyshko*. Cum on my cock."

I'm oxygen starved, but I don't care. I can only gape up at the sky as Edmond sinks his teeth into my throat. Biting me right as he gives my clit another cruel pinch. Coinciding with the ruthless, unrelenting piston of his hips.

I die. Because there is no way to survive the explosion that tears me apart.

I scream as pleasure ripples through me. The passion of *us* forces me to clamp tightly around his shaft. The tension makes him grunt. The smooth roll of his hips turns jagged. His already brutal thrusts become something more. He takes, holding me against the tree while he saws between my thighs.

Pounding.

Thrusting.

Violating.

I hear his bellow as he whips his mouth from my throat. He buries himself as deep as he can go before I feel the spasm and pulse of his shaft swelling inside of me before he stiffens. Then there's heat. Searing and insidious as he seeds my bare pussy.

I cling to him, sobbing with relief and the emotional crash that comes after such a rough bout of sex. Because Edmond has shown me the truth.

He is my damnation.

And my salvation.

Chapter Thirty-Nine

Edmond

Ipant against Rina's throat, feeling the jagged spasms of her pulse against my lips. Flicking my tongue out, I taste the salt and sex now staining her skin.

Rough, primal sex has made the anger I feel fall to a low simmer. She still needs to be punished, but I can't do that while we're in the middle of the forest.

I slide out of Rina's cum-flooded pussy. The post-orgasm sensation is almost too much, bordering on pain, and I can't stifle the groan as her aching sex clenches. Then the muscles relax until I'm free. Looking down, I can't help but grin at the stickiness and pink sheen on my dick. She's bled for me. But not enough to satiate the beast she'd woken.

"Edmond," she whispers, reaching for me.

I curl my fingers into her hair, wrenching her head back so that I can look down into her sex-drunk features.

"You ran from me."

I don't mean to say it. I hate the wounded tone that serrates my voice, making it feel rough. But it's been the insistent war-drum driving my actions for the past half-hour.

Wetness glimmers in Rina's eyes. Her makeup is fucked. The eyeliner drips like Harlequin's tears down her cheeks, inky strokes that run from just beneath her eyes to a wavering point along her cheeks.

"I'm sorry."

"I don't want to hear it." I shove her back into the tree and take a step away from her. Busying myself with tucking my still-hard dick back into my trousers, I try to sort my thoughts. Fuck. What is it going to take to get this girl out of my system?

"Please, Edmon.."

My anger flashfires, and before I can stop myself I'm tearing off my tie. The one that costs almost three-hundred dollars because it's pure silk. Then I wind it around her face, shoving the length between her lips and past her teeth until she's gagged. She batters at me, trying to claw it off her mouth.

"Move it, and I'll tie you up and gag you with your panties."

She freezes, trembling before me. But she wants to be a good girl. I know she does. Because she leaves it in place.

Raking a hand through my hair, I turn away from her, trying to figure out what I want to do.

My cock wants to punish her some more, and I can't see how that's a bad idea. I've spent weeks in blue ball hell trying to be the prince in her story.

Now that I've revealed my real face, I need to continue to shed her misconception about who I truly *am*. The only way to do that is by taking her home with me.

With that settled, I turn toward her, wrap my arm around her waist, and fling her over my shoulder in a fireman's carry.

Rina squeals as I hike her hips onto my shoulders, jarring her as I make my way back the way we've come. She has zero sense of direction or self-preservation. We're barely inside the woods' perimeter. She ran in circles before I took pity on her and caught her. It takes us only a handful of minutes for me to emerge from the dusk, with me carrying my prize as if I'm a Viking marauder. The globes of her soft ass look like a golden full moon atop my shoulder.

Leon and Marcus stand by the Rolls Royce. The other men are gone. But the Bugatti is right where I wanted it to be. The restaurant's floodlights are on, picking out the satiny gleam in the car's unique paint job.

For a moment I think about stowing her in the trunk, like I would if Rina was any other victim. But I don't, because I'm still too fucked up in the head where she's concerned.

Growling under my breath, I jerk my head toward the passenger door.

Leon is quick, and he yanks it open before stepping back.

Realizing we're not alone, Rina lifts her head. No doubt trying to get eyes on one of the guards. Maybe plead with them with those fucking hazel doe-eyes to help her. She even squirms, and my jealousy surges that she's asking *them* for help from *me*.

Crack. My hand stings from how hard my palm ricochets off her ass. Rina squeals, writhing against me before I drop her in the front seat.

Her eyes are flooded again, staring up at me with shock.

"Behave." Then I kiss her across her gagged lips and shut the door.

Marcus shakes his head. I split his lip pretty well, but a crust of bloody serum is already clotting the cut.

"I never thought I'd see the day."

I narrow my eyes and take a step toward him. Before I can hit him again, Leon slips between us, placing a hand on my shoulder.

"What the fuck does that mean?"

Marcus grins as if he knows something I don't; a secret he refuses to share.

"You'll figure it out, Boss," he says cryptically.

Then he grins like a loon, smacks Leon on the back, and disappears around the boxy back end of the Rolls Royce.

I brood after him, before pushing my questions away.

My chattel awaits me.

Chapter Forty

Rina

I wait for the anger to come as Edmond drives us in silence. While I have no idea where we're going, I figure it's his lair.

Then I flinch at my uncharitable thoughts. No matter how angry I should be, I can't muster the emotion. Not when every time I close my eyes, I see the pain in his eyes when he enunciated how I ran from him.

It wasn't him I ran from, per se. But what he represents. He is the antithesis of all the ethos I try to teach my students.

Be good.

Be kind.

Don't stab people with your freakishly beautiful knife.

I swallow a sigh as I work my tongue against the fabric he's wadded in my mouth. My throat is parched as all the moister gets sopped up by the material. I consider tugging it loose, maybe make it look as if it's still in my mouth but its really just lying across my lips.

Edmond must have ESP because he cuts a look at me that makes my hands scurry and hide beneath my thighs.

The silence between us is thick, filled with unspoken things that rattle around in my head. A few key phrases are bumped up from the depths by the occasional dip of a tire rolling on the edge of a pothole. It's the post-winter terror for asphalt roads, the expanding and contracting of cement, and the erosion of snow-melt and liquidized salt creating pockets beneath the asphalt; the perfect breeding ground for potholes. The ride is jerky, bopping my thoughts around until I finally settle on one.

I feel something for Edmond. It wraps around me, curling and plucking at my heartstrings as if this attraction between us is fingers on the harpsichord of my emotions. He's violent, but whenever I think about the things he's done - including defiling me against a tree in the middle of the Washington forest - I don't feel disgusted.

I feel protected. Safe. As if I finally have someone at my side who can - and is willing - to help me shoulder my burdens. That I came so hard my legs still ache over something so brutal isn't his fault. That's my own fucked up psyche.

I want more. A lot more. I want to feel Edmond pin me down. He spanked me *once* and my skin tingles as I think about the percussion of his hands and how it would feel to have him smack other parts of my body.

Closing my eyes, I lay my head against the rest. I need to give my brain relief from my tormented thoughts. There is no use fretting about it when Edmond won't listen to me until he purges his anger.

I must have drifted off because before I know it, the car stops. The engine ticks quietly as it cools in the frosty air. When I open my eyes, I realize there is a whole other section of Echo Bay. I mean, I knew that. Where I live is for the working class; those whose entire existence caters to the wealthy who populate the city.

When Lucia and I first moved into the area, we drove

around, wanting to get a feel of this new land. We explored the different subdivisions from afar. A lot of the mini-mansions were protected behind gates and enormous privacy walls. Then there were the larger mansions, set miles off the main roadways with towering walls that indicated a big house, but prevented voyeurs such as myself from seeing beyond the tops of the trees.

Had I known that a place like *this* existed beyond the wrought-iron gates and privacy walls, I might have tucked tail and begged Lucia to pick another school. Another career.

Edmond has a *literal* castle in the rolling, evergreen hills above Echo Bay. The estate perches high, almost on a mountaintop, and offers all within a panoramic view of the entire area. It overlooks the quaint, glittery heart of Echo Bay. From where I sit, I can see the curvature of the waterfront, and just beyond it, the lights of the nearest island.

There are honest-to-goodness turrets, multiple chimneys, a hedge wall, and so much ambient landscaping light that it almost seems like it's midday instead of evening.

I stare, barely able to take in the whole scope. Zoe and I joked about how wealthy the Vasiliev family is. But this is a whole other level.

Crime pays extraordinarily well.

Edmond doesn't look at me as he jerks open his door and pours himself onto the cobblestone. There's an actual governor's drive, a big circle constructed of columns and flagstone that navigates around a fountain. Water trickles from the top of the three-tiered, old-world display, creating a tranquil melody whenever the droplets patter off the granite.

Overwhelmed, I clamp my eyes shut. Only to have them pop open when Edmond hauls open my door and drags me out. I expect him to force me to mush into the mansion like a whip-wielding slaver. But he's still feeling like a caveman. He hauls me right back over his shoulder, as if I can't be trusted to walk on my own two feet. Then I realize he's showing me his care, because I'm barefoot and it's cold out.

This time I don't fight him. I sag against his shoulder. Some wild part of me giggles, the noise seeping into a bubble of mirth I can't contain. I wonder if there's a tower in this place. Does Edmond plan on locking me up?

His fingers trail up the back of my thigh, the ticklish, arousing touch stealing my humor and leaving breathless anticipation behind.

"What is going on in that head of yours?"

I catch snippets of the interior as he carries me into the enormous foyer. There are golden veins in the Italian marble floor, the silhouette of a crystal chandelier reflected in the mirror-like finish. Though they could also be diamonds, I wouldn't put it past him to encrust everything he owns with the precious gemstone.

Then he sweeps me up a staircase that seems to go on forever. Eventually, he turns down a carpeted hallway, his footsteps muted in the thick pile. He stops, and shifts me closer as he opens a door, and then I hear the soft thud as it's closed.

Finally, Edmond drops me. I expect to land on the floor and squeal in terror, bracing for the impact. Instead of the harsh ground, I sink into an enormous bed.

I blink as my surroundings come into focus.

The walls are papered with charcoal and silver which create a vine-like design around the whole room. Crown molding adds elegance to the spacious height of the bedroom. Everything seems to have a touch of glitz to it, the designs on the wall are foiled and pick up the gleam from the wall sconces. There are threads of silver in the throw pillows sitting in a high-back chair beside one of the windows. The same silver embroidery match the lavish comforter I'm laying on top of. Though the color scheme is not quite black, it is a monochromatic palette that exudes *noveau* wealth without even trying.

I'm mad at you, but I would never hurt you."

I cock a brow at him because what we did in the woods *had* hurt.

His grin is wolfish as he leans over me and pulls the sodden tie from my mouth.

"You liked that." A statement of fact, and I want to bury myself in the cool, light-gray, and white sheets. As if that would get me away from the truth.

"I didn't think sex would be like that."

Edmond watches me warily. His jaw is set as he unbuttons his shirt. I've never seen him look so rumpled. Sure, I've seen his casual side, like when he came into *Timberhaus*. But every time he's touched me before, he would leave, looking completely unruffled.

Right now, he looks unhinged. Deranged.

I did that to him.

And I love it.

Feeling safe despite how I arrived, I wriggle on the sheets and watch him with hooded eyes.

"Did you have a fantasy about how you would take your first cock, *solnyshko*?"

The anger is back, but it's welded onto something else. Something dark and hot that leaves my bare toes curling and the heat blooming in my belly.

Jealousy.

The buttons pop as he finishes tearing off his shirt. Leather and metal clang as he jerks on his belt, and then it too is free of his pant loops with the ends snapping in the air with a *crack* like a bullwhip.

I swallow hard as he stalks toward me, wrapping the belt around his knuckles.

"Did you have someone in mind? Maybe someone nice and kind. Whose hands aren't bloodstained?"

Oh, my god. *He is jealous.*

"I di-didn't...."

He cuffs my chin with his fingers. His thumb digs into my bottom lip, forcing my mouth wide before he shoves his middle and ring finger in. There's an acrid tang to his flesh, and I realize with a jolt what it is.

Blood.

"Suck."

The fear is back, crawling through me perversely as it mates itself with my lust. My heart throbs in my chest. My pulse is so loud that I can hear nothing but the rush of it. But my nipples pebble, tightening against my bandage dress, and my core clenches. Sending an ache that's double-edged; soreness and arousal.

I tighten my cheeks around his knuckles, sucking on them until he pulls them free with a lewd rush of wetness. Saliva spills down my chin.

"You are mine," Edmond growls, the words gritty and violent. They resonate deep in his chest like a guitarist thrumming the heaviest chords on his bass, sharing the vibrations with me from how tightly we're pressed together.

Edmond pushes away from me, the material in his slacks bunching around his thighs as he straddles my prone body. This is what dancing with the devil causes. The absence of all my good sense. The well-honed survival instinct evolution bequeathed us fades away until I willingly allow myself to be trapped - pinned - by the dark god above me.

I moan, shamelessly drowning myself in the spicy scents he exudes; the coalition of cologne, sweat, *death.*

"Please," I gasp.

"Begging already? I haven't even begun." He draws his fingers along the length of the belt, snaring my attention.

"Put your hands above your head, wrists crossed."

Goosebumps quiver to life along my skin. My nipples tighten further, sending spikes of pleasure trembling from my curling toes, all the way into my hairline. Even my scalp feels tight as if a soft stroke of the strands would send me hurtling into the ether.

I don't think of disobeying. This Edmond I barely know, but he's always been beneath the surface. Peeking out from behind his steadfast gaze, seducing me with the darkness and wildness that Edmond tried to keep at bay.

Now it's free, let loose and I am his most willing victim.

I pant as I lift my arms, the position hiking my breasts up against the triangular cut-out that teases my cleavage. Edmond's eyes dive, locking on the rigid outline of my nipples.

"You like this."

He sounds mystified, but isn't this why we're so drawn to each other? Why I can't convince myself to resist? There's a darkness inside both of us. His well-honed, mine a fledgling eaglet testing newfound wings.

I want to fly.

"Yes," I breathe.

Edmond groans and his mouth finds mine. The kiss is meant to punish me with how he abrades my tender lips with the grind of his teeth and the undulating pressure of his tongue. I am all soft sweetness, inviting him in deeper. Encouraging him to hurt me.

"Fuck, Rina. You don't know what you do to me. I feel unhinged when I'm with you."

He shakes his head as he returns to trussing up my wrists. The leather is softer, more supple than the zip-ties had been. Though I secretly mourn that I won't have the bruises tomorrow. I'd worn them proudly, like love contusions made into bracelets.

Edmond curves the free end of the belt over the top of the headboard. The bed's frame is made of some kind of dark wood, maybe mahogany lacquered with a satin ebony finish. It's clever because until I'm stretched out and laying right there, I didn't see the separation in the headboard, as if it's made of two slats with an opening just for this purpose. He threads the leather through the middle of the wood, pulling it tight so that a slight ache tugs on my arms. Then he tucks the leather lead in my hand like a leash.

"Don't let go of this. If you do, I'll start over."

"Start what?"

"Your punishment."

I swallow a nervous whimper, even while my pussy floods with another surge of pleasure. God, I'm sore, but I want what's going to happen too. Edmond has demons to purge, ones I made rear their ugly, abandonment-issues head. If the magic power of my pussy can help exorcise them? He can punish me *all* he wants. I'll even promise to like it. Though that won't be too hard, because the steady drumbeat of arousal inside of me keeps encouraging me to push him further.

Edmond kneels above me. Gone is the aloof businessman, the all-powerful mobster. This man is wild, his wavy hair tumbling over his brow. A few curls touch the tips of his ears. His eyes are mercury, bewitching to behold, but toxic to those stupid enough to drink it.

"I couldn't have imagined anything as perfect as this." His fingers ghost over the shape of my body. Tracing the lines from my breasts, down to the dip of my waist, and over the flare of my hips. "You tied to my bed."

His grin sharpens. "Completely at my mercy."

I shake beneath that grin. Knowing that Mr. Hyde is now

coming out to play. It amazes me how Edmond says the sweetest things. Making me melt. Making me *fall*. Then he switches, and I fear. It's a heady, intoxicating combination that has my instincts see-sawing between the two vastly different emotions. Blending into one potent, whole-body throb that seems focused on the greedy, aching epicenter between my thighs.

Whatever Edmond has planned for me, I vow I'll survive it.

But when his hand dips into the pocket of his slacks, and he pulls out that damn knife, all thoughts of survival scatter. Left behind is the need to escape, the *flee* emotion burning in muscles.

I know what he's done with that blade. As he said, I'm completely at his mercy. Except I know Edmond, and he doesn't have a merciful bone in his body.

Chapter Forty-One

Edmond

The fear that brightens Rina's heavy-lidded hazel eyes rushes through me. It's a high not unlike an adrenaline rush, spiked not from my adrenal system. But fully through the external stimuli that my girl gives me.

Sometimes, I feel like a sadist when she looks at me like that. They show the same gleam as the the terror-stricken irises of my victims. When she's like this, it's as if I am her god, her savior, the fucking planet which her brilliant sun rotates around. I should feel bad, I should feel terrible, but I can smell the sweet musk of her pussy from how wet she is. The proof still stains my cock from how hard my little virgin came for me when I brutalized her in the forest. She's barely lost her v-card a few days ago, and we're already playing kinky sex games.

Licking my lips, I run my thumb across Iustina's handles. The metalsmithing worked in the steel is a work of art. Roses are etched across both handles, the design darkened intentionally so they stand out against the bright, shiny steel.

"Edmond, please don't." Tears glimmer to life in her eyes, threatening to spill over like captured stars.

"Say you're mine, *solnyshko*."

"I'm yours. Just yours. Please, Edmond." Her fear is so hot that it heats her face, makes her eyes brighten, and her hair crackle as if offering proof of life that she's alive.

I rotate my wrist, freeing the blade from where it sits between the handles. Diligent. Dutiful. Obedient until I need it.

Rina is not obedient.

"I thought it was me you feared when you ran earlier." I tilt the knife before her eyes, watching her focus on it. The lights are low, creating a surprisingly cozy ambiance. There's just enough illumination to catch and spark a len's flare across the razor-sharp edge.

"I'm sorry I ran from you. What I saw scared me."

"I know, baby." I do know, but that doesn't mean I'm going to go easy on her. "You know what I'm capable of. You've seen me at work. But I don't think I've ever properly introduced you to Iustina."

Rina gapes up at me, her gaze flicking like the shutter on a camera between my face and my knife.

"Iustina?"

I lay the flat of the blade against her cheek, letting the cold steel grow warm against her cheek.

"This is Iustina, and she thirsts for a taste of you."

"Oh, my God. Oh, my God," Rina pants. For a second, I think she's going to misbehave, either let go of the makeshift leash, or else struggle and fight against me. I see the war march to her frantic heartbeat as her thoughts flash across her face.

I wait for it, feeling the seed of disappointment sinking in.

Then, she surprises me. Because even as cries quietly, she holds onto the leather, keeping herself still just as I told her to.

Pride bursts through me, freeing me from some unspoken

concern. Moving my hand away from Rina's face since my hand isn't steady, I let her see my delight.

"You are such a good girl," I praise. My free hand caresses her other cheek, encouraging her to nuzzle into my palm. "My good girl."

Some of the fear and tension melt out of Rina. I briefly mourn it, but I know it's for the best. I only want a tipple of fear, it makes the pleasure I'm going to give her be much more potent.

Clenching my thighs around her hips, I draw the dull side of my blade inward, pressing it to her bottom lip. Only then do I apply pressure, hatching a divot into her flesh. A minor, painless nick. Perfect to give bloody kisses.

"Give her a kiss."

Rina's eyes widen as if she can't quite grasp the things I'm urging her to do. She needs to know, to understand, that being in my bed isn't all rose petals and candlelight.

A fat ruby droplet dribbles down Rina's chin, marring her flesh like Amazonian warpaint. Light facets the blood, and I groan as I think about fucking her mouth when it's raining red like now.

Her lips purse, aware of how close the keen edge of my knife is to wounding her. She gives a polite kiss, one that smears a streak of blood across the glossy surface.

"Good girl. I knew you would be the first moment I saw you on your knees," I murmur as I lift the knife away from her mouth, and bring it to mine. "But I knew I would ruin you."

Licking away the metallic coppery tartness of her blood, I level a half-smile at her.

"Have I ruined you, *solnyshko?*"

"Yes," she moans.

"Good."

The knife flashes as I hook it in the hemline of her dress. I fucking love the look of her in it, but I want a memento, a trophy stained with her sweet blood that I can frame and put on my wall if I want.

Rina screams in fright as the material splits. The knife never touches her, but the metal comes close as I slice the fabric clean through. It falls away from Rina's body as if it were the wrapper on a chocolate bar, exposing the peachy interior of her flawless, silky skin.

A few freckles dot her chest and shoulders, a cute mole bristles beside her belly button that I'll kiss later. She sucks hard on the air, her belly carving beneath her ribcage while her lungs flare. There's a sheen of fear sweat on her skin, but when I smack her thigh with the flat of my knife, urging them open, there's a different kind of wet glistening between them.

She's fucking soaked.

I groan as I stroke her bare pussy, as her juices and my cum were meant to polish my knife. Her panties are a casualty of my forest rampage. A shame I didn't think to pocket them too after I tore them off her.

"Look at this soaked pussy. All for me, isn't it, baby?"

Rina looks undone before me, floating high in the rush of adrenaline and cortisol, a potent cocktail that has her quivering as if she's run a marathon, even as her core burns with denied pleasure.

She's so fucking primed that it makes my cock pulse in its cages of wool and cotton. I take a minute and grind the heel of my palm against it, trying to cool my lust. I feel like a horny fucking teenager. I've already cum once, and my balls are loaded to unleash more inside of her.

I lightly tap her clit with the knife, watching the fearful pleasure, the erotic agony, flick over her face.

"Do you trust me?"

That is what this is all about, after all, now that much of my anger has dulled beneath the tide of pleasure.

Trust. Earlier, when she ran from me, she showed me she didn't trust me. She thought I would hurt her. As if I ever could.

Now, I need to show her just how precious she is to me.

This begins with showing her that while I destroy easily, being ruined can feel good too.

Chapter Forty-Two

Rina

"Do you trust me?"

Edmond's voice flicks around me. But it isn't the words that make me flinch. It's how he straddles me, a wraith in the shadows, an uncrowned king reigning above me.

All I can see is him, a pale outline that captures the icy brutality of St. Petersburg's winters. He intimidates me without touching me. Instead of his hands, he's using that damn knife as an extension of himself. He strokes my clit with the now warm metal, making me half-mad at the hard, unyielding sensation. My thighs tremble, but I can't close them or buck away from the sensation. He has wedged his whole body between my legs, jamming them far, far apart so that I can feel the lustful trickle of my juices ooze out of my poor, tender slit and roll between my butt cheeks.

I am that wet as if the primal games we've been playing have unlocked some secret yearning inside of me.

How am I turned on by a knife?

Better yet, who in their right mind names their knife?

Edmond, apparently, and yet I can't find any fault in it. Because in his hand, the butterfly knife is more than just a weapon. He makes my body sing with it; the maestro wielding the lethal accouterment as a violinist would manipulate a fiddlestick; plying me with danger until I croon for him in octaves of 'fuck' and 'me. There's worry there that he'll slip and cut me, maybe deeper than he might ever intend. But that danger only stretches my nerves tighter, pulling taut sinews and tendons until I am his perfectly bowed instrument.

My bottom lip stings from the taste of death he gave me. Hot blood dribbles down my chin. It doesn't spill any further, but puddles in the nook of my throat.

He strokes between my lips with what feels like the hilt. Threatening to shove the handles inside of me. I groan as his knuckles caress each lip, pressing against the puffy flesh without ever touching where I need him to.

"I asked you a question, *solnyshko*."

There is a pushing sensation, and then roughness as I feel my tender flesh catch on the decorations engraved on the metal. My pussy spasms, a yelp of shock and arousal bursts free.

He can't mean...

He really...

Edmond fucks me with the metal handle. He drags the handle out and then pushes it into my core again. Gently feeding me only an inch of the knife's handle. Fucking me with it, while being one slip, one twist away from slicing myself on the blade. I can feel his fingers whenever he thrusts, protecting me, but how is he not cutting himself?

I pant as tension blooms inside of me. Coiling like a trip-wire in my loins. I'm so turned on that my whole body is shaking. My breasts wobble in the demi-cups of my lace bra, a set that matched my long-lost panties.

"Answer me." He retracts his hand, easing the full sensation out. Making me break.

"Yes." I cry, because he's showing me I can trust him. No matter how he decides to play with me, even if he has a knife in his hand, he won't hurt me. "I trust you. Oh God, Edmond."

His laugh is almost demonic. I swear I smell fire and brimstone, bringing me with him to some carnal hell.

"Good girl." My pussy pulses and flutters, loving so much when he says those two little words. I whimper in the back of my throat, lifting my head from the pillows stuffed beneath it. I watch his hand move, and more of the handle disappears inside of me.

It's so erotic. So, so twisted, that I'm hapless to look away.

"Your pussy is drooling for me. Fuck, I'd hoped you would be wild, but you are a kinky thing." Slowly, he pulls the knife free. His wrist swirls and fills the air with a metallic melody as he shuts the blade away.

"How did you remain a virgin? Mm? Were you waiting for me?"

Edmond leans over me, until we are forehead-to-forehead, nose-to-nose, and the sweltering heat of him promises to smear me in sex-sweat. He's shuddering as I am. Both of us are on the cusp of something violent and beautiful.

"Yes," I moan. Because how else do I explain this madness between us? It's as if the universe created him for me, and me for him, molding us from the same fucked-up clay. "I was made for you."

He groans at my admission, and playtime is over. He unsnaps the button on his slacks, ripping the zipper down. I watch as he pushes them over his narrow hips, and then draws his boxer-briefs down, tucking the gray flex-waist beneath his heavy balls. His cock is a beautiful thing. Hard and thick, big enough to give a virgin pause, but not enough to break me. Though he's ruined me for any other man.

Folding his hands on my thighs, he pins me down, making sure my legs are as locked as my arms are. He grinds the entire length of his shaft against my slit, making me gasp when I feel the way the meaty head nudges my entry.

"Fuck," he moans, and I'm deliriously thinking the same thing.

Then he thrusts, burying his cock in me with one rough pump. Turning our shared moan into a rhapsody; his growls; my half-scream.

"So tight. Whose pussy is this, *solnyshko*."

"Yours," I chant. "Yours."

Edmond's fingers tighten. Leaving love contusions on my skin. His body is sharp, a tightly muscled weapon itself, as he pounds into me. Until the air is filled with the cadence of silky wet sex and the smack of skin-on-skin.

He's kept me pinioned on the razor's edge of lust since dropping me on the bed. I can't last. I don't want to hold back. Even though I'm sore, my core clamps around him. He uses all of those velvety inner muscles to squeeze and massage his shaft. Clenching tightly, I feel his heart - and mine - throbbing through the thin flesh.

"I'm so close," I gasp, shivering not from cold. But from the rolling cascade of tingles that are building at the base of my neck. Edmond thrusts, and they spread, filling me with dizzying lights that have my head sinking into the pillows. As if it's too heavy for my neck to support.

My lashes flutter. Then Edmond's hand is right there. Rolling his fingers against the needy bud of my clit. Before he clamps down, pinching it.

I scream as those flutters spike, becoming all-consuming. I climax, rocking mindlessly against the delicious torment of

Edmond's body. I beg for him to continue slamming into me even as my body grows too sensitive, too sore.

He tweaks my clit again, and what I thought were the ending jolts of my orgasm, burst again. Extended on and on and on until I don't know anything but how good it feels.

If I had my way, I would never leave Edmond's bed.

As he fucks me, holding me down with leather and skin, I realize he knows it too.

Dimly, I'm aware of him releasing inside of me. His smooth motions grow stilted. His body tenses, before the rush of heat fills me up. I know I should be worried. That's four times he's flooded me with his seed. But I don't seem to care. Not about the possibility. The worry of what might happen should the contraception fail. I know I should. Maybe in the morning, I will.

Right now, I feel as if there's warmth filling me; beginning from where Edmond's seed swirls inside of my bare pussy, and spreading all through my veins like the roots of a rose bush until its latches on and coils around my heart.

I don't fall asleep as much as pass out. My body is exhausted, wrung dry, from the emotional highs and lows.

Edmond's hands stroke across my face, holding me close as he brushes his lips over mine. And I think I hear him say three magical words that make those roots wrap tighter around me.

I must have already been dreaming, but for a moment I think I hear him say 'I love you'.

Chapter Forty-Three

Edmond

When I'm in Rina's arms, when she looks at me with her light-dappled eyes, I don't feel like a monster. Nor do I feel like the abandoned little boy who somehow still exits inside me, living in a festering, untouchable nightmare. If I didn't remember a time when my mother was *normal* I might not have these issues. But I do. I have always felt the the absence of her and Pops when I was most impressionable. It would be easier to hate her.

Rina though. She makes it easy to forget that I'm not just a regular guy. I'm the *pakhan* of a multi-billion enterprise whose chains go all the way back to Russia. But for a while, I can pretend, and that alternate reality me can love Rina. Because binging her into my life would be dangerous, it would imperil her life that I have a hard time being comfortable with. I tell myself, that in the dark, I can love her.

The *Bratva* life is not easy for women. All you need to do is look at my mother and sister to know that. I'm petrified about how it will chew up Mila when she's older. Which is why I protect her as if she's a precious, priceless Fabergé egg.

I slip out of the heat of Rina's cunt, groaning as her body pulls away its snug, glove-tight fit. The's a visceral pleasure when I see my second load of seed spill out from between her thighs. I think about leaving the mess, but she's going to be sore when she wakes up.

Still, I'm as proud as a peacock that I fucked her until she passed out.

Gently I unwrap the belt from her wrists and toss it onto the floor. Then I slip out of bed, stripping out of my pants and boxers. I soap my cock up in the sink, sad to wipe away the minor remnants of pink which remain behind. I was rough with her, and she's still untried. But that vile side of my psyche loves seeing the pink sheen of her on my dick. Then I get a soft cloth, wetting it with cool water, and carry it back to my girl.

I press it against her thighs, holding it there to offer her some relief and sop up the signs of our sex without roughing her up further.

Rina barely moves. I've worn my little sunbeam out, and she's sought the grip of slumber to recharge her batteries.

I, on the other hand, am wired. Sex gives me a buzz.

After washing her up, I toss the cloth back in the sink, and then slide under the covers. I tug her against my side, adjusting her from her starfish sprawl in the silky bamboo sheets, to cuddle against my chest. She breathes deeply, a soft, slumberous sound, but curls around me. Turning me into a body pillow with how she flings her leg over mine.

I stroke my fingers down her shoulder, counting the freckles that dust her shoulder. The low light buffs off her skin, leaving a light burnish behind.

Comfort spools around me, and I think maybe I can sleep if it means I'll be sharing dreams with Rina. At least until a light rap of knuckles taps on the closed door.

There are really only two reasons one of my men would interrupt me in the middle of the night: an emergency or Mila.

My phone is on silent, so if an emergency is happening, I'd be out of touch.

I sigh and stare up at the ceiling. All I wanted was one night without being the *pakhan*. Instead, it's been non-stop violence.

Grimly, I set Rina aside, grab a pair of sweatpants from the shelf in the walk-in closet, and then go to see what bullshit is being heaped on my plate.

I crack the door, seeing Victor's pinched face. He's one of my interim guards. With Marcus and Leon handling the mess back at *Merce's*, overseeing the cleaners, and then getting rest, he's in charge of the house.

He looks over my shoulder, and I block his line of sight. Not wanting him to see the precious bundle in my bed.

"Eyes on me," I growl under my breath.

Victor swallows. "Yes, Boss."

"What do you need."

"It's Cody. There's a bit of a problem at Miss Christenson's house."

Rina's love for her sister is the same that I have for my niece and brothers. Naturally, when I stormed through her life - and whisked her off tonight - I put a detail on Lucia. Without her as my ally, this night would not have happened.

Now, Victor's saying there's a problem. I step out of my bedroom, close the door quietly behind me, and push Victor into the thickly carpeted hallway until his shoulders and spine touch the opposing wall.

"What exactly is the problem."

Licking his lips with a nervous tick, Victor stares up at me. It makes me wonder if he's lost a bet to come up here and tell me bad news. While I don't kill the messenger, my reputation among my men is fearsome. If they believe that they will die for saying 'boo' to me, I'm fine with it.

"Alexander. He, uh, he's over there casing the house. Cody thinks he's going to try and break in."

What. The. Fuck.

Why is Alexander sniffing around Rina's house? How does he even know her?

Then I realize the ages, and I close my eyes. Because it's not Rina that Alex is sniffing at.

It's Lucia.

Rina would kill me if I let her little sister get mixed up in my world. Right now, she's on the periphery. In a year or so, she'll be off to college. Hopefully, none the wiser to the brushes her sister has had with the lawless side of life.

Alexander though. He thinks he's a great white of his piddly little pond. He rules over Harbor Crest Academy and Echo Bay High School as if they're his birthright. I don't care about his small-time machinations. They'll help him should he decide to properly enter into the service of the Brotherhood.

But not with Rina's sister. Fuck no. Whatever reason he's over there after midnight on a Saturday night, nothing good can come of it.

"Tell Cody to grab him. Do not let him in that house."

"What if he won't come peacefully?"

"Shoot him in the fucking knee-cap. He's not to bother Lucia. When he's here, come get me."

"Yes, Boss."

I run my hand through my hair and realize I've been doing it a lot more recently. These outward signs of frustration are going to get me killed. I've been letting my emotions bleed out in ways they haven't in years. Back before the Gulag, and the education we all receive in Siberia.

Dropping my hand, I slip back into the bedroom to shower dress, and deal with my younger brother.

***

Alexander sits across from me with a split lip.

Thankfully, Cody didn't have to shoot him. While I'd given the order, I figured that he would come willingly when informed it was me who summoned him.

It almost hurts me to look at him. He reminds me so much of myself, back when I was just going to be Nadia's high-level enforcer. Except I don't remember having that much hate in my eyes.

He's dressed all in black; a black T-shirt with only a small logo on the collar, black jeans, motorcycle boots, and enough silver rings to supply Mikhail's jewelry shop with inventory when he returns. His motorcycle helmet sits in the chair beside him, resembling a disembodied head with a skull painted on the lower half of it.

His backpack is on my desk, the zipper open and spilling out a whole slew of incriminating evidence. The spray can is self-evident. Whatever his beef is with Lucia, it seems he only intended to graffiti the house.

It's everything else that makes me wonder how I missed the shit that Alexander is in. He's waded into a cesspool all the way up to his fucking neck. And if I don't act now, he's going to drown on the sewage.

I wait until Victor returns with an ice pack wrapped in a towel, before dismissing the guards with a jerk of my chin.

Alexander and I are cut from the same cloth; wholesale from our father's genetics. The same dark hair and skin; as pale as the birch trees which dot the Russian countryside.

He has our mother's eyes, thought. His smolder with anger

instead of the drug-addled glaze hers often held. Maybe that's why things are so broken between us.

Finally, he breaks the silence that draws between us, as tight as a bowstring. "What the fuck? You've never interfered in my business before."

My anger spills out of my skin. Had there been a time when I felt as untouchable as needle-dick teenagers do? Hadn't I been a fucking impervious glacier? Now there's all this wrath that's cracking through the veins Rina's warmth has melted in my exterior.

"Business? Is that what you call this shit, *sasha*?" I deliberately use the child-hood nickname Pops and Nadia called him. He has the wherewithal to flinch, but he doesn't back down. Because he's fucking stupid and too pumped up on hormones to realize how badly he's fucked up.

The drugs are candy-colored, a rainbow of pills individually packed in what amounts to a gallon-sized Ziplock baggie. There are even a few smaller baggies of white powder, probably cocaine pre-packed for a good time. With weed and edibles being legal in Washington, it's a waste of time to try and peddle them. What Alex is carrying around are party drugs, stimulants meant to enhance an evening out.

I choke down my rage. I've never laid a hand on my siblings in violence, and I'm not about to start now. Even though my own fucking rules are demanding I put a bullet between Alexander's eyes.

Fuck.

I pinch the bridge of my nose, trying to stave off the headache that is thumping behind my eyes, Rage chomps on my bones, putting me into a precarious position between family fealty and my own rules.

Alexander's blue eyes narrow sharply, as if assessing how angry I am. The infallibility of youth is him thinking he's going to get away with flouting my laws. Honestly, the only thing that's saving him from receiving Fredo Corleone's fate is that there's no obvious heroine or fentanyl product in the mix.

I wait him out, letting him see the psychopathic anger that's out of its cage; the bulging hint of silvery eyes that make grown men's balls shrivel up as if they're facing down a bullet.

He doesn't look away, and I feel my respect grow for him, even as my anger spikes.

"It's not that big of a deal."

"You know my laws. No drugs on Echo Bay's streets, and you're pushing this shit in the high school? What the fuck."

Alexander breaks eye contact. His upper lip curls, showcasing utter arrogance.

How have I failed at raising him this badly? There's no respect. He thinks he's above my edicts.

Nobody is, but I also can't fathom putting a bullet in my brother.

I'm fucked. The whole situation is fucked. Especially if another family gets wind that I can't keep my own house clean. Let alone the streets which I rule.

I don't have the wherewithal or the fucking patience to deal with teenage dramatics. Alexander's a year away from being brought into *Bratva,* but he's old enough to be taught a few lessons from seasoned mobsters.

I know what I need to do, but it feels like a failure. It settles beneath my sternum, as heavy as a three-hundred pound foot digging into my chest. Alexander has tied my hands. I can't let it get out that my own brother's been dealing drugs under my nose, flouting the city-wide ban I've had in place, and making me look like an idiot that I didn't know.

"This is done. You dealing, your little empire? It's so fucking done with. You're going to New York in the morning."

Alexander's head swivels around. Anger erupts in his

wintery eyes, thawing them like ice melt until their sapphire hue reminds me of our mother. What little color his rage created in his cheeks falls away, washing his features into hard slate with two glacial pits for eyes.

"What?"

"What did you think was going to happen? That this." I wave my hand at his pharmacy that's strewn over my desktop. "Was going to be okay?"

Alexander jerks out of the chair. He braces his palms on the edge of my desk. Low light catches on his silver rings, making them gleam where they ring each finger.

"You can't do this."

"It's done, *sasha*. If this is what you want to do, be a low-level, petty drug dealer, then you'll do it under someone else's watch. You're going to fucking learn how to do it right instead of this bullshit."

I don't stand, though I'm tempted to meet his bluster with a right hook to the jaw.

How have things gone so wrong between Alexander and me?

There are a lot of dark things a teenager can get into. It leaves me with only one option.

Re-education.

"You fucking prick." Alexander turns away from my desk and grabs his helmet.

My words stop him. "You're under lockdown until the jet leaves in the morning."

His shoulders square. His spine stiffens.

"I didn't want this for you." Can he hear the regret in my voice? I can taste it, the guilt much like I felt when I sent Mikhail to Russia. "But you've left me with no choice. Now get the fuck out of my sight."

Alexander's fingers tighten on the doorknob. "You're not

my *pakhan*."

His disrespect makes me itch to get out the pliers and mess up his arrogant mouth. Pops is probably turning over in his grave if he's watching this from the afterlife. There's nothing more I can do for Alexander, and I'd rather him hate me than have to bury him. I understand this. He doesn't. That fact is the only thing that keeps my hands from reaching into the bottom drawer of my desk where I keep a spare Glock and other weapons.

"Not yet, and at the rate you're going, you might never be worthy of being one of the *Bratva*. Get out before I show you what I do to betrayers."

Alex yanks open the office door and then slams it as he shoulder-bumps Victor out of the way. The *slam* reverberates through me, tumbling into a pit of despair that knots in my gut.

I sigh and sink back into my chair. Failure is a bitter pill to swallow, and while I hate sending Alexander away, his leaving for New York means he'll survive and hopefully mature.

Right now, that's all I can hope for. That his hatred will be tempered, and he'll understand the rules that govern our life.

I close my eyes and check my watch. It's just about midnight in New York. Hopefully early enough that I can inform Uncle Felix that he has an angry, undisciplined teenager heading his way. He's the head of the Russian Brotherhood on the east coast, having married into the Gusev family around the same time Pops came to Washington. His kids carry the Gusev name instead of the Vasiliev. As is the way of marriage contracts and the intermingling of the families that strengthen the *Bratva*.

It doesn't sit easily, though, and I spend the next hour sipping a few ounces of whiskey and trying to numb the pain left behind by Alexander's bristling anger.

Chapter Forty-Four

Rina

How does one do the walk of shame out of a mansion?

The thought pokes at me as I hide beneath a mountain of pillows and two layers of covers. All the while pretending to be asleep. Usually, I'm at my best in the early morning. Right now, my brain is molasses, slow and dreamy while my mind frantically claws out of the morass to handle the situation I've found myself in.

The main crux of the problem is that I don't want Mila to see me sneaking out of her uncle's house, hair a wild mess, and yesterday's makeup on. I don't even have clothes since Edmond tore my panties off *and* shredded my dress.

I'm going to need to call Lucia and ask her to bring me some clothing. That's a whole other issue there. While I want to berate myself for being so inconsiderate, I really can't blame myself. It was Edmond who trussed me up and carried me like a war prize into his bedroom.

My toes curl as I think about all that happened since Edmond picked me up. Then groan when I think about the fact that I witnessed a murder.

Is Edmond ever going to let me go? Am I going to have to go into witness protection?

God, I can't believe this is my life.

How do the women Edmond dates get through this?

That thought brings up a nasty, bitchy side of my subconscious I never knew existed. I try to think logically, while she trashes the back of my mind with a possessiveness that rivals Edmonds.

I can't see Edmond inviting women over and letting them stay. But maybe I'm wrong, and he has a carousel of those types of girls who strut past the breakfast table – or even sit there with him – and Mila is used to it.

I ignore the angry kernel which feels a lot like jealousy that lodges beneath my breastbone. Whatever they do, that isn't me. That type of behavior is not what I'm getting paid the big bucks for at Harbor View. Then I giggle because my salary is in no way 'big'.

My laughter gives me away. In the next second, the covers are tugged off, and the cool splash of the morning air nips at my naked skin. I squeal, trying to burrow back into a cocoon when an entirely male and very large body lays over me as a living blanket.

"Good morning, *solnyshko*."

Edmond.

His voice is a decadent drizzle in my ears, sending pangs of heat shooting into my core. My toes curl, and I immediately feel the hot flush which informs me that I'm probably beet-red from a full-body blush. That involuntary flutter of muscles makes me intimately aware of the soreness within. Edmond had not been gentle, and my heart throbs in my chest at the memory of him chasing me through the forest.

"You let me stay over."

I don't mean for that to be the first thing I say to him. The words just pop out, brushed on the edges with surprise and a modicum of wonder.

Edmond shifts atop me, sliding sideways into the messy bed. He allows me to roll onto my side to face him. He's casually dressed, much in the way I saw him at *Timberhaus*. It's unfair to the female population how good he looks in simple jeans and a T-shirt. I'm beginning to realize he favors black and monochromatic colors, from his cars to his wardrobe, and his bedroom. Everything I've associated with him embodies that abyssal hue, with flashes of silver and gray like a knife winking in the dark before it bites.

A fitting metaphor for all that I know of Edmond and his fascination with his blade.

"What do you think I was going to do with you?"

The intrusive thoughts about the murder I witnessed swing back around, hacking into my warm, cozy bubble like a reaper's scythe; annihilating it until all I want to do is turn and hide my face in the pillows. There was a point last night where I thought I was going to die. I was sure of it. That somehow it all led to an adrenaline-fueled fuck-fest leaves me on more solid ground. But that small fracture of true mortal fear underlines the experience.

Edmond's arm latches on my waist, not letting me shy away from the hard reality between us now that the morning has stolen away the night. Shining light on the dark deeds that can't be stuffed in a box simply because I want to avoid them.

I close my eyes because I'm a coward.

"Ah," he says.

I blink up at him, hating that he seems to know everything I'm thinking. Being able to mask my thoughts and emotions is something I've never been good at.

"I would never hurt you that way."

"Why?"

"Because you're sweet and beautiful. When I touch you, I feel like I'm holding onto the sun."

I look up at him, letting that transparency I so hate to do the hard lifting for me. There should be more valid reasons to not kill someone other than *I like the way you look.*

Then again, history is filled with mythologies of men who have wrought war just for that very same reason. If beauty can be the banner beneath which men muster, why can't it also be why Edmond chooses to let me continue breathing? I don't know if the thought that I might be Edmond's very own Helen of Troy is depressing or endearing.

His laugh rumbles in his chest. Suddenly, I'm pulled tighter and the cocoon I sought earlier in the sheets is now found in his arms. He smothers me with his attention. Demanding I meet the gray sheen of his eyes, those twin hues honed to a razor's edge that has witnessed and condemned men to an early grave. Yet right now are molten silver, threatening to burn me with their searing heat from the veracity of his emotions.

Those emotions leave me breathless.

I love you.

The ephemeral words from last night. A confession given to the night and not meant for my ears. That I heard them and knew how deeply he cares for me, is immaterial. Edmond doesn't want me to know. Even if my heart soars at the thought that someone other than Lucia cares that deeply for me. The love-starved neediness inside of me wants to reach for the promise with both hands, clinging and grasping greedily.

"I know what you taste like." His voice is gruff, brushing my heat with puffs of humidity when his lips are against my forehead. "I know how creamy your cunt gets when you're coming for me. I smeared your virgin blood all over my cock, proving that I'm the first man to ever have you, and I will be the only."

His possessiveness leaves my insides quivering. Wetness

floods between my thighs, taking away some of the sting from the swollen, bruised tissue between them. There is no way I'm going to be able to have a morning romp with Edmond, but the slick feeling of my arousal leaves a heady high rushing through my veins.

"The only reason I do anything is because I want to. You are mine, and I will never let you go. Never."

His head dips as he presses a kiss to the tip of my nose. Then his mouth seals over mine, reinforcing the vow with the ardent pressure of his mouth. He kisses me, and savors me, for what seems like hours. The bruises marking my skin he gently caresses. But he makes no further move for sex. Leaving me warm and cozy and drifting in his arms. Feeling the strangest sensation of all considering I'm in the arms of a mobster.

Safety.

Edmond doesn't say those three little words again and I don't pressure him to. Because I don't know how I would feel seeing his eyes when he utters them. I'm already on the edge of falling fully into Edmond and his life. I might have been selfish last night, stealing it for myself. And even this morning, I allowed myself to think *what if* in our little love bubble.

But I have Lucia to think about and the year and a half which remain before she's an adult.

Hours pass as we remain locked together. Enjoying the intimate moment of exist together, without the intrusions of the outside world. Both of us realize that the moment I climb out of his bed, reality is going to come plunging down on us.

Eventually, my belly rumbles, reminding me that our dinner last night was interrupted. I don't even know what time it is, nor where my phone and purse are.

Thinking about breakfast – or maybe it's lunch now – brings me back to the thoughts that woke me up.

How am I going to get home without clothes?

Edmond slowly unwraps me from the bonds of his arms. "Go take a shower. I'll have the cook make us something for lunch."

"But..."

His hand falls onto my bare ass with a loud *clap*, sending me squeaking out of bed as he meant it to. I stand above him, feeling the heated flick of his eyes as he assesses my very naked body. There is a second of wanting to cover me, my hands threatening to stray in front of my pussy, or even try and conceal my breasts in that age-old cringe of a maiden.

Edmond sits up in bed, swinging his long, denim-clad legs over the side. He loops his fingers around my bruised wrist and draws me toward him until I'm standing between his knees.

"Don't ever hide yourself from me."

I swallow at the intensity in his eyes. I don't think I will ever get used to it. The look makes me tremble, unable to decipher the motive behind it, but I feel appreciated and wanted.

Cherished.

I exhale a shaky breath while he touches me as if I'm priceless. Roaming his tattoo-marked fingers down the centerline of my body. Goosebumps erupt in the wake of his gentle caress, anticipation burning in my core as my whole body primes itself. He deliberately avoids my nipples, though they are rock-hard and begging for his attention. And neither does he give me that much-coveted stroke between my thighs. His hands stop on my hips, using them as hand-holds to draw me closer and place a closed-mouth kiss above my navel. It is so sweet and endearing that it leaves tears blistering in my eyes. I don't know what to do with this attentive Edmond. I only witness him sometimes, as if the demons in his mind are sated and allowing him to access normal emotions.

"I don't have anything to wear."

"Trust me. Now go take a shower."

I huff at him, before spinning and stomping into the bathroom. With each step, I can feel Edmond's gaze burning into my skin. There's a bit of feminine satisfaction when I deliberately add a swing to my hips, and shoot a smoldering look over my shoulder. Seeing him sitting on the bed with his fingers rubbing the edge of his mouth as if he's mopping up drool makes my heart and confidence soar.

Let him look.

I shut the bathroom door, and face the reality that Edmond lives in a world I can only dream about it.

This bathroom wouldn't be remiss in a high-end spa. It's enormous, with a walk-in shower, a separate soaking tub, and enough counter space that a Sephora could set up a cosmetic shop. It is gorgeous and utterly masculine with black tiling, a gray-mottled and silver-flecked backsplash, and all-white porcelain amenities. There are towels and a washcloth laid out for me. Of course, they are black too. That Edmond surrounds himself with shadows and does not have any color in his life other than Mila, leaves me feeling inexplicably sad.

Solnyshko – little sun.

It's not until now I realized how apt and literal he means my nickname.

I step into the shower, and though it takes me a bit of trial and error to figure out which knob controls what shower-head, eventually I get it working. The water pressure is perfect. The temperature changes with a minute flicker of my finger.

Steam surrounds me, easing into the aches left behind my Edmond's affection. One of the shower heads is detachable, and I direct it where I'm most sore. Groaning slightly, the water strokes and soothes my well-used pussy.

The aches of yesterday fade away, and by the time I step out of the pelting spray and into the steamy bathroom I feel invigorated.

Using two black towels, I wrap one around myself and twist the second in my hair, before slipping back into the bedroom. It's hard to feel bold and confident when one is only dressed in terry cloth.

Edmond is nowhere to be found, but there are clothes neatly laid out on the bed. Not just random pieces, but full-on outfits that complement each other in color and texture.

I blink and look again around the empty bedroom. Obviously, these are for me. Edmond must have a shopper on speed dial or else he's a magician who can conjure up women's clothing on a whim.

Checking the tags, I shake my head in wonderment seeing that everything is in my size; from the silky panties and matching bra, to the sweater dress and tights, and leggings and sweater combination. My choice of attire it seems, and a pair of chunky heeled leather boots that I'm afraid to wonder over how much they cost.

I choose the leggings and tunic-length sweater, feeling more like myself when I bundle myself up in layers of heavy wool and plush cotton. The boots are a bit tight in that way of new shoes that need to be broken in, but I can already tell the dark brown leather is going to mold to my foot like a dream in time.

Edmond returns right as I'm brushing out my hair. He leans in the bathroom doorframe, his slumberous gray eyes roving over the black leggings and beige-and-cream windowpane sweater with a lovely cowl neck that doesn't make me feel as if I'm being smothered.

"How do you manage such things?" I catch his eye in the mirror above the sink.

"Eve."

"Isn't that Mila's nanny?"

Edmond's lips twitch with mirth. "She's a jill-of-all-trades. Keeping tabs on Mila is the least of her skillset."

"Her tastes are impeccable." I can't help but run my fingers down the sleeve. I've never felt anything so soft. "Is this cashmere?"

"Knowing Evelina, yes." Edmond shakes his head, a rueful expression flashing on his handsome face. "She likes the finer stuff. When I send her shopping for you, part of my agreement is that she can pick up something for herself. At this point, I'm pretty sure she has a collection of Dior and Louis Vuitton bags beneath her bed."

I pivot away from the dual-sinks and find myself gravitating toward him. His arms enfold me, making me feel warm and cozy in his embrace.

"Doesn't that bother you?"

"Not at all. All I have to do is look at your face and it makes every penny she spends worth it."

God my heart. He says the sweetest things.

Edmond's fingers curl through mine as he tugs me out of his bedroom.

"Let's get some lunch."

I'm absolutely petrified as we leave his suite that I'm going to run into Mila. Instead, I only see the occasional shadow from the various men who work in the mansion. But I suppose 'work' is a mild term. They're his bodyguards. Because Edmond's life is dangerous, and at any minute his enemies could storm the gates.

"Do you have enemies?"

Edmond's footfalls click to an abrupt stop on the center step in the middle of the twisting, behemoth-sized staircase that connects the upper wing to the central floor.

"That's a pretty broad question. I think everyone has enemies."

"I don't." I shake my head. "I can't name one person that dislikes me, except maybe Victoria Malone, and even that isn't a true enmity. She just thinks she knows better when it comes to her son."

"Tori? She's giving you trouble."

I scowl at his profile. "Of course, you know her."

Jealousy rears her ugly green-eyed head inside my chest. They probably dated before she married her husband. Or worse, maybe he doesn't care about monogamy and...

Edmond's hands brace my hips, and he plucks me up from the staircase and drags me down the final few stairs and into his arms.

"I can hear your brain working, *solnyshko*. Your eyes are shooting fire. What's turned you into a dragon?"

"She's beautiful." I swallow that lingering feeling of *not being good enough*.

Emond grunts. "She's a bitch and if Drew wasn't one of my best men, I'd never have anything to do with her."

My self-doubt and anger deflate, leaving me blinking up at Edmond.

"Her husband works for you?"

"So, innocent." Edmond's finger tucks a damp lock of my hair behind my ear. "I'm the largest employer in the state, let alone the city."

Oh. Well, that answers a slew of questions I'd wondered about Echo Bay.

Yes, everyone is okay with Edmond's criminal enterprises.

"As for enemies. Yes, but it's nothing you need to worry about. You're safe, here and with me. Always." Edmond laces our fingers together, and we walk into the kitchen where lunch is spread out for us. Some kind of protein bowl from the looks of it.

"Mila is out with Evelina. We'll introduce this new relationship to her when you're ready."

Sliding into the chair tucked beneath the overhanging

marble island, I feel the earth shake again. The axis of my world shifts, throwing me out of balance. I keep thinking this is some temporary thing, but Edmond has shown time-and-again that he's all in.

Am I in with him?

"Relationship?" My voice is so faint.

"Relationship," Edmond reaffirms. His smile is secretive, as if he's revealing the blueprints of our future in that single word.

I duck my head, and stare down at the grilled chicken and sautéed greens on a bed of colorful quinoa.

Taking a deep breath, I let my barriers and walls drop.

I let Edmond in and give him the keys to my kingdom with one word.

"Okay."

Chapter Forty-Five

Rina

Time slips away from me. A few days vanish into weeks, and everything between me and Edmond is perfect. I've almost stopped waiting for the other shoe to drop.

Today, I blush as I walk into the dining room where everyone is seated for breakfast. Each time I come down here in the mornings, I feel like I'm doing the walk of shame. Even though I'm fully dressed, Edmond and I have been seeing each other three times a week - evening and morning - for the past couple of weeks.

We've settled into a routine. Work in the morning, with only *one* lunch visit allowed per week at school. Edmond has tried to get me to increase it to twice a week. But I won't allow him to. Mostly because the teachers are already beginning to talk, and I don't want to make it weird for Mila. She already sees way too much of me that is seemly. However, she seems to understand the boundaries - unlike her Uncle - and doesn't treat me with any increased familiarity while in the school setting. She still calls me Miss Christenson there, as if perhaps her Uncle spoke with her about respect, while I am Rina at home.

Home.

It's strange to think of Edmond's mega-mansion as home. But it's beginning to feel like it because it has two of my favorite people there. Lucia likes 'having her own place', as she puts it, during the times I spend the night with Edmond.

Last night was also my final shift at *La Baia Italiana*. Edmond has insisted on taking care of Lucia and me. To the point that her tuition for the rest of her education at Harborcrest Academy is taken care of. I can now afford our life, without feeling the pressure of penny-pinching or stretching a dollar till it screams. Edmond won't let me buy anything. Which is helping me build a nest egg.

His new area of attack is my car. He began on it last night, insisting I should either borrow one from his fleet or get a new automobile altogether. One that he gets to pay for and pick out, of course.

I've held fast to that. The Toyota is my baby, and I'm not about to trade her in because my boyfriend thinks she's ugly. She's provided Lucia and me with a steady mode of transportation for years.

Edmond is sitting at the head of the table, talking in low tones to Mila who sits to his left. He has me on his right. Eve is absent. Mikhail is supposed to be arriving soon from Russia, and Alexander went off to New York a few weeks ago.

None of Edmond's guards are in the dining room. It's almost like the three of us are a little family. Though Mila isn't my daughter and Edmond and I are still figuring it out.

I slide into my seat, staring at the hot serving dishes filled with buttery eggs, toast, and bacon. Edmond is big on bacon, as I found. He won't have sausage for breakfast. He also likes cottage cheese and fried tomatoes on the side. Two things I haven't quite worked up to add to my breakfast routine.

"Good morning." Edmond catches my eye, giving me a smile that sends warmth basking through me. Especially between my thighs, where I'm nice and sore from last night's activities.

Mila gives me a tiny smile but picks at her food. Her uncommonly low mood has me tilting my head at Edmond, asking him silently and with brow movements what's wrong with her.

"Evelina is sick with a migraine," Edmond murmurs above the rim of his coffee. He takes a sip of the black liquid, and I grimace. Still unable to grasp that he drinks it black without any benefit of sugar or creamer to cut the acerbic taste.

Mila exhales a long sigh. It's not quite a pout, but it could turn into one if she was less well-behaved.

"We were supposed to go to the butterfly garden today."

Ah, I mouth at Edmond.

Mila is absolutely rabid about butterflies. It has finally warmed up enough that Bis' Butterfly Garden is opening again to the public to show off the newest batches of freshly emerged butterflies.

"You can go next week when Eve is feeling better."

I know Edmond can't do it. He's still dealing with the 'Irish problem'. Whatever is going on, it's been escalating in scale. A few times last week he's been woken in the middle of the night, and he and a cavalcade of his men vanish for hours on end. I don't ask, because whatever is going on doesn't involve me. At least I tell myself that. I know that as Edmond and I grow more serious, I'll have to learn more about his business. I'm not ready for that, yet. I might never be.

Edmond educates me at my own pace.

Mila and I don't often hang out alone. Edmond or Eve is

always there. Along with her guards, Dom and Pasquale, who are practically shadows. Invisible, quiet, and dangerous.

I've had to learn how to deal with having a security detail. I'd tried telling Edmond 'no' when he insisted on sticking men on me. He didn't agree or disagree. And I thought I'd won the fight until I returned to visit Lucia, and saw a car stopped beside the SUV that's been routinely parked in front of my house. Then I realized there have been multiple bodyguards on me the whole damn time, and on Lucia too.

Grabbing the teapot, I pour a spot into my cup. The cook has been surprising me with different blends. I take a tiny sip, seeing if this needs any sort of addition or if I can drink it straight. I'm surprised when something herbal and flowery touches my tongue. A nice astringent taste that doesn't need sugar. But a squeeze of citrus will really enhance the flavors. I open the small dish next to the pot and grin. Two lemon wedges wait for me.

"Well," I hesitate as I squeeze the lemon juice into my cup. "I could take her."

I'm a coward because even as I suggest it, I don't look up from my teacup. I don't want to see rejection on either of their faces. There's intimacy, and then there's trying to step into shoes that aren't meant for my feet. I'm not Mila's mother. I'm not her caregiver. I'm Edmond's girlfriend, who just so happens to also be Mila's teacher. At least for this year. Next year she moves on to fifth grade. Who knows if I'll even be in Edmond's life then?

"Do you mean it?" Mila's voice rings with excitement, startling me enough that I look up.

She looks positively ecstatic. I wonder if it's because she gets to see the butterflies and doesn't care who will be taking her.

"You don't mind that you'll be stuck with your boring old

teacher?" There's a knot in my throat, something that feels kind of like tears. I don't know why I'm suddenly so emotional at the thought that Mila seems happy to spend time with me.

I don't dare look at Edmond. I can't. My heart's on my sleeve about how much he - and his niece - mean to me.

Mila is out of her chair and bouncing around the table. She wiggles into my side, demanding a hug. She's such an affectionate sweetheart, and I squeeze her back.

"I would love it if you take me, Rina. I like it when Eve goes, but I know that Uncle Edmond pays her to be there for me. She's not there because she wants to be, but because I want to. She's kind of aloof."

I look over her head, widening my eyes at Edmond. Did he know that Mila knew the intricacies of Eve's employment?

Edmond sets his coffee down and pulls a face. "Evelina is Russian."

As if that explains the matter. Which, I suppose, it does. A Russian governess. That doesn't sound exactly like a warm or ideal upbringing.

Mila spins to face her Uncle. "Can we go? Can we? Please!"

Edmond's face is unreadable. I can't tell which way he'll fall out on this. I almost think he's going to say 'no'. But then those frosty silvery hues warm, and he favors the two of us with a rare smile that makes my heart kick over in my chest.

"Yes, *pcholka*. You two can go. Make sure you wear your rose necklace."

"But I want to wear the butterfly one!"

His voice grows stern. "The rose one."

"Why don't you wear both," I suggest.

"That's a good idea. Wear both."

Mila squeals and flings herself at her uncle, bouncing

happily in a way that makes her seem so much younger than she is.

Then she flips back around and hugs me just as tightly.

"Thank you," she whispers, her voice soft against my shoulder and sending those warm stabs of happiness into my heart.

I manage not to cry until Mila scampers out of the dining room to get ready. Then a few tears trickle, and I wipe them away. Hoping Edmond doesn't see them.

"Why are you crying, solnyshko ."

"Because she likes me." The tears come faster, and I feel so silly for bursting into tears that are a tangy twist of bittersweet and happiness. "She reminds me of Lucia when she was younger before she began hating me for not being able to bring Mom back out of the bottle. And now that Luce is a teenager. God, I wouldn't wish that on my worst enemies."

Edmond seems to understand as he gets out of his chair and kneels in front of mine. He urges my thighs apart so that my knees brace his sides. Then he pulls me close, letting me have my moment in the protection of his arms.

"Love in any form is a wonderful gift."

His hands stroke my spine as I come down from the emotions. I cup his precious, handsome face in my hands and kiss him.

Just like that, we weather the emotional storm and I return to breakfast.

"What was that about the necklace? Why were you insistent about the rose one?"

"Because it matches your bracelet."

I look down at the red diamonds and gold secured to my wrist. I haven't removed it since he put it on me weeks ago. Though it feels like a lifetime.

"That's an expensive gift for a ten-year-old."

Edmond finishes his coffee. He laces his fingers overtop his plate and gives me a smile that sends heat shooting straight through me. Until my toes curl at what that look does to me.

"It is, but it's not only a pretty-looking bauble. There's a tracker inside one diamond."

He stands and buttons his suit coat, letting his words sink in.

Wait.

Does he mean...

Edmond is already kissing me when I grasp the subtle hint.

He pulls away, heading toward the door, followed by my sudden shriek.

"Edmond! Does that mean there's one in mine too?"

His laughter is demonic and tells me all I need to know as I sit and ruminate on how best to get back at him.

Despite knowing that he's tracking my every movement and has for weeks without telling me. I'm not angry. I understand his safety precautions, even if he's militant and old-world about it.

Mila has hold of my hand as she drags me through the last room of Bis' Butterfly Garden.

It's surprisingly spacious, made up of interconnected greenhouses full of flowers, and plants that entice the butterflies within to thrive. Wide brick edging delineates the different species, though they intermingle, flittering to share the flat-topped leaves. The hothouse environment is warm, a jarring contrast to the colder outside. By the time we've made it to the end, there's a fine layer of sweat gathering on my skin beneath my sweater.

"...and that is an Indra Swallowtail." Mila points to a

gorgeous black butterfly with white squares along the edges of its wings.

She's spent the past hour teaching me about the twenty-two different Washington state butterflies.

How funny is it that our roles are reversed?

I lean close to the bright flowers the insect is resting on. Taking out my phone, I snap a photo of it. Because it's simply gorgeous against the hot pink petals.

"Oh, will you send me that!"

"Of course!" As if she hasn't taken a million photos on her phone. What's one more?

Mila doesn't let go of my hand as we head toward the exit. A huge sign details the steps the Garden wants us to go through before leaving. Just past the door, we step into what looks like a clean room in a science building. A white-walled space nestled in between two vacuum-sealed, locked doors for us to make sure there are no winged hitchhikers trying to escape their sanctuary.

I turn around, looking in the full-length mirror. Double-checking my hair, I then give Mila the same careful, diligent once-over. While I know Mila would love to take the butterflies home with her, it's still a bit too cold outside for them to survive in the wild.

"I can't wait until summer. Uncle Edmond promised me that he was going to have Misha plant flowers to attract the butterflies in the garden this year." She talks a mile a minute as we push the double-bared door and exit into the giftshop that anchors the garden.

"Then I won't have to come here all the time. I'll have my own butterfly garden!"

We look through the wares presented at the gift shop. A lot of it is frames with butterflies pinned to a corkboard backing.

Mila makes a sound in the back of her throat. "I don't like those."

I look at the poor creatures caught eternally behind glass. Hopefully, they were dead before they were mounted, but I doubt it. Some of them look too beautiful and young to have perished naturally.

"I don't either," I whisper back.

Mila's guards are waiting for us beside their SUV. Edmond wanted us to take both sets, two to each Rolls Royce, plus my car. I thought that was a bit much for a quick excursion. We are only five from the mansion, and six miles from downtown Echo Bay.

Begrudgingly, he agreed. Probably because he has us both digitally tagged like a gamesman with a prized deer.

I'm still disgruntled knowing that the gorgeous, expensive bracelet has a dual, insidious second purpose.

Dom and Pasquale wait as we climb into my Toyota. Mila buckles herself in, continuing her one-sided conversation about all the different species of butterflies.

I check my side mirror, give a hand wave to the security detail, and pull out into traffic.

"I want to go to the Mariposa Butterfly Festival in California next month. Uncle Edmond says it might be too grown-up for me. Until I pointed him to the website. It says family-friendly. We're a family and I'm friendly!"

I laugh softly, giving her a look out of the corner of my eyes while keeping the bulk of my attention on the road.

"We'll talk him into it. I think having a road trip down to California would be great."

"He'll make us take the jet. Uncle Edmond hates driving. But don't tell him I told you that. He thinks it's a big deal that he would rather fly everywhere or walk than drive."

Oh really?

I file that tidbit of attention away.

"Are you hungry?" I signal for the next turn, the one that takes us to the far end of Willowbrook and onto I-5. The highway twists and turns through the forest. Along one side, through the trees, we can see the water. There's a bridge further up, and ferries to take you to a few of the islands. Others are ultra-private, allowing none but personal ships and jets to land on them.

"It's too cold for ice cream."

"Who says?"

"Uncle Edmond."

"Psh. It's never too cold for ice cream."

I'm not sure where the nearest ice cream store is. Dairy Queen is probably still closed for the season. I hand Mila my phone. "Why don't you look up to see if there is an ice cream shop around, maybe a Menchies?"

Mila flashes me twin dimples as she taps open the map app.

We approach the intersection that will take us right toward the center of the state, straight if we want to head to Canada and west for Echo Bay's harbor and boardwalk.

I look over at Mila and see she's narrowed down the location of one that is only a couple of miles away.

There is a sound like a train roaring nearby that jerks my head around. The noise confuses me because we're not anywhere near the tracks.

A flash of sunlight glinting off metal makes me whip my head around, and I stare toward the harbor. I catch the sight of a truck grill, chrome-plated and massive, and enormous tires as it hurtles straight towards us. I don't think I've ever seen a truck like this before. It's a four-wheeled, monster-killing machine on lifted suspension, big enough and perched high enough that it easily dwarfs my sedan.

I think I manage to scream, and fling myself across Mila before the truck rams into us.

Pain lashes into my shoulders and across my waist as the seat belt bites into me. It does its job though, and I'm only flung mildly forward before it snaps me back. I hold on tightly as the other car pushes and barrels us off the road.

Mila's scream joins mine. Her voice is impossibly high and shrilled with fright as she clings to me.

Panic lodges in my chest as the vehicle lurches. I slam my foot on the brakes, desperate trying to get them to lock. But we're being slammed sideways. There's no way the tire tread can grip the asphalt.

Over Mila's screaming, the *rat-tat-tat* of gunfire peppers the air. The constant, unending *burr* is something semi-automatic. I hear a sudden whoosh that makes me think of a war movie, before a fireball fills the road behind us. The ground shakes from the impact of whatever just blew up.

I don't have time to panic. Even as my ears ring and my eyesight narrows down at Mila's terrified eyes. Her face is sheet white.

I clutch onto her, shielding her as the massive RAM truck shoves us off the road. The engine roars like a dragon until the edge of my tire clips the berm.

Suddenly, we're airborne as the Toyota rolls over the cliff. Metal crumples as we're jostled about inside. Glass shatters. My head bounces along with the motion of the car as we plummet over the ravine and into the forested terrain below.

I don't know how far the drop is, but it happens quickly. I scream as I see the rising impact. Pine needles swish from the branches battering the car, scattering and spraying like green bullets across the windshield.

Mila's tiny body trembles in my arms. Her head is cushioned by the softness of my chest and the way I have her barricaded from the metal by my arms. There have been stories of mother's holding onto their child, saving them from the impact with their own bodies. This I do, because I would never be able to live with myself if Mila died and I lived.

The car's backend lifts, pushing the nose into the ground. It causes the whole thing to roll, and I don't have time to think as it slams into the earth; a crumpled tin can that has been swatted low by a giant's cruel hand.

Chapter Forty-Six

Rina

Mila's screams pierce through my head, bringing me to painful consciousness. All at once memory floods back. The sound of an engine revving. The impact of something much larger than my sedan slamming into me.

"Let me go!"

Though it's agony to open my eyes, I force the lids up, and try to take stock of my situation. My Toyota is upside down, bobbling on the roof. The engine hasn't stopped running, the now sky-bound tires trying to find traction but obviously can't. The precariousness makes the whole thing rock and shake.

Mila, being small, has slipped out of her seatbelt, and she's trying to wiggle through the half-cracked glass of the back window. Except someone is holding her back. A man's arm, clad in black with hands wrapped in leather gloves, grips her ankle.

No.

Wetness dribbles down my face from my hairline. I can't focus through the blurry, double vision which makes the whole world seem to swim as if through distorted glass. But I know I need to stop this man. I need to save Mila. Because Edmond won't survive losing his niece. He'll blame himself.

Fumbling for the buckle on my seatbelt, I click it, praying that the mechanism isn't messed up. Thankfully, it unlatches, and I tumble out of the driver's seat and hit the roof.

My whole body throbs as if I'm one giant bruise. My left hand doesn't want to work. But I don't focus on that as I push myself between Mila and the man trying to wriggle his way in.

"Let her go." I want to shout, but my voice is thready as I force it past bruised lips and a dry throat from lungs that can't quite get enough oxygen to project. The pain in my side makes me think I broke a rib, and it is preventing me from breathing properly.

I grab the man's wrist, trapping it and prying his fingers off Mila's ankle by wrenching his pinkie finger back. Hard enough that if he doesn't free her, it'll break.

He yells something, not quite English, but with a familiar accent. One I've heard before. He tries grabbing for me, but I kick him at him, jabbing my boots at his face, hands, and any part of his body that dares enter the car. Finally, he scuttles back, retreating to consort with his buddies just beyond my vision.

For now, the car is a safe spot. But it won't stay that way.

"Rina," Mila whimpers. She reaches for me, wanting comfort, and needing me to tell her it's going to be okay.

There's more noise outside. Shouts. A few curse words. There might be a whole army out there. There's at least one carload of bad guys. Maybe two. If I stay with Mila, she's going to get taken. Or worse. They may kill her just to make a point to Edmond.

I hold her trembling body close, feeling her tears wet my blouse. My own eyes blur. This time not from the accident, but my tears. They sting. My nose burns with the impounding threat of crying.

I hold it back, sniffling as I press a kiss to her forehead. "Mila, look at me."

She burrows tighter, and I'm reminded of Lucia when she hugs her body pillow and stuffed animals when she's scared.

My heart. It cracks. Leaking grief out into the world. She is just a child. She's barely had a chance to live.

And Edmond.

I never got to tell him I love him.

The realization is piercing. As if a thousand swords are jabbing at the bleeding ache in my chest. I'd been too frightened to tell him how I felt. I hadn't felt worthy of his attention. His love.

But the two of us? We're the same. Broken inside. Carrying the multi-generational wounds fostered by our parents. Somehow, though, he's made me realize I deserve to be loved. I'm worthy of someone taking care of me. Of helping me. Of carrying my burden.

I'm barely holding back the tears as I stroke Mila's dark hair away from her face. The waves remind me of Edmond, and the tears start to leak from the corners of my eyes.

"Mila. Please." I cup her shoulders, pulling her out my arms. She clings, desperate for safety. But this isn't safe. Not with the men stalking around the car. Through the shattered windows, I see flashes of boots in the headlights.

"I need to distract them. They want to take you. They don't care about me. But you? You're precious to your Uncle Edmond. You need to be safe, and you need to tell him all about this when you see him. But you need to be brave, sweetheart. Can you do that?"

This is not a situation a ten-year-old needs to be in. She's both sheltered and so much wiser than her years.

The tears dry up, and her jaw tightens, firming in a replica of her uncles. As if she's seen him make that same brave face a hundred times and is mirroring him.

Edmond might not think so, but he's an excellent father. Mila is so well-adjusted that I wish I could see him one more time just to praise him for the hard work at raising his niece. To Kiss him. To Love him. Tell him to stop doubting himself when it comes to Mila.

But I can't.Instead of drowning in regret, I'll do the best thing I can by saving Mila.

"I don't want you to go out there."

"I know, but I need to. I need you to make yourself small, and when you see an opening, you run. As far and as fast as you can until you find a good place to hide. Your uncle will find you. I know he will."

That he has a tracker on Mila, buried in her necklace, makes me positive he will. It might take him an hour or so. But eventually, as long as she stays safe, he'll come for her.

I don't know what these men have planned, but that they could have killed her in the crash makes me think they want blood and not a hostage/bargaining chip.

Hugging her once more, I turn toward the broken window. I curl my fingers around a broken shard of glass, hiding it in my shirt sleeve, and then I begin crawling out of the car.

"Oi, who the feck is this."

The accent assails my ears a moment before hands grab me. I'm lifted to my feet and spun around. The movement makes my head swim. My ears ring, and I almost pass out again as my brain feels as if it is sloshing around inside my skull again. I know I probably have a concussion.

When I open my eyes again, I stare at a face I recognize. I know this man. I saw him at *Timberhaus* with Barrett.

I realize just as recognition sparks in his eyes, that this is bad. This is worse than I thought. If they were with Barrett, this is about the drugs, the arson. The murder of his man in *Merce*.

This is revenge.

As long as Mila is safe.

Gripping the glass, I surprise the man behind me as I stab my hand backward. I am for flesh, and slash him in the thigh, gouging through cloth flesh and muscle. Hopefully I hit his femoral artery. He deserves nothing less. I scream like a banshee as I stab, and the man holding me lets me go. He howls as he falls to the ground, clutching his thigh. A heavy gout of blood squirts from between his beefy fingers, where he's trying to apply pressure.

Not letting myself get distracted, I launch myself at ol' blue eyes, and slash at him with my makeshift weapon.

The asshole laughs. His teeth are big, tombstone-shaped things. Then he pulls a gun out and cold-cocks me right across the face with it.

As I fall, I take note that all the men are focused on me, or trying to help the man I stabbed. None of them see the small shadow slip out of the car, and run into the forest. She's not safe. Not yet.

I struggle to remain conscious. Planting my hands on the damp ground, I push up onto my palms. I don't get far, because a lug-sole jackboot encompasses my vision right as it slams into my face.

Blinding pain flashes in my head. Bright lights burst behind my eyelids. I crash into the ground again, and am carried away on a blood-tinged wave of darkness and agony.

Chapter Forty-Seven

Edmond

I'm in the middle of a phone call with one of the harbor masters near Olympia about a disturbance in our distribution when the alarms blare.

Living in the age of cutting-edge technology, there's an application for everything. As long as you have enough cash flow to hire a software engineer, both for the coding and the secrecy.

This particular application, and the alarms tied to it, are synchronized to Mila's trackers. Plural. My family, along with Rina, are the most precious things in my life.

The noise is akin to an amber alert. But it's not tied to the federal government/state agencies. It's solely for Mila. Until now, I'd almost forgotten what it sounded like. We might test it yearly, but it's never been triggered in an emergency.

I hang up the call, cutting the man off mid-word.

Eve races into my office, with Marcus a half-step behind her. Every man, woman, child, and fucking pet in my organization has this application. All through Echo Bay, the alarms are screaming, followed with a mass-text notice to muster.

I thumb the alarm, muting it for the moment so that I can see the notifications popping up like chat bubbles at the top of my screen.

My heart stops beating in my chest when I pull up the topographical map of Echo Bay. Throughout the day, Mila and Rina's rose-shaped icons had been overlapping as they'd had their 'girls' day out; lavender for Mila, rose gold for Rina. With the green thorns marking their guards staying in the vicinity.

The green is completely gone, and the roses are far, far apart. The lavender one is stationary, tucked in a swathe of forest preserve off I-5.

Rina is speeding in the opposite direction, heading away from Echo Bay.

An uncharacteristic blankness fills my head with silence. My ears are packed with mud, muting Evelina's worried, teary cries. I know, deep down, that Rina would never leave Mila alone. Especially in a forest known for brown bears and coyotes.

For my entire adult life, I've micromanaged my emotions. Fear is not something I'm well-acquainted with. When Nadia's plane went down, it wasn't fear I felt, but rage, sorrow, grief. A potent cocktail that iced over the sister-shaped hole in my life.

Now, a strange rush is surging through me, a jolt of vitality that has my heart racing like a herd of thoroughbreds on the final stretch of an important race. I'm tense, muscles coiled like a spring. But the usual adrenaline rush is twisted, the exhilaration latching onto fear that has me feeling as if I'm traveling through a tunnel. Time around me is warped and slow. I know it's only been a second since I looked down at my phone, but it feels as if hours have passed in a heartbeat; I'm caught in a nightmarish limbo that robs me of my senses.

I've never felt all-encompassing fear like this, and paralyzes me. My brain is a sputtering engine unable to kick over no matter how much external stimuli demand it to start.

Then the time-lapse shatters, and I draw a breath in. I use the deep gulp to get my body working.

"Boss!" Marcus is never frantic, but right now he's snapping his fingers in front of my face. Behind him, a literal horde of my men have poured into the hallway outside of my office. A lethal mixture of AR-15 and AK-47 type rifles are in hand. They are ready for war. All they need now is my command.

I stare down at the map and the growing distance between my roses. Right now, I can only secure one.

Bile coats the back of my throat as I lift hard eyes to my men.

"Mila is in a knot of woodland off of I-5. Secure her, by any means necessary."

The choice gouges into me. I feel as if I've suffered a mortal wound, bleeding out from a soul-sucking wound in my chest. This anguish is un-fucking-bearable. But I can't go after my sunbeam until I know what war is waiting for me.

The logic doesn't soothe the pain. It's salt in the wound, leaving me white knuckling my phone as I stand slowly.

I touch the icon on the screen, pinning the path that's shifting further and further north-east out of Echo Bay and into the unknown.

My heart.

My love.

I'll come for you.

I fucking swear it.

Chapter Forty-Eight

Rina

I come to in what I suspect is a rich man's finished basement. I'm sprawled across a black leather sectional with my head pillowed on something soft with the recessed lighting creating a muted shimmer. Oddly, I can hear something like balls clacking together and male laughter.

The mother of all headaches thumps inside of my skull, making me smother a moan of sheer agony against the cushions beneath me. I can't quite piece together how I got here. There are flashes of memory scattered amongst the shattered puzzle pieces of my thoughts. It takes painstaking, nausea-inducing minutes to put it together.

Then I remember, and I wish I hadn't. Because remembering the attack. The gunfire. Meant I left Mila alone in the forest.

The thoughts prod at me, surly pitchforks that force me upright too fast. The basement and its low lights spin, as if I'm on a carnival ride, whirling and twirling around until the colors, lights, and sounds mutate into a painfully loud shriek that pierces my eyes and eardrums with icepicks.

I sink back into the couch, panting through the pain. I think I drift again, slipping out of consciousness. But retain enough thoughts to pick up snippets of voices. Whoever has me, they aren't speaking English.

I remember the deep blue eyes of the man who grabbed me. The Irish brogue from the first time I met him at *Timberhaus*.

Gaelic. They're speaking Gaelic.

Then I recall a vital piece of the puzzle, and icy terror cramps my stomach. I know what being a prisoner of the Irish means for me. I don't forget my first thoughts of O'Malley. If that is even his name. He has the look of a brutalizer, the type of man who gets off at a woman's suffering.

I don't want to cry. I remember enough to know I chose this. I traded my life for Mila's.

Please let her be safe.

That doesn't mean knowing my death - my torture - is imminent makes me feel brave. It leaves me trembling in heart-stopping fear. While I enjoy the games that Edmond and I play, I'm not into genuine pain. Tears flood my eyes, and I turn my head to try to smother the sobs against my scratched forearms.

The lilting voice of my captor brutally intrudes on my dark, pain-soaked sanctuary. "Ah, the princess awakes."

Rough fingers dig into my hair and yank my head up. The rough movement causes the kaleidoscopic lights to pop and sway behind my eyes again. I can barely crack them open to look at the blurry form of the man above me. I don't need to see him to know that O'Malley has come to torment me.

"Got a bit of blood on you." He sounds gleeful as he strokes his nails across my scalp. Probing for, and finding, the head wound caused by the car accident.

I scream as he fingers it, interfering with the clotting process, and sending a fresh wave of blood trickling down my hairline.

"So you're his woman. Not much to look at, are you? Fucking pitiful that we lost his little girl and got you instead."

He crouches down in front of me, pulling me close to his face by the pressure of his hand in my hair. There's a gold crown capping a bicuspid. The metal flashes in the low lights whenever he talks. I stare at it, trying to anchor my thoughts with that gilded gleam.

"You cost me one of my men. That stunt with the glass was smart." He bops me on the nose with his finger as if I've been a bad pet. "Do you think he'll come for you? Or will he leave you to us wild boars? We have a bet. I think he won't. Pussy is common for men like he and I. We fucking drown in it."

His eyes narrow, turning their baby blue sheen into beady lapis lazuli pinpricks.

"My boys, the ones that have been watching you and him since he took out Barrett. They say he'll rescue you. If he doesn't. Well. What's left of you is going to be passed around to my men. They got a lot of anger to work out over how much time, money, and men this foray into Washington state has cost us."

My neck screams as he wrenches my head to the side, causing new thudding pain to blur my vision. He points toward the shadows, directing my gaze to a cluster of men enjoying the playroom the house's owner has kitted out. A pool table, foosball, and some built-in card tables are all taken over by a group of heavily tattooed men. Quite a few almost look like Vikings, their hair long and beards even longer.

A man stands up after sinking a striped ball into a corner pocket. His eyes eviscerate me as if he's already plotted my murder.

"That's Finn, Patrick's brother, the man you killed. He wants first dibs, but I'm not sure you'll survive his revenge."

As swiftly as he grabbed me, he drops me. My bruised face

bounces off the leather cushions, and I sob noiselessly at the pain in my head.

"You better hope he comes," I hear from far, far away as the world around me recedes into a bottomless pit of shadow from which I'm not sure I'll ever escape.

Chapter Forty-Nine

Edmond

The ride to Mila's location is the longest journey of my life. I don't know what I'm going to find when we reach the purple-hued rose on my screen.

Our caravan is five cars long, a fleet of Rolls Royce SUVs with a flank of two Mercedes-Benz motorcycles front and back. We cut through Echo Bay, scaring the local townsfolk off the streets and sidewalks. Quite a few cars pull over, watching our procession as if the president himself is being escorted through town.

Those who have lived in Echo Bay since my father's rule know that something bad is in the air. They will scurry home, locking up their shops, and shuttering the windows of their houses, as if there is a chance the brewing war will spill into their simple lives.

I don't use cannon fodder. I protect my people. The men who have brought violence to my doorstep - my family - won't care about collateral damage. Not all of the Irish mafia are as violent and uncaring of the rules that govern interactions amongst other factions of organized crime.

O'Malley's gang is a splinter of a splinter of the Irish Mob, having become little more than petty thugs instead of the more esteemed gangsters that still control the drug trade from their glass towers in Chicago.

I don't have a beef with the Irish Mob as a whole. This fight is between me and that Gaelic pissant. It has taken a graveyard full of bodies the past few weeks to tease out the scheme that O'Malley had put into play.

Finally, we arrive at the accident site. The burning wreckage of the Rolls Royce is already being handled by the firefighters. Cop cars are parked on the brim above what I assume is the pathway down to where Rina's car is.

And Mila.

"We can't get there this way, Boss," my driver says.

"Find a way down there."

Chief Rogers stands beside his white, labeled pick-up truck. The lightbar whir amber. But the sirens are off as they douse the flames that have turned one of my Rolls Royce SUVs into a blackened husk of twisted metal.

They used a fucking rocket launcher. Maybe a bunker buster. It's the only hand-held weapon capable of taking out an armored vehicle and leaving a crater like this on asphalt. They could have hit Rina's car, vaporizing both of them. Their recklessness tells me that they don't care if they kill Rina. They're probably planning on it. Which means I don't know what I'll find when we reach Mila.

I stuff the sudden surge of grief down beneath my breastbone. Now isn't the time to mourn. If she's dead, I'll fucking rain fire-and-brimstone on any mother-fucker who dared touch my niece.

Rogers steps in front of my bumper, and I'm almost tempted to tell Marcus to run him over. Or shoot him through the window.

I don't have time for this.

But I'm going to need his assistance when it comes to flushing those Irish rats out of their bolt hole.

I roll down the tinted window. The Chief hovers near my door, bending low to talk to me.

"What's going on here, Mr. Vasiliev."

"Hostile takeover. They have my niece."

"Mila? Fuck." This is his worst nightmare and I'm sure he has contingency plans for contingency plans.

I don't mention Rina. Or that Mila isn't the one kidnapped. He's on a need-to-know information diet. Right now he doesn't need to know anything but to get out of my way.

"Contain this scene. The men in the SUV were Dominic and Pasquale. Treat whatever you find of them with dignity."

I swallow the grit speaking their name fills my mouth with. The grim reality of working for me is this: death. I doubt there will be enough of their remains found to bury them. Maybe an ash pile to scoop into urns to send to their family. They had been Mila's bodyguards for years. Never tiring of her endless chatter and inquisitive nature.

The Chief swipes his hard hat off his head, half-turning to look at the smoking mess.

"Alright," he says. "Will there be more scenes like this?"

"Just one more."

Rogers closes his eyes. His face grows florid, as if he's two seconds away from having a heart attack and keeling over from the stress of being corrupt. "Please don't turn this into a war."

"It already is."

I roll the window up, and Chief Rogers jumps away from Rolls Royce as my caravan rolls on, heading toward the still icon on my screen like a heat-seeking missile.

Another ten minutes later, and we've navigated to the lower elevation. I try not to think of how many feet Rina's car crashed. Or how impossible it is going to be to get an emergency vehicle into the wooded copse.

We're forced to park on the outskirts, having driven into the trees as far as possible, and off-roading before the narrow valley between the trees forces us to stop and get out on foot.

Mila's marker is ten yards in front of me. I don't dare call out to her until I know she's alone.

She's managed to run a whole two miles from the accident site. When we push through a rather thick chunk of pine trees, we come upon a small lake. A boat, half-rotted through, is upturned on the shoreline.

I hold my hand up, phone in my fist as I approach. If the accident caused internal injuries, Mila might have gotten away, only to die here. Hiding. Waiting for me to come find her.

I'm fucking terrified as I walk around the decrepit rowboat.

Mila is snuggled on her side. Eyes closed. There's blood flecking her face.

Please don't let her be...

I kneel beside her, and gently lay a hand on her shoulder.

"Mila." I give her a light shake. "*Pcholka.*"

Her eyes open, bulging with fear. Before her gaze clears and she realizes who I am.

Then she dissolves into sobs, crawling out of her hidey-hole.

My heart breaks and then re-knits together as I lift her. She wraps around me, a little spider monkey as I carry her toward where my men wait. Their fingers show incredible trigger control, not even a twitch or accidental misfire. I know if anyone but Mila had popped out from behind the wreckage, they'd have been turned into a bloody mist.

Marcus' hand finds my shoulder. He squeezes, his affection expressed in a single touch. Then my men fall into formation around me as I carry my precious cargo out of the woods.

"She saved me."

Mila looks up at me with her dirty, tear-streaked face as we travel back to the cars.

I know who she means, and I can't force the words past my glued tongue.

"Rina," Mila continues. "The man was trying to drag me out of the car. She was hurt really bad, but then she woke up when she heard my scream. She kicked and stabbed at him until he let me go."

Her voice quivers, shaking with remembered terror that fills my head with violence. I'd never wanted this life to scar Mila. Nadia had thought long and hard about bringing a child into this life. It's one of pain and violence. Ultimately, the decision had been taken out of her hands by her arranged marriage to Anton.

Nadia didn't regret having her daughter, nor do I regret caring for my niece. But sometimes I wish I could spare her all of this, and the future pain that is going to color her future.

I squeeze her tighter.

"She told me to run, and then she crawled out of the car and fought with them. I did what she told me to. I ran and ran, and then when I felt safe I did what you taught me with the necklace."

"You did so good, *pcholka*." Fuck. My eyes are wet, and the tears I don't want to shed are beginning to burn through the cage I have wrapped around my emotions.

It's my tears that make Mila tremble again. Her lower lip quivers. I know she's trying to be so brave, but the sobs crack through again as if she is realizing the weight of the sacrifice Rina has made for her.

An exchange that I want to yell at Rina for and thank her for in equal breaths.

She gave me Mila, but at what cost?

This knowledge - the gravitas of it - ages both of us, chiseling away a fraction of Mila's childhood innocence.

And a sliver of my heart.

If I'm too late, I might never get those shattered pieces back.

Hold on, solnyshko.

I'm coming.

Chapter Fifty

Edmond

Waiting for the cover of darkness is the hardest thing I've ever had to do.

I would have raced to rescue Rina the moment Mila was secured if Lev hadn't proved why he was my interim second-in-command. I hope that Mikhail is as diligent as Lev has been.

"They'll see us coming, Boss. We don't know how many men are in there. You know the Irish, packed like fucking rats in a ship when they get together."

He's right. I know he is. That doesn't mean I have to like it.

The plan comes together easily. This isn't the first threat the Vasiliev OCG has faced. During my father's later reign, and the earlier years of Nadia's, our enemies pushed the boundaries. Checking to see if any of our security and personnel had lapsed during the leadership switch.

They hadn't, and those who dared had died for their hubris.

I pace around the warehouse closest to I-5. We're using it as our staging ground for when night falls.

Mila is safe and sound, secure in the compound with Eve

and another retinue of guards. I don't know how to tell her about Dom and Pasquale's death. So far she hasn't asked for them. Perhaps in her little grown-up woman brain, she realizes that if she was in danger, they fell protecting her. As was their duty.

There've been a lot of tears, and Eve is already looking for a child psychologist who can handle the trauma inflicted on Mila. She's a fucking godsend. I know she loves Mila, even if she doesn't show it in a warm, motherly way.

Finally, the sun sinks below the waterline. I stand in the open doorway of the warehouse, the wide corrugated door pushed open. The sunset is splendid, a fiery showcase of red and gold that paints the sky above the water. It's as if nature mocks me, flashing its bold, blood-red palette that reminds me of Rina's hair; shimmers of copper that glow with the warmth of a setting sun.

I turn away when Lev approaches me. Followed by another of my men who is going to be the head of the spear that I batter through O'Malley's defensive forces.

"We're ready."

I already know where we're headed. After gathering a virtual fucking army of men and weapons at the warehouse, I've done nothing but stare at Rina's rose-gold icon. It hasn't moved. A quick surf through real estate records pulled up the owner. Of course, it's fucking Barrett Hanson. This whole cluster-fuck with the Irish is his fault.

The need to dig his ashes up and kill him again rides me hard. It's a futile urge. You can't kill what's already dead. I just wish I'd killed him slower. Made him suffer through the fire in his club instead of simply slitting his throat.

"There's an auxiliary road here." Lev traces a shallow line on the map he's pulled up on his phone. He zooms in the view, his tattooed fingers stretching across the small touch screen.

"It's probably leftover from when Barrett built the place and the construction workers needed to truck in material. The road shouldn't be too overgrown. The real estate listing shows the house is only two years old."

"We should take a fleet of the four-by-fours."

"I agree."

Lev taps another icon, and a satellite view of the surrounding landscape above Barrett's house gives me the topography.

"There's a lot of glass on the topside of the house. But the foundation looks solid, maybe an underground bunker. Everything here in the upper levels is easy. It's when we breech down here that we're going to be going in blind."

"But," he says and holds up a hand, beckoning to two men who carry a case between them. They lug it right up to the front of the car, place it flat on the hood, and then slowly open the lid to show me the contents.

"Remember that deal with did with the Mancini's? Well. We still have a few of these bad boys."

A half-dozen RPG-7 anti-tank rocket launcher are nestled inside. They are warheads in handheld form, the big daddy of the one O'Malley used to take out my men's vehicle.

I laugh, because it's fucking beautiful. O'Malley isn't going to know what hit him.

Thinking back to what else is in the armory we've stockpiled, I say, "There's also those infrared cameras and military-grade night goggles you've been wanting to play with."

Lev's smile is ruthless. "You read my mind. We'll be able to get an accurate count through their heat signatures."

I turn and look toward the direction that Barrett's house - and Rina - is.

"What do you think we're looking at? I know you can't give me an accurate number. Nobody can until we're on site."

Lev scratches a hand through a scruffy beard. "Maximum ten. Any more and we'd have heard about an influx of Irish in the area. Our people are fucking diligent."

I grit my teeth, feeling my pulse skyrocket again that O'Malley managed to get under the wire of my security with such a paltry fucking force. Ten men roaming unchecked around my territory is an embarrassment. Later, I can direct the anger where it needs to be. Right now, it's a useless, wasteful emotion that won't get me any closer to rescuing Rina.

"Make it happen, Lev."

His voice is wry, and a quick look is darted my away. "Are you going to give Rogers a head's up?"

My gums ache from how I grind my molars together. I blame this hand-holding bullshit on Nadia. She wanted a working relationship with the local mayorship and his government. While there isn't really any red tape, just being forced to play nice with Chief Rogers and his cronies makes me homicidal.

"Yeah," I say. Because even though I want to begrudge the whole fucking contract. When I need Chief Rogers, he's been there.

Lev whistles sharply, giving the signal to my men.

It's as if a hive has been kicked. They are armed to the fucking teeth. Kevlar and black fatigues, dark paint, and masks pulled over their head. Enough weaponry and ammunition to take over a small country. It's a show of force.

And it's not enough. I want to fucking decimate O'Malley and his entire bloodline.

I inhale deeply. Then exhale and climb into the passenger seat. Men pile in behind me, and Marcus slides into the driver's seat. Leon is directly behind me.

"Let's go get my girl back."

Chapter Fifty-One

Rina

A sudden frenzy of motion packs the basement stairs with bodies and guns. The billiard-playing playing men shove out through the door behind the first wave. They're trying to reach the gleam of cars I see just beyond. Probably the rich man's garage.

My pulse pounds as O'Malley stalks toward me, his face stretched into a jovial grin.

"Well, shit. You cost me money. Your man's come for you."

I want to gloat. Tell him that, of course, he did. The words die in my throat as he drags me off the couch, suddenly hauling me in front of him like a human shield.

The blood in my veins freezes when he presses the muzzle of his gun against my temple.

"Be a good girl and stand right here." He nooses his free arm around my neck, holding me hostage by the throat.

I flinch as an explosion booms through the upper levels of the house. Down in the basement, it sounds as if a bomb's gone off. The artwork decorating the walls rattle. Dust and plaster particles drift from the ceiling where the crown molding is affixed. I don't know how deeply the basement goes. Or how many stories the house soars above us.

O'Malley seems confident that we'll survive whatever attack is happening.

Another roar shakes the very house. Whatever weaponry Edmond brought, it hammers O'Malley's hideaway with destructive fury. The Irishman's anger heightens. His tension manifests in the chokehold he wraps me in. But as Edmond's men chip away at his defenses, there's a new emotion I can practically taste in the air.

Fear.

I close my eyes, almost savoring the flavor of O'Malley's unstable emotions. Anxiety radiates from him like nuclear fallout. A nigh invisible aura of unease that's so palpable I almost choke on it. I try to push it away, but the fear is threatening to become my own. Fear for me. Fear for Edmond. It makes my heart throb, a quick, unsteady symphony in my chest.

O'Malley's hand shakes as he thumbs off the safety. Putting my life in a precarious balance between Edmond's arrival and the Irishman's shaky nerves. I swallow, trying to moisten my mouth. My tongue feels like a wedge of cotton stuck in my throat.

There are only a few men left in the basement. The rest are running up through the house, trying to clot what sounds like a relentless flow of Edmond's men rushing through the building. The staccato of automatic weaponry is constant. A spate of gunfire that makes my nerves tighten, followed by the anguished screams of the wounded and dying.

There is a moment of silence, followed by plumes of smoke and debris as another explosion rocks the rooms adjacent to the basement. A breech in the garage. Maybe the entire house is collapsing on top of us.

O'Malley curses in Gaelic, then barks orders I don't understand to the men hovering near the smoky doorway.

They hesitate. There's desperation in their faces. An exchange of looks as if they want to deny O'Malley's orders.

The braver one, who O'Malley says was Patrick's brother Finn, tries to argue. While I can't follow the language, the tone of voice is pretty unmistakable. As are the hand gestures.

O'Malley ends the argument as he tilts the gun away from my head and plugs a slug a few inches away from Finn's head.

They're going to die tonight. Either by Edmond's hand or O'Malley's.

The last remaining guards rush out to meet Edmond's forces.

O'Malley nuzzles his weapon against my hairline.

"You're going to die tonight." I don't know where the bravery comes from. Or why I've chosen to taunt the man holding a gun tonight. I don't have a death wish. Maybe I just want him to feel a modicum of the terror he's put me through.

"Maybe." O'Malley tries to sound bored over the idea. Except his hand trembles, his body tightening behind me as if he's trying to force bravery into his shaking muscles. "But I'm taking your boyfriend or you with me. Either way. I fecking win."

I breathe through my nose. I inhale deeply to calm my heart rate. There's another commotion on the stairs, two quick gunshots, and then silence.

My eyes burn as I stare through the miasma of smoke seeping into the basement. I hadn't noticed it before, but the air is growing thicker. Filled with the acrid tang of burning plastics, fabrics, and a reek that I know, deep down, is flesh.

Movement shifts beyond the haze, until a silhouette I recognize steps into the basement.

I nearly sag to my knees when I meet Edmond's eyes. For a

gunfight as brutal as it sounded, he's completely untouched. His hair is mussed, and a few of those wavy locks tumble across his forehead. A sooty streak darkens one of his high cheekbones. But he's utterly perfect. My black knight dressed head-to-toe in jet-black fatigues with a matte-black gun of some sort in hand.

"Stop where you are," O'Malley snarls.

Edmond's eyes are intense and searing as he looks me over. I can only imagine how terrible I look from the car accident because his face takes on a murderous cast that he pins to the man behind me.

"You did all of this to get me here." Edmond looks deranged as he spreads his arms. The stance resembles Christ on the cross with how the smoke and shadows pay homage to his shape. "Well, here I am. Let her go."

O'Malley strokes my face with the rough edge of the gun. Unerringly finding all the wounds of my battered skull. I can't stop the pained wetness filling my eyes, or the soft, leaking whimper that spills free. I'm trying so hard to be brave, but my whole body is one big, throbbing mass. It hurts to breathe, and I'm sure if I wasn't being forcefully held up. I'd be on my knees.

"But I can keep you on a leash with this bitch here." O'Malley tightens his arm around my throat, restricting my breathing until I'm only getting snippets of air. "Drop the gun."

No!

I whimper, desperate to tell Edmond not to. That I'm not worth his life. Mila needs him. But I can barely breathe, let alone talk.

Edmond's face is an unreadable mask. Save for those burning gunmetal eyes. He holds my stare, not even bothering to look at O'Malley. I watch with growing horror as he thumbs the safety on, and then tosses the gun onto the ground between us.

O'Malley doesn't even wait for the weapon to clatter.

I stagger as he shoves me away. I hear the shot and then see Edmond stagger back from the impact.

Landing on my hands and knees, I scream with horror as Edmond falls backward.

No. Oh please, no.

God no.

O'Malley's laugh is pure deranged as his long legs eat up the distance. Pausing enough to kick Edmond's gun away before he stands over his body.

"Fucking Russian Dog. Did you think you can beat me? Fuck you and fuck that whore."

I want to crawl toward Edmond. But I'm frozen beside the couch, staring with tear-blind eyes at where he lays unmoving.

The anguish in my heart is almost too much.

Get up. Edmond, please. Please get up. I love you. Oh God, you can't die on me.

I realize I'm babbling, saying everything aloud when O'Malley turns toward me. His victory is forgotten as he sneers, "Love? Love doesn't mean shit. There's only power."

Edmond forgotten, he turns toward me, swiveling the gun around to me.

"As for you, you little slag." He advances, and I crab-crawl backward, ignoring the spasms of pain in my fingers.

With a sudden malevolence elegance, the body on the ground rises, like a ghostly phantom manifesting itself. The devil coming to earth. I bite back a scream when my terrified eyes meet the cold, merciless glare of Edmond's.

There is a metallic clang behind O'Malley, barely any warning. But one I recognize so intimately that I can only stare at the brutal tableau unfolding before me.

O'Malley turns too late, and I watch as Edmond jabs his wrist forward. The point catches skin, and then Edmond slashes that *fucking blade* across the Irishman's throat from behind. He stands there, a puppet with his strings violently cut. Before his mind - his body - catches up with the lethal wound. In an instant, flesh ruptures. There's a hint of spinal cord visible, the garish red of sundered meat yawning open, and the deep scarlet of arterial blood drenching the mobster's chest before I turn away and gag.

I hear O'Malley's breath gurgle from his slit throat, followed by the thud of his body hitting the floor.

"Fucking Irish talk too much."

I have completely lost my mind. There is no way that Edmond is alive. I watched him take a bullet. Maybe I'm already dead, and my mind is showing me what I wish would happen in my last moments.

"*Solnyshko.*" Gentle fingers press against my shoulder, urging me to turn and look and realize what's right in front of me.

I stare up at the ghost. Wondering how he's moving. How he's talking. Before my brain, my body finally gives up.

From far away, I feel the familiar pressure of Edmond's thickly muscled arms wrapping around me. A feather-light kiss brushes my temple.

"I got you, *solnyshko.* I got you."

Chapter Fifty-Two

Edmond

Getting shot hurts like a bitch.

Even through a bulletproof vest, I can feel the bruises spreading from where the .22 caliber impacted. I'm not an idiot. Going into a gunfight without protection is asking to die. I don't have a death wish, and I kitted all of my men out with vests and Kevlar helmets before we breached O'Malley's stronghold.

Not that there was much defense. Two clusters of men, and regular residential construction. I'm still mystified that Barrett thought to get into bed with the mob without allotting funds for his security detail or reinforcing his home.

A cracked rib is nothing compared to the torment that I felt while playing dead. Listening to Rina sob and beg me to live, telling me how much she loved me, nearly gave the ruse away.

Part of me wishes she'd known it would take more than a bullet to kill me. She calls me the devil, her demon. Anything less than fucking holy water and a silver stake is ever going to take me away from her. Just because I might not have a gun, I'm never weaponless.

Iustina has saved me more times than I can count.

Carrying Rina out of the burning home almost makes me feel like her savior. I'm not. We both know I've done more to interfere with her life than enhance it. But for a moment, I feel that I'm worthy of what fate has given me. Until I look down into Rina's battered face and the guilt returns, gnawing away my feelings of warmth.

"How is she?" Marcus is the first to meet us. The rest of my men hang back, surveying the way fire consumes O'Malley's repurposed stronghold.

"I don't know." On the surface, she's banged to hell and back. One-half of her face is bruised and swollen. Dried blood turns her rose-gold hair crimson. A couple of the fingers on one hand look broken, the knuckles swollen double.

She could be bleeding internally, and I wouldn't know it.

I swallow. "We need to get her to the doc."

Whenever I'm hurt, or my men, we visit the in-house doctors. Those men and women on my payroll for house calls. I have one fully outfitted infirmary, which rivals the local hospital's ICU, and two medical bays stashed around the area for less serious injuries.

"I'll call ahead."

Gingerly, I carry Rina to the SUV and lay her down in the back seat. She hasn't stirred since she passed out after I killed O'Malley.

Brushing a finger down the unbrutalized side of her face, I press a soft kiss to her lips.

"Don't die on me, *solnyshko*. Lucia needs you. Mila needs you."

I swallow, tasting the bitter salt of tears and truth. For the first time in my life, I'm not sure how I'll survive losing another person in my life. I'm pretty fucking sure I won't. Already I feel the fault lines of devastation threatening to tear my heart asunder.

I let a single tear drip down, watching it splash on Rina's face like a baptism.

Finally, I give in to the truth.

"I need you."

Chapter Fifty-Three

Edmond

What Nadia liked calling her "Mobsters Red Cross" is a wing of a completely isolated office building a few miles east of downtown Echo Bay. Dr. Murphy is one of the two professionals we keep on call. She's standing in the parking lot, with two nurses and a gurney.

Marcus is driving, while I sit in the back with Rina's head on my lap, lightly stroking the ends of her hair that are matted with blood. While I'm fairly sure that most of her injuries are from the car wreck, I saw the horror show that was the cliff-side plunge. I can't be sure if O'Malley added to them. Sometimes, like now, I wish death wasn't so permanent. Just so I can continue to torture the men who have thought to extinguish the light of my life.

Dr. Murphy opens the car door, her demeanor all business.

Her attention focuses on the blood on her head, and the bruising that has spread from her hairline, down over her temple, and has swollen one eye shut.

"What happened?"

"Car accident. Her vehicle plunged over a hundred feet in a ravine and ended up on the roof."

"Alright. Obviously, shits happened that we can't mobilize her and hope she doesn't have a spinal cord injury." Dr. Murphy glares at me, as if that's somehow my fault and not the fuck-wits who kidnapped her.

I take her ire because I deserve it. Rina wouldn't be in this state if it wasn't for me.

The Doc beckons over her orderlies, and the three of them gently pull Rina out of my embrace. My fingers clench, flaking away bits of the blood which has dried on my fingers.

Rina's. O'Malley's. Mine.

It doesn't matter. In the end, it's all the same. I'm blood-stained and I should never have touched someone as pure as her.

I climb out of the car, standing at a distance as the Doc and her minions rush Rina into the building.

"Are you okay, Boss?" Marcus is all eyes on me. Funnily enough, he was the first one who realized what was going on between Rina and me.

"I get it now."

"Boss?"

"What you meant earlier. I get it. You saw how I felt about her long before I did."

Marcus sighs. He scrubs a hand at the back of his neck, following my line of sight.

"She'll be alright, Boss."

"Yeah," I say, but I'm not sure I believe it.

Chapter Fifty-Four

Rina

The beeping wakes me.

It's an annoying, incessant rhythm that makes me mutter in my sleep.

Who the hell has an alarm going off at this hour?

It takes a few minutes to struggle awake. My head feels stuffed with cotton. Cement bricks in my ears, and there's the taste of roadkill in my mouth.

Finally, though, I am awake. Except I'm not in Edmond's bedroom or my own.

I have no idea where I am. The lights are off, blinds drawn, creating a filmy gray haze in the room. One I don't recognize with its soft, cream-colored wallpaper. It makes me jerk in a panic.

The beeping intensifies, rising into an agitated wailing that feels like an ice-pick jabbing into my ear.

"Shh. It's okay." Lucia's voice cuts through my panic, followed by the sound of fabric shuffling. Her voice is muffled as if she's just waking up too. Or maybe she's been crying. She has that thick, clotted tone to her voice like her sinuses are stuffed up and her throat is raw from the salt.

Why is Lucia crying?

Pieces are missing in my memories, and the disorientation is real.

Finally, Lucia is there above me. Her fingers brush against my hand. She has been crying, cause her face is puffy and her eyes are red-rimmed. She sees me looking at her and then starts bawling again. Plucking a used tissue from her sleeve, she presses it to her nose.

"You're awake."

I try and talk, but I can't get more than a hoarse croak out.

God, I'm so thirsty.

Lucia reaches to the bedside table, grabbing a glass of water, covered with a straw. I suck happily, tasting the ambrosia of the gods as the cool liquid washes away the dryness and foul taste.

"Where am I?" This time I managed to speak.

"You're in Edmond's hospital."

Does Edmond have a hospital? I'm not surprised.

I close my eyes, the words 'hospital' conjuring up images of 'doctor'. Suddenly, a million branches of connectivity spread out. Tugging memories out of boxes. The butterfly garden. Mila's attempted kidnapping. My actual kidnapping.

Edmond. Gunfire. Blood. O'Malley.

I lift a hand to my head, then pause when I see the IV taped to the back. That Lucia looks like she's been put through the wringer, and is surprised that I'm awake, makes me wonder just how long it's been since my rescue.

"Three days," Lucia says, as if reading my mind. Though she was watching me intently, and no doubt saw the question form on my eyes and lips.

No wonder I feel like resurrected death.

"Is Mila..." I don't know if I have the strength to know what happened to Edmond's niece. Panic causes the beeping to spike, and I tilt my head to look at the heart-rate monitor which is causing the racket.

"She's okay. You saved her." Lucia shakes her head, and the tears are back. They don't fall, but they make her blue gleam like morning dew on periwinkle flowers. "She's been checked over by the Doc and complete bill of health."

I close my eyes and exhale, listening to the EKG meter blips smooth into a more sedate rhythm. There isn't a second of doubt in my head that knowing that Mila is okay, unscathed, makes it all worth it.

O'Malley would have killed her without a second thought. I would do this all again. Even if the outcome is worse than what it feels like now.

I open my eyes, and Lucia has an expression on her face I've never seen before. She's gazing at me like I'm a hero like I used to be to her when she was four and I was fourteen and we were two inseparable pods and she wanted to be like me.

The expression sends tears gathering in my throat. I hadn't realized how much I missed our bond until it broke.

"How bad am I? On this side of the bed, I have to tell you I feel like Humpty Dumpty."

"You have a concussion. There was some swelling on the brain. Dr. Murphy considered putting you in a chemically induced coma and cutting out some of your skulls to let the swelling ease. But you started to make progress, so she held off. Still, you've been completely out of it for three days."

Lucia chews on her inner lip. "Cracked rib, you broke two fingers on your left hand. Between your face and body, you look like you cozied up to Conor McGregor. They had to clip a bit of hair in the back to stitch up a really gnarly gash."

"Not the hair," I mutter, which makes Lucia laugh because

I'm not vain at all. They could have shaved me bald and while yes, I love my hair, it wouldn't be the worst thing alive.

Then Lucia starts crying, and I feel terrible for putting my sister through this.

"Come here." I hold my arms open as best as I can, and Lucia sinks into my hug. Her tears wet the hospital gown I'm wearing. The position puts a strain on my injured arm. But I hold on because I have my little sister back. Not the emotionally stunted goblin who has been wearing her face for the past six months.

Sometimes, trauma can tear families apart.

Other times, it can bring people closer.

I hold onto Lucia, feeling my eye tears well in my eyes.

Chapter Fifty-Five

Rina

During the three days I spent in the pseudo-hospital ward I saw everyone except the one person who means the most to me.

Lucia is a constant presence. Eve brought Mila to see me. That was a rough visit. She cried the moment she laid eyes on me, seeing me black and blue and propped up by pillows in the bed. Mila curled against my side, whispering her thanks for saving her. She gave me a delicate gold necklace, with two butterfly pendants: one enameled in lavender. *That one is me she said.* And one in pink.

I cried after she left because it was sweet, and I was so relieved she was okay.

I slept a lot. My body was healing and needed rest. But during those moments when I was awake, staring out through the blinds toward the scenic landscape that surrounds Echo Bay, or playing on my phone. I never saw Edmond. Neither did he text. There was a huge silence and a massive lack of communication that crawled under my skin.

There were echoes of his presence. Dr. Murphy could

open a flower shop with how many bouquets I received. From roses and lilies to a wider range of red poppies and hot-house exotics.

Sometimes, I would open my eyes and see a hint of a shadow, a whisper of fabric, as someone left my room. Haunting me with the fading remnants of his peppery, vanilla wood cologne.

But not once did he visit me while I was awake. Which makes my anger grow until it seethes beneath my bruised skin.

His avoidance is obvious. But as I am stuck in the hospital bed. There's nothing I can do about it until the last day.

"You can leave today." Dr. Murphy says, sliding a copy of my chart into the tote bag that holds all the other items I arrived with.

"Thank you for." I want to hug her. Maybe cry a bit on her shoulder. But I'm not going to embarrass either of us but blubbering into a hot mess in front of her.

I'm wheeled down to the foyer, where I find that Edmond has arranged a driver, and Marcus as my bodyguard. I sit in my wheelchair, eyeing the Rolls Royce through the tinted window from the front lobby. One of the nurses fusses around me.

"Don't overexert yourself. Dr. Murphy thinks another week before you can easily go back to work."

I have a pretty bad concussion, and my broken fingers are taped together in a splint.

Finally, after what feels like an hour of waiting, she wheels me out the front door. I look up, realizing that the building looks like a four-story professional kiosk. Except I know that only one floor, and one room, of the whole building are being utilized. Edmond's secret hospital is hidden right out in the open.

Marcus opens the back door of the Rolls-Royce. I brace my hand on his arm, and he leverages me in.

"You good?"

"Yeah." I crack a smile. "It takes more than being kidnapped by a deranged, wanna-be Conor McGregor to bother me."

Marcus laughs, his face crinkled up in amusement. Then he helps buckle me in, and slides into the passenger side.

I wait until we're all cozy before deciding to throw a wrench in their plans.

"I'm not going home."

The driver's head turns toward Marcus. Some silent communication is exchanged between them. Then Marcus turns in his seat, lowering his sunglasses to stare at me.

I don't flinch away. "I want to see him."

Marcus looks away. Indecision on his face. "I don't think that's such a good idea, you know."

"Why is he avoiding me?"

"He's been to see you every day". Marcus says evasively.

"I know he's been here every day, but I haven't actually seen him. He waits until I'm sleeping to sneak in. And runs before I wake up."

Marcus flinches, looking over at the driver who is pretending he's deaf. I guess me badmouthing their Boss isn't a common thing.

"He is feeling guilty," Marcus says.

Of all the stupid things.

"What is he feeling guilty over?"

"Well, you're gonna have to ask him that."

I laugh because we're about to go in circles. "How am I going to ask him that when you won't let me see him, and he's avoiding answering my texts?"

A dimple appears on Marcus's cheek. "You have me there"

He looks over to the quiet driver who has a smirk on his

face as he listens to us banter. "Take us to see the Boss. I take responsibility."

The driver nods and pulls away from the curb.

I settle back into the cushy leather seats and close my eyes at the smooth cadence of the Rolls Royce carrying me to my destination.

I don't know what I want to say to Edmond when I finally see him. Not until I know why he's avoiding me.

There's a tiny kernel of worry that he's mad at me. Mad that I got Mila injured. Mad that I made such a big deal about taking all four guards. Now two of his men are dead, Mila is traumatized, and I might have helped start a war with the Irish.

I sigh and stare out the window. Unsure of what I'm going to find when we reach the estate.

Chapter Fifty-Six

Edmond

orking has been impossible since Rina's kidnapping.

For the past few days, almost a week now, I've sat behind the enormous walnut desk, slumped in my leather executive's chair, and stared out over Echo Bay's harbor. It's nearly spring, and the fishing and sailboats are trawling the waterways. The warmer the weather, the more people will flood the harbor. Until the whole strait of Georgia and the Pacific Ocean are sprinkled with a confetti of lacquered hulls and brilliant white sails.

I have a yacht named *Voda*. A sleek Nordland motor yacht that I wanted to bring Rina to and seduce her with freshly caught fish off the bow, and the views of Echo Bay at sunset.

Now, I'm not sure I'll ever get the chance.

I close my eyes, feeling the familiar pang of guilt that's burned itself into my chest since the incident.

I never should have brought her into my life.

That is the crux of my self-recrimination. I know at a level most can never imagine, what can happen when dealing with the mafia. But in my greed, I snatched Rina from her comfortable, quiet life, and put her in the crosshairs of my enemies.

Seeing how badly injured she'd been saving Mila, I could barely look at myself in the mirror. It was like seeing the Mona Lisa defaced. Something horrible and shocking.

And I only have myself to blame for it.

It's why I've stayed away. So that I can hold onto the memory of how happy she looked that morning. Her eyes were bright and flaming with dewdrops of amber in an emerald thicket. I even think about her delirious sobs of how much she loved me.

I know trauma makes people say crazy things. So I try not to put too much weight on it. But my heart thrills over the knowledge that, for a time, Rina Christenson loved me.

Though she probably hates me now. Or at least is disgusted by me.

I would regret meeting me too.

The sound of tires on the stone outside stirs my attention. Flicking my watch face about, I notice the time and am filled again with longing.

Rina's out of the hospital. Safe at home with Lucia.

I sigh and spin away from the window. While she was infirm, I've taken care of everything. I added quite a few more zeros to her bank account. Took over the lease on her apartment, paid off Lucia's schooling, and replaced her car. She will never want for anything, never again. Our association might have been brief, but she deserves the world.

I wanted to give it to her.

Gritting my teeth, I focus on the E-mails that have built up. I skim through one before my attention shatters again as my thoughts go right back to Rina.

For the three days and nights she was unconscious, I sat by

her bedside, clinging to her hand, Quietly ordering - then begging - her to wake up.

When she did, I ran like a fucking coward. Afraid of the reflection of myself, I'd see in her eyes. She had run from me the first time I killed someone before her. I couldn't handle that again. Not when this time I wouldn't blame her at all for abandoning me.

So I left. Letting her free of me without consequence.

It is the least I could do for her sacrifice.

That doesn't mean I like it. Or that I chafe against the self-restrictions I've placed on myself.

Shoving away from my desk with a curse, I pace to where a snifter of liquor and a tumbler wait for me. I've given up my whiskey penchant. No, it's only vodka. Pouring a glug, I stare at the picture frames and artistic knickknacks that decorate the shelves.

I reach for a handout, lightly touching the family photo. Back before Adina's birth and death. Before Mila. The last time I felt like a family was when Alexander was a baby and mom still smiled.

Bitterly, I kick back the vodka and slap the frame face-down.

That type of life isn't for men like me.

A light knock on the door draws me away from pouring another shot. I lick my teeth, prying my lips from them before I resituate the glass and bottle.

"Enter."

Marcus pokes his head in. His introspective gaze sweeps the room, then lands on me hovering near the booze.

I narrow my eyes at him. Daring him to say something about it.

He shakes his head at me.

"Is everything settled?"

"Well," he says. "About that Boss."

The door slams open, and a small form limps in behind him. I freeze as my stare collides with Rina's. Her face is a mottled patchwork of black and blues, turning yellow around the edges as it heals. There are enormous bags beneath her eyes, and her hair is uneven on one side from where they cut it to suture her wound.

And she's never looked more beautiful to me. Because she's whole. Alive. Walking.

And angry.

I blink as she stomps inside. Or tries to. It's the thought that counts. She makes it to the chair in front of my desk, before she braces herself on the arm.

"You, get over here," she snaps at me, before sinking into the leather standalone. "I want to yell at you but you're too far away."

Marcus holds his hands up, palms out, and then slinks away with his tail between his legs. With a soft click, the door shuts.

"I'm not repeating myself, Edmond."

I hesitate. I'd wanted to avoid a situation. A showdown. I don't need to hear her ire or how much she hates me.

But if that's what she needs. So be it.

I square my shoulders and move to stand in front of her. As penitent as any one of her students ready to face her wrath.

"What do you need, Miss Christenson."

"Miss." Rina mouths the title. I expect anger. I expect hate.

I don't understand the sudden tears that shatter her composure. She bends over, burrowing her face in her hands.

"I'm sorry." Her voice is as shattered as her expression, and the shock of it sends me to my knees in front of her.

Why Is she sorry?

"*Solnyshko.*"

I want to touch her. I want to hold her close and take away whatever emotional pain she's suffering.

Will she let me? After she nearly died because of her association with me?

Hesitantly, I lay my hand on her denim-clad knee.

She cries harder but doesn't push me away.

Exhaling a shuddering breath, she drops her hands and stares at me with her flooded eyes. The look on her face skewers me. Not because she's angry, or because she hates me.

No.

She looks at me with love, and loss that I don't understand.

"I'm so sorry that I got Mila hurt."

Who knew words could be arrows? Rina shoots eight of them into me, unknowingly decimating me.

I stare at her before I realize that she's not angry with *me* for getting her into the situation. She thinks I'm angry at *her* for Mila's attempted kidnapping.

The walls I've spent the past week re-building shatter in a sheet of ice as if the polar icecaps have melted. Sending a sudden wave of emotion, of terror, of love, slamming into me.

"No, Baby. That wasn't your fault. There's nothing to be sorry for. You didn't force that fucking Irish ass-nut to kidnap Mila. He's been sniffing at my territory for months."

Rina rubs her nose on her wrist before I yank a handkerchief out of my pocket and pass it to her.

I crawl forward, gently urging her knees apart so I can slip between them. The position lets me pull her into me. Holding her like the precious, beautiful woman she is.

"You don't hate me?"

"God no. Did you think I could?" I pull back, cradling her face in my hands.

Her tears have slowed, but there's still a steady trickle that dribbles over her lashline.

"Why didn't you visit me?" Another emotional crack breaks in her voice, and I feel their pieces lash at my heart.

"I did."

"No." Her eyes narrow at me, her undamaged hand reaching between us to jab her finger into my shoulder. "You skulked in while I was sleeping, and then left at first light. I never actually saw you."

I flinch away from the accusations, even though she's right.

Gathering her fingers with mine, I stroke her battered knuckles with a gentle rub of my fingertips.

"I didn't want to upset you. I thought you would hate *me* for bringing you into this life. I was trying to let you go, let you return to your safe life without me fucking it all up."

Rina rolls her eyes at me, shaking her head as if what I've said is a bunch of nonsense.

"Edmond," she sighs.

Her brow furrows as she looks out toward the vista of Echo Bay just beyond my window. A kernel of tension radiates from her, whatever she's thinking makes her anxious. Before she lets it fall away, she meets my eyes again.

Soft. Sweet. Glowing eyes.

"I love you." Her lower lip trembles, but there are no more tears. Just the hoarse voice of choked emotion. "I think I have for a while. But I didn't realize how much until I came awake in the car and saw that man's hands on Mila. I didn't want you to suffer, I couldn't let you suffer, losing her too."

She slides into my arms, sinking into the width of my chest. Fucking tears are contagious because I can feel them burning in my sinuses.

"You were going to leave me."

"Not if I didn't have to. I knew that you'd save us both. Do you know why?"

She pulls away, letting me drink in her love-struck eyes and the sparkle of impishness igniting in their depths.

"Why is that *solnyshko*?"

"Because you love me, and you would move heaven and hell for those you love."

I laugh softly, amazed that this woman loves me.

Curving my fingers against her unmarred cheek, I gently caress her bottom lip with my thumb.

"You've got me there."

Her eyes grow warm, and I pull her tightly into me as if I could fuse us into one being.

My lips skim the baby-fine hairs that tickle her forehead. Disturbing them as I breathe her in.

"I love you, Rina. With everything I am. Every breath. Every drop of my blood in my veins. Until there's nothing left of me but dust. Even then, I'll love you still."

Epilogue

Two months later

An orgasm rips me from my dreams, and I barely have time to smother my cries into the pillow before I explode in a million, fiery pieces. My hands seek the dark head that's between my thighs, gripping the soft, short curls as Edmond eats me for breakfast.

I lay splayed beneath him, gasping in the early morning twilight.

Edmond wiggles out from beneath the covers, until he's hovering above me with his Cheshire-cat smile.

"Good morning, *solnyshko*."

God *damn*.

I gape up at him, trying to piece together my brain. But all of the endorphins have my mind drifting happily in the stratosphere. Eventually, I come down, landing in the cocoon of his arms.

"Wow," I whisper. Because no matter how many times Edmond gets between my thighs, each time is as good and even better than the last. "What was that for?"

He has his covert smile on. The one that doesn't let me read what is on his mind, as if his mental needle is stuck between *evil mafia bastard* and *sweet loving boyfriend*. I've gotten better at reading Edmond and his moods in the time we've been together. When he's in his *pakhan* mood, I usually know to run because Iustina is coming out to play. While people would probably be scandalized over the sex games and kinks that we're sharing together, I love every bit of it.

My pussy does to.

Then there's his sweet phases, that I call his *dark knight*. Because that's when I love him the most. He'll go up to the meanest, largest bully and slug him to protect his loved ones. The world will burn before any of us will know fear or pain. Lucia is in that bubble now too, and she's finally relented and is moving into Edmond's enormous mansion with me. Though that's still a month away.

Last night we stayed over at the old apartment since I have an earlier than usual morning today. It's that time again.

Victoria Malone is coming to pay me a visit.

"Don't think about her."

Edmond growls down at me as his mouth sinks, letting me taste the flavor of my musk that lingers on his gruff and delectable lips. I hadn't planned on telling him my woes about my student's parent. One because her husband works for him, and two I want to find my bad ass inner bitch and handle her myself.

Except despite all the self-confidence I've gained with the many orgasms and adoration that Edmond slathers on me, I haven't quite managed that level yet.

It'll happen in time. You can't fix Rome in a day, and it'll take more than a few months to fix the love-starved hole inside of me.

Edmond and I individually are works in progress, while together we're a complete puzzle.

"I can't help it. She's terrorized me for months." I feel a blush coming on over how immature I feel. But it's the whole mean girl thing. Some people never grow out of their need to bully others, and the wounds they inflict on their victims are for life. Victoria and I are each trapped in our roles, with her grinding ruts over the badly healed scars of my youth.

"Do you trust me?"

"Yes." *Completely.*

"Good."

The questions I might have over what I'm supposed to trust him over dissolve as Edmond slides between my thighs. His cock seeks my slipper wet heat. Then he fucks deeply into my bed, making me bite his shoulder so that Lucia doesn't wake up to my cat-in-heal wailing as I have break into another heart-pounding orgasm.

I'm still wrapped in the afterglow hours later as I sip tea from my thermos and wait for Victoria to show up and begin her antics. I have my mental mantra on repeat in my thoughts.

We do not feed narcissists.

Thou shall not give Victoria emotional kibbles.

Edmond's method of relieving my stress and anxiety worked. Because I'm not as keyed up and anxious about our showdown as I was earlier.

I have new guards with me today, though I was in such a rush I didn't catch their names. Both are standing outside the classroom, on guard until they melt in with the other security details when my day begins. They've been rotating lately because Mila is still adjusting to the loss of Dom and Pasquale. She's working through what happened to her with a therapist from Seattle. Edmond flies out with her three times a week. Though he hasn't told me yet, I believe he's thinking about family therapy for the whole Vasiliev family when Mikhail returns. That has been weighing heavily on Edmond. Though he didn't outright tell me, Mikhail was supposed to be back stateside weeks ago. Instead, he seems to have vanished. Edmond doesn't know if he's been disappeared into Russia's penal system, or if the *Bratva* are still working on Mikhail.

The kids aren't do for another hour. Victoria is do any minute.

Think of the she-devil and she appears.

As if on cue, I hear a ruckus outside my classroom door. There's no mistaking Victoria's shrill voice, but then a man answers her, and I have to wonder who in the heck she's speaking with.

The answer comes a minute later when Victoria *and* one of my guards walk in. Victoria's heels are sky-high, and her anger has her stabbing them into the hardwood as if she wants to leave divots behind.

"What is the meaning of this?" Her whole body is shaking with anger. I have no idea what has her so outraged. I haven't laid eyes on this psycho chick in months, and now she's looking like she wants to carve my eyes out like a mythological harpy.

"I don't know what you mean."

Victoria thrashes her fists against my desk. "You called my husband you fucking bitch."

Okay, what?

I blink over her shoulder to my ashen-faced guard. He's good looking in a bland way. His hair is dirty blonde, and Adam gets his blunt features and heavy brow from him. But he has gorgeous blue eyes, and a buff body beneath his tailored, navy suit.

"I'm Drew, Drew Malone," he says when he sees my look.

I breathe a quiet 'oh', because now I understand what's going on.

Edmond called in Victoria's husband to get a handle on her.

"I have nothing to do with this," I hasten out. I don't want her to go on a rampage.

"You little..."

"Tori." Drew's voice is an audible smack as he grabs his wife by the arm and reels her away from the desk. "Why have you been meeting so frequently with Ms. Christenson here?"

I'm appeased that Drew isn't as terrible of a father as I thought he was from dealing with Victoria. He apparently has no idea about any of the issues Adam has.

"It's none of your business." Despite Drew looking like he wants to take her over his knee, Victoria isn't cowed. I have a deep respect for the man, but it's obvious that she wears the pants in the family.

"Everything to do with Adam is my business."

The two square up for battle, launching into a bickering, martial spat that leaves me feeling like a referee. They are so loud I'm half-afraid Principal Sawyer is going to bust in, and then dress me down for not being able to handle the parents of my students. As if any normal person could deal with these two.

Good lord.

The best way to deal with this is simply to rip off the band-aid, and let Drew know what's going on.

I plant my knuckles in my dusk, and stand. Trying to leverage my voice along with my non-existent height. I'm in teacher mode now, trying to curtail two adults who probably shouldn't ever have gotten married.

Talk about toxic.

"Adam should be checked for ADHD and other learning disabilities," I half-shout over their rising voices.

"There is nothing wrong with my son!" Victoria screeches.

"What? Why didn't you tell me any of this?" Drew yells in return.

"Will you both shut the fuck up."

Edmond slides in through my classroom door, looking as if he's stepped out of a woman's billionaire boss fantasy. Everything warm and feminine inside of me rears its head and squeals with appreciation. *Mine* my whole being croons. My toes curl in my boots as I watch him stroll toward the pair of them, and I nearly wiggle with delight as I watch his approach.

Immediately, Victoria straightens. Her hip cocks, and she arcs her back to push her breasts out against the skin-tight bolero-length sweater.

Drew hangs his head, and he pinches the flesh between his brows. "Boss."

"Edmond, what are you doing here?"

"I'm here to visit my girlfriend, and to make sure that Drew knows the antics you've been up to."

"Girlfriend?" Victoria's mouth pops on the word, and she looks around the classroom as if she's expected someone else to materialize behind her when she wasn't paying attention. Her attention completely sweeps over me, dismissing me with her doll-like eyes, before scurrying back and landing on me. "You mean her?"

Edmond doesn't answer. He swaggers around the edge of my desk and sweeps me into his arms. I'm speechless as he all but dips me, arching me close so that the whole world fades away. His mouth hovers above mine, and he gives a sharp, dangerous side-smile to Victoria.

"Mmmhmm." Then he devours my mouth, melting my bones until the only thing holding me upright is his body. I wrap around him, forgetting the couple watching. Even though this whole over-the-top ploy is for Victoria Malone's benefit.

A few seconds later, Edmond breaks the kiss. His breath kisses my nose.

"I told you to trust me," he whispers against my flushed cheek.

Then he rights me, and we turn as a unified front to face the Malones.

Drew is glaring daggers at Victoria.

Victoria looks as if she's just had her heart broken. There are even tears in her eyes. I guess she harbored some heavy crush on Edmond. Because the devastation on her pretty face is *epic*.

Edmond is heartless as he ignores Victoria. "Drew, handle your wife. From here on out, I don't want Victoria in this classroom or in the vicinity of my girl. Anything that deals with Adam is on you."

Drew's throat works, his Adam's apple works against the collar of his shirt. He's in deep shit, half-buried in a hole his wife dug for him.

I watch as Drew literally grows a spine. He straightens, casts a hard look at the still-silent Victoria before he nods. "Yes, Boss."

Drew's hand cups Victoria at the elbow as he leads her out of the classroom. He pauses at the threshold and looks over his shoulder at me. "Thank you for dealing with Adam. I'll see he gets tested for the concerns you have." Then he disappears down the hall, and I'm left absolutely reeling against Edmond's side.

The weight I didn't know I carried over Adam Malone and Victoria slides away. I feel so light that I'm giddy.

"Oh my god," I breathe.

I turn to Edmond, and his smile is at half-mast, a ghost of a grin as if he wants to tell me *I told you so* but is refraining. He handled the whole situation perfectly, and together, we've come full circle.

So, I reward him. I push Edmond, catching him by surprise and driving him down into my chair. When he's situated, I sink to my knees in front of him, hidden behind the bulk of my desk so that if anyone – like Principal Swayer – walks by. They won't see what's keeping my mouth busy.

"This is familiar." Edmond's voice takes on a husk as he looks down at me. His eyes ignite, smoldering like the ashen dust that coats burning coal.

"Isn't it? Back then you couldn't have what you wanted." I pinch his zipper and slowly undo his pants. "But now you can."

Then I show him with the ardent attention of my mouth how much he means to me. At least until the kids arrive.

THE END

Thank you for reading Ruthless Lessons. Reviews are an author's best friend. Please consider leaving a review on AMAZON or GOODREADS.

Scanning this QR code will bring up the Amazon.com page for this book.

Join Aria's newsletter to keep Up to Date on her new releases!

Keep reading for a sneak peek of Aria's next release: Stealing Valentina - a Holiday Mafia Romance novel for Valentine's Day.

Stealing Valentina

Blurb

As the only daughter of a *Camorra* Boss, I've lived a life of opulence and extravagance. From afar, I seem to have it made. But all that privilege is nothing more than a gilded cage, keeping me from the one thing I crave the most – freedom. The truth is, I'm nothing more than a bartering chip for the *famiglia*.

My father signed my future away years ago to an ancient *Cosa Nostra* Boss whose sons had all been killed. I'm expected to be obedient, despite the bleak reality that I'm going to be nothing more than a baby-making machine for a nascent mafia dynasty.

Except on the day of my dreaded arranged marriage, I never make it to St. Mark's Cathedral. Instead, I'm kidnapped by a renowned assassin known only by one name: Raith. The hitman is exactly like his namesake, a wraith that seems to walk through walls. He's untouchable, lethal, and sexy as sin. He steals me out from beneath the nose of my security detail, and away from the only life I've ever known.

His motives confuse me. One minute ,he's icy and distant.

The next, he burns red-hot, seducing me with things I've never experienced. Is this some revenge plot with me as the lynchpin in his plans, or are his reasons more personal?

The only thing I know for certain is that war is coming, and I am the prize to be won.

Stealing Valentina

Chapter One

"Holy shit, man, you should see this contract. It's unreal. Someone wants this man dead because this has *Moby Dick* written all over it. It's a fucking white whale that is either going to get you killed or make you famous."

Snack's voice echoes in my head through the small flesh-toned earpiece tucked into the lobe. His tone is filled with palpable excitement. His usual high-energy personality is switched up to ten, and I can hear him practically vibrating as he fills me in on our next potential assassination.

"You could put a down payment on a house in La Jolla if you accept it."

"You're a size queen." We've worked together remotely for the past few years, and the one thing I can say that is an absolute truth about him is that he's a sucker for dangerous jobs. He goes completely ga-ga over them. Mostly because it directly impacts his percentage of the take. He's the type of person that can never have enough money. A bit of psychosis I suspect comes from an early life of hardship and poverty.

In his eyes, the bigger the better. Though the price tag correlates to how lethal the contract is, and it's my ass that's out in the field while he gets to play on his computer from afar.

"Hasn't a girl ever told you, bigger isn't always better?"

Snack snorts. "That's what they say to small-dicked men, mate. If you have a woman telling you that, I hate to say it, but you belong to the itty-bitty-prick-committee."

The mic strapped to my throat picks up the vibration of my laughter, even if the sound is muted. I'm on a stake-out, watching the front door of a dingy, illegal casino in some backwater, hillbilly town in Pennsylvania. I'm out in the sticks, having driven for the past four hours trailing my target, Luca Castillo, as he has tried to find a casino that *doesn't* know him or his reputation.

"Besides, you're not seeing the girth on this one. It's high six-figures. Real high."

The fact is, neither of us needs the cash. I've been in the assassin business for over a decade, and with Snack's computer skills and financial witchery making my money work for me, my net worth is outrageously fat. Another year or two, and I might break into a half-billion dollars in pure assets.

"Who wants to live in La Jolla?"

"Yuppies, rich people. Isn't that the dream, to move to California and have an enormous house and many fast cars?"

Snack isn't American. His nationality is a big question mark that I haven't asked about. Information is a high-cost commodity, and risky for anyone who might acquire it. Snack doesn't know my real name, and I don't know his or where he's from. Whatever accent he might have been born with, he whittled away to a plain, general tone long before I met him. It's only times like these when he slips up. Talking about the American Dream and California as if both things are still the goal of the working-class people.

The Gen-Z wet dream affordable healthcare and a resolution to the housing crisis.

My phone buzzes as Snack sends an encrypted file to it. Simultaneously, a shimmer of movement at the club's doors draws my attention.

"Hold that thought," I murmur, knowing the subvocal vibrations will translate.

"Damn, is he already done? He must have lost his ass."

I carefully screw a suppressor on the end of my Ruger, before rolling the window all the way down, giving me a clear shot when Luca tries to reach his car. The rental I'm driving is wedged up against his driver-side door, preventing him from getting in without first coming to see me.

"How long was he inside, an hour?" I ask Snack. He keeps track of the fine details from afar, while I focus on what sits right in front of me.

"About that, yeah. Anyway, go do you, boo."

Snack silences his mic as I surveil the man.

There's nothing special about him. Luca's your average Northeast mobster with his dark hair and bow-legged swagger, relegated to the lower rungs of any corporation because he's too much of a braggart and can't be trusted. He's arguing with a man just inside the low-lit foyer. Probably a bouncer, or maybe even the owner telling him he's out of money and they won't give him a line of credit. These small-time gambling pop-ups never do. Finally, the person gets annoyed and gives Luca a shove.

My target's arms pinwheel to catch his balance as he steps off a slightly raised stoop and into the hard-packed earth right outside. But he doesn't fall.

The metal slams in his face, and I watch as kicks his foot off the reinforced base. He's distracted as he paces in front of the barred door. I don't feel bad for Luca, even though addiction of any kind is a disease. He ripped off his Don by skimming money off the top of some construction deals, lost a boatload of that cash in a casino in New Jersey, and generally fucked up badly enough that the Sicilians put a hit out on him. Large enough to nudge the blip on my radar. Since I was in the area and didn't much care one way or another about the paycheck, I took the job.

It's the *thought* that counts for me. Luca will be one more criminal feeding the fish. He's a criminal, and this is what I do. Though I'm no vigilante. I'm being paid decently to take this guy out.

Luca gives up his fruitless pacing, and stomps toward his Nissan. Only when he's right at the bumper does he realize he can't get in. He rakes his hand through his hair with frustration, before realizing I'm inside, pretending to look at my phone. When in reality I got my eyes glued on him, and my Ruger down by my side.

He leans over and looks into the window I so generously left down for him.

"Hey man, I can't get into my..."

Luca doesn't even get the words out as I raise the gun and shoot a 9mm slug into his right eye in one fluid movement. We're close-up, which makes it a through and through. Though the bullet won't travel too far. The area contains more than enough trees for a trunk to stop its trajectory.

He drops like a sack of bricks, the bare, half-frozen ground absorbing the impact without kicking up noise.

Popping open the door, I grab my cell phone and snap a picture, sending it off to where it needs to go so the money that's held in escrow for Snack and I gets deposited into our accounts.

I *love* how technology makes my job easier. It used to be all clandestine deals and hushed face-to-face meetings where you never knew if you were walking into a trap set by the FBI. Now it's nearly all digital and anonymous. I never meet my employers and I prefer it that way. Once the funds are paid, it's all untraceable, and I vanish into myth only talked about like a scary story.

"What is it that you were saying." I start the Ford, and navigate out of the gravel-strewn field they are using as a parking lot and head down the bumpy road.

"Do you have time to look at the details?"

I glance in the rearview as the lights of the wanna-be casino fade behind me. There's no neon, just a few sad landscape LEDs illuminating a painted, wooden sign. Easily missed if you didn't know the place existed.

"Yeah, I'm almost to Route 6."

Before I merge onto the highway, and head to the turnpike, I check my phone and skim through the dossier.

I read through the important facts. There aren't many, just the target's name, contract price, and itinerary for the next few days. Only amateurs try and set up a mission in that sort amount of time. Along with a slew of pictures and a sketchy video taken on the down-low that lets me memorize his gait and body movements.

People can conceal almost every aspect of themselves with a change of clothing, some hair dye, and a few prosthetics. But it takes concentrated effort to alter how you move. It's a major reason the study of body language is becoming more popular in certain circles, from policemen to petty criminals and high-ranking kingpins. Any leg-up on not getting shot or caught helps.

Many times, the person I've come to kill rarely looks like their photograph, but I find them because they never thought to change how they walk, or a particular tick with the way they eat or even talk on the phone. Everyone has a tell, which makes my job infinitely easier when I discover it. This man favors his right leg when he walks, but he refuses to offset his limp with a cane.

I don't recognize the man's name or his face, but there's a flourish of colorful ink barely visible around the neckline of his black, open-collared shirt. I flick to another picture, this one where he's walking around by a pool in gaudy board shorts. With his shirt off, he's proudly showcasing the full-body artwork that's eternally etched into his skin. A brightly colored koi fish dominates the back piece.

The artist etched the fish to look like it is writhing up the man's spine as if swimming up an imaginary waterfall, then metamorphosing into a sinuous Eastern dragon as it flares out in full glory between his shoulder blades. The tattoos armor the man's body and fold over his shoulders and down his chest like an open kimono in stylish scales and cherry blossoms. They aren't just for decoration but are meant to tell a story.

The man's *irezumi* is elaborate, and it pings on my mental radar. Tattoos are like resumes in organized crime, if you can read the language, you can learn the important details. This man's tattoos bear the sigil of the Ishikawa-gumi, a syndicate of the Japanese mafia.

"Yakuza?"

Snack hums in approval. "Yep."

"No wonder the price is so high." Most people won't touch Eurasian criminals without a few additional zeros for recompense because of the martial arts cliché. In American media, every Asian criminal knows kung fu. That's why a smart person won't grapple with a Yakuza member but shoot them from a distance or sneakily incapacitate them. Poison might be the trademark of women assassins, but I like it just fine too.

"You're not just a pretty face. A+ my man."

I ponder the choices before me. I'm not afraid of the

Yakuza. Fear isn't something I feel much of. Death eventually comes for us all, though often, it arrives by my hand.

My requirements when choosing whether to take a target are both fairly broad and singularly narrow. I only have one caveat: they must be criminals. I like to think of myself as the hitman who watches the hitmen, making sure they walk an acceptable line.

When they don't, I kill them for a price.

The crime families I accept work from don't realize my true motives. They understand that I have the skills to get the job done and that I have never been caught.

Curiosity scratches down my brainstem, leaving behind a phantom tingle that I need to assuage. My jobs always begin like this: with a question and a need to know more.

"Why is the Yakuza fraternizing with the *Camorra*."

"Drugs, probably. Maybe human trafficking. It's one of the shared interests between their clans. Maybe knock-off electronics in exchange for guns." Snack rattles off a few more of their overlapping criminal interests.

The Japanese industrial complex is unparalleled when it comes to mechanical imports and integrated circuits, while the Italians usually go for drugs, gambling, and protection schemes.

"The usual."

"Yep." Snack knows me well enough that there's only one outcome for the questions I'm asking.

I don't realize it now, but I seal my fate with three little words.

"Okay, I'm in."

Connect with Aria

www.ingramcontent.com/pod-product-compliance
Lightning Source LLC
Chambersburg PA
CBHW060610300726
48975CB00005B/1517